THE
LAUNCH
PARTY

Lauren Forry was brought up in the woods of Pennsylvania before moving to New York City to earn her undergraduate degree in Cinema Studies and Screenwriting from New York University. She later earned her MA and MFA in Creative Writing and Publishing from Kingston University in London, England. There she was awarded the Faber and Faber Creative Writing MA Prize for her thesis work, *Abigale Hall*. She is now an Assistant Professor of English at Harcum College in Bryn Mawr, PA, and also adjuncts for Southern New Hampshire University's MFA programme. She resides in Bucks County, PA with her dogs and whatever it is her dogs bark at in the night.

THE
LAUNCH
PARTY

LAUREN FORRY

ZAFFRE

First published in the UK in 2023 by
ZAFFRE
An imprint of Bonnier Books UK
4th Floor, Victoria House, Bloomsbury Square, London WC1B 4DA
Owned by Bonnier Books
Sveavägen 56, Stockholm, Sweden

This is a work of fiction. Names, places, events and
incidents are either the products of the author's
imagination or used fictitiously. Any resemblance to
actual persons, living or dead, or actual
events is purely coincidental.

A CIP catalogue record for this book is
available from the British Library.

ISBN: 978-1-83877-751-7

Also available as an ebook and an audiobook

1 3 5 7 9 10 8 6 4 2

Typeset by Envy Design Ltd
Printed and bound in Great Britain by Clays Ltd, Elcograf S.p.A.

Zaffre is an imprint of Bonnier Books UK
www.bonnierbooks.co.uk

For Cherie and Lindsey
Thanks for giving me books when you put me
in the laundry basket

AN OPPORTUNITY THAT'S OUT OF THIS WORLD!

Have you ever wanted to reach for the stars? Want to show someone you truly love them 'to the moon and back'? Now you can! To celebrate the grand opening of the Hotel Artemis – the FIRST and ONLY hotel on the MOON – the Apollo Group is giving you – YES, YOU! – the chance to experience this once in a lifetime voyage.

Ten (10) lucky winners will receive an ALL-EXPENSES PAID, two-week stay at the brand-new Hotel Artemis. You will be the FIRST to experience the MOON'S FIRST and ONLY luxury hotel and spa. The trip includes the roundtrip three-day flight from Cornwall Spaceport to the MOON on our luxury spacecraft and two weeks at the Hotel Artemis with access to all amenities – Michelin-star chefs, spa treatments, guided moonwalks AND MORE.

HURRY! This could be your ONLY chance to fulfil your childhood dreams and experience the wonder of space travel.

To enter, submit the following information on the form below:

Name: ....

Age: .... Gender/Gender Identity: ....

Address: ....

Phone: .... Email: ....

Current Occupation: ....

A 500-word (maximum) essay explaining why you should be selected for this opportunity.

Note: Entrants agree to participate in background checks as well as physical and psychological evaluations prior to departure. Open worldwide. Submit form only once. Multiple entries will be deleted.

LAUNCH DAY

Chapter 1

Cornwall Spaceport – 11:00 UTC

Opportunity. Opulence. Elegance.

Penelope gripped the sink with both hands as she watched those three words scroll continuously across the flatscreen that hung above the mirror of the first class lounge toilets.

Opportunity. Opulence. Elegance.

Why did they need a flatscreen in the toilets anyway? she wondered, trying to forget how much her hands were trembling.

Opportunity. Opulence. Elegance.

What message were they trying to send? What couldn't wait until someone came out of the toilets?

'And couldn't they think of another word beginning with "O"?' she said out loud.

Below the scrolling words appeared the image of a leggy blonde in a tight-fitting purple and grey Hotel Artemis employee uniform. To Penelope, the model's eyes looked vacant – or dead.

'Or maybe you're just projecting,' she said to herself, looking down at the flight suit she'd been required to change into. The flight suit matched the colours of the employee uniform but had a different design, one with more emphasis on the purple and less on the grey. The purple accents, the PR women had explained, separated those specifically associated with the Hotel Artemis from those who worked directly for the Apollo Group – the consortium that built and owned the hotel – whose logo was the same shade of grey but with steel blue accents. Penelope had only listened to their corporate gobbledygook to take her mind off her churning stomach. It hadn't worked.

She turned on the tap and splashed her face, rinsing away the minimal makeup the PR women had requested she apply. Penelope didn't mind if she ended up looking pale and washed out in the press photos. She was half Irish. Her skin always looked pale and washed out, a stark contrast to her hair – a brown so dark it looked almost black. That hair was now pulled into a tight French plait, the best way to tame it for long journeys. And she was about to take the longest trip of her life.

She patted her face dry with a clean, plush towel that she then pitched into a waiting laundry hamper. The water had done nothing. Nothing could distract her from the fact that each passing minute brought her closer to launch. Her stomach continued trying to make the leap from her abdomen up to her throat. Sweat kept breaking out on her forehead. She felt it in her armpits, too, and hoped it wouldn't be visible on the suit.

Penelope turned away from the flatscreen, leaned her back against the sinks, and took several deep breaths, which also did not help. The cloying scent of orange and cinnamon was being pumped in through the ventilation system. It made her hungry while at the same time the thought of eating anything made her want to vomit. Penelope reached into her pocket for a mint, but her leggings had none. She'd forgotten she wasn't wearing her usual jeans. She crouched down and dug through her holdall for the clothes she'd just changed out of. As she found a mint, a knock sounded on the door. Penelope jumped. The heart rate on her fitness tracker jumped to over 120.

'*Miss Strand?*' one of the PR assistants called. '*It's time for the final pre-flight briefing. Miss Strand?*'

'Yes, one moment!' Penelope took three more deep breaths, gathered her bag and opened the door.

'It's *miz*,' she corrected, handing the PR woman her bag of clothes. The woman took it from her while jotting a correction on her tablet. Penelope admired her ability to whisk the bag into one hand and over her shoulder while holding a tablet in the other and writing a note without missing a beat. Employees of the Apollo Group were nothing if not efficient. Like the models in the promo pictures, the PR woman was young, blonde and empty behind her eyes. That summed up what Penelope had learned about the Apollo Group so far – efficient, attractive and ideals rooted in the patriarchy.

'Of course. I'm so sorry, Ms Strand. If you would, please.' She motioned to the rest of the group. Penelope, the last to have finished changing, almost laughed upon seeing the other nine of her party. They, and Penelope included herself in this, looked ridiculous in their matching flight suits.

'Motley' wasn't quite the word to describe their group, not with all of them dressed identically. They varied in age and nationality, but their body types were remarkably similar – similar heights, similar weights, similar builds – making Penelope wonder if the guest selection had indeed been a random process or if they'd been specifically chosen because they could all fit into the pre-existing suits. One of the travelling party, a woman in her fifties, her hair a bottle-red bouffant, plucked at the fabric as if it personally offended her.

However, the rest of the group shared something that Penelope did not. They all appeared thrilled that they were about to be packed into a fancy metal tube and shot into space.

Penelope crossed the black-carpeted lounge to join the others. The sleek purple leather sofas held the indentations of where some members of the group had been, until recently, sitting. Pinpricks of light dotted the lounge walls, which had been painted black to match the carpet. Penelope supposed it was intended to make them feel like they were already in space, the lights representing the stars, instead of the reality, which was that they were still standing in a room in Cornwall. A pair of doors led to the outer walkway that would guide them to the car that would transport them to the launch pad, but these, too, were tinted black and closed tight. Their view of the outdoors was completely obscured, but the weather had been beautiful when Penelope arrived at the spaceport that morning, and the forecast was predicted to remain perfect. No hopes of a violent thunderstorm or windstorm to delay the launch.

The mint, at least, helped cover the new car smell that permeated the lounge, which while not the primary source of her discomfort, also didn't help. Penelope continued to try and put her fidgeting hands in her pockets and continued to forget that she didn't have any. She glanced at one of the younger men – a man with hair so blond it was almost white. He had his hands in his pockets. All five of the men had pockets, Penelope noticed. All five of the women did not.

'Unbelievable,' she muttered.

The bottled redhead looked at her, but Penelope returned only a closed-lip smile.

This was her first time meeting any of these people in person. Though she'd read the names of her fellow guests, she'd avoided as much of the publicity as possible. She'd not even read through all of the brochures she'd been sent.

'Ladies and gentlemen, gather round please,' the second PR woman said. Penelope had forgotten there were two of them. They both wore matching Apollo Group suits, carried matching tablets that they barely glanced up from, and each wore their blonde hair pulled back in a tight bun; Penelope had difficulty telling them apart.

'Prior to boarding,' said one, 'there are a few additional points we need to discuss.'

'Like why we all have to dress like failed Eurovision contestants?' the red-headed woman asked. Penelope glanced at the Velcro nametag on the front of the woman's flight suit – Burton. So this was Tonya Burton. She looked exactly like Penelope had pictured her.

'Please.' The PR woman's voice became more clipped. She was nervous, but Penelope had no idea why. She wasn't the one about to board a damn spaceship. Or was she? Penelope couldn't remember who else was coming with them. She should have read the documents more closely. 'Ladies and gentlemen, as we previously stated, the flight suits are for the photo op and take-off. Once the ship has safely exited Earth's atmosphere and stabilised its course, you will be permitted to change into your own clothes.'

'I don't know why we have to wear them at all,' muttered one of the men – the most handsome of the five, the textbook definition of *chiselled*. He had a slight accent to his voice that Penelope couldn't place. What was his name? She tried to picture the list in her mind.

Tonya patted the man on the arm. 'Optics, my dear doctor.'

'Dr Wyss,' Penelope remembered, then coughed to try and cover up that she had said his name out loud.

'Our belongings have been loaded onto the ship, yes? They are secure?' the forty-something Japanese man asked, his voice more stern than worried.

'Of course, Mr Uchida!' replied the other PR woman. Penelope then noticed one difference between them. The second woman's voice had a slight Scottish lilt to it. 'Every precaution has been taken with your luggage and I can personally confirm that it has been safely secured aboard the ship.'

Tonya Burton whispered to Penelope, 'Don't see why it matters to him. Not like he couldn't afford to replace the whole bloody ship if he wanted to.'

Penelope stared at her blankly. Ms Burton rolled her eyes.

'Dai Uchida? Billionaire investments firm CEO Dai Uchida?'

It finally clicked.

'Right, yes.' Penelope tugged at the collar of her flight suit. 'I thought he'd be older.'

'Please focus, everyone,' said the other PR woman. 'Time is short. Now remember—'

'When will food and beverages be provided?' asked a woman with a German accent. She had a body in her twenties – athletic with the type of posture only taught in finishing schools – but a face in her fifties, filled with worry and frown lines.

Her body radiated tension. 'I thought we'd have something to eat here, but—'

'Yes, Frau Richter. As soon as the ship has levelled off, food and drinks will be served. As you've been told, eating less than three hours prior to take-off is not recommended, which is why no food was provided here in the lounge. However, I assure you that once on-board all your needs will be met.'

Dr Wyss whispered something in Frau Richter's ear. She laughed and smiled at the doctor. Penelope got the impression the woman had not laughed in some time.

The youngest woman amongst them – whose body type resembled Frau Richter's though she was a bit shorter, her mousy brown hair in a tight bun – raised her hand. The nametag on her suit read 'Crane'.

'No, Professor Crane, I'm sorry but, as was previously discussed, smoking is not permitted on the ship or in the hotel. Complimentary nicotine gum and patches will be provided throughout the duration of your stay.'

Penelope remembered the name Professor Alison Crane from the list. She'd pictured a frumpy, older woman in a tweed suit with a set of pearls not a twenty-something with the body of an Olympic skier.

'Well, how much time is there before we board?' she asked.

'As I was saying, the press are outside now. In just a moment, you'll make your way down the line, posing for pictures and answering questions. The limo is waiting at the end to transport you to the ship—'

'So at least ten minutes.' She pulled a pack of cigarettes and a lighter from a handbag and lit one up. The PR women frowned in unison. The white-blond man quietly asked if he could have one, and the professor happily handed over a cigarette. 'Anyone else?' she offered.

Dr Wyss nodded and winked. Professor Crane palmed one to him. Frau Richter's smile transformed back into a frown.

'We will now be collecting your phones and any other restricted items. These will be safely stored in the private spaceport until your return.'

The PR woman with the slight Scottish accent held out thick, clear plastic bags that locked at the top, the same kind Penelope had seen at concerts where phones weren't permitted. One by one, each of them dropped their phone inside, along with the occasional set of keys and Professor Crane's pack of cigarettes and lighter. The PR woman waited with the professor until she finally extinguished her cigarette and handed over the butt.

The lock screen on Penelope's phone flashed as she dropped it in the bag.

'Sweet dog!' Ms Burton remarked, upon seeing the screen.

'It's one of my parents'.'

'How precious. I'm sorry, what was your name again?'

'Thirty seconds!' the other PR woman shouted.

'Penelope Strand.'

'Oh yes! That's right. Tonya Burton. It's so nice to meet you, Penny. Please call me Tonya.' The woman held out her hand. Penelope kept hers at her sides.

'It's Penelope. And I know who you are, Ms Burton.'

Tonya sighed, nonplussed. 'I do love when my reputation precedes me. Penelope . . . that's a bit of a mouthful, isn't it? I think I'll stick with Penny.'

Before Penelope could respond, one of the PR women shouted, 'It's time!'

The doors opened.

Reporters packed the corridor outside. They shouted questions and clicked cameras before any of them had even taken a step out of the lounge. Penelope had dealt with press conferences before but nothing like this. Near-blinded by the cameras, she could barely see the red carpet that had been rolled out for them, marking the path they were to take from the lounge to the stretch limo which would transport them all to the spaceship.

As Penelope inched towards the exit, the very blond young man grabbed on to her arm.

'You go next,' he hissed in her ear. 'I can't be that close to him, I'll die.' He had an American or Canadian accent. Penelope couldn't tell which with all the excess noise.

'Who?' she asked, taking any opportunity that delayed her having to be out in front of the reporters.

'Robert Rannells! Oh my God, I can't believe we're going to be spending over two weeks together. I hope I don't embarrass myself when we're officially introduced.'

The man identified as Robert Rannells had already made himself at home in front of the reporters.

'Please, please! Call me Bobby!' He smiled at the press.

Penelope recognised him now. Some C-list celebrity from the States who'd made a small name for himself winning a bunch of reality TV competitions. Unlike Dr Wyss, who was handsome by anyone's standards, Rannells – in his sixties, the oldest of the group – had the look of a man who had possibly once been somewhat attractive, but whose body had already started to let him down.

'Mr Smith, Ms Strand, if you please.' The PR woman motioned for them to exit the lounge.

Despite the PR women's urgings, Penelope did not pause for questions or photos. Without trying to look like she was running, she moved briskly down the carpet, occasionally waving, looking sideways at the cameras and muttering the occasional, 'Yes, it's very exciting.'

The flash of the cameras was so bright and so close, she could smell the heat coming off them.

Though she didn't think she'd walked that fast, she reached the limo first. When she went to open the door, one of the PR women interrupted with a smile.

'Not yet, ma'am.'

'But—'

'The group photo.'

'Oh. Right.'

Penelope stood there impatiently, crossing her arms before quickly uncrossing them then trying to stick her hands in pockets that still did not exist. She remembered what the PR people had told her yesterday in their prep meeting, about how Penelope did not want to come across as 'ungrateful for the opportunity' as she had during the initial announcement of the contest winners. Apparently, the fact that she hadn't smiled for two hours straight and gave only monosyllabic answers had not been good for her 'optics'. Some people online were calling for her to be replaced by someone who could appreciate this gift, or so she was told. Penelope didn't know – she went online to search for things like driving directions and new restaurants, not to google herself – and she didn't particularly care what random internet trolls thought of her, either. As she waited for the others, trying to find something to do with her hands and arms, she listened to Bobby Rannells' brash American voice grow louder as he talked to the journalists.

'It really is a great opportunity! I know I was chosen at random like everybody else, but out of everyone here, I'd say I'm uniquely suited for this trip, wouldn't you? *Survivor*, *Big Brother* – US, Brazil, Albania and you know the rest. I mean, who else can handle being locked up in luxury with nine strangers? Though I have to say, if these digs aren't better than what I faced on *Survivor: Botswana*, then I'll be filing one serious complaint!' He laughed. The reporters laughed. Penelope rolled her eyes. As she did, she caught sight of another group of people, outside the fence that surrounded Cornwall Spaceport.

These people, too, were shouting and waving, brandishing signs. But they weren't here to cheer the travellers. Their shouts were filled with anger. Police were already amongst them, trying to break them up. Penelope tried to read the signs, but they were too far away. She guessed, though, based on the online comments she'd glimpsed in the last few days, that they said something about consumerism or capitalism. One protestor started to climb the fence. Police swarmed the person, but before Penelope could see what happened to the climber, her view became blocked as the others gathered around her for the final pre-launch photos. All except Rannells, who continued charming the reporters until one of the PR women went over and whispered something in his ear.

'Thank you, everyone!' He smiled, showing off a mouthful of capped teeth, giving a final wave to the reporters before joining the group at the limo.

Camera flashes went off for ages. Her eyes stung from the lights. She didn't even know if she was looking in the right direction or who was standing beside her. There had been so many camera flashes despite the damnable sunny weather that she could barely see once she got inside the dark limo. She had only just sat down when it sped off towards the launch pad. Penelope kept her eyes closed while the group chattered around her.

'*Look at it! It's gorgeous! This is so amazing. I can't believe it!*'

Someone squeezed Penelope's hand.

'*This is going to be so much fun!*'

OUTBOUND
JOURNEY

Chapter 2

The sounds and smells of space travel were different from a normal flight. Something had to make noise in order for there to be noise. But no wind existed outside of the ship to rattle the windows. The engines were quiet. Occasional vibrations shook the floor, but these were almost imperceptible. The smell, more noticeable after the end of food service, contained a newness, like in the spaceport's lounge. But at least the lounge had been firmly planted on Earth.

Penelope's fellow guests dined and laughed in the cabin around her, filling what would otherwise be utter quiet with the din of voices and clinking cutlery. She didn't want to think of how many – or how few – trips this ship had taken. New should be good. New meant all the parts were in good working order, nothing ageing or rusting or falling off or bursting into flames like the *Challenger* explosion videos she'd watched on YouTube the night before travelling to Cornwall, which was an admittedly stupid thing to do but she'd started by watching successful launches and fell victim to auto-play. YouTube's algorithm apparently thought someone who wanted to watch successful shuttle launches would also want to watch unsuccessful ones and for some reason she hadn't pressed 'stop'.

But everything would be fine. She knew that. The ship was new. But new also meant untested and, while she trusted the scientists and engineers who put all this together, was anyone really aware of how many things could go wrong? If their smooth, event-free first day of travel was anything to go by, everything would be fine. But they still had another entire day of travel ahead of them and—

The ship gently tilted to the right, adjusting course. Penelope clutched her stomach.

'One more day. Just one more day,' she whispered. She grabbed her glass of sparkling water, took a few slow sips, and tried again to eat some of her salmon fillet.

Someone bumped her elbow on his way back from the bar – the ultra-blond young man who'd since been introduced to her as Jackson Smith, an accountant from Canada. He didn't bother apologising as he squeezed his way through the tables, two fresh glasses in hand, to reach Robert 'Call Me Bobby' Rannells. Jackson seemed to have recovered from his shyness around the celebrity, given how much his mouth wouldn't stop moving whenever they were together.

Penelope pushed the salmon aside and decided to give the lemon pudding a try, grateful that of all the phobias she did have, claustrophobia wasn't one of them. The spaceship was luxurious, that was certain, like the fancy private jets she saw in films – leather upholstery, silver-gilded edges, thousand-thread Egyptian cotton sheets. She thought it would be more like the old SpaceX capsules or other space shuttles she'd seen – a bunch of seats and some aluminium panelling. But she supposed this ship better suited the Apollo Group's directive of providing the highest luxury holiday in existence. This was typically going to be a trip for the 'one percenters'. They'd expect more than a few ergonomic chairs.

But despite the glamorous interior, this ship wasn't spacious. In fact, although she was literally in space, Penelope had less space here than when she was a student sharing a two-bed flat with five people. Each of the ten guests had their own small cabin, barely bigger than the length and width of a single bed, and most of the ship was dedicated to crew and cargo. The only two public areas outside of their cabins were the embarkment/disembarkment chamber where they strapped themselves in for take-off and would do so again for their re-entry into Earth's atmosphere just over two weeks from now, and the communal lounge that the crew referred to as 'the Deck', where all the guests now found themselves along with several flight attendants and the two head PR women who, it turned out, were joining them on the trip because . . . well, Penelope wasn't sure why. To watch their every move and document it in stirring press reports, probably. Penelope had done her best to avoid them after they had chastised her after the launch for not smiling enough on departure day. Penelope hadn't even bothered to try and explain that normally when she did a press conference, smiling was very much *not* encouraged, especially that last non-hotel related press conference in which she'd been involved.

The Deck reminded Penelope of aeroplane pictures from the heydays of international air travel. One rounded bar and counter occupied the cabin towards the bow (though she didn't know if boat terminology applied to spaceships), where non-alcoholic drinks and snacks were served around the clock. Padded booths paired with rectangular tables with rounded corners lined either side of the long, narrow space. Three standing circular tables occupied the centre of the room, so if one didn't want to eat while crowded in a booth next to others, they needed to eat while standing. Which was why Penelope currently stood alone at the table closest to the bar.

Normally, Penelope loved small spaces. They gave her comfort. But every time she began to feel at ease, the ship would move, reminding her they were hurtling through the universe in a man-made metal tube.

She felt the ship move again and took another sip of water. What she really needed was a proper drink, but there wouldn't be any alcohol until they reached the hotel. She forgot the exact reason. Something to do with Health and Safety. No doubt there was a whole section in the brochures she had never read. Struggling to zone out her thoughts, she focused on the conversations around her. Dai Uchida's voice came through the clearest.

'They promised Michelin-star meals. This . . . this is fast food.' He nodded for an attendant to take his plate away. Penelope noticed that, despite his complaint, he'd eaten the entire entrée.

Penelope hadn't exchanged much conversation with Dai Uchida yet – what does someone who makes barely £35,000 a year talk about with a billionaire? She wasn't even sure how to address him. 'Dai' seemed too informal but calling someone her older brother's age 'Mr' also didn't feel right. Penelope wasn't alone. Most of the other guests hadn't spoken to him, either, except for Sasha Eris, who sat beside him in the booth.

'To be fair,' Sasha said, 'they promised Michelin-quality food at the hotel. Not on-board the ship. But I love this pudding. I could eat a dozen more.'

The church architect seemed to be the only person not intimidated by Uchida's wealth. The two had struck up a conversation about Victorian-era art and architecture shortly after take-off and hadn't stopped since. They seemed an odd pair despite both being in their forties. Sasha – dark hair and dark eyes – looked and dressed much younger than she was. Her clothes reminded Penelope of what she herself wore at age fourteen. Sasha, who said she was born in Turkey but now based in Luxembourg, spent most of her time smiling at Uchida while sketching in her notebook. Uchida, on the other hand, seemed a decade older than he was, dressing in expensive suits with old-fashioned cuts that looked like they would be more fitting for a man twice his age, while also wearing a perennially serious expression that deepened the lines around his mouth. Yet, when Sasha would tip her notebook towards him and show him a design, Uchida would smile like a schoolboy.

'See?' Sasha was saying. 'If I take the atrium and expand it slightly further into the narthex, that will allow me to fit a spiral staircase leading up to the choir loft while maintaining the original dimensions of the church walls.'

Uchida nodded. 'Yes, yes. I see. Could you do this with other buildings? I mean, do you design buildings other than churches?'

Sasha tucked a loose strand of hair behind her ear, absent-mindedly marking her cheek with her pen. 'No. Not anymore. I've always done mid-sized buildings like these – restaurants, vineyards, tourist centres – but churches, that is my true passion. Using architecture to create a space that brings peace and serenity.'

'May I?' Uchida used his thumb to wipe the spot of ink from Sasha's face then held out his hand for her pen. Penelope watched as he scribbled on a napkin. 'Perhaps I could get your professional advice. I would like to create a new building for our Fukuoka office. I was thinking . . .'

As Uchida and Sasha continued their conversation, Penelope gave up on the lemon pudding. Nothing wanted to settle in her stomach. She turned her attention to the booth on the opposite side of the Deck.

It was absolutely no surprise that Dr Erik Wyss – 'the Swiss doctor with the Greek physique,' Tonya had remarked at one point – found himself sandwiched between two of the other women, young Professor Alison Crane, who had swapped her cigarettes for nicotine gum – packs of which she shared with Sasha and Jackson Smith – and Frau Charlotte Richter, the German lawyer, who was enjoying her third cup of lemon pudding, judging by the empty bowls in front of her. Frau Richter had been the first awake this morning, exercising outside Penelope's cabin, making loud grunts as she did some callisthenics in the corridor. When Penelope had poked her head out of her cabin and looked at her funny, Frau Richter had merely stared back before continuing her set of jumping jacks. Now, Professor Crane chomped on her gum, her mouth close to Dr Wyss's ear as she leaned into his side while Frau Richter kept her back ramrod straight, with her body angled towards the doctor's. Though the women shared a similar body type, their taste in style was very different. Professor Crane dressed in loose-fitting silks and caftans that made her lithe body appear to be floating as she moved through the corridors. Frau Richter preferred boxy suits that both seemed to restrict her movements while hiding the body the form-fitting flight suit had first revealed. Dr Wyss

– who could've been anywhere between thirty and fifty – gave the women equal attention, turning to each one as she spoke, offering nibbles from his plate, which Professor Crane accepted with relish while Frau Richter blushed with embarrassment.

'Emergency medicine? No. Podiatry?' Frau Richter – who refused to let anyone call her by her first name – was guessing. This game had become a competition between the two women by the end of the first day. After Alison, who told Penelope she didn't care what anyone called her, had deduced that Frau Richter specialised in divorce law, Frau Richter had guessed that Alison was a professor of psychology. Now they were both trying to figure out what Dr Wyss was a doctor of. Their guessing had quickly turned to flirting and the flirting was quickly becoming more competitive. Aggressively competitive. And while Alison wore no jewellery, Penelope couldn't help but wonder about the wedding ring on Frau Richter's finger.

'God, we need to get off this ship.' Tonya plopped her elbows on Penelope's table, almost spilling Penelope's drink. 'The stench of the hormones is overwhelming.'

Penelope took a sip of water to avoid answering and tried to subtly shift her body away from Tonya's, but there was nowhere to go.

'And look at poor Bobby over there.' Tonya nodded at the man, stuck with a worshipful Jackson by his side.

All Penelope knew about Jackson so far was that he was an accountant from Saskatchewan who now lived in Toronto because, at any given opportunity, he would only talk to or about Bobby Rannells. The two sat towards the rear of the Deck, Bobby regaling a few crew members with yet another anecdote.

'And that's when I said—'

'You said, "I guess I should've said yes to the Port-a-Potty after all!"' Jackson burst into laughter, but no one else around them did. Penelope could feel their second-hand embarrassment from across the room.

'That's the fourth time today Jackson's finished one of Bobby's stories,' Tonya said. 'Out of all the people in the world who could've won this trip – people who couldn't give a shit that he won *Survivor* Series 74 – and he ends up with his Number One Fan.' Tonya shook her head but her hair remained in place. Somehow, even in space, she'd managed to perfectly coif her cloud of bright red hair. Penelope kept silent, and Tonya kept talking. 'Let's hope our Jackie-boy is able to contain his inner Kathy Bates for the next few weeks.'

Someone snickered. The youngest person on the trip – Freddy Nwankwo – a twenty-something Black man from New York City – stood at the bar, meal finished, his nose in a book – *Murder on the Orient Express*.

Hell of a choice, Penelope thought.

'Sorry,' he apologised. 'I shouldn't have laughed.'

'Don't apologise!' Tonya said. 'See? Young Freddy gets it. In fact, thank you for laughing, Freddy. You know, Penny, it wouldn't kill you to smile once in a while. We're on our way to the moon, for heaven's sake!'

'Penelope.' Her stomach rumbled.

Tonya rolled her eyes. 'Are you like this with everyone or is it just me?'

'Maybe I just don't want to give you anything to write about,' Penelope said.

'You're a writer?' Freddy asked, setting his book down.

'I am, darling.'

Freddy left his book on the bar and joined them at Penelope's table. Three people was a squeeze, and Penelope found herself sandwiched between them, elbows bumping. It made her feel even more as if she was packed onto a life raft.

Freddy leaned across the table to speak to Tonya. 'What do you write? Fiction?'

Penelope answered, 'Yes' while at the same time Tonya said, 'No.'

'I'm a journalist,' Tonya said.

'If that's what you want to call it,' Penelope muttered.

'Don't mind her. She's just jealous because I have better sources than she does. Maybe you've seen some of my articles in *Heat* or *OK!*?'

'No, sorry,' he smiled politely, 'We don't get those in the US. I don't think. But now I know you, I'll be sure to check some out! Once we're, you know, back on Earth. With, like, internet and everything.'

'You know that almost stopped me from entering,' Tonya said. 'Over two weeks without the internet? Without any connection to the outside world? God, two weeks is a lifetime in the entertainment news business. It'll take me ages to get caught up.'

Penelope brought her water to her lips before she could say, *what a pity* out loud, but she drank too fast and choked.

'And what do you do, Ms Strand?' Freddy asked as she coughed. 'Are you a journalist, too?'

'I help my parents with their dogs' home,' she wheezed.

'Your dog has its own house?' he asked.

32

'Shelter.' She took another sip of water. 'They run a shelter for elderly dogs.'

Tonya laughed and patted Penelope on the back. 'She's teasing you, darling. Penny here is a real-life detective with the Met. You know, Scotland Yard.'

Freddy's eyes lit up. 'Oh my God. Really? That's amazing! You're a detective and I'm a criminology student. How cool is that? I go to NYU. New York University? Everyone thinks of it as a school for arts or business but it actually has a great criminal justice program. Oh man. Scotland Yard. I've been wanting to do a study abroad in London. Or maybe my Master's degree, once I finish my Bachelor's. I'm a huge fan.' He pointed over to Agatha Christie's name on the cover of his book. 'Christie. Conan Doyle. And I'm in a modern crime book club, too. But not, I mean, a fan like . . .'

They looked down the room where Jackson continued to talk over Bobby, who patted his admirer on the back with a grin that could've been a grimace.

'Anyway, at some point during the trip, could I . . . I mean, would it be all right if I talked to you? I mean about police stuff? Only if it's all right with you. If you have the time. And if you want to. I mean I met some detectives with the NYPD this one time, but it was all really formal and—'

'Oh, Penny couldn't be bothered, I'm sure,' Tonya said. 'She's on holiday like the rest of us.'

'Actually, I'd be happy to,' Penelope said. 'We've got two weeks. I'm sure I can find the time.'

'Thank you so much, Ms Strand! I mean Detective Strand.'

Tonya smirked. 'The detective has a heart after all.'

The ship adjusted course, curving slightly to the left. Penelope's stomach turned with it.

'Sorry. If you'll excuse me.'

'Oh, don't run, darling! We were having a good chat.'

But Penelope kept walking.

'I know, I know,' she heard Tonya say. 'Every Englishwoman hates me.'

Penelope didn't stop until she made it halfway down the corridor that led to the guests' cabins. She leaned back against the wall and rubbed her stomach. The Dramamine had been utterly useless so far. In an effort to focus on something other than her nausea, she focused on the colours around her. White dominated – white walls, white doors, white floors. Would the hotel be this white? she wondered. Why hadn't she just read the bloody materials? If she'd read them, she would've been prepared. She would've known what to expect. If she was honest with herself – though since the Bevan case she'd been a little too honest according to the police therapist – reviewing the materials would've made the trip real. It would've frightened her out of coming. But she needed to be here. Even if it hurt. Especially if it hurt.

All this white plus the narrow corridors made her feel like she was stuck inside a tube of toothpaste. The only thing that wasn't white was the view outside the small porthole windows. There, black reigned. Utter black, flecked with distant white stars. If she focused on that view, she could imagine she was at home, sitting at her kitchen table, looking up through the window above the sink, listening to the neighbour's dog barking, her feet firmly on solid ground. But she didn't want to be there, did she?

She wanted to be here. She wanted to be on the moon. She just had to get there first.

The door to the Deck slid open and shut, and Penelope was no longer alone.

'Oh! Sorry,' Bobby said. 'Just came to get some air, so to speak. I didn't know anyone was out here.'

'It's fine. I was about to go down to my cabin anyway.'

'And miss all the fun in there?' he laughed, throwing back his head. His white teeth gleamed.

'Your voice is very loud, do you know that?' Penelope shook her head. 'Sorry. I shouldn't have said that.'

'Ah, don't worry. Doesn't hurt if it's true.' He shrugged and stuffed his hands in the pockets of his linen trousers. He looked like a retiree headed to a tropical resort. 'Speaking of true, you look a little pale. Can I get you anything?'

'No, I'm all right. Cheers.'

'Are you sure? Because – no offence – you're the same colour as one of my teammates from *Survive All-Stars* right before he passed out in a puddle of his own urine.'

'Thanks for that image. But no, I'm all right. It's just, well, airsickness. I . . . I'm afraid of flying.'

Bobby burst into another laugh. It was a deep, welcoming laugh, like that of an uncle who could always keep the party going. Penelope couldn't help but smile, too.

'So that's what's been bugging you! Charlotte – sorry, Frau Richter – and Alison have a bet going. Alison thought it was morning sickness.'

'Dear God no,' Penelope recoiled.

'Well, if you feel like messing with them at all, just let me

35

know.' He winked. 'Out of curiosity then, if you're afraid of flying, why did you enter to win a trip to the moon?'

The image of a body in the water flashed through Penelope's mind.

Penelope forced a smile. 'Let Alison and Frau Richter take bets on that.'

She bid Bobby goodbye and continued down to her cabin. One more day on the ship, and then the spaciousness – and privacy – of the hotel awaited.

'One more day,' she whispered.

Chapter 3

01:00 UTC

The ship was winding down for the night. No day or night existed now, not really, but the automated lighting system mimicked a typical 24-hour day to keep everyone's circadian rhythm in check and, like the International Space Station, they followed Universal Coordinated Time. Most of the guests and crew had already left the deck. As members of the flight crew cleared up the tables from dinner and wiped down the bar, the two PR women chatted in a corner, comparing information on their tablets. Tonya watched them while sipping her umpteenth orange juice. Bobby joined her in the booth, slipping into the space next to her with a fresh glass of something clear and fizzy.

'They're going to have every aspect of this trip planned down to the last minute, aren't they?' Tonya nodded to the two women.

'I wouldn't expect the Apollo Group to really give us regular folk free rein of their very shiny, very *expensive* new toy, would you?' He sipped his drink. 'But hey, it's still a free trip to the moon, right? And at least there won't be any reporters there. Present company excluded.'

'How do you handle it?' Tonya asked. 'Living life in a fishbowl?'

'Real drinks help, for starters. Thank God it's just the ship that's dry. But, really, I don't know. I've been doing it so long, to me it's as natural as breathing. I wouldn't worry, though. Speaking of fishbowls, the public has the mind of a goldfish. Look, I overheard some of what you said to Penelope. Don't worry. Whatever they're on you about now, they'll forget it soon enough. Something shinier will catch their attention. It always does.'

Jackson reappeared on the Deck, immediately spotted Bobby and waved. Bobby smiled and waved back.

'Almost always, anyway,' he said. 'You write for the UK papers, right?'

'The glorious world of tabloid journalism.'

'You probably know some people then? Agents and—'

'Bobby!' Jackson squeezed into the booth on the other side of Tonya, then leaned over her like she wasn't even there. 'You never finished your story about auditioning for *The Masked Singer* spin-off.'

'Sorry, Jacks. I'm beat. Was just about to head to bed. We'll talk tomorrow, OK?'

'OK!'

'Goodnight, Ms Burton. See you folks tomorrow.' Bobby nodded and took his glass with him.

Jackson bounced his knee up and down as he watched Bobby leave, saying nothing to Tonya.

'Oh Bobby wait!' He sprang up and ran after him.

'That poor man,' Tonya sighed, and took her time finishing the orange juice she desperately wished had vodka in it.

Freddy had returned to his cabin to read, but afraid of knocking over his glass of water in the night, had carried it back to the Deck. Now he felt bad leaving his empty glass on the bar after the crew had already cleaned everything up, but decided that was better than accidentally making a mess in his cabin.

When he turned back around, he saw Dr Wyss taking something from a table and slipping it into his pocket. The man caught Freddy staring and came over.

'Just between you and me,' he whispered, and showed Freddy what he'd taken – one of the ship's drinks coasters. 'What's a holiday without a few souvenirs? Make sure to get one for yourself.'

He patted Freddy on the arm and flashed him a smile, then headed to the cabins.

Freddy thought smiles like that only existed in old Cary Grant movies. Encouraged by Dr Wyss, he leaned over the bar and saw the stack of coasters there. He reached for one, but as soon as he had it in his fingers, he couldn't do it.

'No. Nope. Maybe I can ask someone? I bet if I ask—'

He righted himself and turned round, accidentally bumping into the German lady. The remnants of her drink spilled from her glass and onto her shirt. Freddy only knew English, but he was pretty sure that what she'd shouted was a curse word.

'I'm so sorry, Mrs Richter. I mean Frau Richter. Do you need a napkin?'

She stepped back from him as if burned.

'I'm so sorry,' he said again.

She set her glass down hard on the bar. 'Let the monkeys out of the zoo and what do you expect to happen.'

Freddy no longer felt sorry. 'What did you just say?'

Without another word, Frau Richter spun on her heel and marched from the Deck. Freddy kept his eyes on her until she was gone. He supposed there always had to be one – at least one. Not like people would just leave their prejudices behind when they got on the shuttle. And at least he knew one person to avoid for the next two weeks. Still, Freddy knelt down and rubbed vigorously at the spill on the floor with an increasingly tattered napkin until his anger ebbed away.

Sasha made the sign of the cross then slowly got to her feet. Only forty, and already her knees were like those of an old lady. Like her mother, she would likely need a knee replacement by forty-five, but even the pain wasn't enough to dampen her mood. Not today. With a smile, she limped from the disembarking chamber – the only place on the ship with enough space and quiet to pray – and found Uchida in the corridor, watching the stars through the porthole window.

'You didn't need to wait for me.' Her smile grew wider as she spoke.

'It's no trouble. Besides, I admire the view.' He smiled at her and reached for her hand. Sasha blushed.

'It's beautiful,' she said, taking his hand and joining him at the window. The peace that came from prayer resonated through her and became amplified by her view of the stars.

'I never thought I would get to do something like this. I never thought I deserved something like this,' she said. As she went to rest her head on Uchida's shoulder, she noticed the sombre mood that had come over him.

'Neither did I,' he replied. He looked at her with a recognisable melancholy, one she had seen in the mirror far too many times.

'But we're here now,' she told him. 'Wouldn't it be worse to dwell in a personal darkness than waste the beauty of all that light?'

He smiled again, but his smile lacked the spark it had held before. He gently withdrew his hand and bowed.

'Goodnight, Ms Eris.'

Sasha returned the bow.

'Goodnight, Mr Uchida.'

She watched him continue down the corridor to his cabin.

'*I'd be careful.*'

Sasha spun round to see Alison in pink silk pyjamas, leaning in the doorway of the toilets, the ship's complimentary toiletry bag swinging from her fingers.

Alison stepped forward, her eyes not on Sasha but on the path Uchida had taken. 'A man like that? A man with that kind of money? They don't even know when they're hurting you.'

'I know how to protect myself,' Sasha said.

'I'm sure you do. But out here . . .' She looked out of the same window Sasha and Uchida had been admiring the view from moments before. 'People often try to be someone else on holiday, don't they? When they're away from home. Away from the people who know them. And we are far, far away.'

'You think he is being nice to me only because we're on this trip?'

Alison sighed and shrugged. 'I don't know. I hardly know the man. But that's just it, isn't it? All of us hardly know each other. We're all just strangers floating in a metal tube.'

'You and Dr Wyss seem friendly enough.'

'Erik isn't worth billions. But also, whatever fun I'm going to have up here, I know it'll just be that – fun. A fling. It'll be back to Earth and the real world soon enough.' She placed a hand on Sasha's shoulder. 'Woman to woman, I would just be careful with him. You don't want to get yourself hurt over a man like that.'

Sasha stepped away. 'Thank you, but as I said, I know how to protect myself. Have a pleasant evening, Professor Crane.'

Sasha hurried away before Alison could say anything else. Once in the privacy of her small cabin, she retrieved the battered Bible from her bag. Professor Crane could keep her negativity to herself. This trip was a miracle. A renaissance. A sign. Nothing would dampen her spirits. She opened the cover of the Bible, revealing the hollowed-out pages filled with folded letters. She unfolded the most recent letter.

Ma chère belle, je t'aime . . .

She tore the letter in half then quarters and set the scraps aside. She did the same with the next letter and the one after that until each letter had been reduced to pieces, her spirit lifting with each whispered rip. She deposited the pieces into her room's waste receptacle then retrieved the paper napkin Uchida had given her, the one on which he had doodled the shape of a building he wished to develop. She ran her fingers over the ink, then delicately placed it into the hollowed centre of the Bible.

Penelope woke to a darkened cabin. According to the ship, it was around 3 a.m. All was quiet. Or was it? Had there been a crash? Something falling? What had woken her?

Out of habit, she reached for her phone, but it wasn't there. Then her tired brain remembered. All of their phones were back on Earth. She tried to tell herself it was nothing. Her body had woken of its own accord, courtesy of this strange environment. While it was unusual for her to wake up for no reason, she was in an unusual situation.

As she tried to return to sleep, the voices approached her door. The words were muffled, but she could now tell it was an argument. Two women. Penelope climbed out of bed to get closer to the door. She recognised the voices now – the PR women.

'. . . *don't like this.*'

'*It'll be fine.*'

'*Who gave the approval for this . . .*'

'*. . . .do what we're told. And don't say anything to the . . .*'

Penelope tripped over her suitcase. It wasn't loud, but loud enough for a time when everyone was expected to be asleep. Penelope froze, but it was too late. The PR women's voices went silent and the footsteps quickly faded away.

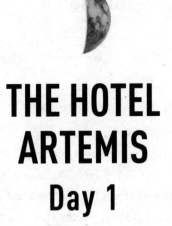

THE HOTEL
ARTEMIS
Day 1

Chapter 4

A flurry of activity surrounded the group as they prepared to disembark. After the ship had safely docked at the hotel, the group had been told to wait in the embarking/disembarking chamber, while in the corridors around them, the crew rushed to and fro with carts, unloading the supplies the ship had transported for the hotel along with, Penelope assumed, the guests' luggage. During their ship meeting yesterday, the guests had been informed that cargo unloading would happen concurrently with the guests' disembarking. There was a separate crew-only area of the ship that had docked with a parallel entrance to the hotel so that the cargo and luggage could be unloaded out of sight of the guests. The main hotel staff was already inside the hotel – sent ahead on a transport ship a week prior to the guests' departure so that they could prepare the hotel and also acclimatise to their surroundings. All of the ship's crew, with the exception of the PR women, would be returning immediately to Earth.

The guests had also been told that they were supposed to be welcomed into the hotel while this cargo and luggage unloading process was underway. However, they seemed to have been forgotten in the hustle and bustle. Even Uchida could not get their attention. Only a few quiet words from Sasha kept him from further anger and further action.

'They were supposed to allow us out,' Uchida said.

'Maybe they forgot?' Sasha said. 'Or they're running behind?'

Suddenly, a pair of flustered flight attendants hurried into the chamber, each carrying five shoeboxes, each one labelled with a guest's name.

'Please change your footwear prior to disembarking,' one told Penelope as he shoved a box into her hands. 'You may place your current footwear into the box.'

Penelope lifted the lid to see a pair of trainers in the grey and purple Hotel Artemis colours.

'We have to change our shoes? I don't remember this from the meeting,' she said.

'Is this like the flight suit thing?' Alison asked, popping a fresh piece of nicotine gum into her mouth. She offered a piece to Frau Richter, who grimaced and turned away.

'These are hideous,' Frau Richter said, examining one of the shoes.

'You are required to wear the hotel-approved footwear,' the flight attendant said. 'All will be explained in the on-boarding video.'

'What on-boarding video?' Frau Richter asked. 'You said you told us everything we needed to know in the meeting yesterday. Where are those women? The women from public relations?'

Dr Wyss placed his hand on Frau Richter's arm. 'I'm sure they just forgot.'

He whispered something else to her in German, which calmed her enough so that she began to put on the shoes.

A third flight attendant appeared, whispered to the other two, and then all three were gone without further explanation. While the guests changed footwear, the rear door of the chamber slid shut, trapping them all inside. Complaints rang out. Uchida even banged on the door until an automated voice spoke over the intercom.

'Ladies and gentlemen, thank you for your patience. Please wait. Disembarking will commence momentarily.'

Nothing happened.

Some of the guests jockeyed for position near the chamber exit, but Penelope was content to wait at the back. Now that the flight was over – that the ship had stopped moving – a sense of calm had come over her. They were here. They had docked safely.

The opposite, however, seemed true of her fellow guests. The usually calm Freddy shifted from foot to foot. Tonya kept complaining about tightness in her neck and shoulders and repeated loudly to anyone who would listen that the first thing she was doing was getting a massage at the hotel spa. Sasha constantly clicked her pen and tapped it against her notebook, which she gripped so tightly in her hand, her knuckles were turning white, as she listened to Uchida's continuous complaints. Frau Richter and Alison were being snippy with one another as they jockeyed for Dr Wyss's attention while the man himself pretended to be oblivious. Penelope knew he was pretending because whenever Alison or Frau Richter made a particularly sharp barb, Penelope caught him smirking. Jackson talked a mile a minute, but only to Bobby, who nodded politely but clearly wasn't listening.

Finally, the room went dark. A large screen lit up on the front wall and a pre-recorded video began to play. 'The Hotel Artemis' appeared on the screen in bold script, replaced with the face of a white, blonde, blue-eyed model.

'Welcome, travellers, to the Hotel Artemis! Please pay careful attention to the following instructions. At the Hotel Artemis, all that comes second to our luxury is your safety. In just a moment, you will disembark and enter the pressurisation chamber. Once the doors are sealed behind you and pressure is equalised, the doors in front of you will open onto the lobby.'

A computer-rendered image of the decadent hotel lobby, bustling with guests and staff, appeared.

'Complimentary champagne will be available in the lobby and will also be brought to your suite upon request. Your luggage is already en route to your private suite and will be waiting for you when you arrive. Once you enter the lobby, please proceed to Reception, where your personal attendant will meet you and escort you on your own private tour of the hotel. Your biometric data has already been assigned to your suite. That's right! No key cards needed. Your handprint will be your key.'

The video continued, informing them of the various hotel amenities, including the infinity pool, spa, restaurant, cafe, library, casino, piano bar . . . Penelope lost track. The hotel seemed massive. She might not need to see any of these people until the return voyage.

'For your own safety, specially designed, weighted footwear has been provided for all guests. Various types and styles await you in your suite. While the Hotel Artemis aims to mimic Earth's gravitational pull as closely as possible, these shoes are necessary to provide further stability for guests. If you require an additional size or style, speak to your personal attendant who will be happy

to assist you. Please remember that there is no cellular or Wi-Fi service at the hotel. You are here to enjoy your time away from the hustle and bustle of Earth. In the event of an emergency, staff may activate a signal to call for assistance from Earth. Assistance will arrive promptly in three days' time. You can be assured that all staff are fully trained in emergency procedures and protocols. Your personal attendant will show you to your muster station during your private on-boarding tour. Now, welcome to the Hotel Artemis! We hope you enjoy an out-of-this-world stay!'

The video ended and the lights immediately came on. The door to their right slid open and the automated voice directed them to calmly exit the ship and enter the pressurisation chamber.

'Why does this remind me of the line for The Haunted Mansion?' Freddy asked.

'Because I think they used the same engineers,' Tonya quipped.

'Will it be the same crew on the return trip?' Sasha asked, glancing around. 'I didn't leave a tip.'

'The trip is all expenses paid,' Jackson said. 'Why would you leave a tip?'

'Because it's the nice thing to do.'

No one saw them off the ship. Not even the ever-present PR women appeared. Soon, the ten of them were all clustered in the pressurisation chamber. Without warning, the doors slid shut behind them. Another automated announcement came over loudspeakers.

'Please wait. Pressurisation in progress.'

The anxious annoying chatter that had filled the ship all morning and afternoon now turned to excitement. Everyone was smiling, even Penelope. She looked down at the metal floor.

Underneath that metal was the moon. She was standing on the moon. Her five-year-old self with the glow-in-the-dark stars on her bedroom ceiling would never have believed it.

'*Pressurisation complete. Welcome to the Hotel Artemis.*'

The large double doors at the front of the chamber slid open.

There, in all its glory, awaited the lobby of the Hotel Artemis.

They moved forward as a group, awed into silence. Penelope thought she was still looking at the video. How could this be real?

An orchestral version of 'Fly Me to the Moon' played softly in the background. The floor was made from a special type of see-through material that mimicked glass but was much sturdier, so that the surface of the moon could be seen beneath their feet. Slightly to their right, a large, curved reception desk of grey marble dominated the lobby. On the left-hand side of the reception desk rose a grand staircase that led up to a balcony above. The staircase, also made from grey marble, mimicked the moon's surface. To the right of the desk was the hotel shop, a glistening display of silver and gold shining objects lined up to commemorate the Hotel Artemis experiences, all available for purchase.

What drew the eye, however, was the far wall beyond the staircase. A seamless, two-storey window revealed the moon's horizon and, beyond it, Earth. Earth like they had only seen it in pictures. An illuminated blue globe, a beacon of light in the utter blackness of space. The view was so clear, it was like there was no separation between them and space. Like they could walk right out of the hotel and onto the moon.

Something smacked against the hotel's floor.

'Ow!' Alison exclaimed. She'd tripped over a suitcase. 'What the—'

Initially lost in the magnificence of the view, no one in the group had noticed their luggage piled near the pressurisation chamber. All ten bags, clustered together, like a wart on a beautiful face.

'Weren't our bags supposed to be taken to our rooms?' Alison asked.

'Perhaps,' said Dr Wyss, 'there are a few kinks in their system that remain to be worked out.'

'Yes,' Tonya said, staring at the vast, spacious, and – as Penelope was realising – very empty lobby. 'Like the staff remembering what time they're supposed to turn up?'

Save for the ten of them, the lobby was completely empty. Except for 'Fly Me to the Moon,' the hotel was silent. Everything *looked* exactly as it was supposed to according to the video, except no one else was here.

Bobby called out a booming *hello*.

The only response was an echo.

Slowly, they drifted to various parts of the lobby, too shocked, too unsure, to say anything. Bobby and Jackson walked towards the main restaurant – the Harvest – located to the left of the pressurisation chamber, its entrance facing the reception desk. Dr Wyss and Alison went over to the hotel shop. Sasha remained in the centre, chewing her pen while Uchida examined the reception desk.

Penelope ended up at the observation window, staring at Earth. But instead of being awed at the sight, of feeling the gratitude for Earth being so far away, the fear that had plagued her for the last three days re-emerged.

Freddy joined her at the window.

'I don't like this,' she said. 'Is the ship still here?' Her voice caught in her throat. She turned from the observation window and said it louder. 'Is the ship still here?'

Though she didn't shout, her voice echoed as much as Bobby's had. The group all glanced at each other, as if they hadn't before considered the possibility of asking that question.

'No,' Frau Richter answered. 'Look.'

She pointed to a screen on the wall by the doors to the pressurisation chamber. It showed the view outside the docking station, the ship already in the distance.

'They moved fast, didn't they?' said Jackson. 'I thought they weren't due to depart until tomorrow.'

'Is there any way to reach them?' Penelope asked. 'Any radio or something?'

She curled her hands into fists to hide the fact they were shaking and looked at Uchida, who remained near the reception desk.

'The emergency signal!' Alison called out. 'The video said there was an emergency signal somewhere, right?'

'We need to find it,' Penelope said.

'Wait!' Bobby shouted.

'For what?' Penelope asked. 'If we don't call them back now, it'll take days for anyone to rescue us.'

'She's right,' Freddy said.

'I agree with Detective Strand,' Uchida said, which surprised Penelope. Not that he agreed with her, but that that he knew her name and occupation.

'Rescue us? From what?' Bobby spread out his arms. 'From the most luxurious hotel in the world? No, sorry. Not the world. The universe?'

'But something's wrong,' Penelope said. 'Can't you see that?'

'What's wrong? OK, so there's no staff here. That we can see, anyway. But do you know what is here? Our luggage.' He patted the pile of cases then crossed the lobby. 'And the champagne. Freshly poured. See? It's still fizzing for God's sake. And here, do you smell that?' He flung open the doors to the Harvest Restaurant. Inside sat a large round table set for ten, appetisers already plated, with a steaming buffet to the right, overflowing with food.

'That to me looks like dinner is served, don't you think?' Bobby said.

The guests looked uncertain now. Penelope glanced at Alison who shrugged.

'What I mean is, we don't see anyone. But does that mean there's no one here?' Bobby smiled. 'Oh, come on. I might be the only one here who's been on a reality show but it's obvious, isn't it?'

No one said anything.

'This has all been staged! It's part of the plan!'

'What plan?' Penelope asked. 'Whose plan?'

'The company that owns the hotel, the Apollo Group. Come on, you saw the media hoopla they put us through ever since our names were announced. The amount of coverage we've gotten on the news? You think they're gonna give up all that publicity now that we – the first group of commercial travellers to the moon – have arrived? Everyone and their mother wants to know what we're doing up here.'

'Are you saying they're filming us?' Penelope asked. 'That everyone else who's supposed to be here is hiding because they've set us up for some sort of reality television . . . thing and they're going to broadcast this on Earth?'

'That's exactly what I'm saying. Ten strangers, on the moon, living in the kind of luxury they'd never have in their regular lives?' He glanced at Uchida. 'Well, most of them, anyway.'

'But why,' said Dr Wyss, 'pretend the staff is not here?'

''Cause every show needs drama! Reality TV is scripted as hell. I don't think I need to tell you that. Even shit like *Survivor*. They have to set up these scenarios to give the audience something interesting to watch. It'd be boring as hell if we were just eating or swimming or whatever. They need to manufacture conflict. And what better way to do that than immediately shake up our expectations on arrival? Shows pull shit like this all the time – starting the game before the cast *thinks* it's started. Starting a game when the cast *wasn't expecting* a game at all.'

'But don't they need our permission?' Sasha hugged her notebook to her chest. 'To broadcast our faces on television, don't they need permission?' She directed the question at Frau Richter.

'Not my area of the law,' Frau Richter said, 'but I believe so, yes.'

'You wanna talk permission? OK,' said Bobby. 'How many of you signed that fifty-page contract they sent us?'

Everyone, including Penelope, raised their hands.

'Right. And how many of you actually read all fifty pages?'

Everyone lowered their hands.

'Not even you?' Sasha asked Frau Richter.

'It's a trip to the moon!' she said. 'I could never afford anything like this. There wouldn't have been anything in that contract that would've changed my mind about coming. Not even having my whole trip televised.'

'The ship is almost out of sight,' Freddy said.

'I still don't like it,' Penelope said. 'We should get some sort of confirmation that we'll be safe here. That this was planned. Can't one person, a producer or something, come out and explain everything?'

'It won't happen, I'm telling you,' Bobby said. 'You watched the introductory video. The only way we can communicate with anyone outside of this hotel is that emergency signal. We press that, they show up. It's over. You think they'll let us stay after wasting their time with a false alarm?'

'We don't know it's a false alarm,' Penelope said.

'It's almost gone.' Freddy glanced between the screen and the group.

'Well, I agree with Bobby,' said Jackson.

'Of course you do,' Alison said.

'What's that supposed to mean?'

'Hey,' Bobby stepped in. 'Here's a good ol' democratic idea. Why don't we take a vote? All those in favour of staying, raise your hands.'

Bobby's and Jackson's hands went up first. Then Dr Wyss, Tonya and Sasha. Uchida did not raise his hand but nodded in the affirmative. That gave Alison and Frau Richter the confidence to raise their hands. And then, finally, Freddy.

'Sorry,' he apologised to Penelope. 'I mean, it's the moon!'

'All those opposed?' asked Bobby.

Everyone lowered their hands and looked at Penelope. She kept her arms crossed, closed her eyes. Settled her breathing.

Focused on the firm ground beneath her feet. She didn't want to be the bad guy, didn't want to make the wrong choice, not again. And if everyone else was comfortable with staying . . .

'All right,' she sighed. 'But if anything happens that even seems to threaten our safety – anyone's safety – even if the two weeks aren't up, we press the button. Agreed?'

Bobby smiled. 'Agreed! Now, c'mon, guys, we're on the goddamn moon! Let's have some fun!'

He grabbed a glass of champagne, hoisted it in the air and led the group into the restaurant. One by one, they grabbed champagne and chatted, picked their spots at the table, the heavy weight of their strange arrival lifted.

Penelope stood alone in the lobby.

'Right.' She picked up the last glass. 'If you're watching just . . . just keep everyone safe, OK? Not like we can step outdoors if there's a fire drill or something.'

She downed the champagne in one go and joined the others.

Chapter 5

To Penelope, the Harvest Restaurant's theme appeared to be 'classy *Star Trek*'. The floor was made of the same material as the lobby, so that the moon's surface could clearly be seen. The large tables at which they sat each bore the image of the moon, but it was no simple graphic. The moon's image had been recreated in what appeared to be moon dust and encased in glass. Dozens of antique-style lights affixed to the ceiling cast light into the darkness. They were of all different shapes and styles but all glowed a burnt orange colour reminiscent of a harvest moon. To the left of the entrance, the entire wall was a viewing window that revealed the view from the dark side of the moon. No Earth here. Only the moon's crust, the guest ship loading dock, and billions and billions of stars. A massive bar, somewhat reminiscent of the one Penelope remembered from *The Shining*, occupied the entire right side of the restaurant, backed by glass that reflected the view from the opposite window, giving the illusion that they were surrounded by stars.

They'd all devoured the pre-plated appetisers – bacon-wrapped prunes, blini with caviar, shrimp and cucumber canapés – then helped themselves to the entrées waiting buffet-style on the bar

– roasted duck with braised cabbage and apples, beef Wellington, pan-seared scallops with roasted mushrooms, pastry-wrapped salmon with raisin herbed rice pilaf. So much food for ten people, and they'd all had seconds. Penelope stared at the buffet as she wiped up the last bit of red wine sauce on her plate with a piece of bread, thinking a) it felt good to have an appetite again, and b) they should pack up the leftovers so they wouldn't spoil. Or would the unseen staff do it? Were the guests supposed to pretend like they were completely alone up here – cook and clean and fend for themselves – or would food magically appear and disappear, rooms magically become clean from invisible hands?

Or was it not pretend? Were they actually alone up here?

Penelope shuddered then looked away quickly, hoping no one had noticed. She focused on a large dessert cart parked by the bar that made her mouth water despite how full she was. No one had gone to it yet and she didn't want to be the first. She'd wait.

That was what everyone else seemed to be doing – waiting.

For something.

For someone.

Sitting around the large, round table in the otherwise empty restaurant, Penelope felt like she was at a wedding where all the other guests had already left. She kept looking over her shoulder, expecting to see a bored waiter encouraging them to finish up. But there was never anyone there.

'A greenhouse?' someone was saying – Tonya. Penelope had lost track of the conversation ages ago. 'There's a greenhouse in here somewhere?'

'That's what I heard,' Alison said. She finished her wine and popped another piece of nicotine gum from its blister pack.

'I never heard anything about a greenhouse,' scoffed Frau Richter, neatly laying her knife and fork across her almost empty plate.

'It's true,' Freddy said. 'Sasha told me about it.'

Frau Richter glared at Freddy, apparently displeased at having been corrected.

'Sasha, tell them what you told me,' Freddy said.

Sasha blushed as everyone looked towards her, but animatedly began speaking. 'Yes, well, it's not a greenhouse exactly. But there is a hotel garden based off the research done by NASA's Veggie programme – the Vegetable Production System – although it's more than just vegetables. The Hotel Artemis has created an Advanced Plant Habitat similar to that on the International Space Station. It's self-sustaining and self-contained with little human intervention needed, with its own water recovery and distribution system, automated temperature and moisturisation levels—'

'I do not remember seeing it on the map,' Frau Richter interrupted.

'It's not open to guests,' Sasha said. 'Except for guided tours. I was so looking forward to seeing it in person. But I suppose that's impossible now. If they're pretending we're alone, I suppose they won't suddenly reappear in order to run the excursions.'

'Something else to cross off the list,' Tonya sighed. 'No spacewalks, no anti-gravity chamber, no moon-rock hot stone spa treatments. What do they expect us to do up here? Read? I should have known they'd find a way to cheat us common folk out of the full experience.'

'Well, the library is supposed to be amazing!' Freddy said.

'I had planned on going on the excursion to the *Apollo 11*

landing site,' Uchida said. Penelope detected a hint of genuine disappointment in his tone.

'Me too,' Alison sighed. 'And they were also going to offer trips to Eugene Shoemaker's grave.'

'Who's Eugene Shoemaker?' Jackson asked.

'Some sort of geological scientist,' Alison answered. 'But he's the only person interred on the moon. How cool is that?'

'More like morbid,' Frau Richter said.

'Hang on.' Bobby held up his hand. 'I'm still stuck on the whole food thing. So they grow their own veggies and stuff up here, but how do they get the fresh meat? You think they have a hidden barnyard up here, too? A few space pigs and space cows?' He laughed. Jackson joined in, so loudly that no one else bothered.

'I believe,' interjected Dr Wyss, 'that much of the meat is actually plant-based.'

Bobby gaped. 'Are you telling me this goddamn delicious beef Wellington I just ate came from a tree not a cow?'

'Well, not a tree, but in all likelihood, yes.'

'Goddamn. I would've ate more veggies as a kid if they'd all tasted this good.'

'Can you imagine how much it must cost to supply the hotel with fresh food?' Tonya asked. 'Just this seafood, for example. I mean these scallops, my God, I've never tasted anything so good. But they can't possibly be planning supply runs every three days. That's the quickest they could get food here from Earth. How do you keep fish fresh for three days on a spaceship? And even if they did, the fuel costs alone?' She shook her head.

Penelope spoke up. 'This is actually more like a cruise, isn't it? The hotel? It has its own self-contained ecosystem with clearly established boundaries. And everything we need must be contained within those boundaries. It's even more of a bubble than a cruise, really, because there's no atmosphere outside. No oxygen. If we go outside, we're dead.'

'Unless we go on a spacewalk,' Bobby said.

Tonya picked up her glass. 'Well, that's a cheery thought. Thanks ever so much, Penny.'

'I didn't mean it like that.'

'Detective Strand is right, though,' Freddy said. 'Food, water, air. It all has to come from within the hotel. There's absolutely nothing out there to help us if something happened.'

Frau Richter glared at Freddy over her glass. 'Do you expect something to happen?'

'Of course not,' Freddy replied, a bit more firmness to his voice. 'It's just interesting to think about. This whole place, it's an illusion, isn't it?' He motioned to Bobby's empty plate. 'The illusion of real meat. The illusion that everything here is as safe as it is on Earth. That everything functions in the way we're accustomed to. Do you know how much effort is going into making this look like a normal five-star hotel when it's basically a space station? It's so crazy! In a good way. Like, we're finally living like they do in *Star Wars*. It's so cool!'

'This is no illusion,' Uchida said. 'It is here. It is real. It is a palace. A monument to man's achievements.'

'And to his pride,' Alison added, stretching her arms above her head, the sleeves of her silk blouse falling to her shoulders. 'I mean, no offence, but this place wasn't built to help advance mankind.'

'What do you mean by that?' Uchida asked.

'She means,' Tonya said, 'that it was built so a bunch of man-boy billionaires could play-act at being explorers and astronauts while stroking their own dicks.'

Uchida's face went red. Nervous coughs echoed around the table.

Tonya held up her hands. 'Present company excluded.'

'And I'm not complaining,' Alison said. 'I would've given my left tit to be here. Thankfully, I didn't have to. But Tonya's right. Let's not pretend we're all Neil Aldrin or whoever doing some sort of service for mankind.'

'Neil Armstrong,' Penelope corrected under her breath.

'The hotel is going to invite scientists,' Uchida said. 'They're going to run experiments here as they do on the ISS, experiments that will help many on Earth who—'

'Relax.' Alison waved him off. 'I'm serious! I don't care. I'm happy to be here. You don't need to justify this place's existence to me. I'm not your mother.'

She downed the rest of her drink while Uchida narrowed his eyes.

'If you cannot appreciate the opportunity you've been given—'

'Who said I didn't appreciate it?' Alison interrupted.

'She never did say that,' Dr Wyss said.

Sasha placed a hand on Uchida's arm. 'All Dai meant was—'

Alison laughed. 'We know exactly what he meant. He said it clearly enough.'

Their voices overlapped one another as the conversation dissolved into bickering, avoiding an all-out argument only because Bobby loudly cleared his throat.

'You know what I think we should do?' His voice rang out. 'We should break this place in properly. We're the first ones here and, quote–unquote, the 'only' ones here. Christ, it's like getting locked in a mall after it closes! Or an amusement park! I mean, who hasn't imagined being in Disneyland after it closes?' He leaned forward as if whispering a secret. 'We can do whatever we want! And I think we should kick things off with a party.'

'That's a great idea!' Jackson shouted – directly into Sasha's ear. Sasha winced but said nothing.

'A party?' Penelope asked. 'Isn't it already . . .' She checked her watch, but her battery had died on the flight and she hadn't had a chance to recharge it yet. There were no clocks in the restaurant that she could see, either. 'Late?'

Bobby waved her off. 'Time is a construct, right? Especially here. There aren't any real hours or minutes, are there? Not up here. And it's not like we can bother anyone next door. Plus, they're expecting us to put on a show. Why do you think they've given us access to that very glorious bar?'

Bottle after bottle of all varieties of expensive drinks were stacked in front of the mirrored wall. The crystal glasses – washed right out of the box, never yet used – were polished and waiting. Penelope spotted a bottle of Macallan – the fifty-year-old Anniversary Single Malt, which on average went for £140,000. She knew that because at last year's department Christmas party she'd almost accidentally ordered a glass of it instead of her usual ten-year-old Macallan.

'Come on,' Bobby encouraged. 'It'll be fun! Let's all check out our rooms then meet back here in an hour for drinks and dessert. Celebrate being here and being off that tiny-ass ship. What do you say?'

Filled with food and feeling safer – or at least feeling the comforting illusion of safety – not even Penelope could object.

Chapter 6

The Hotel Artemis consisted of five main floors with additional mezzanine levels between ground and first, and first and second, which Penelope had yet to explore. The ground floor consisted of Reception and the hotel's managerial offices – off-limits to guests – the Harvest Restaurant, shop, casino, meeting points for outdoor excursions and a medical bay. The twenty guest suites were situated on Levels 1B and 2B – ten suites per floor – while the penthouse suite took up all of Level 3 and the public observation deck occupied Level 4. What the building lacked in height, it made up for in width and depth. Rather than build up, as many luxury properties on Earth were wont to do, the Hotel Artemis had been built out, covering a larger surface area. From the outside, it was octagonal in shape. Every exterior wall was made from glass so that guests could always look out at the vastness of space, the exceptions being the various airlocks that occupied the ground floor. The interior spaces were a maze of passageways, staircases and lifts. Ample signs directed guests to wherever they wanted to go, but as Penelope tried for the third time to find her assigned suite, she wished that maps had been available at Reception. All of the hallways looked the same – grey carpet patterned to mimic the moon's surface, black hallways with pinpricks of light meant to mimic stars, like the walls of the spaceport lounge. Plus, she found it difficult to walk in the weighted shoes. Every step was like picking her foot up out of a puddle of cement while the rest of her body felt light and airy by comparison. All the technology that existed to construct this place and transport them here, and the Apollo Group couldn't have come up with a better solution for counteracting the weaker gravity?

'Or is this all part of the show?' Penelope asked out loud, looking at the ceiling for whatever cameras were following her, though she saw none. There had to at least be CCTV cameras somewhere, but they had been hidden well within the hotel's design. After what felt like an hour, but was probably closer to half, Penelope finally located her suite. It did not help that the twenty suites were not numbered but rather named after various lunar deities, and there was no rhyme or reason to their arrangement. Penelope had been placed in the Auchimalgen Suite. She had no idea what that meant and wondered if there might be a book on it in the library Freddy had mentioned, which she had seen the sign for at some point during her search.

The name 'Auchimalgen' decorated her door in silver letters. It was pretty, but Penelope's tired body cared more about getting through the door than admiring what was on it. She placed her hand on the biometric scanner located next to the door and held her breath. A light on the scanner turned green and the door slid open.

'*Welcome, Ms Strand,*' a pleasant-sounding automated voice with a London accent announced as she wheeled her suitcase into the room.

As soon as the door slid shut behind her, various lights

throughout the suite glowed to life, and a large curtain on the far side of the room automatically opened to reveal the view of the moon and Earth beyond. The window then became illuminated with glowing labels that pointed out specific constellations, satellites, and locations on Earth.

'OK, that's neat,' she said.

'*If there is anything you need as you get settled, please do not hesitate to request your personal attendant – Armand.*'

'Yeah, I don't think Armand is going to be able to help much,' she said.

'*I'm sorry. I didn't catch that. Could you please repeat your request?*'

Penelope thought for a moment.

'Could you ask Armand to come to my suite?' she asked.

'*Request processing . . . I'm sorry. Armand is currently unavailable. If there is anything you need as you get settled, please do not hesitate to request your personal attendant – Armand.*'

'Well, that's fun. Can you have any personal attendant come to my suite?'

'*Request processing . . . Your personal attendant is Armand.*'

'Can I talk to Armand, please?'

'*Request processing . . . I'm sorry. Armand is currently unavailable. If there is anything you need as you get settled, please do not hesitate to request your personal attendant – Armand.*'

'OK, that's enough of that. How do you turn off? What are you? Voice activation?'

'*Earthshine will be silenced as per your request. To reactivate Earthshine, say, "Hello, Earthshine." Goodbye, Ms Strand. Have a pleasant evening.*'

'I'm not sure I like that you said goodbye. That seems pretty . . . final.' Penelope waited and listened. 'Are you there, hotel? It's me, Penelope.'

The room remained silent.

'Oh, thank God.'

Penelope shuffled further into the room – finding shuffling her feet to be far easier than trying to lift them – afraid of touching anything, of soiling it in some way. She knew hotels always wanted guests to feel as if they were the first person to stay in a room, but in this case, it was true. Penelope would be the first to sleep in the king-size bed that took up the right side of the room and that resembled a sleek, rounded space capsule. The first to leave her things on the large circular table in the centre that was decorated with fresh sunflowers – her favourite flower. The first to sit at the desk which faced Earth and sit at the upholstered bench that ran the entire length of the window.

She already felt bad about the temporary tracks her suitcase left on the plush, grey carpet. Most of the room was decorated in shades of grey and white, with the occasional accent of what Penelope had started to call 'Artemis purple'. Even the ceiling had been painted in a way that resembled the moon's surface. It was as if the suite was a cavern carved into the face of the moon itself.

Her bladder full from the drinks at dinner, she ventured into the bathroom. Here, too, the lights came on automatically, and grey and white colours dominated – a large, grey-marble double sink, a rainfall shower and separate plunge bath. The towels were pure white, soft and fluffy enough to be used as blankets. On the back of the door hung an equally soft robe with Penelope's name embroidered in gold.

'I guess that's coming home with me,' she said.

The bathroom also held the faint whiff of jasmine – another of Penelope's favourite flowers – though she couldn't tell where it was coming from. Despite her name being on the robe, Penelope couldn't shake the feeling that she was trespassing. This type of luxury wasn't meant for her. The last time she had felt even close to being this posh was when Mum and Dad had taken her to tea at the Ritz for her twenty-first, and she'd slightly soiled the experience by eating her weight in cream eclairs and nearly being sick on the way home.

'Note to self – do not eat all of the profiteroles you saw on that dessert trolley, no matter how good they taste.'

Some of the hotel's sheen came off when the toilet wouldn't flush properly. It took four times before it finally flushed with a sudden *whoosh* similar to that of an aeroplane toilet. It made Penelope feel a little more at home, knowing this place wasn't as perfect as it seemed.

After washing her hands, she leaned in the bathroom doorway. There was so much space. Too much. If she laid out all the rooms of her semi-detached terrace house side by side, the square footage might have been the equivalent to the size of the suite. But her rooms weren't all side by side. They were arranged on two floors – tight, cramped spaces blocked in by walls. Penelope found comfort in the walls being so close, a protective barrier at every turn. The tight spaces on the ship hadn't brought her much comfort because, at the time, all she could think about was that she was flying – flying in outer space – and on her list of fears (and she did keep a list) flying ranked higher than open spaces. Now she was stationary, which was an improvement, but the space around her was vast.

As she pictured her tiny, lovely little house, the suite suddenly felt too big. She couldn't even look out of the window without becoming dizzy or nauseous. With her eyes half closed, she hurried to the window and found the button that closed the curtain. The fabric drew itself across the view with a gentle hum. Some of the vertigo dissipated, but not all, and she wondered if it would be bad form not to show for the post-dinner party.

Her mum's voice echoed in her head. *A few minutes, at least. Get to know them. You'll be with them for two weeks.*

Mum was right. It would be good to show a little more of her real self and not the terrified, antisocial person she'd been on the ship.

'You won't be here again. Enjoy it while you can. Plus, there were mille-feuilles on that cart not just profiteroles.'

Deciding the hotel could not fault her for anything after pulling this stunt, Penelope rearranged what furniture she could, bringing tables and chairs closer to the bed, which was too large to move, in order to make the room seem smaller around her. After that, she unpacked her things, getting more accustomed to the suite as she did so. In the walk-in closet, she found the other hotel-approved footwear – flats, slippers, an extra pair of trainers, sandals. But no heels, which she never wore anyway. There was, however, a personalised dressing gown to match the bathrobe she'd found earlier.

Even though the hour since dinner ended had already passed, Penelope decided to read through the welcome pack she'd found on the desk before heading back downstairs. The pack included personalised stationery with her name printed at the top of the letterhead above the Hotel Artemis logo, pens, a map of the hotel and printed instructions for how to use the hotel's automated concierge service, Earthshine. She read about how she could adjust the temperature, lighting and control the in-suite sound system from the panel beside her bed. The lights could be switched to manual from automatic, if she preferred, and she could also request amenities, like room service, using Earthshine.

'Well, if Armand is the one who's supposed to be delivering all of that, I don't think that's going to work.'

The pack also referenced a Hotel Artemis tablet being available for Penelope's use, but she couldn't see it anywhere. However, in the pack, she did find a description of her suite's namesake:

> *Auchimalgen, a lunar deity of Chilean origin.*
> *Auchimalgen is a protectress against evil spirits and*
> *disasters. If death is near, she shines red. She was the*
> *only deity of the Araucanian Mapuche that cared*
> *for the human race.*

'Well I like the sound of you.'

Penelope neatly rearranged the information back into the padded leather folder then checked her watch. The others had been back downstairs for at least fifteen minutes already, unless they'd also got lost. She closed her eyes and took a deep breath.

'Think of the profiteroles.'

As Penelope had expected, she was the last to arrive. She stood in the doorway of the Harvest Restaurant while 'Fly Me to the Moon' continued to play in the lobby behind her. The song appeared to be on an endless loop. Inside the restaurant, everyone else had freshened up and changed into evening wear, and she felt decidedly underdressed in her jeans and jumper. However, no one seemed to care. The magic of the place had won them over. They were here. They were special. They were the first.

Though their dirty dinner plates remained on the large circular table at the front of the room and the remnants of their buffet had been left to cool and congeal, the lighting had changed from orange to a soft blue that helped conceal the mess they'd made. In addition to seating at the bar, the restaurant had several black leather booths shaped in half-circles. Each booth had a round table that bore an image of the moon composed out of what appeared to be actual moon dust encased under glass.

Penelope made no grand entrance, instead making a beeline for the dessert trolley, grateful to see that there were plenty of profiteroles and mille-feuilles left. After filling a plate, she looked for a place to sit.

Dr Wyss had taken over bartending duties, so skilled at spinning glasses and bottles and mixing drinks, it was obvious he'd had some sort of professional experience. He served Uchida, who seemed to have warmed to someone other than Sasha and sat near him at the bar. The two were also joined by Frau Richter.

Bobby had struck up a conversation with Tonya, Alison and Freddy. From what she could hear, they were discussing the psychological games employed by reality TV producers. Jackson, seated next to Bobby, floundered at the edges of the conversation, unable to keep up or contribute. Penelope nibbled on a profiterole as she watched Freddy try to get Jackson involved in the conversation by asking him about his work as an accountant, but Jackson didn't seem interested in speaking to anyone but Bobby.

Penelope stood with her plate, unsure of where to go. Everyone seemed so at ease in their conversations. She pictured herself like Jackson – trying too hard to shoehorn herself into a group – and debated sneaking back to her room with her desserts before anyone noticed her. Then Freddy spotted her and, with a big smile and wave, called for her to come over.

'Oh my God, those are so good, aren't they?' He pointed at her profiteroles, whispering as Tonya spoke.

'The Bahloo Suite,' Tonya was saying. 'Apparently, it's an Aboriginal lunar deity most often associated with serpents. And I can't help but think they chose it for me on purpose! I mean, everything else has been personalised. I don't even remember telling anyone I liked blue daisies. And there they are – a whole vaseful right there, as soon as I walk into the room.'

'They should have spent more time on the functionality aspect,' Alison said, swirling a glass of wine. 'It's great having an embroidered robe and all that, but I can't get that automated concierge thing to shut up!'

'Have you tried "Earthshine off"?' Freddy asked. 'That worked for me.'

'Only about five times.'

Bobby leaned forward. 'I thought I'd try a shower and, when I pressed the button, the damn tub started to fill up instead!'

Jackson laughed too loudly. 'I guess any bath or shower is better than scuba diving in the sewage pit on *Survivor: Botswana*, right?' He laughed again, but no one joined in. Even Bobby didn't force a smile.

'It took me four tries before the toilet flushed,' Penelope said, hoping to course-correct the conversation.

'I'm not sure I can get my curtain to close,' Freddy said. 'You know the one for the big window? Not that I'm not mad about the view, but I don't know if I'll be able to get to sleep with it open. I'll just be staring at Earth all night.'

Tonya finished her drink. 'Maybe we can keep a running tab of our complaints and ask for our money back.'

This made everyone laugh, except for Jackson, who took his leave from the group without a word. Penelope considered calling after him, but then Freddy was asking her questions about her suite and she got lost again in conversation.

Suddenly, several hours had passed and many more desserts had been consumed. Alison, Bobby and Tonya had all drifted away to other conversations, but Freddy and Penelope remained in the booth discussing the differences between US and UK policing, what fiction got right and wrong about forensic work, and their mutual crush on Daniel Craig. Perhaps it was the alcohol and the desserts, but Penelope felt more comfortable than she had since travelling to Cornwall for the launch.

Four or five drinks in – Penelope had lost count – Freddy excused himself to find the toilets. As she waited for him to come back, a snippet of angry conversation caught her attention. Bobby and Jackson were just outside the bar, arguing in hushed voices. No one else seemed to notice. Penelope couldn't hear what they were saying, but it ended with Jackson storming off towards the lifts and Bobby returning to the restaurant. The alcohol had slowed her reactions and she didn't look away fast enough when he glanced her way. He'd caught her staring and was coming over.

'Sorry,' she said. 'I didn't mean—'

He waved off the apology. 'No. I'm the one that should be sorry. In fact, I meant to say it earlier. I shouldn't have put you on the spot about sending the emergency signal. I guess I'm used to this sort of shit happening to me. Stunts like this are what I get paid for. I should've realised how uncomfortable it was for the rest of you.'

Penelope had had enough to drink that she couldn't tell if his apology was sincere or scripted. But in the interest of being a good sport, and because they had to spend two more weeks together, she decided it was sincere.

'Buy you a drink?' he joked.

'I think I'm just about done for the night.' She shook her half-empty glass. 'But cheers.'

'Would you mind if I sat here for a few minutes anyway? I can't tell you how nice it is to have a conversation with someone who isn't . . .' He trailed off.

'Jackson?'

'So you noticed?' His voice was filled with sarcasm.

'Well, it must be nice to have a fan. Someone who appreciates your work.'

'True. I guess. But there are fans and then there are . . .' He smiled and closed his eyes. '"It is the very error of the moon. She comes more nearer the earth than she was wont. And makes men mad."' He opened his eyes. '*Othello*. Can I tell you a story, Ms Strand?'

He looked at the doorway as if expecting to see Jackson there.

'I'm gonna tell you story. So, I had this girlfriend once. Maybe twenty years ago? Or, God, thirty? Christ, it was *at least* thirty. Anyway, back then, I was still trying to be a real actor. She was an actress, fairly popular at the time. Doesn't matter who. But we broke up because I found out the only reason she was dating me was because there was this guy – this fan – that she said was stalking her. The only time he'd leave her alone was if he saw her out with another guy. That was the only reason she wanted to be seen in public with me. He'd never done anything to physically hurt her. Not yet. But if she was alone, he'd always want to talk to her, be near her. She couldn't go anywhere without him turning up. At the time I was between jobs, my agent was about to dump me, no one recognised me on the street. My only fan was my mom. So when she told me this, I thought she was . . .'

'Crazy? Overreacting? Ungrateful?'

'All of the above. I mean, number one, I'm a guy, so I didn't get it. I wasn't as enlightened to the daily plight of women as I am now.'

'Uh-huh.' Penelope tried not to roll her eyes.

'But mostly, I thought it would be great to have people who were that interested in you. Anyway, I got mad that she was using me, so I dumped her. Then she went on to win an Oscar. But anyway . . .' Bobby looked again over his shoulder. 'Now? Now I know exactly what she was afraid of.'

Penelope's police brain kicked into gear.

'Has Jackson threatened you?'

He laughed and waved her off. 'It's fine. I just told him it's been great talking to him these last few days but, now that we were here, I wanted my time alone. Just like everybody else. And he, uh, didn't take it so well. Thought I was joking. So I told him if he spoke to me again other than a simple "good morning", I'd send the emergency signal and tell everyone it was his fault.'

Penelope studied his face. 'You mean that, don't you?'

Bobby smiled. 'Don't worry, I think he got the message.

And I also think it'll do him good. Once he gets over it. I mean, I got the impression that he doesn't get to be on his own a lot when he's at home.'

'No better time to learn than being stranded on the moon.' She looked around the restaurant. 'I guess if they are planning on turning this into a show, you've given them some of that drama they're looking for.'

Bobby raised his glass to her. 'Now you're getting it. Speaking of which, now you owe me.'

'I'm sorry. I owe you?'

'Yeah, I told you something personal about me, so now you have to reciprocate. They'll weave the storyline from us being enemies to allies. People love that shit. But you have to tell me something about yourself – something important. Otherwise they won't have anything to work with.'

'All right then. I suppose I'm just tipsy enough to agree.' She leaned on the table. 'I'm afraid of flying.'

'Doesn't count. You already told me that on the ship. How about this? Why did someone with a fear of flying enter a contest to fly to the moon? Three days to get here, three to get back . . .'

'Go back? Don't fancy hotels like this need in-house detectives?' She finished her drink and examined the empty glass in her hand, how the expensive crystal reflected the lights in the restaurant. 'OK fine. It's not just flying. I'm also afraid of open spaces, the dark, heights, snakes and trampolines.' She counted them off on her fingers.

'And you're a detective?'

'You'd be surprised how little snakes and trampolines come up in police work.'

'But flying, open spaces, heights and the dark? You realise you're on the moon, right? How are you not comatose?'

'It seemed like a good place to think,' she said.

'What is it you need to think about?'

I'm telling you the honest truth, Detective. Please.

Penelope tried to shake the memory of the voice from her mind, but though she no longer heard it, its effects lingered. Suddenly, she became very tired. She noticed that Freddy, on his way back from the toilets, had fallen into conversation with Tonya, so had no guilt about making a French exit. She set her empty glass on the table.

'That will have to wait for another day. Have a pleasant night, Mr Rannells. And if I see you early enough, I'll be sure to keep any conversation to a brief good morning.'

Penelope, full of pastry and whisky and guilt, made her way to her suite alone. She was only the second person – after Jackson – to leave the party. She had never experienced a stranger day in her life and probably never would again. While the alcohol and conversation had served to quell some of her anxieties at the time, now alone in the utter quiet with that voice repeating in her head, they flittered back to the surface. Once inside her room, she double-checked that the door was locked behind her – a red light indicating the deadbolt was engaged – changed into the embroidered dressing gown and reclined on the large bed.

'Tomorrow is going to be fine,' she told herself. 'You're going to enjoy yourself. You're going to have a good time. And you're going to make a final decision.'

Chapter 7

Tonya was lost. Again. She swore her suite had been right here. On this floor. She blamed the gin. The gin had moved her room. She stumbled down the corridor, pressing her palm against every door scanner, hoping to see a green light. They kept turning up red.

She stared at her ineffectual palm. 'I haven't lost my key, but I've lost the bloody room.'

'What are you doing down here?'

Tonya turned around too quickly. The entire hallway spun and she had to lean against the wall until the three people in front of her merged into one.

'Oh! Alison, darling! I didn't know we were on the same floor.'

'We're not. I'm on the second floor. You're on the first.'

'Am I?' Tonya looked from her palm to the doors that had all refused to open. 'Well that explains everything! So I just need to go one floor down? Excellent. Which way is the lift?'

Alison pointed back down the hall from the direction Tonya had come.

'Ta, darling.' Tonya stumbled past her then paused. 'By the way, which floor are we on again?'

'The second,' Alison said.

'So I need to go to the first. Bahloo! I'm on my way! Alison, you're a star.'

'Bahloo. Associates with serpents, you said?' Alison asked. 'I suppose Dalia Joy and her mother would find that fitting.'

Tonya paused, sobered by the name. But not enough to come back with a proper response. She continued towards the lifts, refusing to look back at Alison. As she waited for the lift to arrive, she decided she didn't need her room. She needed more alcohol.

Alison watched Tonya disappear around the corner then slipped into her room – the Igaluk Suite. Once inside, she used the control panel to turn on the ambient noise machine, selecting the sounds of a busy city street. How could people think in such an oppressive silence?

She'd had a healthy amount of whatever the gorgeous Dr Wyss had called his 'Moonshot Surprise' cocktail and wanted nothing more than to change into her pyjamas and spread out on the king-size mattress with the Egyptian cotton sheets. But she had work to do. She shed her silk blouse and trousers and slipped into a pair of jeans and a neoprene hoodie. She could always think better in jeans.

Alison closed the curtains, took one of the hidden cigarettes from her suitcase, lit it up with a match and got to work.

Frau Richter stormed through the hotel. She didn't even bother with the lifts and instead took the stairs, needing to burn off some energy. *How dare* . . . She stopped herself. It did no good, cycling into bad thoughts like that. No good at all.

On her way from Level 1 to Level 2, she tripped over Jackson, who was sitting in the middle of the stairs.

'What on earth are you doing there?' she snapped. She felt a little bad when she saw he'd been crying, but not bad enough to apologise. She had her own problems to deal with.

'Sorry,' he said.

'It's fine. Just . . . just watch where you sit. There's plenty of space. You don't need to block the staircase.'

'No, you're right. Sorry.'

Before she could say anything else, he got to his feet and exited the stairwell through the nearest door. Frau Richter continued up to her floor.

'Some people . . .' she muttered then began searching her floor for a vending machine. Did a hotel like this have vending machines? There had to be some place where she could get something to eat without going all the way back to the restaurant. Something salty. That would make her feel better. That would help her forget how horrid some people could be.

Dr Wyss and Dai Uchida stared down at Freddy, asleep in one of the restaurant booths.

'Should we wake him?' Uchida asked.

'I'm not sure if we can. Freddy?' Dr Wyss nudged him.

Freddy laughed at something in his sleep then rolled over onto his stomach and started snoring.

'Is it safe to leave him here?' Uchida asked. 'He will not . . .'

81

He made a gesture that indicated vomiting and choking.

'I think he'll be all right. He didn't drink that much.' Dr Wyss paused then took a bin from behind the bar and left it by Freddy's head. 'Just in case.'

The men left the restaurant together and paused in the lobby at the observation window.

'It's quite a sight, isn't it?' Uchida said, admiring the blue and green globe of Earth.

'Indeed. It makes one feel . . . quite small, don't you think?' Dr Wyss turned away and strolled over to the gift shop. It had no doors, but almost everything for sale was encased in glass. 'An iPhone case made out of moon dust? A twenty-four-karat gold coaster with the Hotel Artemis logo? A sterling silver necklace with a ruby, embedded in moon rock? And look at those price tags. I live a comfortable life, but spending so much on a single item such as these would not be in my budget. Tell me, Mr Uchida, as someone who could afford to do so, do people who have this type of money really spend it on these things?'

Uchida continued staring at Earth. 'Tell them it is exclusive. Tell them no one else in the world can afford such a treasure. Then, yes, they will buy it.'

Dr Wyss shook his head and started for the lifts. Uchida remained by the window.

'Aren't you coming?' he asked.

'In a moment. I would like to admire the view for a little while longer.'

The doctor nodded.

At the bank of lifts, the doors to one opened and Sasha stepped out, wiping something from her eye as she bumped into Dr Wyss.

'Oh! I'm so sorry.' She smiled.

'Sasha! I thought you went to bed for the evening.'

'I did. I just . . . I forgot something. I'm sorry. I'm in your way, aren't I?' She stepped aside, giving him space to pass. 'Have a pleasant night.'

'You as well.' Dr Wyss stepped into the lift as Sasha walked quickly towards the restaurant. As the doors closed, he saw that Uchida had disappeared.

Bobby Rannells stepped out of the bath and wrapped himself in one of the oversized hotel towels. God, he hadn't felt this good in months. The freedom to move around without worrying about a goddamn camera in his face. At least, he assumed there wasn't a camera. He'd done a check when he first got to his room, but he did another sweep now. No cameras hidden in the usual places. None in any of the unusual places, either. They could be sneaky, though, producers. Catching you when you least expected it. When you thought you were alone. When you thought no one would be able to see or hear your private conversations.

He sat on the edge of the bed, tapping his fingers against his knees. Maybe it was the alcohol talking as he sat there, but the lack of cameras became more concerning than comforting. Despite what he'd told the others, despite what he'd been told, he'd yet to see any of the normal signs that indicated they were being recorded. And if it wasn't that type of set-up, where *were* the staff?

What if, he thought, as he dressed for bed, what if they really were up here all on their own? What if . . . ?

There was a knock on his door.

Day 2

Chapter 8

Penelope experienced a quick rush of adrenaline when she opened her eyes. She had never slept so well in her life and thought something might be wrong with her, that she'd overslept and lost half the day. But the hotel clock informed her it was just past 8.00 UTC. Like the ship, in order to maintain the guests' circadian rhythm, the hotel ran on Universal Coordinated Time. The lights in her suite simulated sunrise, but when she looked out of her window, it was Earth, as bold and beautiful as always, that shone the brightest. Seeing it from this perspective, it was easy to forget all of the terrible things that could happen down there. That did happen down there.

The welcome pack in her room informed her that breakfast was served from 7.00 to 11.30 in the Sunrise Lounge located on Level 1A – the first mezzanine level. Thanks to the map, she knew now that Level 1A contained the Sunrise Lounge, a piano bar and the library while mezzanine Level 2A contained the swimming pool, spa, anti-gravity chamber and gym. She thought about which places to visit first as she showered (after adjusting the water temperature with some difficulty) and dressed. The thought of so much free time was almost terrifying. Days at the Met were spent in mountains of paperwork or tracking down leads on a case. Days at her parents' dogs' home were spent cleaning kennels, walking and training the animals, and completing mountains of paperwork for adoptions. She couldn't remember the last time she'd had something akin to 'free time'. But that was one of the reasons she'd wanted this trip. Time to fully think about her life and what she wanted to do. What she wanted to be. Time to fully process the Bevan case on her own, away from everyone else it had also affected.

As she made her way to Level 1A via the lifts – 'Fly Me to the Moon' played here, too – she decided that after breakfast she'd start with a spell in the library followed by a swim in the infinity pool.

She'd stayed in plenty of hotels over the years and was used to hearing the clatter and din of breakfast service. But all was eerily quiet as she emerged from the lifts. Only the sound of 'Fly Me to the Moon' coming up from the lobby below broke the silence. When she entered the Sunrise Lounge – decorated in warm yellow and orange tones, the opposite of the restaurant, with simpler tables that sat only two or four – she was first drawn to the terrace at the back of the room. The terrace jutted out into space and was contained within a glass-domed roof, allowing patrons to literally breakfast under the stars. The floor was translucent as well. The tables and chairs almost looked like they were floating in space.

Tearing her eyes away from the terrace, she realised that the room was empty. She should not have been surprised, but a part of her was still hoping that some staff would appear. The hope remained when she noticed that, like last night's dinner, a buffet was set up on the far side of the room. Perhaps she would be able to catch a quick glimpse of someone clearing a tray or exiting the room. But as she lifted the metal cloches to see the options, all the food – bacon, eggs, beans, oatmeal – was stone cold, as if it had been sitting out all night. She moved down the table and pressed her hand to the glass jugs of milk and juice. Room temperature. The milk even smelled like it had begun to sour.

Footsteps sounded behind her and she turned to see Dr Wyss enter the room. He looked flushed as if he had just come from working out.

'Morning!' he said. 'How was your night?'

'Um, fine.'

He joined her at the buffet and grabbed a plate.

'So what looks good?' he asked.

'Nothing, actually.' She didn't have to say anything more. He quickly realised what she already knew.

'This . . .' he said. 'This is strange, isn't it?'

'What's strange?'

Penelope and Dr Wyss turned to see Alison and Frau Richter entering together, Alison in a turquoise silk blouse and white linen wide-legged trousers, Frau Richter in expensive black active leisurewear.

'I hope you don't have an appetite,' Dr Wyss said and explained what Penelope had found.

Alison stabbed at cold scrambled egg with a serving spoon. 'Well, this seems to fit with Bobby's reality show theory, doesn't it? "The guests must now make meals for themselves as if they've never had to cook anything before in their lives."' She plopped the spoon back down. 'At what point do you think they'll make us mud wrestle in bikinis?'

Tonya stumbled in next, a large pair of sunglasses shielding her eyes. After they had filled her in on what they'd found, she slumped into the nearest chair, popped two tablets from a blister pack, and dry-swallowed them.

'This must be the most expensive reality show in the fucking universe,' she said, her voice hoarse. 'Do you know how much it cost to send the ten of us here? They'll never recoup that money. Not from a TV show. Not unless they splice us into a Marvel or *Star Wars* film.'

'Maybe they don't care about the money,' Frau Richter said. She picked up an unsliced bagel and began searching for something to cut it with.

'Oh, they care,' Tonya said. 'If anything, they care about what people like Dai Uchida think. Sure, the novelty of the moon will attract the rich folk for a little while, but how sustainable is it? If the filthy rich don't feel like they've been treated particularly well, it won't matter if this place is on Mars or Atlantis or fucking Asgard.'

As if on cue, Uchida hollered in the corridor. '*I requested room service!*'

'Case in point,' Tonya said. 'We're in here, darling!'

Uchida's face was red from shouting, which illuminated an old white scar on his neck that Penelope hadn't noticed before.

'I specifically requested breakfast room service for the duration of my stay. A hotel of this supposed calibre should not expect its patrons to rely on *buffets*.' He spat out the last word as if it personally offended him just to say it.

Alison dropped the serving spoon onto a table. 'I'm not going to be the one to tell him,' she said.

'Mr Uchida,' said Tonya, 'keeping in mind the extraordinary and other-worldly location we find ourselves in, at this moment in time, would you recommend the Hotel Artemis to your friends?'

'Absolutely not.'

'See? I told you. Sometimes bad publicity is bad for business.' Tonya took up the burden of explaining to him the state of the food. Uchida listened carefully. His anger turned to worry.

'Is there really no one here to look after us? What if something goes wrong with the life support systems? Do you think we should activate the emergency call signal?' He addressed the questions to Penelope. Now, everyone stared at her.

'Well,' Penelope considered, 'we should speak to everyone first. We did agree that we'd only press it if we felt our lives were in danger. The hotel appears structurally sound and there have been no oxygen level warnings, so that's no cause for concern.' She remembered what she'd read in the welcome pack about the hotel's various warning sirens. 'There also appears to be plenty of water and food, even if it's not the food we were expecting. And we don't know that there isn't anyone here. It could still be that this is just another trick to convince us we're alone.'

'So you don't think we should press it?' Tonya asked.

'I don't think it should be my call to make. Not alone. We need to talk to everyone. And I'd rather do that on a full stomach. Does anyone remember where the kitchen is? I know I read something about the kitchen in the welcome pack.'

'They have several,' Frau Richter said. She'd given up trying to separate the bagel and bit into it. 'I believe at least one per level.'

After a brief search, they found a door to one of the kitchens in the corner of the room. Alison, Frau Richter and Uchida elected to stay in the Sunrise Lounge while Penelope, Dr Wyss and Tonya searched the kitchen.

Penelope found the lights and flicked them on. The gleaming metal almost blinded her. It was clear straightaway that this kitchen wasn't just clean, it had never been used. Protective wrapping still covered some of the appliances and a few weren't even plugged in yet. No unseen staff had been working here overnight, or ever, it seemed.

'Well, this is fun,' Tonya said.

'The refrigerator is working,' Dr Wyss said, and opened the massive doors. 'But there's nothing in here.'

'Maybe they weren't planning on using all of the kitchens until they're open to full capacity?' Penelope asked. 'It can't be cost-effective running every kitchen for only ten people.'

'There must be food somewhere,' Dr Wyss said. 'Perhaps a large central pantry and walk-in fridge and freezer. They would probably keep it all in one place whether they were using this kitchen or not. And there needs to be enough to feed all of the staff as well as the guests. This kitchen doesn't offer enough space for that.'

'Surely there must be a kitchen downstairs that serves the restaurant,' Penelope wondered.

'Just what I love, reverting to hunting and gathering for survival,' said Tonya. 'So, should we go be the bearers of bad news?'

As they left the kitchen, Penelope glimpsed a flash of red on the floor near one of the ovens and paused. The colour scheme of the hotel was all greys and whites and purples. This was the first red she'd seen since they left Earth. She bent down and touched it with her fingers. Spray paint. Dry but fresh, as with most things in the hotel. But there was no reason for this splotch to be here. It looked accidental. A mistake.

A scream echoed through the hotel.

Penelope forgot about the paint and ran back into the lounge. The rest of the group was already on their feet and rushing to the door.

'It came from downstairs,' Tonya told her and they ran out together.

Coming down the grand staircase from the floor above was Freddy, still in his pyjamas.

'What is it? What's happened?'

'We don't know,' Penelope said.

'But who screamed?'

'One of the women, I think,' Tonya said. 'But we were all in that lounge.'

'Not all of us,' Penelope observed.

'Sasha,' Tonya remembered.

The three of them ran down the final steps into the lobby where the crowd had gathered. Sasha was indeed there, crying and trembling in Uchida's arms, but she appeared physically unharmed. She kept pointing to the Harvest Restaurant. No one seemed willing to go inside.

'Sasha,' Penelope said. 'Sasha, look at me. Tell me what happened.'

'I thought,' she said between tears. 'I thought breakfast was in there. I thought that's where we were supposed to go. So I went in. And he was just . . . he's just . . . oh my God.' She broke down again and could no longer even stand. Dr Wyss and Uchida helped her down to the floor.

Penelope cautiously made her way to the restaurant's entrance.

'Stay back,' she warned the others. She didn't know what she was about to see, but she was at least trained for situations like this, for seeing terrible things. They weren't.

Still, even she gasped.

Bobby Rannells lay in the middle of the restaurant floor on his stomach, arms and legs spreadeagled, his face turned towards the entrance, his cloudy, lifeless eyes pointed at Penelope. He wore only boxers and hotel slippers. But what shocked Penelope was the pole protruding from his exposed back. It had been shoved into his upper torso and out through his chest, pinning him to the floor. A white sheet had been attached to the pole and stretched out with rope that connected to the nearest wall, holding the sheet aloft so that the message scrawled in red paint could easily be read:

THIS IS FOR MANKIND

Chapter 9

Penelope dismissed every protocol she knew as soon as it entered her head. She could not call in any backup. She was on the moon. She could not call in SOCO. She was on the moon. She couldn't even examine the scene properly because she didn't have any protective gear. She was on the moon. All she could do was stare into Bobby's lifeless eyes and remember their conversations from last night, his big booming voice now silenced forever.

Uchida muttered something in Japanese. His voice jolted Penelope into action. She wasn't alone. There were other people here. And one of them was stepping forward to enter the restaurant. Penelope flung out her arm and stopped Uchida from going any further.

'Stop! No one goes in there.'

She couldn't assess all of their reactions at once. There were too many of them, but at a glance everyone seemed shocked.

Sasha vomited all over the polished floor. Uchida ran to her side, but Penelope's attention was drawn away to Dr Wyss, who was reaching for the doors of the restaurant.

'Don't!' she shouted.

'You said no one goes in there. We should be spared the sight of . . .' he motioned.

'Yes, but you can't touch anything. Not even the doorknob. This is an active crime scene.'

Dr Wyss quickly drew back his hand. Penelope looked around until she spotted the velvet ropes near Reception.

'Here,' she said, grabbing one of the metal poles. It was lighter than it looked. 'Someone grab that end. Freddy. Freddy!'

The young man blinked rapidly as he came back from wherever his thoughts had sent him.

'What? Oh. Right!'

Together, he and Penelope used the velvet rope to cordon off the entrance to the restaurant. Time slowed to its normal pace, and Penelope could examine the group more closely: Uchida kneeling by the trembling Sasha, Tonya with a hand pressed to her mouth in shock, Alison with her hands wrapped around her torso, Dr Wyss looking solemnly at the body, and Frau Richter glaring at Freddy, who was shifting from foot to foot.

'Does anyone have any reservations about activating the emergency signal now?' Penelope asked.

No one objected.

'It should be in the office behind Reception,' Freddy said. 'I'll find it.'

'No, you won't. Not alone. I'll go with you,' Frau Richter said. There was no hiding the suspicion in her voice.

'What? You think I won't press it? You think I—'

'Tonya,' Penelope cut him off. 'Go with Freddy and Frau Richter. The rest of us will wait here.'

The three of them cautiously approached the closed door behind Reception that led to the managerial offices.

'It's unlocked,' Tonya said. 'There's a keypad here, like our suite doors, but this door's unlocked. Do you think it's supposed to be?'

'Who cares?' Frau Richter said. 'I want to find that signal. Move!'

Tonya opened the door and the three of them then disappeared inside.

'It will take three days,' Alison said, pressing a palm to her forehead. 'Three days before anyone will reach us. Three days while his body . . .'

She closed her eyes and shook her head. Sasha stood up with Uchida's help.

The others re-emerged from the office.

'We found it,' Freddy said. 'There's a whole maze of offices back there, but we found it in a communications centre. And, this is kind of weird, but it's not just this door that's unlocked. All of the office doors are unlocked.'

'And there's no one there,' Tonya said. 'There's no sign that anyone's been there. Anyone at all.'

'We are alone,' Frau Richter said. 'Truly alone. No staff would have allowed this to happen. No production crew,' she spat the words as if they offended her. 'And if they had, they would show their faces now. No, we are alone as we first thought. Alone, and trapped here for three days. With a murderer.' She looked at Freddy.

And then everyone else began looking at one another. No one was willing, or ready, to say anything more. Penelope could feel

Bobby's cloudy eyes on her back as she counted the people in the lobby and realised they were short one guest.

'Has anyone seen Jackson?'

According to the hotel register, Jackson was staying in the Coyolxuahqui Suite on Level 2B. The group travelled there together, squeezing their eight bodies into the lift. 'Fly Me to the Moon' played over the speakers.

'We've got to figure out how to turn that off,' Tonya muttered.

Sasha remained pale and could barely stand. She leaned on Uchida's arm for support as they all filed out of the lift.

All was quiet on Level 2B. On Penelope's floor, the suites were to the left of the lifts, so she went left. The group followed her as if she knew exactly where she was going, which she didn't. She read the names on the doors as she passed, hoping the right one would materialise.

'The Coyo . . . Coyle-axle . . . I can't even begin to pronounce it properly,' she said.

'Coyolxuahqui,' Alison said effortlessly.

'Impressive,' Dr Wyss said, ignoring the glare from Frau Richter.

Alison shrugged. 'I like languages.'

'Here it is,' Penelope said. Like with her suite, the suite name was scrawled across the door in an elegant embossed silver script. She knocked.

'Jackson, it's Detective Strand. Open the door, please.' She had immediately switched into her police voice, though it was rusty from disuse. She cleared her throat to call again, but Uchida pushed her aside and banged on the door with more ferocity.

'Mr Smith, open this door immediately!'

Nothing.

'What if . . .' Freddy hesitated. 'What if something's happened to him, too? What if he's . . .'

Penelope nudged Uchida to the side and knocked once again. 'Jackson, we need to know that you're all right. There's been . . . there's been an incident.'

'There's been a murder!' Uchida shouted.

'Out of the way.' Tonya pushed her way to the front of the group. 'Here.'

She handed Penelope a magnetic strip key card.

'It's a master key. We found it in the communications centre.'

Penelope took the silver card and tapped it against the scanner. The light turned green. As the door slid open, she secured the master key in her trouser pocket. She motioned for the others to stay back as she stepped over the threshold. Though she sensed them moving closer, no one else crossed over.

Perhaps because she had used the master key, all of the lights immediately clicked on to full brightness, instead of the gradual soft glow which occurred when she entered her room. Earthshine also remained silent.

'Jackson?'

The Coyolxhuahqui Suite was a mirror image of Penelope's own. Instead of sunflowers, Jackson's centre table contained a large, blossoming house plant – a Japanese peace lily – and his room smelled faintly of pine. While her bed was against the right wall, his was on the left. The large bed was empty and perfectly made, like it had never been slept in. The curtains of the window were drawn shut, hiding the view of Earth. Jackson's suitcase had been placed on the luggage stand but remained zipped shut. No other personal effects were visible. He hadn't unpacked anything. She checked the closet. His hotel dressing gown was there as were all the pairs of hotel-provided footwear. He had the same styles as she except for a pair of men's loafers instead of flats.

Since Penelope's bathroom was on the left, Jackson's would be on the right. Her trainers made no sound on the plush carpet as the crossed the room.

'Jackson?'

She pressed the button that opened the pocket door. The lights automatically came on.

The bathroom was empty. A hand towel had been used but otherwise everything else appeared untouched. Not even a bar of soap had been unwrapped.

The others waited expectantly in the hall.

'Nothing,' she said.

'He must be somewhere,' Uchida said. He held Sasha, who had stopped crying and seemed more cognisant of her surroundings.

'I'm sure he is, but he's not in there.'

'Then we must search the entire hotel! We must find him and—'

'And what?' Penelope asked. 'Like Freddy said, something may have happened to him, too. We have no idea what's going on and I will not be jumping to any conclusions.'

Her voice was stronger now, and she must have made her point clear because no one argued with her.

'Did anyone see him last night?' she asked. 'After he left the party?'

Everyone shook their heads.

'Did he say anything about what he wanted to see in the hotel? Any place he particularly wanted to go?'

'All he ever talked about was Bobby,' Tonya said.

'Isn't there an emergency transport ship?' Dr Wyss asked. 'Maybe he went there?'

'Or to his muster station?' Freddy offered.

'No one was here to show us to our muster stations,' Frau Richter snapped.

'The information was in the welcome pack if you had bothered to read it,' Alison said. 'Maybe we should split up into groups? Half of us could check the emergency transport ship and the other half could check—'

Alison was interrupted by a muffled crash from the floor below.

Most of the group rushed for the lifts, but Penelope and Uchida ran for the stairwell. They raced down one level – racing each other more than they were racing to the source of the sound. Uchida reached the door first, but when he opened it, Penelope slipped through and beat him into the Level 1B hallway. She didn't need to go far after that.

Jackson stood over a broken picture frame he'd knocked off the wall. The red blood on his hands contrasted with the silver of the carpet.

Chapter 10

Before she'd been promoted to the murder squad, Penelope had once investigated a series of thefts near the Savoy. During her investigation, which involved speaking with the hotel's loss prevention manager, she learned the difference between a hotel's front of house and its heart. The front of house was any space visible to guests. The heart of the hotel referred to everything that existed behind the scenes.

The heart of the Hotel Artemis resembled more of a complex brain. The single door behind Reception led to a beehive of managers' offices – general manager, guest relations manager, food and beverage manager, head of housekeeping, front of house manager, director of operations, building manager, loss prevention manager. Only one door – the general manager's – had a person's name along with the title. Every other door stated the title only. There were also different offices for the hotel's lesser roles. Freddy, Tonya and Frau Richter had only located the communication centre so quickly because it was the first door on the right after one entered from the lobby. Penelope had yet to explore all of the other offices because they had found what they needed behind a door within the loss prevention manager's office. This door first led to a security centre, though all of the security monitors were switched off. Another inner door in the security centre led to a room that contained a pair of cells, which also required either the master key or handprint to enter.

Sasha, being an architect, had thought of it. It was only logical, she said, still recovering from the shock, that this hotel – the only building on the moon – would function as its own community. This meant it would include any necessary community services, such as a medical facility, worship space and a jail. And here was its jail. The two identical cells contained a metal bench and toilet. They were enclosed by bars with a single slot wide enough to insert a food tray. This place was not meant for guests. More likely, the cells were intended as a place to hold employees caught stealing or who had drunk too much.

Jackson, in the first cell, sat on the edge of the metal bench. Penelope stood outside the bars. It seemed old fashioned that what was, in essence, a space station would use bars but it did make Penelope feel more at home. She could believe, standing here with Jackson, that they were on Earth. That when their conversation ended, she could walk out of the building and take the Tube home. Or at least go down the street for a coffee from Costa.

Jackson was entirely different than he'd been on the ship. The cocky, brash man had disappeared. His voice, once loud enough to rival Bobby's, had been transformed into a harsh whisper. His long sentences extolling stories of the great Bobby Rannells reduced to monosyllabic answers. Penelope couldn't tell if his haggard look was because he'd murdered someone or because the group had locked him in a windowless cell. He wore loose-fitting tracksuit bottoms and a white long-sleeved T-shirt – not the clothes he'd worn to the party. His hands remained covered in blood. He hadn't asked for a towel nor had Penelope offered one. Jackson himself was evidence and he would have to remain as he was, even though the blood had dried and was starting to flake.

'I didn't do it,' he repeated. For a few questions, it was the only complete sentence she could get out of him. She decided to change course.

'Jackson, I'd like to know more about Bobby.'

At first, he said nothing. Then he sighed and leaned back against the wall.

'I don't know what to tell you.'

'Let's start with the basics. Date and place of birth. Family. That sort of thing.'

'His birthday is September fourteenth. He's a Virgo. He was born in a small town outside of Allentown, Pennsylvania. He was the firstborn. His dad was a shift supervisor at a manufacturing company and his mom worked at an Amazon warehouse. He paid off their mortgage with his first big pay cheque.'

Jackson spouted off the facts in a monotone, like a computer reading a Wikipedia page.

'You said he was the firstborn. So he has siblings?'

'A sister. But they're estranged. He never said why. Not publicly.'

'Did he ever tell you?' she asked.

'Why would he tell me?' Jackson snapped.

'You two seemed close.'

Jackson shook his head. 'We weren't close. We talked a lot but not about anything real. Anything personal. I was just a fan. He made that very clear.'

The hurt in his voice was unmistakable. Jackson didn't try to hide it.

'May I ask why you were such a fan?'

Jackson shifted uncomfortably on the bench. 'Why is anyone a fan of anyone?' he asked.

'For all sorts of reasons, I suppose. I mean I once had a thing for Benedict Cumberbatch that started because I went through a phase where I was actually obsessed with Alan Turing and the code-breaking work he did during the war. I was really into the history of Bletchley Park. But anyway, why Bobby? As far as he told me, he hasn't done any real acting in years. Just the reality TV shows. I guess I'm just wondering, what made you notice him?'

Jackson shifted again, mumbled something Penelope had to ask him to repeat.

'I said I never told him. I never told him why I was a fan. I wanted to but I . . . I was too . . . I was embarrassed. And now it's . . . now I can't.'

Penelope waited for the silence to fill up the room. Then she said, 'You can tell me.'

Jackson sighed, looked even more deflated.

'*Big Brother US*. His first season. I'd never heard of him. Barely heard of some of the B-horror movies he'd been in. I was fourteen in a small town in Saskatchewan and all the other kids seemed to know I was gay before I did. School was rough. Lots of jokes about hockey sticks. My little brother was only eight at the time, so he had no clue, but my parents . . . my parents didn't want to know. I stayed home as much as I could. Watched a lot of TV. I stumbled on *Big Brother* one day, and it was the perfect mindless escape I needed. But then a few episodes in, one of the cast members was harassed for being gay. This one jackass in particular making jokes. And the others were either joining in or ignoring it and I thought, I can't even watch TV anymore. It was like the bullies from my school had reached into the TV to torment me at home.

'I was about to turn it off when Bobby walked into the room. He'd been in the confessional or something and came back in the middle of this harassment. And Bobby, he just laid into this guy. Called him a bigot, an ass, lots of other things. Called out the others for not saying anything. Shut the guy right up. And not only that, Bobby was able to manipulate the group to vote that guy out next. I don't remember anything else that happened that season. I don't even remember who won. But I remember watching that moment, all alone in my little bedroom, wishing that guy could come to my school and do the same thing to my bullies. It was like I'd discovered my superhero.' He looked at his blood-covered hands. 'It's stupid.'

'It's not stupid,' Penelope said. 'But you didn't tell Bobby any of this?'

'I told you I didn't. God, I should have, shouldn't I? Because if he'd known, then he wouldn't have thought . . .' Jackson didn't finish his sentence.

'Wouldn't have thought what?' Penelope asked.

Jackson wouldn't look at her. He kept staring at his hands.

'Jackson, last night, at the party, what did Bobby say to you?'

'We hardly spoke at the party.'

'But when the two of you stepped outside? What did he say that caused you to leave?'

'He said . . . he called me a money-grabbing sycophant. Said I was shit out of luck because he had no money left to grab. That if I didn't leave him alone, he'd have me thrown out of the hotel.'

'Were those his exact words?' Penelope asked.

'I've only been replaying them in my mind every other minute.'

She paused before asking her next question. 'Jackson, where did you go last night after you left the party?'

'I don't know.'

'You don't know?'

'I wandered around for a while.'

'Where?'

'Inside the hotel, obviously. What? You think I went for a stroll around the block?'

'But you don't remember where you went or what you saw?'

Jackson threw up his hands. 'I didn't know I was meant to keep track! What else are you supposed to do when your childhood idol threatens you?'

'That's what you thought it was? A threat?'

'I don't know! But he was serious. At least he seemed serious. I didn't want to have to leave the hotel. But I didn't care so much about that. It was . . . he made it clear he hated me. That he didn't give a shit about me.'

'That must've hurt.'

Jackson lowered his head into his hands, like he didn't even notice the blood on them anymore. Penelope listened as he took three deep breaths.

'Where did the blood come from, Jackson?'

She waited. Let the silence between them build to a crescendo.

Finally, he sat back up, dropped his hands into his lap. 'I guess this is the part where I say I want a lawyer.'

'Or where you say you didn't do it.'

'I've already said that. But you don't believe me. Neither will the others. You've already made up your minds.'

'That's not my job,' she said. 'That's for a jury to decide.'

Jackson laughed. 'Yeah, sure. If the Apollo Group lets me face a jury.'

Penelope slowly made her way upstairs to the Sunrise Lounge where the others were waiting.

I'm telling you the honest truth, Detective. Please. It weren't me that hurt Janice. I'd never. You've got to believe me.

Penelope paused at the top of the staircase and took a deep breath, like the police therapist had taught her to. Jackson sounded nothing like Bevan. Jackson hadn't confessed, but he wasn't professing innocence, either. This situation was completely different, and it wasn't up to her to decide how much of what Jackson was saying was the truth. She closed her eyes, nodded to herself, then marched confidently into the Sunrise Lounge.

As soon as she entered, the other guests bombarded her with questions. She couldn't keep track of who was asking what.

'Did he confess?'

'Was he planning on killing the rest of us?'

'Are we safe?'

She held up her hands and waited for them to quieten down.

'He'll stay in the cell until the ship arrives. I'll make sure he has food and water. None of you has to worry about him.'

'But did he confess?' Uchida asked. 'We have a right to know.'

Several of the others chimed in with their agreement.

'We spoke until he requested a lawyer and then I terminated the interview.'

Another outpouring of voices bombarded her.

Penelope held up her hands again, urged them to be quiet.

'This will never be considered an official interview anyway. I'm a witness to the incident just like the rest of you. Not to mention this isn't my jurisdiction.'

'Whose jurisdiction is it?' Freddy asked.

'Good question,' she said. 'I guess we'll find out when the ship gets here.'

'Do they even know there's a body?' Alison asked. 'Do they even know there's been a murder?'

'We couldn't send any details,' Tonya said. 'All we could do was activate the emergency distress signal. Everything else, it's all shut down.'

'So if they don't know there's been a murder,' Alison said, 'how will they know to send the right people?'

'It is a murder, correct?' Frau Richter asked. 'He is actually dead, and this is not some trick for his . . . his show?'

'The body was still there when I left Jackson to come up here,' Penelope said. 'Bobby is very much deceased.'

'How long is his body going to lie there?' Sasha asked, which triggered another round of murmurs.

'Listen, everyone,' Penelope said. 'We've done everything we can. I know it's hard but the best thing we can do now is just wait. When the ship arrives, then we'll find out the next steps.'

'So what now?' Frau Richter asked. 'We're just supposed to go about our day?'

'Does anyone have a better idea?' Tonya asked.

'Well, I haven't had breakfast,' Alison said. 'Does anyone know how to cook?'

'How can you eat after this?' Sasha asked.

'Because I'm hungry.'

'I have to call my mom each time I need to boil an egg,' Freddy said.

'Fifteen minutes in boiling water, leave set fifteen more minutes, then rinse under cold.' Alison sighed. 'There must be something in a kitchen somewhere.'

'I'll go with you,' Frau Richter said.

Like that, the group began to split up, departing in singles and pairs. Uchida was the last to go. He seemed like he wanted to say something to Penelope but decided against it and left without a word. Before long, she was alone in the Sunrise Lounge with the table of cold, dry eggs, uncut bagels and sour milk, trying to accept the same advice she had given the group – wait.

You believe me, Detective Strand, don't you?

Chapter 11

Tonya had several reasons why she wanted to get away from the others. The first was her hangover, which was like someone was taking a fistful of needles and jabbing them between her eyes. The second was a worse feeling – groupthink. The mob mentality that had made her, like the others, want to lash out at Jackson. It was good he was in that cell, yes, but the euphoria she'd felt as they'd grabbed him? She paused in the lobby, leaned against the Reception desk for support. Helping restrain Jackson had felt good, righteous. The same way she felt when she dug her nails into a good story, and when she saw that story go to press, and when she saw how public fury could be swayed by her words. She loved it. It made her sick. She needed another drink. Or several. But it was morning. Except it wasn't, was it? Like Bobby had said last night, hours and minutes up here weren't actually real, were they?

Bobby.

If she turned round, she'd be able to see him lying there in the restaurant. She looked towards the hotel shop instead, the display cases holding items that would cost her a year's salary or more. Even the Hotel Artemis-themed carry-ons probably cost £50,000 or more, just because they could. Funny, she remembered seeing four of those silver suitcases displayed out front when they arrived yesterday. Now there were only three.

Voices sounded on the landing above as more people exited the Sunrise Lounge, amplifying the throbbing in her head. The entire hotel was open to them. There had to be somewhere she could go for peace and quiet and another drink. She slipped away before anyone could see her, wanting to put as much distance between herself and the lobby as she could.

Dr Wyss followed Alison out of the lounge, glimpsing Tonya Burton's red hair as she hurried somewhere else. He was speaking to Alison, asking her if she was all right, but he wasn't really listening to what she was saying. He glanced over the railing, to the entrance of the restaurant, remembering what lay just behind his sight.

'I'm fine, Erik, really,' Alison said. 'You can let go of my hand.'

He hadn't noticed that he was holding it. He rubbed his thumb over the back of her hand.

'I just want to make sure,' he said. 'Seeing something like that, even if you're used to seeing dead bodies . . .'

'Are you?' she asked. 'Used to seeing dead bodies?'

He smiled and tucked a loose strand of hair behind her ear, let his hand linger there.

'We should talk,' he said, 'about last night.'

'I told you there's nothing to talk about.'

'But I want to explain . . .'

Alison took his hand and gently removed it from where it rested on her cheek. 'I said I didn't see anything. Your business is your business.'

He opened his mouth to say more, but she pressed a finger to his lips.

'I mean it.' She let her hand fall. 'Now, I think I might go for a swim. There's supposed to be an infinity pool on the second floor. They say it juts out over the edge of the moon, so it feels like you're swimming in the stars.'

'The moon is a sphere. It doesn't have edges.' He grinned to let her know he was teasing. She slapped him playfully on the chest. 'Although swimming in the stars sounds like a delight. Maybe I'll join you later.'

'Maybe *I'll* join *you*. The Mayari suite, right?'

'A deity of beauty and strength. Or so I read.' He smiled.

'I wonder why they put you in there.' Alison returned his smile then blew him a kiss.

As she hurried up the stairs to her suite, the doctor watched her go and let his smile fall.

'Dr Wyss.'

He turned and forced the smile back onto his face. 'Hello, Frau Richter.' He stepped closer and rested his hands on her shoulders. 'How are you doing? Are you all right?'

'I'm fine. Everyone here is acting as if they've never seen a dead person before.' Despite her brusque response, she leaned into his touch.

'Perhaps some of them haven't.' He rubbed her shoulders. 'What are your plans for the day?'

'I've not yet decided. Everything I wanted to do, the staff is required. The anti-gravity chamber. The spa treatments. The excursions to the original moon landing sight. I may as well be trapped in the Hotel Vier Jahreszeiten Kempinski.' She closed her eyes as she spoke, relaxing underneath his touch.

'I'm sure it is much quieter here, at least. Maybe, later, we could find something to do to occupy our time. Together.'

Her eyes snapped open. 'I thought you were busy making plans with the young professor?'

He leaned in. 'Plans can change.'

Frau Richter began to smile then seemed to think better of it. She quickly stepped away and cleared her throat. Regained her upright posture. Rubbed the ring on her left hand.

'Yes, well,' she said. 'Perhaps I can find you later.'

'Perhaps you can.'

She gave him a polite smile then hurried down the stairs just as Alison had. Dr Wyss let out a long breath, looked once more down into the lobby, then hurried in the opposite direction.

Freddy stared at his well-loved copy of *Murder on the Orient Express*.

'Of all the books you own, why did you have to bring this one? You thought you were being cool, didn't you? Idiot.'

He'd finished rereading it yesterday, before the ship docked at the hotel, and now it filled his head with no doubt erroneous thoughts about Bobby's death. His murder.

'There is no conspiracy. Jackson did it. He's in custody. It's over.' He tossed the book on top of his open suitcase and paced his suite. 'Nothing feels off. The message on the flag didn't mean anything. Don't pretend you're in a story. Don't bother Detective Strand. You don't want to screw everything up.'

He took a deep breath. He didn't know how the hotel had done it, but his suite smelled like his mother's apartment in Brooklyn. Not overwhelmingly, but it was there. She loved the Wallflowers scent bulbs you could buy at Bath & Body Works, particularly the clean linen one, and that's the smell that seemed to permeate his room. That had to be coincidence though, didn't it, he thought. There was no way the hotel could know what scents she bought, or that the hotel suppliers also shopped at Bath & Body Works. Still, the smell calmed him. He stopped his pacing.

'You know what you need? You need to read something else. That's what you need.' He hurried over to the suitcase and dug through for one of the other books he'd brought. He couldn't help it; eBooks weren't for him. He needed the feel of the pages under his fingers, the smell of the paper. He always left room in his suitcase for books. The hotel had said it was fine as long as his suitcase stayed under a certain weight, and he'd weighed it three times with the digital luggage scale his mom had bought him, just to be sure.

He pulled out the first book he laid his hands on – *And Then There Were None.*

He sighed. 'What is wrong with me?'

Once the door slid shut behind her, Sasha slapped her hand blindly against the inside scanner until she heard the deadbolt engage. She stood there catching her breath, trying to think if anyone had seen her. If anyone had followed her. In lieu of a spyhole, there was a small monitor affixed above the scanner. Sasha turned it on. The hall outside her was empty, at least as far as she could see. Why would anyone be following her? she chided herself. Jackson had killed Bobby and was now safely secured in the cell. Detective Strand wouldn't lie about something like that. It had been horrific for her to find Bobby like that, yes, but she was safe. No one was coming for her. He could not reach her. Not here.

With a deep breath, she finally stepped away from the door. There on the centre table lay her Bible. Though she had destroyed all of his letters, she had read them so many times, the memory of them remained. The Bible only served to remind her of their contents. She had grabbed the book intending to hide it in a drawer, when she noticed a piece of paper sticking out of the centre. She set it back on the table and opened it slowly. The space she had so carefully hollowed out no longer contained the napkin upon which Uchida had scribbled his note for her. The napkin was gone. In its place was an envelope – thick, cream-coloured stationery bearing the Hotel Artemis logo on the front. She held her breath as she slit open the envelope with her finger and removed the letter inside.

His handwriting assaulted her.

Je te deteste . . .

Sasha's hands trembled. It was impossible. He couldn't reach her here. He wasn't allowed to. And where had this come from? Even if he'd smuggled this letter onto the ship, even if he'd paid someone to plant this letter in her room, no one knew about the Bible. And there were no staff. If he hadn't bribed the staff, then that meant one of the other guests . . . Jackson? But Jackson was already in the cell, and this letter hadn't been here this morning. She would have seen it. She would have noticed.

She wanted to tear it to pieces as she had the others. It would do her no good to read it. But he drew her in, as he'd done before. She needn't be told this letter was a warning. His letters always brought danger. She read it anyway.

Dr Wyss's touch lingered on her shoulders as Frau Richter marched down the hall to her suite. She tried to ignore it, tried to push the image of his smile from her mind, and instead tried to plan out a series of ordered events that could occupy her day. First, a shower. Just seeing that body had made her feel violated. It would erase the feel of Dr Wyss's hands on her as well, for better or worse. Then she would run a few laps around the hotel. The gym had a treadmill, she knew, but running on a treadmill never felt the same for her. She needed real movement. She needed to see the scenery change. Running on a treadmill made her feel like a hamster on a wheel. Instead, she would do laps around the hotel's perimeter. Keep her view on the stars. After her run, another shower. Then perhaps lunch. After lunch, she would decide what to do next. Anything that would keep her away from the others. Jackson might have been in custody, but that didn't mean she trusted the others. At least, not all of them. Perhaps she would see if Dr Wyss was available.

She slapped her palm onto her suite's scanner and marched inside, making sure the door was deadbolted behind her, just in case. She wouldn't let them drag her into their nonsense.

Undressing for the shower, she paused to look at her wedding ring. She twisted it and twisted it until she could finally yank it off her finger. Then as she rolled it between her thumb and forefinger, she decided what to do. She settled for placing it inside the bedside drawer. It rattled as she pushed it shut.

With some difficulty, she adjusted the temperature of the water. By the time it was hot enough, she had wasted too much time already. The shower was more rushed than she'd planned, but she needed to keep it short to keep on track with her schedule, her list. She had spent too much time in her room already.

She towelled herself off as she stepped out of the bathroom then stopped.

A paper stork sat on the centre table underneath the vase of roses.

She stepped closer. She had already thrown that away, hadn't she? Maybe she'd only meant to and forgotten. The shock of this morning had tampered with her memory. No matter. She would throw it away now. She reached out to grab it then stopped.

Hanging around the paper stork's neck was her wedding ring. The ring she had most definitely placed in the drawer before her shower.

Uchida looked out of the hotel's rear observation window, near the moonwalk airlock, the one that faced away from Earth, and looked at the endless stars. This was not how this trip was supposed to go. It had all been ruined.

'*Something will go wrong,*' his mother had warned him. '*Something always goes wrong.*'

He swore to her then that it wouldn't. He swore that she would be wrong. And now there was a dead body in the restaurant. Why had Jackson Smith killed him? What sort of message was he trying to send? Did he think this would ruin the Apollo Group? Nothing would stop this hotel from opening. All Mr Smith had done was ruin this trip. Ruin it for Uchida, for all of them.

'No. You are wrong,' he whispered, and he put the view of the stars behind him.

Chapter 12

Penelope left Jackson a tray with a banana, a bagel and a few bottles of water. She said she would check on him later and bring him a hot meal. He said nothing. She asked him if he had any food allergies. Again, he said nothing. He would no longer even look at her. But three days in a cell was a long time, especially with nothing to occupy his time. She considered going to the library to gather a few books for him, but first she wanted to further explore the maze of managerial offices. If she could find some sort of clue as to why they had been abandoned here, some message, maybe figure out how to log on to the computers or turn on the security monitors and find the CCTV footage . . . She had just opened the general manager's office when a voice echoed through the lobby.

'*Please stay put!*'

Penelope emerged from the office corridor to see Sasha fighting with a sheet. Sasha had found what looked like two hat racks (though why a hotel on the moon would have hat racks, Penelope didn't know) and was trying to hang the sheet between them. But she barely got one end of the sheet clinging to the hat rack before the other end would fall down.

'Why can't you please stay put?' She wiped a tear from her eye.

'Sasha?'

The small woman looked up, surprised.

'Would you like some help?' Penelope asked.

'Oh hello!' Sasha pretended she was scratching her cheek instead of wiping away a tear. 'I came down to clean up my mess . . .' She waved to where she had vomited. 'There's no one else here to do that is there? And when I finished, I thought . . . I thought I could make a screen so we could cover . . . so that we wouldn't have to see . . .' She motioned to the open dining room behind her, Bobby's body clearly visible. 'I remember what you said about not touching the door. But I can't . . . he deserves some privacy.'

'You're right,' Penelope said. 'It's a good idea. Let me help.'

Together, the two of them managed to string the sheet up using the hat racks, blocking Bobby's body from view. Sasha said nothing while they worked. The entire hotel was silent, despite there being seven other people around, though only six free to wander about. Penelope hadn't realised how little ambient noise there would be during the day. She wondered if it would be different when the hotel was fully operational, when it was filled with guests and staff, or if it would always have this heavy, underlying silence.

When they'd finished, Sasha thanked her then reached for a small coffee cup on the Reception desk.

'Is that . . . is that hot coffee?' Penelope asked.

'Espresso. There's a machine in the room upstairs. Not where we have – where we were supposed to have – breakfast. Next door. The Cold Moon Piano Bar, it's called.'

'Damn. I don't really know how to work those machines. Did you notice if they have any instant?'

'I don't know about instant, but I could make you something, if you like.'

'Oh, I don't want to impose.'

'It's the least I can do. For all you've done.'

'Honestly, I haven't done anything,' Penelope said.

'You helped me.' Sasha placed a hand on Penelope's arm. 'That, to me, is something.'

They headed upstairs together. Penelope noticed that Sasha did not seem to struggle as much with the weighted shoes as she did. Or maybe Sasha had simply gotten used to them. Penelope did find it was somewhat easier to walk today than yesterday, and hadn't thought of them much when running through the halls looking for Jackson, earlier.

The Cold Moon Piano Bar was next to the Sunrise Lounge, as Sasha had said. The long left and right walls were plain white. Penelope could see projectors mounted on the ceiling that must've been able to shine images onto those walls but were currently switched off. Small glass-topped tables were spaced out throughout the room, each with a pair of small circular chairs that faced the back of the room where an elevated dais jutted out into a space. The glass walls that enclosed the dais revealed the stars and in the centre sat a black Steinway grand piano, though one of the keys appeared to be broken. The bar was on the right side of the room. Behind the counter was a row of coffee machines, as well as a wide selection of croissants, Danishes and other small pastries.

'Are they fresh?' Penelope asked, her stomach rumbling.

'I don't know, I haven't had the stomach to eat anything.' Sasha manoeuvred behind the counter and waved at the machines.

'Any preference? I was a barista while at university. I can make pretty much anything.'

'I'm not fussy. If it has caffeine in it, I'll drink it. Thank you.'

Sasha busied herself with the buttons and knobs while Penelope came around the counter to scope out the pastries. Used glasses lined one end of the bar.

'So you've made a few drinks so far?' Penelope asked.

Sasha glanced at the glasses. 'No, just the one. Those were there when I arrived this morning. After . . .' She closed her eyes.

'How are you feeling?' Penelope asked. 'Seeing that must've been quite a shock. I'm sorry.'

'You don't need to be sorry unless you're the one who killed him. Jackson deserves whatever is coming to him. There is nothing more horrific than taking another's life. Nothing.' A sharp tone entered Sasha's voice that had not been present earlier. 'I'm sorry. It was – it is – a shock. Maybe it wouldn't have been, not so much, if we were home. On Earth. The police would be taking care of it. Not that you aren't the police. But we would be sent home. Or at least not forced to stay in the same place where . . .' She stopped, and again forced a smile on her face. 'Anyway, nothing we can do about it, is there? So we must . . . we must make the best of it, I suppose. If such a thing is possible.'

'I was afraid of malfunctions at take-off, mechanical issues on the ship, getting sucked out of an airlock. All sorts of things crossed my mind. But this – what happened to Bobby – never occurred to me. Did you get to know him at all?'

'We didn't speak much,' Sasha said. 'Only a few words here and there. We didn't seem to have much in common. But he was always very polite to me.'

'Do you remember the last time you saw him? I left the party early. But I can't help thinking, if I'd stayed longer, if I'd been awake, maybe . . .'

Sasha nodded then continued prodding the machine. 'I know. I spent most of the night worrying because . . . because there was no one else here. Or we thought there was but we couldn't see them. The thought that I was being watched, it made me uncomfortable. I wanted to enjoy myself at dinner and the party, but I couldn't relax. I went up to my room not long after you. I tried to wind down, get ready for bed, but I couldn't even get undressed. In the room, I felt . . . trapped. I came back down to the lobby. I thought a walk would ease my nerves.'

'And you saw him then?'

Sasha shook her head. 'No, I didn't see him once I left the party. When I came back down, Erik and Dai were in the lobby. But I never saw Bobby again.'

'When did you go back to bed?'

'I wandered for a bit until I found the spa on the second floor. The anti-gravity chamber is there. It's turned off, of course. I thought about turning it on, but I didn't. Instead I . . . I'm sorry, this is embarrassing. But I sat there in the anti-grav chamber. On the floor. It felt . . . it felt safe. There are no windows. I didn't see any cameras. That's what I kept thinking about all night. How Bobby said there were cameras everywhere. That they were watching us. Recording us. Even though I wanted to be here, even if, without realising it, I'd agreed to someone filming, I wanted privacy. I was upset and—'

'Why were you upset?'

'Oh, nothing.' She laughed and waved it off. 'Frau Richter had made a comment, but never mind now. Too little sleep and too much alcohol, you know?'

The machine began to whir. The aroma of the dispensing coffee made Penelope's mouth water. She bit into a croissant and decided to let Sasha's comment about Frau Richter go for now.

'I still can't decide if Bobby's theory was right,' Penelope said between bites. 'Or if . . . well, the ship will be here in a few days, so I don't suppose it matters. Were you able to get any sleep in the end?'

Sasha hesitated. 'I did. In . . . in the anti-grav chamber. I didn't even realise I'd fallen asleep there until morning. Well, so to speak. I guess there is no morning here? Anyway, I went to my room to shower and change clothes. Then I went down to the restaurant because I thought breakfast would be served there and opened the door and saw . . .' She closed her eyes again and shuddered.

'So the door was closed when you got there?' Penelope asked.

'Yes.'

'All the way?'

'I think so. I remember grabbing the handle to open it. Oh God! My fingerprints will be on the door. You told us not to touch the door and I touched it.'

'It's OK, Sasha. You didn't know.'

Sasha clenched her hands into a fist and Penelope thought she was about strike the counter. But instead, she took a deep breath. Her body relaxed.

'You're right,' she said. 'I didn't know. But it's going to be OK. Everything is going to be OK.'

Penelope didn't know exactly what Sasha was referring to. Before she could ask, Sasha whisked around and served Penelope an espresso in the type of small, delicate porcelain cup that probably cost more than all the dishes in Penelope's house.

'Does it taste all right?' Sasha asked. 'It's been years since I've used one of these. It tasted OK to me, though I've been told I don't have a particularly refined palate.'

'It's delicious, cheers,' Penelope said. 'Some things you don't un-learn, I suppose.'

'No, I suppose you don't. If you don't mind, Penelope, I think I need to go and lie down. Surprisingly, spending the night on a hard floor does not do wonders for one's back and neck.' She smiled.

'Of course. Get some rest.'

Sasha nodded then hesitated, as if she was going to say more. But she only smiled again and left the bar.

After Sasha left, Penelope pulled her hotel stationery from her pocket and wrote down what Sasha had said about her movements last night. She wasn't investigating. Not really. But it wouldn't hurt to keep track of what Sasha had said and pass on any info she had to whatever authorities did arrive. When she'd finished, she tapped her pen against her notes and looked again at the ceiling. It probably wouldn't hurt to speak to the others, either, just to establish a timeline of last night's events while they were fresh in people's minds. A lot of information could be lost or confused in three days' time. Of course, she could just access the CCTV footage on the hotel's system . . . A cloud descended over Penelope's mood once again.

'Because relying on CCTV footage has never got you in trouble in the past, has it?' she said to herself. 'But where are the cameras? The hotel has to have cameras.'

She sipped the espresso. 'Oh my God. This really is amazing. What type of coffee is this?'

As she knelt down to read the label on the bags of coffee beans, her eye was instead drawn to a familiar gold bracelet lying knotted on the floor.

Sasha shoved her hand in her pocket as she hurried away from the piano bar. And the detective. She knew why Penelope had asked all those questions. She knew it wasn't only because Penelope cared. She crumpled the envelope and letter that remained hidden in her pocket, checked over her shoulder and then deposited them in the first bin she passed without missing a step. That was it. It was over. It was done. Whatever else happened, at least now she would be left alone.

Chapter 13

A casino on the moon seemed like something out of a Bond film to Penelope. It also seemed pointless. People had already gambled enough with their lives just to arrive at the hotel safely. Why gamble away more once they got here? Why take such unnecessary risk? She supposed it didn't matter to the hotel's intended clientele, people like Dai Uchida, where they could experience the thrill of winning without the threat of real loss. What must it be like, she wondered, when losing thousands in a single night was like chancing a tenner on a scratch card?

The casino was on the ground floor in the north-eastern corner of the hotel, diagonal to the Harvest Restaurant, if one were looking at the map that had been included in the welcome pack. Penelope hadn't been surprised to find Tonya here, sunglasses on, a cocktail in hand, dealing cards to herself at the blackjack table. The rest of the casino – the roulette wheels, slot machines – all sat silently. Whatever magic a live casino held for some people, it was certainly absent now. Despite the glamour in the design and decoration, the room was lifeless. And, like most casinos, there were no windows. No view of the outside world – or the outside universe – to distract from the games inside.

As Penelope approached Tonya's table, she saw that Tonya was playing solitaire.

'Deal you in?' Tonya asked. 'We can play doubles.'

She patted a stack of card decks, still in their plastic, the backs emblazoned with the Hotel Artemis logo.

'I've decided I'm taking these home. I think we're owed a few souvenirs, don't you?'

Penelope slipped onto one of the stools at Tonya's table. 'There are some pastries in the piano bar upstairs, if you're hungry.'

'Cheers, but I can never eat much in the morning. Especially mornings where I've seen a dead body.' She sipped her drink.

'And you've already been to that bar anyway, right?' Penelope dropped the bracelet on the table.

'I was wondering what happened to that. Cheers. Yes, I stopped in there for a few drinks after the party last night. So, what on earth was Jackson thinking? Although I suppose he wasn't. Nice of him to ruin the entire trip for us, wasn't it? This is exactly why I decided to take unpaid leave from work, risking losing my footing with my contacts while other journalists scoop them up like sharks.'

'It's certainly not what I was expecting.'

'Well, someone was. I mean, what are the odds we have a murder squad detective amongst us when there's been an actual murder?' Tonya flipped over a card.

'How did you know I was murder squad?'

'Because we live in the same city, darling, and I know how to read.'

Penelope shifted in her seat. 'Law enforcement is a popular profession. I'd say the odds of someone in law enforcement being in the group is just as likely as having a doctor. Or a journalist.'

'I suppose. Anyway, go on then. Ask what you want to ask. I know you're not here on a social call, so let's not play with each other, Penny. I've already told you I spent some time in the piano bar last night. What else do you want to know?'

'How well did you know Robert Rannells?'

'I know that he preferred to be called Bobby,' Tonya said. 'He said that "Robert" reminded him of his mum yelling at him.'

'So you got to know him well these past few days?'

'No more than anyone else. The man didn't have much of a filter, if you noticed. Would tell anyone and anything about his life. Professional hazard, I guess.' She finished off her drink.

'How about before the trip? Ever do any stories on him for the papers?'

'Never. I'd heard of him, vaguely, but British readers don't care much about C-list American celebrities. I think he was trying to get into our market, though.'

'What makes you say that?'

'Work in America was drying up, I think. He mentioned something, when we were on the ship, about looking for a UK agent. I think he was going to butter me up for some of my contacts, but well . . .' She lifted her glass for another sip, realised it was empty and slid it away from her. 'Jackson might know more about it than me. They were always talking, those two.'

'Did you ever see any arguments between Bobby and Jackson? Or Bobby and anyone? One of the other guests or any of the crew?'

Tonya shook her head. 'As far as I know, he was charming to everyone. A bit loud. But never rude, not like some can be.'

'Some Americans or some celebrities?'

Tonya smirked than sighed. 'The only problem I know of

for certain is that he had a bad divorce recently. The wife got everything, including the kids. He was so excited to be here, though. I could tell. This trip seemed to be exactly what he needed. So of course he ends up dead.'

'Do you remember anything out of the ordinary from last night?'

'It was our first night on the moon. Was anything supposed to be ordinary?' Tonya rubbed her forehead. 'I left the party sometime after one thirty, when the doctor stopped mixing those fabulous drinks. I was going to go straight to my room, but I got lost. I may have been somewhat . . . inebriated.'

'Do you remember where you went before you made it back to your room? Any place other than the Cold Moon Piano Bar?'

Tonya started massaging her temples. 'I bumped into someone. Frau Richter? No. Professor Crane. It was Alison. On whatever floor her room is on. Then I took the lift up. But I was supposed to go down, so after it went up, I took it right back down. Somehow ended up in that bar with the piano. Saw the coffee machines and thought that sounded good but couldn't figure out how they worked and mixed some cocktails instead. Then there's a bit of a blank space there. I vaguely remember making it back to my suite. And I must have because that's where I woke this morning.'

'Did you wake at all in the night? Hear anything or . . .'

'Penny, Martians could have invaded and I wouldn't have heard a thing.' She picked up the bracelet. 'Thank you for returning this. Now is that all or can I get back to my rousing game? I'm on a hot streak here.'

'It's Penelope. And I didn't come to find you just because of the bracelet. Something doesn't feel right.'

Tonya stopped flipping cards. 'You don't think Jackson did it?'

'I don't know. It could be nothing. Maybe it's as simple as Jackson was hurt and jealous and let his anger get the best of him.'

'I'm sensing a "but" there,' Tonya said.

'It's the staging. If Jackson had lashed out at Bobby in anger – an unplanned act of passion – why bother with the staging? Why not leave his body alone? It's a lot of effort for little purpose. In fact, it's counterproductive. If Bobby didn't have a pole with a message sticking out of his back, Jackson could at least argue it was an accident or self-defence.'

Tonya drummed her fingers on the card table. 'I see your point. Although we literally caught him red-handed. But the pole and the sign? You're right. What's the point of it if he was going to deny murder after the fact? Jackson's motive is in line with an unplanned act but the circumstances make it seem more like premeditation.'

Penelope paused before asking her next question.

'Tonya, I know what I said to you on the ship. But I also know what kind of journalist you were before the tabloids.'

Tonya stilled. Penelope continued.

'Someone killed Bobby, whether it was Jackson or, well, someone else. Normally, when investigating a murder, I'd have a partner. Be part of a team. I don't have another detective here, but you have investigative experience.'

Tonya looked at Penelope over her sunglasses. 'You want me to help you investigate? You don't even like me.'

Penelope shrugged. 'I don't always like the people I'm partnered with. But I don't have to like someone to trust them.'

'I'm almost flattered. But you know what they say. Keep your friends close, and all the rest. You could want my help. Or you could just want to keep an eye on me.'

'Guess you'll have to find out.'

'Detective Strand, that was dangerously close to friendly banter.'

Tonya gathered up the cards in a neat stack, removed her sunglasses and held out her hand.

'Consider me onboard. God knows I need something to do while we wait.'

They shook on it.

'So, Detective, where do you want me to start?'

Bobby had been housed in the Dewi Ratih suite on the first floor, a few doors down from Penelope. Penelope used the master key to gain entry, and the door slid open without a sound.

'Is everything in this place so quiet?' Tonya asked.

'My toilet is fairly loud. But you're right. I've noticed the silence, too. In all this quiet, you'd think someone must have heard something last night.'

'Did *you* hear anything?'

'No, I was asleep as soon as my head hit the pillow. And I'm a fairly light sleeper.'

'See? And your room's not far. There are only ten of us spread out in this massive maze. Maybe it's not so unlikely.'

'I won't know for sure until I've asked everyone. Why don't you start over there at the desk? I'll start over by the bed.'

Bobby's suite was configured exactly like Penelope's. The only obvious indicators that this wasn't her own room were the bonsai tree on the table and the scent of sandalwood in the air.

Penelope slipped on the rubber gloves and booties she had located in a cleaning cupboard and instructed Tonya to do the same. If Bobby's suite was a potential crime scene, she wanted to disturb it as little as possible. Really, she shouldn't have been going in it at all, but if there was even a chance Jackson was innocent, she wanted to be sure. Another face came to mind, but she pushed the image away as she started searching Bobby's room.

Unlike Jackson's suite, signs of Bobby were everywhere. Used towels, bottles of personal grooming products, shaving kits and various hairbrushes littered the bathroom. The closet was already filled with his unpacked clothes, neatly hung or folded in the drawers.

'Well, I don't see any blood,' Tonya said. 'Do you?'

'No. Nothing.'

The question of the blood had been bothering Penelope since she finished speaking to Jackson. Though she'd wanted to avoid it, it seemed increasingly likely that she would need to return to the restaurant.

She continued her search of the suite. The bed was turned down but not unmade – no wrinkles in the sheets or duvet. No impressions on the pillows. His hotel dressing gown was laid out at the bottom of the bed. Had Bobby been preparing to go to bed when he was interrupted? Or had he chosen to sleep somewhere else?

'Listen to this,' Tonya said. She stood at the desk, holding Bobby's welcome pack in her gloved hands. 'Dewi Ratih is a Balinese deity. Apparently, she gets chased and sometimes consumed by the floating head of a demon called Kala Rau. It was their explanation for an eclipse. Consumed by a floating head. That sounds fun.'

As Tonya continued reading, Penelope noticed something sticking out from under the bed – a file box. She slid it out. Inside were standard A4 Manila file folders. Each file was numbered – one through nine. She flipped one open and there was Dai Uchida's face. The first page listed his basic background information. The following pages went into more detail. She chose another folder – Charlotte Richter. Another – Freddy Nwankwo. They were all there, including her. All except Bobby. A dossier on each of them, detailing all of their lives.

'Penelope?' Tonya called.

Penelope quickly slid the box back underneath the bed. She would return for these later. Fortunately, Tonya hadn't noticed what Penelope had found. She was too preoccupied with the notepad she was now holding.

'Is this Bobby's handwriting?' Tonya asked.

Penelope came over to look.

The pad was the white Hotel Artemis stationery with Bobby's name embossed across the top. On the top of the page, someone had written a single question:

Why aren't they filming yet?

Chapter 14

'So are we or aren't we being filmed?' Tonya looked up at the ceiling in the hallway outside of Bobby's room.

'Bobby was at least questioning it.' Penelope also searched the ceiling for cameras she did not see. There were no signs of CCTV cameras – let alone television cameras – anywhere, yet the set-up in the security centre, all those monitors, indicated there should be.

Penelope took out her notepad and scribbled down the results of their search. 'Well, there's no sign that anyone else has been in his room. The door was locked. No sign of forced entry. No indication that a struggle took place or that anything's been taken.'

She also made a note about the file box but didn't say that part out loud.

'But I'm sure yours isn't the only master key,' Tonya said. 'And you didn't even take possession of that one until this morning.'

'Good point. We should search the offices. See if we can find any others, or at least some record of how many there are supposed to be.'

'Jackson didn't have one on him, did he?' Tonya asked.

'No. I had him turn out his pockets. He didn't have anything on him except what he was wearing.'

Tonya leaned back against the wall. 'Bobby is – was – a fairly big man. Even if he was drunk, it would've taken some effort on Jackson's part to take him down. He's skinny as a rail, that one.'

Penelope drummed her fingers on her thigh. 'Freddy's a criminology student, right?'

'You want to bring another partner into this investigation? Or do you think Jackson had an accomplice?'

'I'm not closing the door on any possibility, but I also haven't had a chance to talk with him yet, alone. Not since Bobby was found. Plus, I need to take a closer look at Bobby's body and Freddy might be a student, but he'll have some crime scene training.'

'So you want to go into the restaurant that you said no one should go into and potentially disturb the crime scene you said you didn't want anyone to touch?'

'You looked in the restaurant. You saw his body,' Penelope said.

'And?'

'How much blood do you remember?'

'I . . .' Tonya paused. 'Actually, I don't remember seeing any blood. The sign, it was such a shock. And the sign was red, like blood, but no. There wasn't any blood, was there?'

'So why did Jackson have blood all over his hands? I stood close to him. That wasn't paint on his hands. You could smell it.'

'I think Freddy said he was going to spend some time in the library,' Tonya said.

'I'll find him and examine the scene in the restaurant. I'd like you to keep looking into the hotel's security system. We saw CCTV monitors even though they weren't on. So even if we can't see any cameras, they must be somewhere.'

'Aye aye, Captain.' Tonya saluted her.

'Please don't.'

They agreed to meet in an hour in the main kitchen off the Harvest Restaurant. When Tonya departed for the lift, Penelope only pretended to go to the stairwell. As soon as the lift doors closed, she doubled back to Bobby's room, let herself in and grabbed the box of files from under the bed. If she trusted Tonya enough to let her in on her doubts, she should've trusted her with the box, but Tonya wasn't a detective. She was a journalist. A tabloid journalist who made a career from exploiting the secrets of others. Tonya had once had some integrity when she was a true investigative reporter, but the tabloids had been her life for some time now. Penelope did not know which side of Tonya would win out – the true investigator or the tabloid reporter – and wanted to know exactly what was in those files before she allowed Tonya to see them.

After hiding the box in her room, she started for the library. As she walked, she realised that throwing herself into an investigation kept her from thinking about where they were and exactly everything that could go wrong. Her instincts had taken over, muffling her other fears. As long as she kept busy like this, she would be OK. But hadn't she come all the way here to get away from investigative work?

A loud *clang* rattled through the hall. Penelope ducked. *The hotel had been breached. A meteor had shattered a window and all of the oxygen was about to be sucked into space. They had only seconds, maybe minutes until . . .*

Another *clang*.

Penelope realised she was crouched in the hallway with her

hands covering her head but nothing else was happening. There were no warning sirens. No sound of the oxygen getting sucked out of the hotel. She slowly straightened up, took deep breaths.

Clang clang.

She followed the sound.

In a hallway off the lobby, she discovered Uchida attempting to prise open a door with what appeared to be a crowbar. Penelope hadn't spent much time in this hallway, yet. Like the upper floor hallways of the hotel, this one was carpeted, with the twinkling star patterns on the walls, and it bore that new car smell that permeated most of the public spaces in the hotel. Nearby signs indicated the way to the casino, moonwalk airlock and medical bay.

Hiding her shaking hands in her pockets, she approached Uchida, who hadn't noticed her.

The door he was trying to open simply said 'Staff'. Where had he found a crowbar? She pictured it connecting with Bobby's head, cracking it open. Is that where the blood on Jackson's hands had come from? But there was no blood around Bobby. A crowbar could have caused internal injuries, however. More importantly, what was Uchida doing with it now?

Penelope cleared her throat.

He spun around, surprised, but quickly composed himself as he adjusted the cuffs of his shirtsleeves.

'Detective Strand.'

'Mr Uchida. Looking for something?'

'My business is my own.'

Penelope leaned against the wall. 'Except when someone's been murdered.'

'I thought that matter was settled.'

'It'll be settled when the rescue ship arrives,' she said. 'Speaking of that matter, would you mind telling me what time you left the party last night?'

'Mr Smith is the one you should be interrogating. He should be the one suffering. He's destroyed every dream I wanted to achieve here. There was only ever going to be one first trip, and now he's ruined the experience and brought my stay to too brief an end. And yet, if I don't answer your questions, I suppose you'll suspect I have something to hide, which is untrue. So to save us both the trouble, I will tell you it was approximately three. Dr Wyss and I left together. We were the last two people to leave, with the exception of Mr Nwankwo, who was asleep in one of the booths.'

'Great. And then?'

'The doctor and I separated. He took the lift. I took the stairs.'

'Any particular reason?' she asked.

'I prefer stairs.'

Penelope noticed his neck redden around his collar, the old scar seeming to shine against his skin.

'And then?' she asked.

'I went to my room and retired for the evening.'

'Which room is that?'

Uchida clasped his hands behind his back. 'The Ix Chel Suite.'

Penelope recalled the suite from her map, which she pulled from her pocket to double-check. 'The Ix Chel Suite is the penthouse.'

'You do not sound surprised, even though you were told we would all be staying in the same type of suite.' Uchida raised an eyebrow.

Penelope shrugged and stuffed the map back into her pocket. 'You're a billionaire, Mr Uchida. I don't expect you to be bound by the same rules as the rest of us. And I do appreciate you telling me the truth. Although, now that you mention it, how were you able to secure the penthouse?'

'Like you said, I am a billionaire. Now if you would excuse me . . .'

Penelope straightened up and crossed her arms. 'Just a few more questions, if you wouldn't mind. When was the last time you saw Bobby?'

'At the party. He left approximately half an hour prior to myself and Dr Wyss. Before you ask, I will tell you that we hardly spoke over the past few days. I found him boorish. Although, naturally I wished him no ill will.'

'Naturally.' Penelope, with very deliberate motions, pulled her notepad from her bag and jotted something down. Uchida casually stretched his neck, trying to read what she had written. 'And what did you do after you returned to the penthouse?'

'I performed my evening ablutions and went to bed. I fall asleep quite quickly.'

'Did you hear or see anything during the night?'

'The penthouse occupies Level 3. There is no reason for anyone else to be there.'

'So is that a yes or a no?'

Penelope waited, pen poised above her pad. Uchida's face flushed again. He adjusted his grip on the crowbar.

'I slept all night, Detective. Then woke at five, used the gym facilities on Level 2A and returned to my room to shower before arriving at the Sunrise Lounge, as you recall.'

'Right.' Penelope made another note. 'So how long did it take you to realise room service wouldn't be arriving?'

'Pardon?'

'When you came down for breakfast this morning, you were yelling that your breakfast hadn't been delivered by room service as you'd requested. How long did you wait before you realised it wasn't coming?'

'I don't know.'

'You don't know?'

'I wasn't watching the time. I only know that it wasn't there when I returned to my room to shower, and it wasn't there after my shower. I assumed by then it wasn't coming. Anything else?'

Penelope held up a finger and took her time writing another note. From the corner of her eye, she noticed Uchida shifting from foot to foot. She kept writing until he tried to start speaking again.

'One more thing,' she interrupted. 'You described Mr Rannells as "boorish". So you didn't like him?'

He shifted the crowbar to his other hand. 'I have already given my opinion on the man.'

'Right, but was there any particular reason you didn't like him? Anything that really rubbed you up the wrong way?'

Uchida smiled patronisingly. 'Detective Strand, I know what you are implying, so allow me to state, for the record, that if I were to murder everyone that has ever annoyed me, the population of the planet would be significantly less than it is now.'

'Interesting.' She made a note. 'One more thing. You're doing what exactly with that crowbar?'

'Good day, Detective.'

He walked away without another word, clutching the crowbar tightly. Penelope watched him until he was out of sight. Then, she used the master key to open the door he'd been trying to force. There was nothing behind it but a white, windowless hallway – a staff passageway. She made another note, then shut the door.

Uchida returned the crowbar to the open utility closet in the managerial hub from where he had first taken it. There had to be another way in. Detective Strand had held on to the master key, but that didn't mean there was only one, or that there wasn't another access point that would be more yielding.

Chapter 15

Books filled the floor to ceiling shelves of the library. The ceiling had been decorated to look like stars, and the only windows were small portholes that occupied various reading nooks nestled in the stacks. The sense of closeness provided by the stacks of books and minimal exterior view made Penelope feel somewhat more grounded and gave her a sense of peace. Unlike the casino, the library's sense of purpose remained unfazed by the lack of hotel staff. She half-expected a librarian to appear and shush her as she walked through the stacks. Space travel was about making things as light and ergonomic as possible, that much she knew, so how much effort and cost had it taken to ship all of these books up here? She picked a random title from the shelf, something by Dickens, and opened it, wondering if the insides would be hollowed out, that the library was a façade. But it was a real book, the prose as dense as always. She closed it and returned it to its shelf, catching a whiff of coffee.

Around the corner, Freddy had taken up residence in one of the reading nooks built into the bookshelves, a mug of steaming coffee on the little table in front of him alongside a crumbling croissant, his nose in a book. She barely managed to say hi before he jumped, nearly knocking over the drink.

'Oh jeez! Detective Strand. It's just you. Sorry.' He looked for a napkin and, not finding one, dabbed up the spilled drops of coffee with a piece of croissant.

'No, I'm sorry,' she said. 'I didn't realise you were so absorbed.'

He brushed the crumbs off his fingers and showed her the cover. 'It's the newest La Plante. This isn't even released until next month. I've got to finish it before the ship arrives. My book club is going to freak out when they find out I've read it already.'

'Well, if you don't finish it, you can always take it with you.'

'Pretty sure that's stealing.'

'Pretty sure the Apollo Group can afford it.'

'But stealing? From a library?' He shuddered. 'My average time for a book is three days, so I should be fine. Especially since, without the staff, there's limits to what we can to do.'

'I guess I know where to find you until then.' She looked around the library. It was incredibly calming, not having to be reminded of the vastness of space all the time.

'It's so cool, isn't it?' Freddy said, joining her. 'Not the murder. That's not cool. But this.' He waved his arm. 'I mean, first I thought it was weird they'd put a library in a luxury hotel, but then I was like, well the *Queen Mary* has one and that's a luxury ship, so . . .' He shrugged.

'You've been on the *Queen Mary*?' she asked.

'No, but my mom's always wanted to go.'

'Maybe one day.'

'Yeah, like I could afford that. I wanted her to take my place on this trip. We both entered and she loves to travel, too. But when I asked Apollo, they said no. I couldn't swap and, if I declined to go, they'd choose someone else. I can't believe it's only going to be for a few days now instead of the full two weeks. It's, like, thanks a lot, Jackson. This really sucks.' He picked at a piece of his croissant. 'This tastes so good. I can't afford food like this at home. Not, like, all the time. New York is super expensive. I'm mostly eating ramen noodles and whatever I can get at the bakery down the street when they're closing and everything is half off. But London must be the same, right? I've heard it's crazy expensive. I wanted to spend a few days there before the launch, but I would've had to pay for it myself and I couldn't afford it. I found this in the kitchen and found some instant coffee in there, too. Probably for the staff, I guess, but I like instant anyway and it is OK that we just take food from there, right? Because we have to eat and they would've probably fed us way more if they were here. Sorry. I'm rambling. I'm just . . . this is exciting. It's exciting, isn't it? Well, not for Bobby. It's pretty horrific for Bobby. For everyone, I guess. Sorry. I'm rambling again. And when I said exciting, I didn't mean I wanted someone to get murdered. What happened sucks and I just keep thinking, how many times did I talk to Jackson? And our rooms were next to each other on the ship and now he's murdered someone and it's like, wow, you know?'

Penelope wasn't sure if Freddy said all of that in one breath, but it seemed like it.

'It's OK to be nervous, Freddy. I think everyone is.'

He flopped back in his seat. 'I just keep thinking, if I hadn't drunk that much, if I'd been awake, maybe I could've, I don't know. Done something.'

'You fell asleep in the restaurant, right? Did you hear anything?'

'Passed out more like. And I woke up sometime before Bobby was . . .' He drew a line across his throat. 'I would've seen him. I walked, like, right over that spot on my way out. Wait. Are you interviewing me? Is this an official police interview?' He sat up in the seat, an eager look on his face. 'I'll tell you everything I can think of. What else do you need to know?'

'It's not an official anything, no. I'm just trying to gather a few facts about everyone's whereabouts.'

'Like establish a timeline?'

'Exactly like that. So do you know what time you woke up?'

Freddy slumped in the seat again. 'I honestly don't. I was so groggy. The lights were dimmed. It was dark out. That's all I remember. Except we're in space. It's always dark, isn't it? I remember it was quiet, though. I kept thinking how quiet it was while I went to my room.'

'Did you take the stairs or the lifts?'

'The lifts? I don't . . . Oh! You mean the elevators? No, I took the stairs. The big main staircase because that's the one that was right in front of me. There's actually another staircase that's closer to my suite but I couldn't remember how to get there from the lobby. I didn't see anyone, either. I just went into my room and fell into bed. I didn't hear anything until I opened my door this morning.'

'So what do you think?' Penelope asked.

'What do you mean what do I think?'

'You know criminology. Based on the evidence you've seen, do you think Jackson did it?'

'You're really asking my opinion? OK. Wow. Well, um, I'm not

146

a detective. And I'm still a student not a professional. But I guess I'd say it looks that way. Considering how we found Jackson. But it's weird, isn't it?'

'How so?' Penelope asked.

'Well, how Bobby's body was left, that looked pretty premeditated to me. If Jackson killed him, why not stage it to look like an accident? It's not like we can get a full forensics team up here to document the scene. Accidental death – tragic but not illegal. And probably the Apollo Group's responsibility, considering they've left us alone up here. Accidents are bound to happen, right? At least that's what Jackson could argue. But he went out of his way to make it clear this was murder. He *needed* us to know it was murder. So I guess . . .'

Freddy paused. Penelope waited for him to finish.

'I guess, that makes me want to know why. Why let us know it was murder instead of trying to pass it off as something else, especially considering you're going to get caught? And I don't know. Maybe people are just weird. I mean, why kill anyone anyway? I know the typical motives. Money. Greed. Lust. Jealousy. Love. Revenge. Usually something personal. Over fifty per cent of people are killed by someone they know.' He paused for breath. 'If I were Jackson, and I was going to kill Bobby for any one of those reasons, I would've made it look like an accident or self-defence. Or if I wanted people to know I did it with a giant, hand-painted flag, I would own it. I wouldn't stage the body like that, get caught literally red-handed, then try to deny it.' He leaned forward in his chair, a worried look on his face. 'And you know I'm speaking metaphorically, right? Like, I didn't kill Bobby. I've never killed anyone! I swear. So when I'm saying *I* what I mean is—'

Penelope held up her hand. 'Freddy, how far along are you at university?'

'I'm a junior.'

'What's that in English?'

'My third year.'

'Out of three?' she asked.

'Out of four.'

'Good enough. Would you mind if I interrupted your reading for a little longer?'

Penelope had decided her basis for trusting the others was whether or not they accepted wholeheartedly that Jackson was guilty or not. Anyone who noticed and was willing to admit that something seemed off, that they were open to other answers, likely had nothing to hide. Anyone who wanted to keep that door shut – those were the people she wanted to keep a closer eye on, just in case. Freddy, like Tonya, had passed her test and, a few minutes later, she stood with Freddy in front of the entrance to the Harvest Restaurant, behind Sasha's makeshift curtain.

Freddy stared at his feet, but Penelope made a point of looking at Bobby. She wanted him to know she wouldn't let him down.

'We don't have any full protective gear or anything,' Freddy said.

'I know. So don't touch anything and just watch where you put your feet.' She handed him the same kind of protective booties she'd worn going into Bobby's suite, and they both donned rubber gloves that she'd found earlier. With a deep breath, Penelope unclipped one end of the velvet rope, and she and Freddy stepped inside the restaurant.

She'd been to countless crime scenes in her career, starting with her years in uniform, several of them murders or suspicious deaths. But never had she been to a crime scene for a victim that she had a personal connection with. Less than twelve hours ago, she had been sitting with Bobby in this very room. Now he was dead and impaled on the floor near the table where they'd all eaten together.

As they went further into the restaurant, she focused her attention on the makeshift flag. The murderer had knotted the ends to the pole, which Penelope saw now was the same type of pole used for the velvet ropes, except with the base removed. The 'flag' she recognised as the same type of bedsheet in her room.

'Do all of the rooms use the same sheets?' Freddy asked. So he had noticed, too.

'I would think so. There must be a linen cupboard or laundry somewhere.'

'More than just a cupboard, don't you think? Or does that mean something different in British?'

She followed the path of the pole down to Bobby's body and examined where it penetrated his shirtless back.

'I was right,' she said. 'No blood.'

'The pole could have plugged it up some.'

'True, but a wound this size? There'd be something. Yet he didn't bleed out onto the floor, and there's almost no blood around the entrance wound, either.'

'So, he was already dead when . . .' Freddy made a two-handed jabbing motion.

'Fortunately for Bobby, that seems to be the case.'

'That's good. I'm glad. I mean, I'm not glad he's, you know, but I'm glad he wouldn't have felt, you know, Jackson go all horror-show on him. You know.' He wiped his eyes.

Penelope patted him on the back. 'I know.'

She knelt down and examined Bobby's hands and face.

'No defensive wounds. No apparent injuries. At least, none I can see without moving the body. No bruising that I can see, so probably no crowbar.'

'Crowbar?' Freddy asked.

'Nothing. His skin . . .' Penelope continued. 'He looks a bit puffy, doesn't he?'

'I can't tell what killed him,' Freddy said. 'Maybe Jackson shoved him and he hit his head? Are his pupils uneven? Or maybe he was suffocated or strangled? I mean, I thought he must've been stabbed, but I don't see any injuries except for the pole. But I'm not an expert.'

Penelope stood up and looked around the room. Their many used glasses from last night were stacked on the bar and tables. Their dirty plates were exactly as they'd left them, the uneaten bits of food hardened and cold. Nothing appeared otherwise disturbed. Simply the remnants of a party.

'Whatever it was, I don't think it happened in this room,' she said.

'So Jackson killed him somewhere else and placed him here. Then, after he was dead, did all this.' Freddy let out a long breath. 'That is a lot of trouble. And a lot of risk. I mean, sure this is a big hotel, but it's not like the Burj Al Arab in Dubai or something. There was a good chance one of us would've heard or seen something.'

Penelope looked again at the flag. 'Someone didn't just want

Bobby dead. They wanted to send us a message. Do you remember those protestors? The ones outside the spaceport?'

'Oh yeah. I tried to ignore them. I mean, I'd already had to set all my social media accounts to private, but even then . . .'

'They were harassing you online?' Penelope asked.

'Yeah. Most of it was pretty standard. The typical racist, homophobic shit. But others . . . I mean there was at least one death threat. Still, at least I didn't get doxed like Sasha.'

'Doxed?'

'You know, when trolls post your address and phone number online. She was telling me on the flight here. She had to stay at a friend's place for a week before the trip because people were showing up at her house. Didn't you get any, you know, threats?'

'I saw some of the comments online but no one personally threatened me, no. Then again, all I have is an email address.'

'No social media? Not even, like an old Facebook account you don't even use anymore?'

Penelope shook her head.

'Wow. And you're not even, like, that old or anything.'

'Cheers, Freddy.' She motioned that they should leave the room.

'Have you done a lot of murder cases?' Freddy asked as he struggled to pull off his rubber gloves.

'Enough. London's a big city. Lots of crime.'

'Yeah, like New York. Probably mostly muggings. Domestic abuse. The normal stuff, right? Have you ever seen anything like this? I mean I've read a few stories about bodies turning up in duffle bags and—'

Penelope grabbed the used rubber gloves from Freddy's hands and walked them to the bin behind the Reception desk.

'Sometimes the domestic stuff is enough,' she said.

'I didn't mean it like that.'

She dropped the gloves in the bin. 'Freddy, do you think you could ask the others if they received any online harassment? If they can remember any specific threats? Maybe there's more to that we can look into.'

'Sure! I can totally do that. So you think Jackson was part of one these protest groups or something?'

'I won't speculate, but I do know there's another reason why people kill – a cause.'

Freddy hurried away with a smile, apparently pleased to have a purpose. When he was gone, Penelope sat in one of the chairs behind Reception and took a moment to gather herself. She tried not to think of young women bleeding out on the pavement in front of their tower block and of bloated bodies being pulled from the river – of one young woman and one body in particular – and reminded herself why she was doing this. She had to be one hundred per cent certain that Jackson was indeed the person responsible. There could be no mistakes. Not this time. She stood up, tightened her ponytail and went in search of a doctor.

Tonya had walked the hallways on most of the floors, but had not seen a single security camera anywhere. There had to be some way of monitoring the staff, at least, if not the guests. Not that the guests wouldn't get into any mischief, but they were the kind of guests whose mischief could be paid off. But the fact they had built a pair of cells showed they had considered the possibility of people breaking the law. So they had to have CCTV.

She passed through the silent lobby into the managerial hub. She entered the security centre and switched on the computers. While they loaded, she noticed the door leading to the cells was open. Inside, she could see Jackson. She was debating whether or not to say hello when he looked up and spotted her.

She waved.

'Did Penelope leave this open for you?'

He said nothing, simply stared at her but not in a threatening way. In fact, he looked rather terrified.

'I'll just . . . I'll just close it for you, shall I?'

She tried pressing the button, but the door wouldn't shut. A little light indicated a key card was needed. Finally, she gave up and left the room without another word, feeling Jackson's eyes on her the whole way.

Chapter 16

Penelope was not in the habit of ogling men, especially those she was interviewing, and Dr Wyss wasn't even her type. But she couldn't deny that he was fit. Tall, muscular but trim, blond hair and blue eyes and a jawline even Bobby would have envied. As the doctor knelt down near Bobby's head, Penelope thought that this was exactly the type of person who could manoeuvre a dead body.

'I'm not a coroner,' he said, 'but I agree with your assertion that if he were impaled while still alive, there would be far more blood.'

'Any idea of what might have killed him?' Penelope asked.

'Without being allowed to move the body and examine it more closely, it's difficult to tell.'

'Sorry. I wish we could. But nobody even has a camera to document the scene. We can't move a thing. Not to mention the possible evidence contamination.'

'Do you really think they'll send a forensics team up here?' he asked.

'It's a murder,' she said. 'Although I don't have any idea whose jurisdiction this is.'

'Maybe it will be treated the same as a crime committed in international waters.'

Penelope couldn't tell if he was making a joke or not.

'What I can see,' he continued, 'is there does not appear to be any head injury, and there are no marks on the face or neck.'

'So we can rule out his being clobbered on the head or strangulation.'

Dr Wyss sat back on his heels, his gaze on the body. 'I think we can also rule out firearms. I can't see how anyone could have smuggled a gun onto the ship. Besides, a firearm presents other dangers here. A spark from a bullet firing – it could cause a catastrophic reaction.'

'How about stabbing? There are plenty of knives in the kitchens.'

'The only visible wound is the post-mortem impalement. If there are stab wounds, they're currently concealed by the position of the body.'

'But somebody could've stabbed him in the back then inserted the pole there to hide the wound.'

'Elaborate. And possible. But they would've had to clean up the blood from that initial wound. And his underpants.' Dr Wyss gestured to Bobby's boxer shorts. 'No blood dripped there, either.'

Penelope nodded even though she had already come to that realisation. She'd just wanted to know what he'd say.

'What about poisoning?'

'Again, possible. But without doing any tests . . .' He shrugged.

'What could've caused the puffiness in his face?' she asked.

'A multitude of things, but also it could be a side effect of his body decomposing in space. The hotel maintains a suitable atmospheric pressure, but it's not exact. As these damned heavy shoes keep us well aware.' Dr Wyss dusted off his hands, even though he hadn't touched anything, and rose to his feet.

'So you left the party last night with Mr Uchida?'

'I was wondering when you'd ask. Yes, Freddy was passed out in that booth.' He pointed. 'Very much unconscious, in my professional opinion – and the two of us exited into the lobby together.'

'What time was it? Two?'

'Close to three or three thirty, I believe. I went to the main lifts, but Uchida remained at the observation window.'

'Did Mr Uchida show any interest in exploring the hotel? Looking around the staff-only areas, for example?'

'None that he expressed to me.'

'So you went to the lifts. Did you see him leave? See which way he went?' Penelope asked.

'No, I got distracted because when the lift opened, Sasha came out. She seemed upset but didn't want to discuss it. I went up to my room, but then came back down to the lobby almost immediately.'

'Forget something?'

'It seemed wrong to leave Sasha alone if she was upset. When I returned to the lobby, I found her seated on the lowest step of the main staircase.'

'Did she still seem upset?'

'She was no longer crying, but she seemed worried. I asked if there was anything I could do. She said no.'

'Did she say anything else?' Penelope asked.

'Only that she shouldn't let others upset her so much for so little.'

'She didn't say anything more about it?'

'No, she didn't.'

'What did you do then?'

'I returned to my room. Where I remained all night. And before you ask, no I didn't hear anything. And I do have an alibi. If you'd like to know more, I suggest you speak with' – he coughed, to cover some embarrassment – 'Professor Crane.'

'We're all adults here,' she answered, as she escorted him out of the restaurant. 'One more thing. You said you aren't a coroner. What is it that you're a doctor of? What's your specialty?'

Dr Wyss's face became a mask. 'Jackson Smith has committed murder, ruined an experience that we will never be able to replicate, and you still want to play guessing games like Alison and Charlotte? Good afternoon, Detective.'

With that, he jogged up the stairs. Penelope watched from below as he went in the direction of the Sunrise Lounge. On her notepad, she added him to the list of the people who didn't seem to want answers.

'Sasha. Sasha!' Freddy ran up to the woman in the hall outside her suite then regretted it. She looked frightened half to death.

'Sorry! I'm so sorry. I didn't mean to freak you out.'

'No, no. It's fine.' She laughed it off, but Freddy could still see the worry in her eyes. 'You just startled me is all. It's so quiet up here, isn't it?'

'Until I came running down the hall.'

They both smiled.

'Is there something I can do for you, Freddy?'

He stuffed his hands in his pockets and shrugged. 'Actually, I just wanted to ask you about the harassment.'

'Harassment?' Suddenly she looked terrified again. 'What harassment?'

'You know, the online harassment you were talking about on the ship? How you got doxed and stuff?'

She relaxed a little. 'Oh yes. Why do you want to ask about that?'

'Well, I . . . that is Detective Strand and I, we're sort of working together. And she, and we, well, we're trying to figure out if, I mean why, Jackson might've killed Bobby. And I, I mean we, were thinking that maybe he's part of one of those environmentalist, anti-capitalist groups, you know the ones that have been protesting against the hotel?'

'You think it was Jackson harassing me at home?' she asked.

'I don't know. Maybe not Jackson, but members of the same group? If he is a member of a group.'

Freddy knew the look Sasha was giving him. She wanted to get away but was too polite to say it.

'It's just a theory.' He took a step back, giving her an out.

'It wasn't any group,' she said.

'It wasn't? Sorry. 'Cause on the ship, I thought you said some of those groups had sent you threatening messages and stuff and that's why you had to go stay at your sister's.'

'I did receive some messages from those groups, but their harassment is not why I had to go to my sister's. I . . . it was an ex. I have an EPO against him and he wasn't supposed to contact me but—'

'Sorry, what's an EPO? Is that a European thing?'

'Yes, a European Protection Order.'

'Oh, like a restraining order?'

Sasha nodded.

'Oh wow. So you can get a restraining order against a person in one country and it applies to all of Europe?'

'You can, yes.'

'I didn't know that! That's cool. You can barely get a restraining order enforced in the US in one state let alone across states. Sorry, I shouldn't have said cool. It's not cool that you had to go through that. My mom says I say "cool" way too much.'

'No, I understand what you meant. And I'm sorry for the confusion. So, does Penelope not believe it was Jackson alone who was responsible?'

'Um, I don't know. Maybe? I mean, yes. It's just we were – she was – interested in his motive. Because of the message on the flag?'

'Yes.' Sasha nodded. 'Very strange, isn't it?'

'Anyway, sorry for bothering you. And thanks for talking to me. Hey, do you know if anyone else mentioned getting any online threats?'

'I don't know. Alison, I think, might have mentioned it.'

'Great. I'll, uh, I'll go see her. Thanks again.'

He awkwardly waved goodbye and hurried away to give Sasha the privacy she so clearly wanted.

Chapter 17

Penelope had seen infinity pools in commercials for all-inclusive resorts, but this was her first time seeing one in person. One side of the pool bordered a giant window that gazed out over the dark side of the moon, and the water looked like it was falling right off the edge into space. The floor of the pool room was slate grey, like most of the other floors in the hotel, while the bottom and sides of the pool were black, so that it looked like it was carved out of onyx. Deckchairs bedecked with towels depicting the Hotel Artemis logo lined the wall while access to the private changing rooms was at the rear of the room.

'There's one for each of us.'

Penelope jumped. She hadn't noticed Alison climbing out of the pool, but there the professor stood at its edge in a black bathing suit, water dripping from her hair and skin.

'The changing rooms,' Alison continued, dripping water on the floor as she crossed to one of the deckchairs for a towel. 'There's one for each suite. You need to scan your palm to open it and inside there's two bathing suits, sandals, a robe, bathing cap, goggles. How cool is that?'

'Very. I was thinking about going for a swim.'

'Have at it! Although just to warn you, I don't think what's in there is purely water. It feels, I don't know, denser? I guess something to do with the lesser gravity or something.' Alison towel-dried her hair. 'But I get the feeling you came in here for another reason.'

'What reason would that be?'

'To interview me, obviously. You're a detective. Even if this isn't an official investigation, I can't imagine you just sitting around, waiting for help. No matter what you told us.' She reached into a bag by her chair and popped out a piece of nicotine gum. 'I could kill for a real cigarette. Sorry, not actually kill. Poor choice of words.'

'Don't worry about it. By the way, I meant to ask you on the ship, but your accent is unusual. Where are you from?'

'All over. I was born in France but my parents were real mutts who just happened to live there at the time. My father moved us around a lot. Mostly Western Europe but with some time in India and Asia. I guess that's why I chose psychology. I met so many different people growing up, I was fascinated with all their different opinions and ways of thinking.' She flopped her body onto the chair and let out a sigh as she gnawed on the gum.

'And where are you a professor at?'

'Kingston. Just outside central London. Mostly teaching intro courses to first years. I'm considered "relatively young"' – she used air quotes – 'by academia's standards. That translates as I'm not an old fart, so it'll be a while before I'm allowed to teach the juicier courses.'

Penelope sat on the deckchair next to Alison's.

'Do you do any practical work? Therapy or anything?'

'No. No patient-facing stuff. I couldn't handle people spouting their problems at me day in, day out. Although that's basically what my students do to me anyway. No, my entire career has been in academia. I teach and I do some research. Well, I *did* teach and I *did* do some research.' Her face suddenly became downcast.

'What do you mean?'

Alison sighed. 'I couldn't get leave from work. You'd think they'd love the publicity. One of their lecturers getting selected for this once in a lifetime opportunity. But when they found out, their only reaction was, "What about your courses?"' It was either the trip or the job. So here I am.'

'I'm sorry,' Penelope said.

'It is what it is. Maybe someone will have use for a psychology professor who's been to the moon. Or maybe now I'll be so tainted by this murder, no one will touch me. *Comme ci, comme ça.*'

'Alison, I know you just said your experience is mostly academic, but what I've been trying to figure out is why Jackson would want Bobby dead.'

Alison rolled onto her side to look at Penelope. 'Well, I'm not a profiler. But, if I had to guess, first, the positioning of the body along with the flag is a cry for attention. This is someone who wants to be noticed. Has a possibly pathological need to be noticed.'

'And the words on the flag?'

'Just trying to be clever. But also usurping the words of a powerful, celebrated man. He might have a need to see himself in the same way. Which could also be reflected in his decision to murder poor Bobby. Bobby had his own brand of celebrity and, has-been or not, he exuded a certain presence that perhaps Jackson was jealous of.'

'And the act of penetrating Bobby with the pole?'

Alison smirked. 'Personally, I've never bowed to the altar of Freud, and most in the profession don't. Sometimes a stabbing is just a stabbing.'

'So is that your hypothesis on the motive? Jealousy?'

'Possibly. Jealousy could be one of Jackson's subconscious desires. But he might not have seen it that way. Maybe he just got very angry with Bobby for some reason. Or . . .' Alison pursed her lips then sighed and rolled back onto the chair. 'Or less likely, but still possible, is that he's simply a raging psychopath who wanted to kill for fun. There is a certain disturbing playfulness to the crime scene.'

'There's a fun thought.'

'Honestly, the chances of that are low. Full-fledged psychopathy like that is rare, despite what TV would have you think. Though, given your profession, you're probably already aware of that. I'm more inclined to the intimidated male theory.'

'So you agree that it's likely Jackson committed the murder.'

Alison launched herself up from the chair and wrapped the towel around her waist. 'All I know about crime-solving, I learned from podcasts, but I know what I saw this morning.' She walked towards the changing rooms then stopped. 'But I also know Jackson wasn't the only one angry with Bobby.'

She waited for Penelope to ask who.

'Frau Richter was muttering things about him when I bumped into her last night.'

'When was that?'

'Around two? I'd left the party and was headed upstairs. When I asked her what she was doing, she said she was looking for something to eat. I . . .' Alison blushed. 'I may have been somewhat intoxicated and made an unkind comment about her weight.'

'Where were you headed?'

Alison cleared her throat and looked away. 'I decided to see what Dr Wyss was up to. And we enjoyed an evening in each other's company. Which is probably the other reason she isn't so fond of me at the moment.'

'No, I don't recall the young professor making any such comment,' Frau Richter bristled. 'We passed each other in the hall, said good evening, and that was all. I have no idea why she would say such a thing.' She rubbed her left ring finger, but there was no ring there anymore.

'It is a strange thing for her to make up,' Penelope said.

'She is a strange woman.'

Penelope and Frau Richter sat at the table in the lawyer's room – the Chang'e suite. Penelope had glanced at the open welcome pack when Frau Richter first invited her into the suite, which had the same set up as Jackson's. Chang'e was a Chinese goddess, banished to the moon for stealing the source of immortality from her husband.

Frau Richter continuously glanced at the cheese Danish Penelope had brought her from the Cold Moon Piano Bar. Penelope had brought one for herself as well and had eaten half of it already, but Frau Richter seemed to be deliberately ignoring it. She sat back in the chair and crossed her arms.

'I thought you two were getting on quite well,' Penelope said, needing to lean around the large vase of red poppies in order to see her. 'You were always together on the ship.'

Frau Richter huffed. 'Who else was I supposed to talk to? You? You hardly spoke to anyone. Tonya speaks too much. Mr Uchida? Why should a billionaire speak to me? Besides, he and Sasha kept each other busy. And I'm sure I don't have to tell you that Jackson only had eyes for Bobby. Professor Crane was the only person who seemed willing to have a conversation. Her and Erik.'

'What about Freddy?' Penelope asked.

'What about him?'

'Nothing. It's just that you mentioned everyone but him.'

Frau Richter looked away. 'I don't think we'd have anything to talk about. He's . . . we're very different.'

Penelope made a note. Frau Richter tried not-so-subtly to read what it said.

'Have you asked Freddy where he was last night?' Frau Richter asked. 'From what I hear, he was out quite late.'

'So you don't think Jackson is responsible?' Penelope asked.

'Oh, Jackson most likely is to blame. But you can't overlook that someone like Freddy is also probably involved.'

'Someone like Freddy?' Penelope repeated.

'You know, his . . . kind. They can't help but get involved in criminal behaviour.'

Penelope pressed her lips together and nodded. 'Mm-hm. Of course. And by "his kind" you mean students? Americans? New Yorkers, specifically?' She looked Frau Richter dead in the eye.

'You work in London. You have plenty of them there. I shouldn't have to explain myself to you.' She grabbed the plate with the Danish and rose, a clear signal for Penelope to leave.

'So why is Professor Crane strange?' Penelope asked quickly.

'She makes up stories about saying outrageous comments for one.'

'Right. Why else?'

Frau Richter set her plate back down but remained standing.

'I don't think it's proper for a woman to be throwing herself at eligible men. It's embarrassing.'

'And has she? Been throwing herself at eligible men?'

'With abandon! Have you seen the way she's been with poor Erik? She couldn't leave him alone on the ship. I bet you anything that's where she was headed last night. To his room.'

'How do you know she wasn't going to her room?'

'Because she was going the wrong way. Her room is on Level 2B and we were already on that level and she was heading for the lifts. The set at the rear of the hotel that delivers you directly to the suites on Level 1B.'

'So you know your way around the hotel pretty well.' Penelope made another note. 'And her going to Dr Wyss's room concerns you because . . . ?'

'It doesn't. What he does, what she does, it's no concern of mine. I just think it's improper. That's all. He's far too old for her. It wouldn't surprise me if she had started chasing after poor Bobby once Erik rejected her.' Frau Richter finally gave in and picked up the Danish.

'You're a lawyer, isn't that right?' Penelope asked. 'Remind me of your area of expertise?'

'Divorce. I represent women who have been wronged in their marriage and deserve to be compensated for their suffering. That's how I know why Jackson killed Bobby.'

Penelope raised an eyebrow. 'You do?'

'Of course. It's obvious. Bobby's ex-wife. She arranged it. Hired Jackson to kill him while he was on this trip. That's why Jackson made such an effort to get close to him. And perhaps someone else, someone like Freddy, helped him. Case closed.' She bit into the pastry.

'It would be a good motive. Ex-wives hire contract killers all the time.' Penelope exaggerated her speech with sarcasm, but Frau Richter didn't seem to notice. 'But it's a bit risky, don't you think? Why do it here? Why not on Earth, before we launched?'

'Opportunity of course. It was easier to get to him here.'

'You seem very certain,' Penelope said.

'It was a very bad divorce. Very messy. Very nasty.'

'You heard about it?'

'From Jackson. He told me all about it.'

'I didn't think you spoke to Jackson much.'

'It was at that publicity event. Prior to the launch. Before he gathered up enough courage to speak to his idol and forgot everyone else on this trip existed. Now that he's destroyed our holiday, he deserves whatever is coming to him. All bad people do.' Frau Richter rose. 'Now are we done? I came here for the solitude, and I intend to make the most it before we're unduly taken away.'

'One more thing. Did you see Sasha at all last night? After dinner?'

Frau Richter stilled. The skin on her neck and chest began to blush. She cleared her throat and looked away.

'No,' she said. 'I never saw her once she left the party.'

Chapter 18

The main kitchen was empty when Tonya arrived. Penelope had said an hour and Tonya was nothing if not punctual. She was also hungry. She quickly found the main pantry and opened the door.

'Good God. It's all ingredients.'

She'd been hoping to grab a bag of crisps or maybe a microwavable pasty. Something that required little effort. But the wonderfully full pantry contained only bags and boxes of things that could be used to make food. It did not contain any actual food. Tonya picked up a small bag of flour and sighed. She hadn't made so much as a Bolognese from scratch since her university days. She put the flour back and left the pantry doors open before crossing the large kitchen to the walk-in fridge. She'd adjusted to the coolness of the hotel, but the fridge raised the goosebumps on her arms. Here, however, she had more luck – extra portions from last night's dinner, left in the fridge.

As she lifted a dish from the shelf, her foot kicked something on the floor. She reached down and picked up what looked to be a small wheel, the kind that would be on a trolley. The metal end was jagged, like the wheel had been snapped off.

A clank sounded in the kitchen.

'Hello?' Tonya called out.

Footsteps scampered away, but by the time she peeked her head out of the fridge, there was no one there. She followed the path the footsteps had taken to a door at the rear of the kitchen and emerged onto a service corridor. There was no sign of anyone. A light in the corridor flickered.

The broken wheel still clutched in her hand, Tonya returned to the kitchen, and screamed.

Penelope screamed back.

'God,' Tonya said, catching her breath. 'Where did you come from?'

'I came in through the restaurant.'

'Not through here?' She pointed to the door behind her.

'What's through there?' Penelope crossed the kitchen to reach her.

'Staff entrance. A service passage, I guess.'

Penelope opened the door and peered out. 'Why did you think I came through there?' she asked.

'Because someone did. I was in the fridge and I heard them. But they were gone as soon as I came out.'

'What were you doing in the fridge?' Penelope asked.

'I was hungry.'

'Hey!'

Tonya and Penelope both jumped and screamed.

'Sorry!' Freddy said. 'I didn't mean to scare you. Did you guys find something?' He quickly hurried over to them and peeked his head out into the corridor. 'Hey, do you think this is how Jackson moved Bobby's body without anybody seeing?'

'Possibly,' Penelope said. 'The other staff doors require a key, though. I saw Uchida trying to open one earlier today with a crowbar. I could only open it with the master key.'

'Why on earth was he trying that hard to get in to the staff corridors?' Tonya asked.

'He wouldn't tell me. No surprise there. What's that?' Penelope pointed to Tonya's hand.

Tonya had forgotten she was holding the broken wheel. She handed it to Penelope.

'Found it in the fridge.'

'What were you doing in the fridge?' Freddy asked.

'Trying to find something to eat that wasn't a croissant.'

'Did it come off of something in there?' Penelope asked, nodding to the fridge.

'Don't think so. Nothing in there is on wheels. Although I suppose it could have happened when they were unloading supplies.'

'I found something in the other kitchen this morning,' Penelope said. 'It looked like a splotch of spray paint on the floor. The same colour red that's on the sign out there.' She nodded to the door that led to the restaurant.

'How would Jackson have gotten spray paint into the hotel?' Freddy asked. 'That's a pressurised can. Wouldn't it have exploded on take-off or something?'

'Maybe it's not spray paint exactly but something similar,' Penelope said. 'And maybe he found it in the hotel. Could be something left over from the construction. Anyway, let's put the paint aside for the moment. Tonya, were you able to find out anything about the cameras?'

'Well, there's definitely a CCTV system. I went to the security office and was able to switch the computers on, but I can't access it. It's password protected. I looked for a password book or something – even tried "password" – but I didn't find one and I couldn't get in. I also tried looking for any memos or notes about a TV show coming to film, but there's nothing. It's probably all on the computers, but my limited hacking skills amount to guessing the names of people's pets.'

'What if,' Freddy said, 'there isn't any show and Bobby found out and that's why Jackson really killed him?'

'You mean there's a different reason why there aren't any staff here and Jackson knows what it is?' Tonya asked. 'Like he's in on it? Some sort of plant?'

'Did you talk to Sasha about the online harassment?' Penelope asked Freddy.

'Yeah, but she sort of walked it back. I swear that on the ship she'd said people were threatening to kill her. That someone even left a dead bird on her doorstep with a note attached. But when I asked her about it now, it didn't seem like a big deal to her. And she said it was actually an ex-boyfriend or something.'

'Dead birds? That's horrible, no matter who they came from.' Tonya shivered. 'I didn't receive any threats like that. Did you, Penelope?'

'No, but according to Freddy, I'm a Luddite, so no one could find me online to harass me. Plus, I was staying out of London with my parents.' She drummed her fingers on the preparation table. 'So, say Jackson is one of these eco-terrorists. He enters the contest, maybe a bunch of them do, and it's just pure luck that one of them is selected?'

'It doesn't explain how he could arrange for all the staff to leave, though,' Tonya said. 'Either someone in hotel management is also in on it or they were completely duped.'

'Or the missing staff is entirely coincidental,' Penelope said.

'If they were actually planning to film,' Tonya said. 'Bobby seemed to think otherwise.'

Freddy squeezed his eyes shut in thought. 'So wait. Bobby discovered Jackson was up to some sneaky eco-terrorist shit and Jackson killed him and left that message? And either these eco-terrorists arranged for the staff to leave, or the staff was coincidentally gone for some other reason?'

'It would be helpful if we could research some of the hotel employees,' Penelope said. 'The general manager's name is on the door. And there must be employment records somewhere. But without the internet or access to a police database, names alone don't do us any good.'

'Do you . . .' Freddy hesitated. 'Do you think Jackson was planning on killing all of us? And something went wrong which is the only reason we caught him?'

Tonya laid a hand on his arm. 'If that's the case, we're safe now. He won't be getting out of that cell.'

'Yeah, but what if he had an accomplice? I mean, Jackson's a small guy. It was probably hard for him to move Bobby's body on his own. What if someone else was in on it?'

'Frau Richter implied the same thing.' Penelope glanced at Freddy then looked away.

'But why would someone want us all dead?' she asked. 'Sure, if it is eco-terrorists, that would be a reason. Kill us all to make a point. But that's the only thing we have in common – that we're the first guests of the hotel.'

'What if it's not?' Freddy asked. 'What if there is something that connects all of us other than this trip?'

'I'd say you're reading too much Agatha Christie,' Tonya said.

'She's right,' Penelope said. 'We're all different nationalities, different ages, different social classes.'

'But you and Tonya are both from London and you both knew of each other before the winner's announcement. What are the odds of that? And Professor Crane works near central London, doesn't she? So that's three not just from the UK but from around the London area? Plus, Sasha, Frau Richter and Dr Wyss – they're all from Europe.'

'And you, Jackson and Bobby are all from North America,' Penelope said. 'Mr Uchida is from Japan. More likely the Apollo Group decided to be a bit discriminatory about which countries and continents they selected the winners from. And yes, Tonya and I had heard of each other, but finding a thread that connects all ten of us? Complicated plots exist in Sherlock Holmes, but in real policing, the simplest explanation is often the right one.' Penelope made a face as she said it, as if it almost hurt to have those words come out of her mouth. Tonya decided not to press about it right now.

'But if we asked everyone,' Freddy urged, 'If we talk to Jackson—'

Penelope cut him off. 'Policing isn't about entertaining wild theories, Freddy. If you want to do this job, you need to learn to apply what you've learned from school. Not what you read for fun in your spare time. You don't twist the facts to fit a story. You develop a narrative that fits the facts.' She pinched the bridge of her nose then continued. 'I don't want anyone talking to Jackson right now. He's made up his mind that he doesn't want to say anything, and the only thing that's likely to change that is a long, lonely night in that cell. So please don't bring it up again.'

Freddy nodded, though he was clearly hurt. Instead of bouncing on the balls of his feet, as he was prone to do, his body had become still.

Tonya leaned forward on the table. 'Well, the simplest explanation isn't even eco-terrorists. It's that Jackson got mad, killed Bobby in a rage, panicked and dressed up the body. And that the missing staff was part of some separate stunt on behalf of the Apollo Group. Perhaps, if there had been staff here, they could've stopped Jackson or at least apprehended him immediately after the murder. So I have to ask, Penelope: why *are* we doing all this? Yes, it's been fun and a good way to keep ourselves distracted while we wait, but the ship will be here in a few days. Their security team or whoever will be looking into all of this. It's not your responsibility.'

'I know. I just want to make sure we have the right person. That the person responsible is the one taken into custody. I just want to be ... I need to be one hundred per cent certain.' Penelope stared at the table, but Tonya could tell she saw something in the shining metal other than her reflection.

'What if we had a party?' Tonya asked. 'Or not a party, I suppose. Even I admit that would be in bad taste. But what if we all had dinner together tonight? All eight of us? Maybe someone will mention something they hadn't thought of before.'

'Or,' Penelope said, 'something they thought was insignificant.'

'Good food and drinks always gets tongues wagging,' Tonya

said. 'It's why after-parties are such delicious sources of gossip. What do you think, Freddy?'

Freddy, sullen, nodded.

'Excellent! There's just one problem.' She looked at the pantry and sighed. 'Does anyone here know how to bloody well cook?'

Chapter 19

Frau Richter wished she could slam the door of her suite behind her. Instead, it slid calmly shut as she exited, her wedding ring clenched tightly in her palm, the metal band growing warm from her body heat.

She stomped down the passage.

Her stomach rumbled as she continued down the hall, and she did her best to ignore it. She knew she wasn't hungry, not really. She didn't need anything to eat. She was just angry. She needed to fight the urge to eat. She needed to keep her composure. Isn't that what her husband always used to tell her?

Keep your composure, Charlotte. Control your anger, Charlotte. You could be prettier, Charlotte, if you could only keep your mouth shut at the table, Charlotte.

She stopped in front of the door to the Máni suite and banged on the door until it opened.

'You're in there. I know you're in there. Open the door!'

A click sounded and then the door slid open. Sasha stood there, clothed in her hotel dressing gown, arms wrapped around her body like she was trying to disappear into herself.

'Frau Richter! What is it? Has something else happened?'

Sasha looked up and down the hall as if expecting to see some commotion.

Frau Richter thrust her hand into Sasha's chest, the ring resting on the centre of her palm.

'What is the meaning of this?' she asked.

Sasha looked from the ring to Frau Richter, confused, or pretending to be.

'First, you berate me about my husband and next you come into my room—'

Sasha shook her head and held up her hand. 'Charlotte—'

'You can call me Frau Richter. That is the only part of my name I want coming out of your mouth.'

'I don't know what you're talking about.'

Frau Richter kept her hand out, kept the ring where Sasha could see it. 'Your memory is so poor, is it? You do not recall trying to tell *me* about *my own husband* last night? How maybe I could have kept him if only I had been *nicer*? If maybe I wasn't so *angry*?'

Sasha held up both hands now. 'That is not what I said. I'd heard from Alison that you and your husband had separated, and I was only trying to be nice.'

'Oh, you heard that from Alison, did you? Because Professor Crane is a marriage expert? Because you, also, know so much about marriage? About *my* marriage?'

'I'm sure you know far more than me. You are the divorce lawyer, yes? If there's nothing else I can do for you, I would prefer to be left alone.'

Frau Richter grabbed Sasha's wrist and forced the ring into her palm. Sasha tried to pull away but the other woman was too strong.

'I don't know what you're up to. But you better behave.' She released Sasha with a shove. 'And stay out of my room. I don't know how you got in there, but don't ever do it again.'

Sasha recoiled. 'I've never been in your room.'

'Oh yes, continue acting like you know nothing. See where that gets you.'

Sasha stared at the wedding ring as if it burned her skin.

'Hey!'

Tonya appeared at the end of the corridor, waving her hand at them, her dyed-red hair appearing even more garish against the hotel's grey tones. Sasha quickly slipped the ring into the pocket of her dressing gown as Tonya approached.

'I'm so happy to run into you both. Tell me, darlings, do any of you happen to know your way around a kitchen?'

Freddy curled up in one of the library nooks and looked at his list. He'd returned to the library after the meeting with Penelope and Tonya because it was a quiet place to think, and lick his wounds.

Bobby = no blood
Jackson = blood
This is for mankind – red herring?
No witnesses
No alibis?
True motive?
Cause of death?

He sighed and tucked the list back into his borrowed Lynda La Plante novel. It was really a list of questions more than anything else. What he needed was the answers. It always seemed so easy in books. The authors laid out clues like puzzle pieces, enticing clever readers to put them together, and he always could. There wasn't a book whose ending he couldn't guess. A twist he couldn't spot. But if he'd ever needed proof that he couldn't be a real detective like Penelope, he got it today. She was right. He was stupid to think that what he read for fun would help here, and he'd made himself look like an idiot in front of a real detective. Why did he have to be so stupid sometimes?

He had no idea what to look for if it wasn't being handed to him. Sure, he could put a puzzle together if he had the pieces. But he didn't know how to go about finding them. He only knew how to collect the evidence from a crime scene, if he had the right equipment. And despite his grades last semester, he was perfectly capable of applying the knowledge he was learning in class. It wasn't his fault he'd been distracted. But if he helped solve this case, it would be worldwide news. They'd have to let him into the senior seminar with the dean. They'd have to.

Freddy put the book into his backpack and left the library. It had hurt when Penelope shut down his theory, but she was right. She was absolutely right. It was ridiculous to think that they'd somehow all be connected. But something didn't feel right and Penelope knew it, too. If she thought the answer was as simple as Jackson killing Bobby in a rage – like Tonya suggested – Penelope wouldn't have spent all day investigating, would she? She was looking for an answer, too. Freddy knew that if he wanted answers, he needed to look for them. He needed to ask for them. And if he couldn't ask Bobby, he'd have to try Jackson. Penelope had told him to stay away, but maybe Jackson just wasn't responding to her. Maybe he would talk to Freddy. Maybe Freddy could get them to bond, like over how they were both from North America or something. It was worth a shot. If he could get something useful out of Jackson, Penelope would see that he wasn't always so useless. And if he didn't get anything useful, then he wouldn't have to tell Penelope that he'd tried at all.

Outside the library, he heard a noise, like a grunt. A service door was open. Freddy approached, continuing to hear noises from inside. He peeked his head in.

Uchida struggled to push a laundry cart down the corridor. Penelope had said he'd been trying to get into the staff hallways earlier today. Now it looked like he'd succeeded. If Freddy could answer this one question for Penelope, maybe she'd be more comfortable letting him speak to Jackson.

'Mr Uchida, can I help you?'

The man looked up, startled, but quickly composed himself.

'I am fine. Thank you.'

'It's really no trouble.' Freddy approached, but Uchida took a step back. Freddy pretended not to notice. 'Are you trying to move this?'

'It's fine.'

'My high school used to have carts like this, for moving around gym equipment and stuff. If it's not budging, it's probably because the wheel locks are on.'

'I said it's fine.'

Freddy knelt down. 'To take it off, you just have to . . .'

He noticed the cart was missing a wheel. Uchida yanked the cart back, away from Freddy.

'I said it is fine. Now excuse me. Please.'

Freddy got to his feet and held up his hands. 'Yeah, sure. Sorry. Just trying to help.' He paused, unsure if Uchida would say something else. But Uchida merely stared at Freddy, waiting for him to go.

'We're having dinner tonight,' Freddy said. 'All of us. Penelope would like everyone to be there.'

'Would she?' Mr Uchida paused. 'Yes. Fine. I'll attend. If you would please leave me.'

Back in the hall, Freddy pulled out his list and made a new note.

Chapter 20

Penelope paced her suite. If Bobby hadn't been killed in the restaurant or in his room, then that meant somewhere else in the hotel was the primary crime scene. She pictured her fellow guests traipsing around the hotel, making themselves comfortable in whatever room they chose, disturbing potential evidence without even realising it. It made her skin itch. But she couldn't very well tell them they all had to stay put for the next three days. The odds were that Tonya was right, anyway. They had the guilty party in custody. Plus, it was possible that the primary crime scene was the restaurant, even though the evidence and her instincts said it wasn't. But she couldn't trust her instincts. She was missing something now. She had to be. She had before.

The band of her ponytail pulled at her scalp. She yanked it out, taking a few strands with it, slipped the band onto her wrist and shook out her dark hair, pacing the room as she rubbed her fingers over her scalp.

This case was cut and dried. She shouldn't even have been investigating this as much as she was. Jackson killed Bobby, staged the body and got caught. The blood on his hands – did it matter where the blood had come from? Bevan had had blood on his clothing, too, when they picked him up. Janice's blood. Blood he said was old. That had come from a fight they'd had weeks before when he'd slapped her and cut her lip. He'd felt so bad about it, he said, that he'd hugged her to his chest as she'd cried and the blood had stained his shirt. He'd never washed it out. What sort of man wore an old, bloody shirt to run errands in Tesco?

Penelope sat on the bed and kneaded her bare toes in the plush carpet. It felt good to walk without the shoes on. Her body did feel lighter in the room without them on, like it was just about to float away but didn't. Her thoughts about Bobby were the same. Each time she tried to let them go, they only got so far before sinking back down. They wouldn't leave her and she couldn't leave them.

She looked at the box of files on the floor at her feet and couldn't get the image of Bobby's body out of her mind. What would it hurt to retrace Bobby's steps last night? If she could at least determine where the blood on Jackson's hands came from, it would quiet some of the thoughts racing through her head.

Penelope retied her hair then crossed the room, opened her welcome pack and pulled out the hotel map. With her pen, she crossed out the Sunrise Lounge, the piano bar, the casino, the library and the swimming pool. Then she circled the Harvest Restaurant and Bobby's suite because, while the murder also didn't appear to have occurred there, they were still the places of most interest for now. Bobby's clothes from that night were in his suite, so it was highly probable he had gone back there after he left the party. Jackson, or an accomplice, could have taken the clothes back to the room, but why then undress him in the first place? Possible but not probable. So assuming Bobby had returned to his suite, how did he get from there to the restaurant? Where might he have stopped along the way or been approached by Jackson? Had the restaurant been Bobby's intended destination when he left his room, or was he headed somewhere else? There were a few direct paths from Bobby's room to the restaurant, and a few that were less direct. Of course this map only showed her the public passageways. The hotel had plenty of hidden rooms and passages, like the managerial hub, at its heart, meant only for staff. If Jackson once had one of the master keys, he could have accessed these as well. The hotel was not boundless. It had limits. And whatever happened to Bobby had happened within these limits.

She checked the clock. She had plenty of time until dinner. If she could establish whether or not any of the master keys were missing, it could help her narrow her search radius. She tossed the map and pen into her bag and bumped right into Sasha as she stepped out of her suite.

'I'm so sorry!' Penelope said, bending down to scoop up the papers Sasha had dropped.

'No, I'm sorry. I should've been looking where I was going.'

Penelope handed Sasha her papers, noticing they appeared to be blank. Sasha's hands were shaking.

'Everything all right?' Penelope asked. 'I mean, you know, considering.'

'Yes, just too much caffeine. Couldn't stop making those espressos.' She laughed. 'Plus all I've eaten today is sugar, I think. Sorry if I disturbed you.'

She turned to walk away.

'We're having a dinner tonight,' Penelope called after her. 'Has anyone told you? Make sure you're there. You know, to get some food that isn't a pastry.'

'Yes. Tonya told me. It sounds wonderful. Thank you.' She quickly continued on her way with her handful of papers before Penelope could ask her another question.

Penelope's hours of searching, however, proved fruitless. Nowhere did she see any signs of an altercation or struggle. Nowhere did she find any blood. Letting Jackson stew for a night alone in the cells and then re-interviewing him in the morning seemed like the best course of action.

As dinnertime approached, Penelope prepared a tray of food for Jackson and carried it down to the managerial hub. She balanced the tray with one hand while tapping the key card with the other to open the closed door to the cells.

Jackson lay curled up on the metal bench facing the wall as she entered. He looked over his shoulder, saw Penelope and turned back.

'I brought you some of the leftovers from last night's dinner.' She slid the tray of food through the slot in the cell. Then she reached into her bag and pulled out a pair of paperbacks she'd taken from the library.

'I brought these, too.' She slipped them through the cell door. 'I wasn't sure what you'd be interested in, but Freddy said these were good, so . . .'

She stuffed her hands in her pockets and waited. Other than that initial glance, Jackson gave no acknowledgement of her presence.

'Jackson, look. The ship will be here in a few days. I honestly don't know what's going to happen to you when it gets here. If there's anything you want to tell me before it gets here I can—'

'It won't work,' Jackson interrupted, his voice muffled by his proximity to the wall.

'What won't work?' she asked.

'The whole good-cop bad-cop routine. It won't work. I'm not going to tell you anything.' He added something under his breath that Penelope didn't catch.

'I don't know what you're talking about,' she said. 'Has someone else been to see you?'

She waited, but he said nothing more.

'Has someone threatened you?'

He flinched. Or maybe it was an involuntary movement caused by his uncomfortable position on the hard bench. She couldn't see his face, so she couldn't be sure.

She stood there for a little while longer, but he wouldn't speak. Maybe in the morning, she thought, he might change his mind. A whole night in a cell could sometimes change people's minds.

'Goodnight, Jackson.'

With a sigh, she exited the cells and returned to the security centre. Earlier, she had found a logbook – unused as of yet – that included a list of which departments had clearances to which rooms as well as an empty sign-out sheet that indicated there were two coded master key cards for the entire hotel. Penelope had one. On her way out of the security centre, she stopped in the general manager's office and soon found the other in an unlocked desk drawer. Had someone used this other card and gone in to see Jackson? Or had he not spoken to anyone else and was messing with her? She decided to pocket the second master key just in case.

When she returned to the lobby, Freddy was waiting for her.

'Tonya sent me to get you,' Freddy said. 'Dinner's ready. Did he say anything?'

'No.' Penelope glanced over her shoulder then walked with Freddy up the grand staircase. 'You haven't talked with him today, have you, Freddy?'

'No,' he said. 'Why?'

'No reason.'

She spared one more look behind her. From this angle on the balcony, she could see over Sasha's makeshift curtain and into the restaurant, but not far enough to see Bobby's body.

Chapter 21

The lights in the Sunrise Lounge had been dimmed and battery-operated candles dispersed throughout the room. Like the suites, most of the lights in the hotel's rooms could be controlled manually from a panel. Tonya and Frau Richter had moved the breakfast tables together to form a large square around which everyone could sit, and one of them had even found a tablecloth to drape over the top. Places had been set for all eight of them, although no one was sitting yet. Dr Wyss and Uchida were speaking in the corner, Tonya and Frau Richter carried hot trays of food out of the kitchen, while Sasha and Alison stood together, nursing drinks and saying nothing. Sasha kept glancing at Frau Richter as she went in and out of the kitchen.

'Can I help with anything?' Freddy asked. Frau Richter blatantly ignored him, but Tonya called him over and gave him some instructions.

With the two other men engrossed in conversation, Penelope made her way to Sasha and Alison.

'Hello.' She waved, then stood there awkwardly, unsure what to do with her hands. She'd changed into one of her nicer blue jumpers her mum said brought out the colour in her eyes and hoped no one had decided to dress in anything more formal. No one had. In fact, unlike last night, Penelope was one of the nicer dressed ones there. Most people, it seemed, had decided to stay in their loungewear.

'Smells good,' Penelope said.

'Really? I can't smell anything,' Alison said. 'Guess I should quit smoking.' She tapped her fingers against the stem of her wine glass.

'It's so kind of them to do this for us,' Sasha said. 'But I'm not sure I have much of an appetite.'

'Don't worry,' Alison said. 'I can eat your share. I've been positively starving all day. Well, not all day. But since lunchtime at least.' She downed her drink and walked over to the table, the first to choose a seat.

Penelope smiled at Sasha. 'Sasha, you didn't happen to speak with Jackson today, did you? Down in his cell?'

Sasha's eyes went wide. 'No! Of course not. I don't think I could bear to be in that man's presence. Not after what he did.'

Uchida called from the table, 'Have you finished interrogating Ms Eris, or is she permitted to join us for dinner?'

Everyone was gathered round the table now, waiting and looking at Penelope.

Sasha laughed off his comment. 'She wasn't interrogating me. She was just being polite.'

Uchida held out a chair for her then sat beside her. The group sat two to a side at the almost square table. Two of the sides were slightly longer, making the entire table feel somewhat distorted, like a Dali painting. Penelope chose a seat next to Freddy with Frau Richter across from her. Penelope smiled when they made eye contact, but Frau Richter merely scowled and looked away. Bottles of red wine had been found and several adorned the table. Alison – sitting opposite Freddy – grabbed the nearest one and uncorked it.

'You've got to try this,' she said to Sasha, who sat to her left. 'It's an excellent vintage.'

Sasha put her hand on top of her glass. 'No, thank you.'

'You deserve it.' Alison grabbed Sasha's glass and poured anyway. 'I was thinking we should all drink up as much of their cellar as possible over the next three days. It's the least they owe us.' She gestured to Frau Richter. 'Give me your glass. Where is their cellar, by the way? I mean, they don't have an actual cellar, do they? I can't imagine they were allowed to dig a hole in the moon.'

'There's a room near the Harvest,' Tonya said. 'Looks like it has a special control panel to keep the temperature right. Though all I know about wine is that I like how it tastes.'

They passed around the bottles. A few, like Sasha and Frau Richter, glanced at the labels, but others like Freddy simply poured. Penelope declined when the bottle came to her.

'A teetotaller and a detective! Do you not have any fun, Ms Strand?' Dr Wyss, sitting to Penelope's left, said somewhat mockingly.

'No, I just hate wine. It all tastes like cough syrup to me. If I'm going to drink, I'm going to drink something I like.' She reached into her bag and pulled out a bottle of stout she'd taken from the Cold Moon Piano Bar. 'This is more my speed.'

'Spoken like a true Brit,' said Tonya, who had taken the seat next to the handsome doctor. 'Hear hear! Now that we all have a drink, I think a toast is in order.'

'A toast for what?' Frau Richter grumbled.

'For making it through the day. For working together to create a hot meal. But, most importantly, for Bobby. Who deserved a better ending than he got.'

'To Bobby,' Freddy said and raised his glass.

Everyone, except Frau Richter, did the same, though Penelope noticed that Sasha barely sipped her wine.

'Dear God I hope no one's vegan,' Tonya said as she started serving herself.

As Penelope scooped food onto hers, she realised how hungry she actually was.

'Now that we know we're alone, we should probably come up with a rota,' Penelope said. 'You know for the cooking and dishes.'

'Dishes?' Uchida scoffed.

'They certainly aren't going to wash themselves,' Tonya chimed in. 'And while it's not as if the hotel can fault us if we don't – it was supposed to be our holiday after all – nine people can go through an extraordinary amount of dishes and cutlery in a short amount of time. You know, I was also wondering if the Apollo Group couldn't make this up to us by giving us the cash value for the trip. No offence to this beautiful building, but even if they offer us another free trip, I don't think I could stomach it.'

'Nine people?' Frau Richter asked.

'Jackson's still with us. Is he not? He has to eat, too.'

'I brought him some food just now,' Penelope said.

'Is that why you asked me—' But before Sasha could finish her question, Alison interrupted.

'Do you really think the Apollo Group will give us the cash?' she asked.

'I think there's a decent chance of it,' Tonya said. 'Especially if we present a united front.'

'I do not want their money,' Uchida said.

'Don't want or don't need?' Alison quipped.

'Of course they'll give us money,' Frau Richter said. 'They will give us money to keep us quiet. Blood money. So that we say nothing of how Bobby actually died. They will say it was natural causes. A heart attack, most likely. And they will pay us enough so that we will say what they want us to say.'

'What a horrible thought,' Sasha said. 'They can't do that. They couldn't. Could they?' She looked around the table for an answer.

'Frau Richter has a point,' Alison said. 'Do you know how much money the Apollo Group has? Enough to build a five-star hotel on the fucking moon. That's how much. Which means they have plenty to cover up a murder. I'm perfectly happy to name my price, and I'm sure everyone around this table could use that kind of money, couldn't they? Well, except for one.'

They all looked at Uchida. Sasha rested her hand on his knee and gazed at him, but Penelope couldn't decipher her look in the dim light.

'I'm sure they'll find some other way to pay you off,' Alison said.

'I cannot be bought,' he said grimly.

'Right. Sure.' She shovelled a forkful of food into her mouth.

In the quiet that followed, Freddy cleared his throat. 'Well, not to be morbid, but honestly, it might serve them just as well financially to tell the truth and say he was murdered.'

Now it was Freddy's turn to be stared at.

'I mean, do you know how popular true crime podcasts are? Murder shows? Lizzie Borden's house is a B and B. In London you have Jack the Ripper tours. I knew someone who went to Canterbury just so they could stand on the spot where Thomas Becket was assassinated in 1170. We – people – have a morbid fascination with death and murder. It's why we slow down to look at car crashes. And I don't think rich people are immune to it. They could probably make a killing marketing the Bobby Rannells Moon Murder – the first man murdered on the moon.'

'And we'd probably get paid well to tell our story,' Tonya added.

'That is morbid,' Frau Richter said. She reached for the wine bottle, but Alison whisked it away. Intentional or accidental, Penelope couldn't tell.

Freddy continued, 'It's a lot less dark than thinking a multi-billion-dollar corporation is going to pay me to cover up a man's murder. At least to me. And I'm not saying I would take the money either way. Just, you know, putting it out there.'

'Do we . . .' Sasha hesitated. 'Do we know for certain that it wasn't suicide?'

'You clearly are more of an artist than a pragmatist,' Frau Richter said.

'I only want to make sure we eliminate all possibilities.'

'Yes, because he clearly planted the pole onto the floor and threw himself on it.'

Sasha's body tensed in frustration and she opened her mouth to retort, but Alison shoved a wine bottle into her hands.

'More wine?' she asked.

'That would be a nice thought,' Dr Wyss said, speaking for

the first time. 'Unfortunately, there is no evidence to suggest he could have done that to himself. I examined the body alongside Detective Strand earlier today.'

'I thought no one was to go into the restaurant?' Uchida stared at Penelope.

'Maybe Jackson helped him.' Sasha clutched the bottle in her hands like a child holding a toy. 'Maybe he got Jackson to agree to help him die.'

'And maybe' – Frau Richter held up her wine glass – 'Mr Smith simply murdered the old man.' She reached for one of the unopened bottles, but was beaten to it by Alison.

'Has anyone been to see Jackson?' Penelope asked. 'Other than me?'

Everyone shook their heads. Penelope tried to glimpse their faces, tried to discern who, if anyone, was lying, but it was too difficult in the dim lighting. Unlike the previous night, when the conversation dropped off, no one picked it back up again. They were all hungry. They were all tired. The sound of their cutlery against the plates echoed in the room. It wasn't until they were halfway through dessert – ice cream – that someone spoke again.

'So,' Tonya said, 'since Frau Richter and I took care of dinner, who's on for breakfast tomorrow?'

'Animals,' Tonya snorted as she scrubbed the dishes while Penelope stood beside her and dried them. 'Did you see how fast they all ran out as soon as they finished dessert? At least Freddy was kind enough to offer to prepare breakfast tomorrow.'

'I'm not surprised,' Penelope said. 'It's always the same. Whenever I had to do a group project for school, I was always the one who ended up doing all of the work.'

'Well, *that* does not surprise me in the slightest.' Tonya handed Penelope another dish to dry. 'So did you find out anything useful after our team meeting this afternoon?'

Penelope knew that Tonya would ask. What she didn't know was how much she would say.

'There are only two master keys cards and I have both now. I traced the most logical routes from both Bobby's and Jackson's suites to the restaurant, but I didn't notice anything unusual. Tomorrow, I'm going to explore the staff areas. See if I can find the source of all that blood.'

'Here, last one.' Tonya handed over the final dish. 'Well, if you need an extra set of eyes on your excursion, let me know.'

'Sure. Of course.'

Tonya wiped her hands on a towel. 'Do you want me to hang around? Walk up to your room with you?'

'I'm fine, Tonya. Cheers. I'll be right behind you.'

Tonya didn't need any further encouragement, and a moment later had gone, leaving Penelope alone in the kitchen. She set the final dish on the rack, took one last look around the kitchen, then turned off the lights on her way out.

The hotel was as quiet as it had been last night. She could hear the whispers of the machines that kept the air circulating and the atmospheric pressure at near-normal levels and the faint strains of 'Fly Me to the Moon', but of her fellow guests, she heard nothing. Penelope paused at the observation window and looked at Earth. She stared at the continents and vast oceans and wondered what was happening down there. Did anyone with the Apollo Group wonder why they had activated the emergency signal? They had to know the staff wasn't here. Didn't they realise how dangerous that would be? What if something went wrong with the oxygen? What if the hotel walls were breached in some way? She'd read that hundreds of meteors per day struck the moon. And the moon had no atmospheric layer to burn them up like Earth did. What if one struck the hotel? Had the company really been willing to risk their lives for some sort of publicity stunt? Who would do that?

She remembered the words scribbled on Bobby's notepad: *Why haven't they started filming?*

Penelope bid goodnight to Earth and continued up to her room. She took the stairs, pausing and listening on each floor, just to be sure. Inside her room, she double-checked that the electronic deadbolt was engaged and laid the two master keys on the centre table. After she had changed into her pyjamas, she took the files out from under her bed and settled in to read.

Chapter 22

Freddy paced back and forth at the end of the hall. Should he or shouldn't he? Her room was right there. All he had to do was knock. He rubbed his thumb over his notebook. But what if he was wrong? If he was wrong, it would make things worse, wouldn't it? He didn't want to make things worse. And also, he'd made a promise. Wouldn't telling her break that promise? The decisions looked so easy in books. You knew who to trust, knew who to suspect. But it was harder when it was happening to you. When you were right in the middle of it all. When you were trapped inside the maze instead of viewing it from above.

'Freddy?'

He spun around. Tonya stood there in her pyjamas.

'What are you doing here? Isn't your room upstairs?' she asked.

He wanted to ask her what she was doing in the hallway in her pyjamas, but he didn't.

'Oh, um . . .' He needed to answer the question. But did he tell her the truth or not? Earlier in the day, he would've trusted Tonya without question. But now, he didn't know what to believe.

'Freddy?'

'Nothing. Sorry. I thought I'd go to the library to get another book but then I was thinking I should finish the one I have before getting another and then I thought does it really matter if I have more than one book out or not because no one else is using the library. But then I was, like, if I get another book, will I be able to finish it before the ship gets here and if I don't—'

Tonya held up her hand. 'No need to overthink it, darling. Just do whatever you want.'

'Right. Whatever I want. Thanks.' He headed for the lifts. ''Night, Tonya.'

'Goodnight, Freddy.'

Tonya watched Freddy get into the lift. As soon as the doors closed, she continued down the hall on the way to her suite, pausing at Penelope's door.

The detective had found something in Bobby's room, Tonya was sure of it. But she hadn't been able to go back and look for herself because Penelope had pocketed both master keys. Tonya had no way in now. Whatever it was, Penelope must have gone back on her own to get it. But why the secrecy? What didn't she want Tonya to know? And what had Freddy been doing, pacing the hall like that? Had he just come from Penelope's? Had they had some sort of private meeting without her?

Tonya considered knocking, but decided against it and kept going to her room. Instead of confronting Penelope now, Tonya would let this play out tomorrow. Yes, she wanted to see what tomorrow would bring.

Alison checked that no one else was in the corridor, then hurried to Dr Wyss's door and knocked. No answer. She knocked again, a little louder, adjusting the strap of the bag on her shoulder. A second later, the door slid open.

'What are you doing here?' he asked, his voice a low hiss. 'You need to go back to your room. You shouldn't be here. What if someone sees you?'

'No one's going to see me,' she said.

'If the detective—'

'She has bigger problems to worry about, don't you think? Besides, they all know we've been spending a fair amount of time together. At night.'

'Not as much time as they think,' he said, his body continuing to block the doorway.

'Look,' she sighed, 'I changed my mind, all right? I do want to talk about it. I can help.'

She held out the bag. Dr Wyss hesitated then took it.

'Go on,' she said.

He looked inside.

'Now can I please come in?'

Finally, he nodded and turned his back, returning into his room. As Alison started to follow, she thought she glimpsed a shadow move at the end of the hall. She paused and listened, but neither saw nor heard anything. She stepped into Erik's room and closed the door behind her.

Sasha held Frau Richter's wedding ring in one hand and the new envelope in her other. She would burn the envelope if she could, but of course no sources of flame were allowed in the hotel. She had already read the latest letter, already knew what was being asked of her now. She closed her eyes, said a prayer. She would make it through this ordeal. She deserved to make it. She did.

Didn't she?

She looked down and glimpsed her open notebook. Uchida had drawn a little cartoon of an alien in a rocket ship. She remembered how he told her to keep his secret – that he liked to draw even if he was not good. How this was a sweet secret, an innocent hobby he was afraid others would embarrass him for but one he trusted her to keep. She thought of how he would smile for her and only for her. Of how he respected her views and appreciated her sketches and could admit when she knew more about a subject than he.

She ran her fingers over the little cartoon.

Yes, she did deserve to make it through.

She would give in no longer. She would have her new beginning, damn their consequences.

She tore the envelope and its contents into pieces. Along with the ring, she carried the pieces to the bathroom, dropping some, like breadcrumbs, along the way, and dumped them into the toilet. They wouldn't be completely destroyed. They would simply be whisked away to another part of the hotel. But they would be away from her. She dropped the ring in, too, then flushed it all away.

Uchida stared at the photograph in his hand, the corner worn from his thumb where he had held it so many times before.

'I will prove you wrong,' he said quietly in Japanese.

He returned the photograph to the desk and pulled down the roll-top cover, shielding the image from his view and rubbed at the old scar down his neck.

Jackson had quickly got used to the silence of the hotel. He thought rural Canada was quiet, but this was something else. He liked it, though. The quieter it was, the calmer his mind became. His thoughts seemed to swirl less not more. This was probably why his friend Joanie had recommended he try a sensory deprivation tank. He'd brushed her off, but he swore now that he'd try it. As soon as he got home, as soon as this whole disaster was sorted out. Someone would believe him. They had to because he didn't know what he'd do if they didn't.

Footsteps disturbed his thoughts.

Someone had entered the main security office again. He'd heard people going in and out of there all day, but wasn't it late now? The cell had no clock but only a few hours had passed since Detective Strand brought him dinner. It couldn't be breakfast already. He listened, waited for the footsteps to leave as they'd done several times before.

Instead, they approached the door to the cells and paused.

Jackson held his breath.

Day 3

Chapter 23

The sun's rays encroached over the dusty landscape. Penelope had learned that all the windows were equipped with a shield that helped protect them all from the ultraviolet rays and radiation while still allowing a clear view of Earth and the stars. Somewhat clear. Dust had begun to gather on the window.

Unseen threats – Earth was full of them. She imagined all the people down there. Imagined her parents waking in Kent, taking the dogs for walks and cleaning the kennels. Imagined her colleagues in London commuting to work, her desk sitting empty. Her colleagues, who knew little of her phobias, probably thought she was having a grand time. The police therapist had suggested Penelope try being more open about her phobias, and she'd tried but found it too difficult to share with the people, other than family, who knew her. She didn't want them to look at her any differently or think her any more incapable than she already felt. But when Bobby had first asked her on the flight, it had been easy. The words just came out of her. It was easy to admit the truth to strangers.

Her parents, though, were probably wondering how she was coping. They had laughed when she told them she'd entered the contest. Then they'd questioned her when she said she'd be going. She needed time away, she'd told them. She needed space to think. Her dad said that was why he thought she was staying with them in Kent. When she said 'space', he hadn't thought she actually meant space. All that unnecessary risk, they'd said. They knew Penelope hated unnecessary risk.

In truth, Penelope thought she'd be more scared than she was. But ensconced in the hotel, wrapped in warm sheets, the furniture pulled in around her, it was easy to trick her brain into believing that the view outside her window was fake, a projection, a cinema screen.

She stretched out her leg and knocked a folder onto the floor.

The files surrounded her on the bed. She'd stayed up most of the night reading them, slept briefly and fitfully, and now sat watching Earth, waiting for it to be an acceptable hour to be awake. Not that there were real hours up here. The twenty-four-hour day was an illusion. Just, as she suspected, was most of this trip.

Nothing in the files contradicted what she already knew about her fellow guests, and all of the information included in her own had been accurate. What bothered her was why these files existed at all. Who had put them together? And why did Bobby have them? There were no identifying organisational markers on any of them. Nothing with the Apollo Group logo. No production company name or address. There was only one clue she'd found – a Post-it note loose at the bottom of the box, like it had fallen off one of the folders as Bobby went through them. The handwritten note simply said: 'Break a leg!' Even though she wasn't a theatre person, she knew that was slang for good luck before a performance. It implied that Bobby would be putting on a show, but Bobby himself had already been questioning his TV show theory. So had the files been part of the ruse for Bobby? To convince him there was a reality show happening so he'd be comfortable convincing the rest of them to stay? Had Bobby been killed because he'd stumbled on the real reason the guests were left alone? Was Jackson a plant who screwed up and got caught? And if so, what was the reason? Or was there something else going on that had nothing to do with Bobby's murder?

With Bobby dead and Jackson keeping silent, Penelope would have to look for answers elsewhere. If she could find the primary crime scene today, perhaps she could find more evidence that would help her piece this all together. Perhaps this was what she really needed. Not a break, but a puzzle. A reason to remind her why she'd fallen in love with police work to begin with. She threw on some jeans and a long-sleeved T-shirt, the hotel-approved trainers, and slipped both master keys into her pocket.

The hotel was as quiet as usual, just the hum of background machinery, which she was starting to get used to, and 'Fly Me to the Moon', which she was not. She passed no one as she headed from her suite down to the lobby. The large observation window was coated on the outside in a thin layer of dust. An automated window-washer – like a Roomba but for windows – was making its way up and down the glass.

The makeshift curtain remained in place in front of the Harvest Restaurant and she took a peek behind it, to make sure Bobby's body was still there. It was. Although the faint odour that now occupied the lobby had made actually looking at the body unnecessary. If there had even been a sliver of suspicion that Bobby had somehow faked his death, the smell erased it.

She glanced at the hotel shop on her way into the offices. Hadn't there been three silver suitcases on display yesterday? Now there were only two. Or maybe there had only ever been two. She set that thought aside for now and headed back to the offices.

She started with the security office. There had to be technical specs of the building somewhere, for staff reference. Either electronic files or even a paper copy. If Bobby hadn't been killed front of house, then it had happened somewhere in the heart of the hotel. She switched the computer on, but it was password protected like Tonya had said.

How much power did it take to run the hotel, she wondered, as she stared at the glowing screen. The lights and oxygen, however they stabilised gravity and atmospheric pressure, hot and cold running water. And where did it all come from? She'd read something about solar power, but how did it work? What fail-safes were installed? And how long could it all function without professional staff overseeing everything? Penelope could hardly go a week in her house without a leak springing up or a light going out. Granted, her house was not a five-star hotel, but it also wasn't on the moon. No one here was a scientist or an engineer. If something were to go wrong with the life support system, if someone decided to tamper with the life support system . . .

She shut the computer down and decided to see if there were any hard copies of the hotel schematics. The building manager's office was next door, in an office shared with the assistant GM and the front of house manager. As soon as she entered the office, she spotted the black storage cabinet parked along the far wall. It stood out because its doors had been prised open. Penelope crossed the room to examine it. There was nothing inside but a bunch of charging cables that looked like they belonged to laptops or tablets. The rest of the contents was gone. These must have been the tablets for guests that were referenced in her welcome pack. But if the tablets weren't in the guests' rooms, and they weren't in the office, where were they now? Who had been desperate enough to break open the cabinet to get them and what did they want them for?

A thump sounded from somewhere in the complex of offices.

'Hello?' she called.

No one answered.

Penelope left the storage cabinet as it was and entered the corridor that connected the offices. Nothing appeared disturbed. The security centre door remained locked. She kept listening. Hearing nothing, she tapped the key card to open the door. The room was empty. From the entranceway, she could see the door to the cells, and the red light, similar to the one in her suite, indicating that the door was locked. It was silent. She considered calling out to Jackson, but didn't want to wake him if he was still sleeping. She'd get some breakfast for him first then see if a night in the cell had made him any more willing to talk to her. At least if she had his breakfast, it would give her a reason – other than an interrogation – to enter his cell.

She checked over her shoulder as she exited the offices even though she heard no other sounds until she stepped into the lobby where 'Fly Me to the Moon' had restarted the chorus. She took a closer look at the shop. Every item, except the suitcases, was locked in a display case, and all of the display cases remained untouched. She tapped both suitcases just to confirm for herself that they were there, then jogged up the grand staircase.

The lights were on in the Sunrise Lounge, but Penelope suspected this was because of the automated system. No one was in the dining area or back in the kitchen, not even Freddy who'd said he'd prepare breakfast. None of the dishes she and Tonya had washed last night had been touched. Perhaps Freddy had overslept or forgotten about his promise to prepare breakfast for everyone. She found a tray and took a bagel from the stack left out on the buffet table.

Tonya's discussion last night, about having the Apollo Group pay them for the cost of the holiday, was tempting. And wasn't she technically working right now? Trying to solve a murder, handling the suspect's care? But as she'd done last night, she shook the thought from her mind. There was only one way that money would look – like a bribe. The handling of the Bevan case had been bad enough. How could she go back to being a detective if it looked like she'd taken a bribe?

She carried the tray from the kitchen, nearly bumping into Uchida who was on his way in.

'Mr Uchida,' she said, 'you're up early.'

'I could say the same about you, Detective.' He eyed the tray. 'Helping yourself, or is that for the villain downstairs?'

'He's not a villain, Mr Uchida. And he has to eat, just like the rest of us.'

'It may do him good to spend a few days suffering. He deserves to rot for what he did.'

'Well, that's not for us to decide.'

She waited for him to step aside, but he did not.

'There is no greater sin than taking the life of another,' he said.

'I happen to agree with you, Mr Uchida. But it's also not up to me to decide the punishment for that sin.'

'So this is your plan? Bring him meals and clean up after him until the ship arrives?'

'I don't know about cleaning, but yes, I'm going to make sure he's properly fed.'

He stared at her. 'And that's all you plan to do?'

They were the same height, but Penelope still got the impression he was looking down on her.

'What else would you like me to do? I'm not a cruise ship director. I'm not in charge of everyone's activities.'

'No. I suppose you're not.' Finally, he stepped aside.

Penelope managed to keep from rolling her eyes until she was out in the hall. She balanced the tray carefully as she walked down the main stairs into the lobby, remembering her brief waitressing days at uni. Yesterday, Uchida had seemed annoyed by all of her questioning and yet now he seemed to imply that he expected her to do more? Had something happened to him last night that she wasn't aware of, or was he simply fickle? She'd try to find out more later, she decided, after she had dropped off Jackson's breakfast and searched for the primary crime scene.

The lights in the security centre came on automatically when she entered, but when she reached the door that led to the holding cell, she paused.

A stain spread out from underneath the door.

Uchida paced the Sunrise Lounge. Instinctively, he went to check his watch, but he was not wearing one. Knowing he would have no concern for one here, he had gratefully left his favourite timepiece at home before departing for the United Kingdom. His sceptical mother had raised an eyebrow but said nothing. He gripped his wrist now, running his fingers over the spot where it should've been then over the familiar scar on his neck.

The door to the lounge opened. Dr Wyss entered. Uchida could not tell if the doctor had slept well or not. The man was as unchanged as ever, like a slab of granite. Uchida met him halfway across the room.

'Well?' he asked.

Dr Wyss considered for a moment then nodded.

'Good, good. We will need others. Professor Crane, yes? And Frau Richter. We should act as quickly as possible. If they are already awake—'

'Detective Strand,' Dr Wyss cut in.

'I don't think the detective—'

'No,' he interrupted again. 'Detective Strand.'

Penelope stood in the doorway, the tray of food he had moments ago seen her exit with still in her hands. She had not appeared to overhear them, however. She looked at nothing, her face pale.

'Detective?' Uchida asked.

She blinked and cleared her throat.

'We need to get everyone together. Now.' As if just realising she was still holding the tray, she quickly set it down on the nearest table. Then she straightened up and lowered her hands to her sides. 'Jackson is dead.'

Chapter 24

The surviving eight crowded the doorway to the cells. Most were still in their pyjamas, having been roused from sleep by Penelope, Uchida and Dr Wyss.

No one said a word.

When they had looked long enough, Penelope closed the door. Single file, they walked silently, returning up the main staircase and back to the Sunrise Lounge. Penelope waited at the door as everyone filed in then closed it behind them. This door had no lock. The only sound was the hum of the hotel machines that were meant to support life. Life support – yet two of them were dead. So far.

Penelope waited. And watched. She wanted to see who would speak first. The seconds passed, the silence painful. Freddy sat with his head in his hands. Tonya stood near him, arms crossed, looking at the floor. Sasha sat at a table, alone, her knees pulled up to her chest, a child's pose. Frau Richter sat at a different table, bouncing her knee up and down. Alison paced, chewing on a piece of nicotine gum. Dr Wyss stood apart, rubbing his forehead. Uchida, like Penelope, stood and watched and waited.

Frau Richter cleared her throat, the sound like a gunshot in the otherwise quiet room. 'So Jackson did not kill Bobby?' she asked.

Tonya responded. 'If he did, someone else killed Jackson. Which means there's still a murderer here. Somewhere.'

'If there was any doubt that this was murder and not suicide . . .' Dr Wyss didn't finish his sentence.

'He was practically decapitated.' Freddy lifted his head from his hands. 'Was that . . . it looked like wire?'

'The ship arrives tomorrow, doesn't it?' Alison asked. 'We've been here two days already.'

'But we only sent the message yesterday,' Frau Richter said. 'It will take two more days to get here. I don't suppose anyone wants to take any responsibility for this?'

'The responsibility may not be any of ours to take,' Uchida said. He looked around the room. His eyes fell on Penelope. She held his gaze as he spoke. 'No one has completed a thorough search of this hotel. For someone who knows their way, it would be easy to hide from our view. I was discussing the possibility with Dr Wyss just before the young man's body was discovered. We were planning a thorough search today.'

'So you believe there is someone else in the hotel?' Frau Richter asked. 'Someone hiding and waiting to kill us one by one?' She glanced around the room as if someone would suddenly pop out of the walls.

Sasha continued shrinking into herself as if she could disappear just by squeezing her knees more tightly.

'There's nothing to suggest that any of us is in danger. It's possible that this was personal to Bobby and Jackson,' Penelope said.

'We need to be sure,' Uchida said.

'We need to be safe,' Penelope countered. 'If there is someone

213

else here – *if* – and *if* they want to come after us, wandering around this place is the best way for someone else to end up dead.'

'And what do you suggest? We cower in a herd like sheep?' Uchida asked.

'Safety in numbers isn't just a saying. Bobby and Jackson were killed when they were alone.'

Uchida shook his head.

'The ship will arrive,' Penelope said, 'with a full crew, in forty-eight hours. We only need to keep ourselves safe until then. Why create added risk?'

'We need to defend ourselves!' he shouted. 'I will not be trapped here like an animal waiting for death. We can flush this criminal out. Then we truly can be safe.'

'And what if we don't?' Penelope asked. 'What if we can't?'

'We could have been killed at any time,' Alison said. 'Yesterday. The murderer could have killed each of us at any time. Most of us spent a large portion of the day alone. Isolated from one another. It would've been easy. Instead, they waited until night fell – so to speak – and went after Jackson, who had been trapped in that cell all day. Why?' She looked around the room, but no one answered.

'There must be some sort of plan,' Alison continued. 'Because if they wanted us all dead, it'll be harder now. We're more likely to travel in a pack.'

Sasha mumbled something that was swallowed up by her knees. Uchida leaned down and whispered into her ear. She slowly lowered her legs to the floor, so she could speak. Her voice was so soft, it could only be heard because the room was so quiet.

'So they wanted us to know?' she asked. 'They wanted us to know we are all going to die?'

'Don't be so dramatic. We're not all going to die,' Frau Richter said. 'Like the detective said, maybe this person only wanted to kill Bobby and Jackson and will leave the rest of us alone.'

'Or,' Penelope said, 'there is no one to find because there is no one else here.' She paused, let the implications of her words sink in. 'Every person here had a motive for wanting Jackson dead,' she said. 'You told me so yourselves yesterday.'

'Way to make friends,' Tonya muttered.

'And you, Detective,' said Uchida, 'did you also have a motive?' But he didn't wait for her answer.

'As we can see,' he said, 'there are several possibilities. We won't know the truth until we eliminate them one by one. We should take another vote. All in favour of searching the hotel, raise your hands.'

Everyone did, except Penelope and Sasha.

'The people have spoken.' Uchida stared at Penelope, daring her to contradict him.

'Then allow me to make a suggestion,' Penelope said. 'There are eight of us. We search as one or in two groups of four.'

'It will be faster if we split into pairs,' Dr Wyss said.

'Do you really think that's wise? Pairs when we don't know for certain that there is a ninth person hiding in the hotel? One of us could be paired with the' – she held back on saying 'murderer' – 'responsible party.'

'You seem intent on sowing suspicion throughout the group, Detective,' Uchida said.

'And you seem very confident that it couldn't possibly be any one of us. Is there something you know that we don't?'

She waited for a retort, but he had none.

'Two groups of four,' she repeated. 'No pairs. One group will start at the top. The other at the bottom. We'll meet back here when we're done. And tonight, no separate rooms. We stay together. There should be plenty of room in your penthouse for all of us, right, Mr Uchida?'

A chorus of surprised voices filled the room.

'Your penthouse?'

'He's been staying in the penthouse?'

'We were supposed to be treated the same.'

Uchida glowered at Penelope, his gaze only softening when it fell upon Sasha, who was visibly trembling.

'Yes,' he said. 'There is room for all.'

Chapter 25

The group of eight stood as one in the lobby, death on either side of them. The scent of decay drifted from the restaurant, where Bobby's body had entered the early stages of decomposition. Penelope believed it would've been worse if not for the hotel's air filtration system. On the other side, Jackson's body was hidden back of house in his cell. Penelope half-expected to see the blood trickling out from behind the Reception desk, even though it was impossible for it to reach that far.

The lift dinged.

The doors slid open.

Penelope handed one of the master keys to Freddy then stepped inside the lift with Tonya, Dr Wyss and Sasha. She thought Sasha would want to stay close to Uchida, but she volunteered for Penelope's group as soon Frau Richter demanded to go with him.

'We'll see you back in the Sunrise Lounge,' Penelope said. The doors closed on Frau Richter, Alison, Freddy and Uchida.

Penelope's group rode the lift up in a silence disturbed by 'Fly Me to the Moon' tinkling over the speakers.

'We've seriously got to find a way to switch that off,' Tonya grumbled.

It took thirty seconds for the lift to reach the top floor. In those thirty seconds, Penelope couldn't help but wonder if she would see the others alive again. With a ding, the doors slid open, revealing the walkway of the observation dome. Sasha gasped, not because of some terrible sight, Penelope knew, but because of the view. The metal walkway clanked under their feet as they filed out of the lift and down the walkway. A geodesic, glass dome topped the hotel like a cherry. Even though she hadn't been paying attention to the brochures, Penelope remembered seeing pictures of it. Now she stood underneath its magnificence. Very little light existed on this floor. Only a sparse series of lowlights illuminated the path to maximise the view above.

'My God,' Tonya whispered.

The starlit sky above them was completely unobstructed and untainted by light pollution. From the ship, Penelope had glimpsed the stars from the porthole windows, but the glimpses were small. From her room and the lobby, it was the sight of Earth that drew the eye. But here, it was nothing but stars. Endless, endless stars. More at one time than she had ever seen in her entire life. Even those in the Arctic Circle could never have seen as many stars as this.

Penelope's breath began to catch in her chest. She closed her eyes and tried to take deep breaths, but when she reopened them, the darkness and vastness of space remained. Sweat gathered in her palms. She felt it breaking out on her forehead. She looked for the others but couldn't see them. They had dispersed throughout the darkened observation deck. Penelope could hear their footsteps. She forced herself to keep her eyes open so they could adjust to the darkness, but even then could only make out the vague shapes of them.

A sharp blade of panic cut through her. She was defenceless. Exposed. Anyone could be up here in the dark. Anyone could be circling around behind her. She started to edge back towards the lift, except it was no longer behind her like she thought. She thought she hadn't moved, but she suddenly was not where she thought she was. Instinctively, she reached for her baton, but of course she didn't have it. She bunched her hands into fists. Remembered her breathing exercises.

'Tonya?' she called out, her voice shaking.

'Here,' answered a voice to her left.

'Sasha?'

'Here,' came the answer to her right.

'Dr Wyss?'

No answer.

'Dr Wyss? Erik?'

No answer. She took another step back.

'Sorry!' His voice came from all the way across the other side of the observation deck. Penelope let out a breath.

'I think I found the control panel for the lights. Shield your eyes.'

Penelope did so. There was a beep and the room was flooded with light. The sudden influx momentarily blinded her even though he'd given warning. For a moment, all she could see was white. Slowly, her eyes adjusted. She lowered her hands and, squinting, saw the shape of Tonya to her left and Sasha to her right.

Bathed in light, the observation deck lost its magic. It was simply a corrugated black metal floor stretching the length of the entire room, with a glass dome over their heads. Dr Wyss stood on the opposite side of the room in front of what Penelope could see now was a control panel. Penelope's chest heaved up and down as if she'd just run a sprint. She shook her arms out down to her fingers, imagining the adrenaline working its way out of her body.

'That's better,' he said. The four of them met underneath the dome.

'Penelope, are you all right?' Tonya asked. 'You're sweating.'

'Fine. I'm fine. I just . . . I'm not a big fan of the dark.'

'You're afraid of flying *and* the dark?' Dr Wyss asked.

'And large open spaces. And snakes. And thunderstorms. And trampolines. But I'm fine now.'

Tonya gaped. 'What on earth are you doing off Earth?'

Penelope shrugged. 'Well, there won't be any thunderstorms here.'

'What about dogs? Are you afraid of dogs?' Dr Wyss asked.

'Oh, I love dogs. Cats on the other hand . . .' She surveyed the observation deck.

'Well there's no sign of anything or anyone up here,' Tonya said.

'Shall we move on?' Dr Wyss asked.

Penelope circled around, refocusing on the task at hand, getting her brain to focus on the search instead of its own fears. 'What about stairs? If the lift goes all the way up here, the stairs must, too.'

'Here,' said Sasha, who had spoken very little since asking to join Penelope's search party. She'd found a door to the left of the lift. It slid open with the touch of a button. Everything was painted black, but it was fairly easy to spot if you were looking for it.

'Anyone see any other doors?' Penelope asked.

They ran their hands over the walls but found nothing else.

'Next floor down?' Tonya asked.

'Detective,' Dr Wyss hesitated, 'before we continue, I have to ask, do you believe Uchida's theory? Do you believe someone else could be here? Uchida spoke of this to me last night. He seemed convinced to the point of . . . of mania. I was going to reject his proposition of searching the hotel this morning, but now that Jackson is . . . now I don't know what to think.'

They all looked at her, waiting for her answer.

'Obviously it's possible. There are entire sections we haven't seen, like the staff quarters and staff cafeteria. And there's a web of service corridors connecting it all. But I also agree with what Alison said. The time to kill us was yesterday, when we thought we were safe. When we were alone. If that was their goal. But killing Jackson upends that entirely. So either the killer isn't after all of us, or . . .'

'Or?' Tonya asked.

'Or they are very, very confident.'

Chapter 26

'This isn't what we're supposed to be doing.' Freddy shifted from foot to foot, hoping the others might change their minds.

'It will be faster this way,' Mr Uchida said. 'We do not need to take orders from Detective Strand.'

'I'm not talking about orders,' Freddy said. 'We agreed. As a group. We're going against what we agreed on as a group.'

'They won't know if you don't tell them,' Frau Richter said. 'We only need to return to the Sunrise Lounge at the same time.'

'Two of us are dead and now you want us to start lying to the others?' Freddy asked.

Frau Richter glared and opened her mouth to say more but Alison cut her off.

'Freddy's right,' she said. 'Kudos to both of you if you don't suspect us all of being murderers. But even if Uchida's theory is correct and someone is hiding, it'll be easier for them to take two of us out at once instead of four.'

'I have nothing to fear,' Mr Uchida said. 'I know of no reason why anyone should want me dead.' He plucked the master key from Freddy's hand. 'We'll search the staff areas.'

'What about you, Frau Richter?' Alison asked. 'You feeling just as confident? You can't think of any reason someone wants you dead?'

Frau Richter clenched her jaw then turned away from Alison. 'Where would you like to begin, Mr Uchida?'

Alison snorted. 'Come on, Freddy. They want to search in pairs, let them. I have no problem going with you. I don't think you're a murderer.' Alison took his arm. 'You two can start down here where the dead bodies are. We'll take the next floor. See you later.'

She led Freddy up the grand staircase. Freddy looked over his shoulder. Was it too late to say something? Maybe he could at least partner with Mr Uchida, and Alison and Frau Richter could search together.

'They'll be fine.' Alison tugged on his arm to hurry him up. 'Honestly, I don't trust them anyway.'

'Yeah, it's just . . .'

'Just what?'

Freddy pictured the gaping red wound that had once been Jackson's neck. Remembered the words that had been spoken by that now lifeless mouth.

'Nothing.'

She squeezed his shoulder. 'We'll be fine. However, you wouldn't be opposed to us arming ourselves before we have our look around, would you?'

The staff corridors were in stark contrast to the guest-facing areas. Where every front of house detail had been meticulously designed and draped in luxury, the back areas reminded one that the hotel was a space station. Narrow and cramped, they had low ceilings with metal tubes that ran along the walls doing whatever it was they did that kept the station running, and its occupants alive. Penelope and her group had to walk single file. Sasha had reluctantly taken point. She had the strongest spatial relations skills aided by her architectural knowledge, but having the others behind her seemed to make her more nervous. Jackson's bloody death had clearly shaken her more than discovering Bobby's body, or perhaps the conglomeration of both murders had taken their toll. After Sasha came Dr Wyss, then Tonya behind him, with Penelope covering the rear.

'Are you all right?' Tonya asked Penelope as they weaved their way through what felt like tunnels.

'Here? Perfectly. I actually feel more comfortable in small spaces. It's why I don't mind commuting on the Central Line at rush hour.'

'Dear God, you are mad.'

'I don't know about mad. But I will say it probably wasn't a good idea to rewatch all the *Alien* movies just before the trip.'

'Here's another door!' Sasha called out.

Penelope squeezed through the tight corridor to the front of the group and tapped the master key on the scanner. It was an unspoken agreement that only Penelope would handle the key card. The door slid open. They exited the staff corridor and re-emerged into the opulence of the hotel. It was like stepping between two different worlds.

'I would love to see the blueprints for this place,' Sasha said, a hint of her former enthusiasm returning.

'I tried looking for them this morning. Where exactly are we?' Penelope asked. 'I thought that staircase was leading us down to the next floor, but now I'm all turned around. I don't even see the lift.'

Sasha turned in a slow circle, her finger held in the air, like she was tracking the route in her mind. 'It did bring us down one floor, but it also weaved us around to the opposite side.' Sasha opened her eyes. 'Underneath the observation deck is the penthouse floor. This hallway runs around the circumference of the penthouse. The lift is on the opposite side. But the stairs are here, probably so the guests are less likely to see the staff coming and going.'

'Upstairs downstairs,' Tonya said. 'The more things change . . .'

They walked anticlockwise around the loop, their hands searching the walls for any hidden doors. They found nothing until they reached the other side. The silent lift awaited instructions while opposite it stood the closed door of the Ix Chel penthouse. Penelope retrieved the master key from her pocket.

'Should we?' Sasha asked. 'You said Dai is staying here, and he's a very private person.'

'With two dead,' Tonya said, 'none of us has any privacy. Not anymore.'

'But we haven't asked him,' she said. 'We should ask him first.'

'He knew we were coming up here,' Penelope added. 'He knew we'd be searching his room.'

Dr Wyss nodded his agreement.

'But leave his personal things alone,' Sasha said. 'Please let's not snoop just because.'

'I promise to be perfectly professional.' Penelope tapped the key.

As they entered, Tonya gasped. 'Yes, this seems about right.'

The penthouse was open-plan, with an elegant spiral staircase connecting the lower floor to the upper floor and windows bordering three sides. The entire space was open in the middle so that the penthouse's private observation dome could allow the stars to shine down from the ceiling. While the observation deck was on the top floor, it did not span the entire width of the hotel. Like a layer cake, the lower levels of the hotel were wider, so that the ceiling of the penthouse was, in places, the highest point of the hotel. Except for the bathroom, there were no separate rooms. The king-size bed was positioned directly in the centre of the lower floor, so that the occupant could fall asleep underneath the stars.

'So this is how the other *other* half lives,' Tonya said. 'Christ. There's money and then there's *money*.'

Penelope began searching the room as the others gaped, but there was not much to see. Despite the furnishings, the penthouse was quite bare. No flowers, like the other suites, no personal touches. Uchida kept his belongings neat and organised – his shirts hanging in an even row in the closet, socks and underwear folded in the drawers. A roll-top desk occupied one side of the room. Penelope lifted the top to see underneath. There was only a single photograph – a Japanese woman in a cherry blossom orchard. Beautiful but unsmiling and obviously pregnant. She was dressed in a traditional kimono, which made the picture seem ageless.

Sasha and Tonya explored the upper-level walkway, while Penelope and Dr Wyss cleared the rest of the lower floor.

'We were all supposed to have the same suite,' Dr Wyss said. 'We were all supposed to be treated the same.'

'If it makes you feel better, he probably doled out a healthy chunk of money for the upgrade.'

Dr Wyss crossed his arms, his face turning red. 'If he paid for this, what else did he pay for?'

Chapter 27

Uchida used his handkerchief to dab the sweat from his brow. The corridors were more cramped than he had anticipated, and the air did not circulate as well. At least there was plenty of artificial light.

'Where, precisely, are we going?' Frau Richter asked.

'It is important to flush out any rats,' Uchida said. He moved slowly. He didn't want to miss a single door, a single hiding spot.

'I assume you are speaking metaphorically.'

He did not respond, and she muttered a few choice words in German.

'You should not say such things about one's mother,' Uchida said.

Frau Richter froze. Uchida turned and looked her in the eye.

'Or assume that your companions are not fluent in German.' He continued on, allowing himself a small smile.

'Running around like this,' she said, '*we* are the rats, trapped in a maze. Anyone seeking to hide could easily avoid us.'

'Possibly. But they would not be able to hide all signs of their presence.'

'It would be easier if we could simply view the security footage.

If there is any security footage. The hotel must have surveillance cameras, yes? Even if they are not in view? Why else would they have those monitors in the security centre?'

'I would imagine so,' he said.

'Then one of us must be able to figure out how to access it. It would be better than putting our lives at risk sneaking around corridors.'

Uchida paused. 'Do you truly believe your life is at risk? That someone brought you all this way to cause you harm?'

Frau Richter looked as if she were about to tell him something but turned away instead.

'I do not know what to believe,' she said.

They continued down the corridor in silence until they found a door labelled 'Bunk B'.

He moved quickly, which made Frau Richter flinch. But he had simply moved to tap the master key against the keypad. He turned on the light, revealing the staff quarters inside. They were empty, all beds neatly made. There were personal items neatly stored in various compartments, no indication that they had been used recently, but also no indication that they'd been left behind in a rushed departure. So if the staff were not here, had they known in advance that they would be leaving? The bunks continued further than he could see.

'At least, when the search is complete,' he said, 'we will know we have tried. Ladies first.'

'No thank you. I would prefer not to have anyone behind me.'

Uchida hesitated then bowed slightly and entered first, Frau Richter following close behind.

The public passages of the hotel's lower floors were clearly laid out and easy to access. But it wasn't the public passages that concerned Penelope at the moment.

'It feels like I'm in the bowels of the Underground or something,' she said as they emerged out into the spa for the third time. 'It's a maze back there. I know they have the little signs on the walls for staff, but honestly. How did we end up here again?' This was why Penelope preferred to use the grand staircase and the main bank of lifts. While there were other routes through the hotel, these were the easiest by which to orient herself.

Sasha opened her notebook and retraced their steps. She had been sketching her own floor plans as they walked, creating her own map in the absence of any other.

'I think we should have turned right instead of left at that last turn,' she said. 'I think that would have led us over to the guest rooms.'

'Let's try again,' Penelope said. They returned to the staff corridor.

A few minutes later, they emerged into another hallway. This time they had taken the correct path. In front of them stretched the row of doors to the guest suites. Sasha, though, noticed something and ran down the hall. The others followed. She was out of breath by the time they reached her.

'My door,' she said. 'I closed it. I know I did.'

The door was stuck halfway between open and closed. Dr Wyss held out an arm to keep the ladies back.

Penelope stepped forward anyway. 'Excuse me, Dr Wyss. Do you have training in clearing a potential crime scene?'

He opened his mouth then closed it again and lowered his arm. 'Thank you. Everyone, stay back.'

Penelope tried the master key. The door wouldn't budge. It was stuck or jammed, but the opening was wide enough for her to slip in sideways.

Earthshine spoke as soon as she crossed threshold.

'Hello, Ms Eris. Is there anything I can do for you today?'

'Earthshine off.'

'I'm sorry. Only Ms Eris can control her in-suite service. Is there anything I can do for you today, Ms Eris?'

Penelope ignored it. Earthshine had not given her a problem when she'd been searching the other suites. She'd deduced that the system did not respond when the master key was used to access a suite. So if a master key had not been used to access Sasha's room, how had someone gained entry? Had the door simply not closed when she last left, or had Sasha herself been back at some point and not told them?

Penelope's suite and Sasha's were similar, so it was easy for her to navigate and quickly clear all the various places a person could be hiding. There was no evidence that anyone was here, or that anybody had been in here.

'You can come in,' Penelope called.

Sasha did a slow circle, her face filled with fear, even though every item seemed to be in place. The bed was unmade and the desk drawer open, a vase of lilies neatly arranged on the circular table.

'Sasha, is this how your room was when you last left it?'

'No,' she whispered. 'I mean yes. The room, yes, but I know I did not leave the door open.'

'When was the last time you were in your room?'

Sasha stared at the desk, her face blank.

'Sasha?' Penelope stepped into her line of sight, tried to get Sasha to make eye contact.

'I'm sorry. What did you say?'

'When was the last time you were in your room?'

'Oh, this morning. It must've been this morning. When you knocked and said I needed to get dressed and come to the Sunrise Lounge. I haven't . . . I haven't been back since.'

'Can you tell me if anything's missing?' Penelope asked. 'If anything has been moved?'

Sasha thumbed the edge of her notebook.

'Everything seems in order.' She went to the bed and gently shook the duvet, ran her fingers over the circular table, dusting some of the pollen to the floor. At the desk, she paused, eyes on an envelope that she quickly ushered into a drawer. 'No. Nothing's been moved. Everything is as I left it. But perhaps we should find the others.'

Chapter 28

'What do you think everyone else is doing?' Freddy uneasily gripped the kitchen knife as he and Alison made their way through the first floor. Or was it the second? He got confused by the British system of numbering floors. Why wasn't the ground floor the first floor? It was a floor, wasn't it? They had gone up the main stairs and into the kitchen off the Sunrise Lounge, each claiming a knife before beginning their search.

'Same as us, I suppose,' Alison said, walking alongside him. Freddy had not failed to notice that since they had picked up the knives, she always made sure to be directly alongside him. Never behind him and never in front.

Without a master key, they could only search the public-facing rooms of the hotel, rooms he'd already seen twice over.

'Why do you think they built it this way?' Freddy asked.

'What way?'

'Like, why not put all of the guest rooms on one floor, and all of the amenities on another. Why the mezzanine levels?'

'Do you think it has anything to do with why Bobby and Jackson were murdered?' she asked.

'No. Probably not.'

'Then why do you care?'

'Just curious, I guess,' he said.

'Why don't you save your curiosity for the murders? Unless, of course, you don't need to be curious about that.'

Freddy stopped and stared at her.

'Because you already know who killed them.' Alison's gaze was dark and blazing.

'I don't . . . I-I . . .' he stammered.

She burst out into a laugh. 'Relax, Freddy. I'm only joking.'

She kept laughing and continued down the hall. Freddy followed.

'It's not something I think we should be joking about,' he said. He paused and picked at a spot of paint on the wall. It was already coming loose around one of the lights embedded there.

'I can't help it,' she said, though Freddy noticed she didn't apologise. 'When I find a situation uncomfortable, I laugh about it. I've always been that way. I was nearly kicked out of my own mother's funeral.'

'I've read that's a natural response for some people,' he said, brushing the chipped paint away. 'It was in one of my textbooks about human behaviour. The different reactions we have to stress and nerves. A detective once told me that he tried not to judge people who laughed in interviews because sometimes that's just how they reacted to stress. But, he said, it still didn't look good.'

'Remind me never to get charged with murder.' She sighed. 'This all seems so pointless, doesn't it? I mean, do you honestly think there's someone lurking about the hotel?'

'I think I'd prefer to think that. Because the alternative is that one of us . . .' He didn't even want to finish the sentence.

'But maybe that would mean we're not all at risk. Maybe whichever one of us did it had good reason. Penelope said we all had a motive. What was yours?'

'I didn't have one,' he said.

'Really? So was the detective lying or do you not realise what you said to her?'

But Freddy's attention was drawn to the spot on the wall where he had chipped away the paint. He ran his finger over the spot then started picking away some more. He couldn't get much traction, so he took his knife and started digging into the wall.

'Hey, Earth to Freddy. I don't think the Apollo Group's going to appreciate that, do you? Freddy? What are you doing?'

Plaster and paint drifted to the floor until finally Freddy had chipped away enough to reveal what was underneath. Alison stepped closer to take a look.

'What the fuck?'

The eight of them stood gathered round the hole Freddy had created, examining what he'd found.

'So let me get this straight,' Tonya said. 'The beautiful star lights decorating the halls of this hotel are fucking cameras?'

She waved her hand at the hall, where there were dozens of twinkling faux-stars.

'Not all of them probably,' Freddy said. 'But some. That's how they disguised the security cameras. They blended them in with the hotel decor.'

'Does this mean they've been recording us all this time?' Sasha asked.

'So there could be footage of what happened to Bobby.' Penelope looked at Uchida. 'Better than a wild goose chase, searching rooms, wouldn't you agree?'

'All in favour of accessing that footage?' Tonya asked.

Hands went up. Uchida nodded.

They hurried down to the security centre together and gathered around the monitors. The door to the cells was closed, but Jackson's blood was clearly evident on the floor, where it had seeped beneath. No one chose to say anything about it, but everyone carefully avoided that side of the room. Though the system would turn on, none could figure out the password to access the footage, as Tonya had said. Penelope remembered the storage cabinet that had been broken into, but she said nothing about it yet, even as the group paced the room in frustration.

'What about the ship?' Sasha asked. 'Maybe on Earth, they've seen the footage and know why we sent the signal. Maybe it gets sent directly there.'

'If the ship is close enough,' Penelope said, 'we should be able to send them a message, right?'

The group murmured their assent.

They went into the communications centre next door and switched on all of the equipment they could find. Penelope knew communication between Earth and space had something to do with radio waves and satellites, that there was some delay between messages sent and messages received. Scientists could transmit experiment data from the International Space Station to Earth. They should at least be able to send an email. If they could log into the system.

However, unlike the security centre, someone had already

logged onto the central communications computer. Penelope decided to worry about who, how and why later, but having access to this computer didn't solve their problem. Each time they pressed the transmit button, they received an error message.

'Why is it giving an error message?' Frau Richter practically screamed at Freddy, who had transcribed their SOS.

'I don't know. I'm not an IT guy.'

'Maybe you've broken it.'

'Penelope?' Tonya quietly called to her from the other side of the room.

'Hang on!' Freddy shouted as Penelope went over to Tonya. 'Look! There's an incoming message.'

'What does it say?' Frau Richter snapped.

'It's still loading.'

'What is it?' Penelope didn't like the look on Tonya's face.

'The emergency signal. When we activated it, this light came on.' Tonya pointed.

'Make it load faster,' Frau Richter urged.

'It's loading as fast as it can,' Alison said. 'Relax.'

'Don't tell me to relax, you—'

Dr Wyss stepped between them.

'Penelope.' Tonya caught her attention again. 'Do you see what I'm saying? This light should be on.'

Penelope's mouth went dry. 'So why isn't it?'

'It's been switched off,' Tonya said. 'Someone's switched it off. No one's coming.'

'Here it is!' Freddy shouted, but his elation quickly vanished.

'What does it say? Move out of the way.' Frau Richter shoved him out of the chair.

Penelope couldn't see the screen. There were too many heads in the way. Finally, she was able to manoeuvre herself to the front to read the message.

Mistakes have been made, but the true price has not yet been paid.

Chapter 29

Like in the hallways, cameras were likely to be concealed somewhere within the walls of the Sunrise Lounge, but they sat there anyway, wondering who might be watching. Wondering who might be listening. But mostly, they were wondering what the 'true price' would be, and who would pay it.

'We all had plenty of time to search,' Penelope said. She kept her voice quiet. Calm. Emulated the behaviour she wanted from the others. 'Did anyone find any sign that there is a person or persons unknown currently occupying the hotel?'

Feet shuffled. People scratched their heads. Someone coughed.

'We located the staff quarters,' Uchida said, his voice as even-keeled as Penelope's. 'But we could not tell if anyone has been living there while we were here.'

'Someone has been in Sasha's room,' Penelope said. 'Her door was open. Half open.'

'I didn't think doors could be left open,' Alison said. 'Aren't they supposed to automatically shut behind us?'

'Well, we all know the automation here hasn't been perfect,' Tonya said.

'So did someone ransack it or something?' Alison asked Sasha. 'Leave you messages written in blood?'

Sasha shook her head before answering. 'No. No, there was nothing.'

'So maybe no one was in your room at all,' Frau Richter said. 'Maybe you are simply imagining things and did not realise the door did not shut behind you.'

'Or maybe someone invaded my privacy because they're imagining the same has been done to them.' Sasha glared back.

Alison snorted. 'I'd say more than a little.'

'OK, enough,' Penelope intervened. 'We're all a little on edge right now. Speaking of doors and locks, Freddy, do you still have the master key?'

'Um, Mr Uchida has it. He . . . he took it after you'd left.'

Penelope looked to Uchida, who retrieved the key from his trouser packet and handed it over without a word. She had expected more reluctance but decided not to question it, for now.

'Let's be realistic about this,' Penelope continued, slipping the second key into her pocket. 'There is a chance a murderer is hiding in this hotel, one who has been able to avoid us by using the complex series of passages intended for the staff. Which, as we can attest, are indeed complex and require key card or biometric data permission to enter. However, as I've said before, there is also a chance that the murderer is in this very room.'

They had not seemed to understand the gravity of the situation after Bobby's death, and not entirely after Jackson's. But the mood was different now that they'd read the message.

'What we also know,' she continued, 'is that we're all potentially at risk. That message implies someone knows what's been going on and that Bobby and Jackson were either not the intended victims or were not intended to be the only victims.'

'We don't know that. How can you make that assumption? What does that even mean?' Frau Richter snapped. 'The true price? Maybe they are discussing money. Maybe someone is holding us hostage and wants money from the Apollo Group.'

Freddy sighed. 'Everyone knows the phrase "true price" typically refers to someone's life.'

'Oh, so you're an expert now? You alone can interpret this killer's words? Or do you understand their meaning because you are the one responsible?'

Freddy quickly defended himself, but Frau Richter kept shouting back. Both got to their feet, pointing and yelling. Dr Wyss stood in front of Frau Richter, trying to calm her down, while Tonya tried to calm Freddy.

'Look,' Tonya said when the shouting had died down, 'someone was able to send a threatening message on a secure communications network. Maybe the Apollo Group has been hacked, but the easiest answer is that it's an inside job, right? That, plus the ability to get the staff to vacate the hotel? That takes power. Someone with influence has been manipulating this from the start.' Tonya turned and locked eyes with Uchida. 'And let's be honest with ourselves, darlings. Only one person here has enough money to make any of this possible.'

One by one, they raised their heads and looked at Uchida.

He shook his head. 'No. You're wrong. I do not want anyone dead. I came here to experience the beauty of space, like all of you. I came here because this is my dream. I have no desire to see it ruined.'

'Why did you enter the contest?' Penelope asked. 'You can afford this trip.'

'Why pay if I could get the chance for free?'

'Some chance,' Penelope said. 'Tonya's right. How many millions of people entered?'

'I have always been lucky. It's part of being a successful businessman.'

'So is making enemies. I'm sure you've made a fair few over the years.'

Uchida crossed his arms. 'So do you suspect me of being the murderer or do you believe I'm the next victim?'

'I haven't decided,' Penelope said. 'But billionaires are likely to have enemies that are just as rich. Rich enough to manipulate the contest. It would make quite a statement. No one would care much about the rest of us. But a billionaire killed in space? That would be something. That would be enough to gain the level of attention those protestors at the spaceport wanted.'

Uchida sighed. He looked tired. But then again, they all did.

'You told me you didn't deserve to be here.' Sasha's quiet voice echoed through the room. Every head turned to her. 'When we were on the ship. You told me that you weren't supposed to be here. You really meant that, didn't you?'

Uchida closed his eyes. Penelope waited. So did the others.

'No one is plotting to kill me. No one rigged the contest in my favour.'

'You sound very certain of that,' Penelope said.

'Because I never entered the contest!' he shouted.

With a sigh, he stopped pacing.

'I purchased my place. I paid twice what this trip is worth.

I wanted to be the first. To show her . . .' He shook his head, paused. 'I always intended to be in the first group of guests. I placed my deposit the day the first shipload of construction materials reached the moon's surface. I am close to several members of the Apollo Group's board. In all these years, there was never mention of any contest. Never. Suddenly, with no discussion of any kind, no mention to me, the contest was announced to the public. A random group of ten people would be chosen as the first visitors. I am lucky, yes, but I am not a fool. The odds were almost impossible. For a long time, I debated what I should do. In the end, there was no other option. I paid for my seat. It was before your names were announced but after you were selected. I saw the list and I paid them double what the penthouse is worth on top of my initial deposit to have my name replace another's. So you are right, Sasha. I did not lie to you, although I should have been more honest with you. You deserved that much. I am not meant to be here. A housewife from the American Midwest should be standing here. However, I am sure she would be thanking me now if she knew what we were being subjected to.'

Uchida sat down. He kept his head low, seemed to be bracing himself for the backlash.

'Thank you, Mr Uchida, for telling us this,' Penelope said. 'Was there a specific contact you had at the Apollo Group? That you had these discussions with? Someone on the board?

He waved a dismissive hand. 'It was all done through lawyers. I never spoke to anyone directly about my plan.'

'It could be a vendetta against Mr Uchida then, couldn't it?' Freddy asked. 'Someone who knew he would be coming and could make a plan?'

'If Dai's name was changed,' Sasha said, 'does that mean other names could have been changed? That other people could have been removed or added? That we all could have been chosen for a specific purpose?'

Penelope noticed how Sasha kept glancing at Frau Richter as she spoke.

'That's what I was saying yesterday!' Freddy practically jumped up and down in excitement. 'What if the selection process wasn't entirely random? What if there is something that connects all of us?'

Alison coughed and raised her hand. 'I, erm . . . well, since we're confessing things.'

She blushed, her usual self-confidence absent. Whatever she had been going to say, she now hesitated. The others became antsy, eager for Alison to continue. The more the murmurs came, the more she was unwilling to speak. Penelope raised her hand.

'Please. Let her take her time.'

Alison nodded her thanks and chewed more ferociously on her piece of nicotine gum.

'The thing is,' she said, 'I haven't been completely honest with all of you. You see, I've also been in contact with someone from the Apollo Group. Or rather, they've been in contact with me.' She held up her hands. 'Before you ask, I don't know their name. But after I was told I won the contest, someone contacted me and asked if I could, well, not spy on you all, exactly, but take notes. On everyone's behaviour. They said they wanted to know what effects living in the hotel would have on everyone. They said it's really only trained astronauts who have ever spent this much continuous time in space, and they wanted to know what it would do to regular people. I was supposed to get a passcode to the communications centre when I got here, to send my reports, but I never did. I thought it was all, I don't know, part of the experiment.'

'Did you know the staff would be absent?' Penelope asked.

Alison bit her lower lip. 'Yes.'

A chorus of shouts went up, some directed at Alison, others not. Penelope struggled to calm them down.

'So this is why they held the contest?' Dr Wyss asked. 'To run some little science experiment before taking on paying guests?'

'It's one expensive science project,' Freddy said.

'They can afford it,' Uchida said.

'But Bobby and Jackson, they are really *really* dead,' Freddy said. 'That can't be part of the experiment. Can it?'

'So that is why you were chosen.' Frau Richter shot daggers at Alison. 'Because you are a psychologist. Because you'd be willing to act as a spy.'

'I don't know why I'm here,' Alison said. 'I thought I won, same as the rest of you. I thought maybe after they found out I was a psychologist, that was why they asked. They'd have no reason to single out my entry. I'm not anybody in the field. This isn't even my area. And they could've planted their own qualified psychologist if they'd wanted to. It doesn't make sense to ask me to do it.'

'Maybe they asked you,' Penelope said, 'because whoever *they* are knew this was going to happen. I think it's all part of the same manipulation. Someone had been in contact with Bobby also. I think someone told him in advance that we were going to be used for a reality show. He had background information – files – on all of us, in his room.'

Everyone's voices rose again. Tonya shot Penelope a very pointed look that Penelope did not return.

'They're safe in my possession. But Bobby also wrote himself a note; Tonya's seen it. He was wondering why he didn't notice anything filming yet. I think he was starting to question what he'd been told.'

'Is that why he was killed?' Uchida asked. 'He figured the show was a lie? A ruse? And he was going to tell us?'

'Then why kill Jackson?' Dr Wyss asked. 'Did he know, too?'

'I don't know,' Penelope said. 'Jackson wouldn't say much when we spoke. But what we have is a psychologist who was told she'd be observing human behaviour and a reality TV star who was told this would be a reality TV series. So at least two people wouldn't have been shocked by the absence of the staff. Two people who could influence us to stay even though we were afraid. Was anyone else contacted by an anonymous source from the Apollo Group?'

Penelope looked around the room, but everyone other than Uchida and Alison shook their heads.

'Not even you?' Sasha asked Frau Richter. 'We don't think that the Apollo Group wouldn't have a use for an international lawyer?'

'I work only in Germany and France,' Frau Richter said. 'Hardly international. Unless someone in that company is very desperate for a divorce. No.'

'When was the last time you worked in France?' Sasha asked, but Frau Richter ignored her. The lawyer had begun to pace and wring her hands.

'If I'm here it's because I'm the one the killer wants. I'm sure of it. Because if anyone arranged this, it is my husband. This is exactly the type of malicious deviousness he would concoct. I wouldn't give him children, so he divorces me and takes everything from me. Everything! Even the cat! But it wasn't enough. Now he's doing this. Now he wants my life. My life is the price that must be paid.'

'You flatter yourself,' Tonya said. 'You have one man angry at you? Try an entire fucking nation. Oh please, don't act like you don't all know. It was still all over the tabloids the day we launched from Cornwall. And I wasn't trying to destroy Dalia Joy's life, I'll have you know. All I wanted was to know more about the little starlet that's been commandeering every television show lately. The public love her. Can't get enough of her. It's my job to dig up the dirt.' Tonya closed her eyes and shook her head. 'I thought she was eighteen. We all thought she was eighteen! Even her fucking agent thought she was eighteen. It was that God-awful mother of hers. She's the one that added five years to her daughter's age and had her dressing up like some Page Three model. If people should be mad at anyone, it's that woman for doing what she did. Not me for writing about it.'

'Even if it was the media attention that caused her suicide attempt?' Penelope asked.

Tonya looked away. 'Of course I'm angry with myself. Of course I am,' she said.

'I work for Dignitas,' Dr Wyss announced without preamble. 'My job as a doctor is to help the terminally ill end their lives with dignity, in a way that brings them peace. I am proud of the work I do. That I am able to help them end their suffering on their terms. But I know not everyone sees my work in the same light. Not even my patients' families. This is why I did not want to tell anyone my specialty. I've received numerous death threats over the years, which I find somewhat ironic coming from people who are "fighting for life". These include threats from some people wealthy enough, and bitter enough, to orchestrate something like this. The murderer could be after me.'

'So that also means you know how to kill,' Sasha said. 'You kill for a living.'

Her comments started another argument. In the commotion that followed, Freddy quietly approached Penelope.

'Um, Detective Strand? I mean, Penelope, could I . . . could I talk to you in private?'

Penelope followed Freddy into the hallway and partially closed the door behind them. Freddy paced and kept sticking his hands into and then taking them out of his pockets.

'What is it, Freddy?'

'Those files you found. Did you read them?' he asked.

'I've started to.'

'Have you read mine?'

'What is it you want to tell me, Freddy?'

He peeked into the room, checking to see if anyone was eavesdropping.

'I don't want the others to know because I don't want them to think I had anything to do with this because I didn't.'

He stopped pacing, but every muscle in his body remained tense.

'I was a suspect once. Recently. Last year. In New York. A . . . a murder suspect. It was all a misunderstanding. A total misunderstanding. Mistaken identity and me being in the wrong place at the wrong time. The police questioned me. For hours.

Days, actually. But I was never charged. And they've arrested the guy who did it. He lived on my block. The trial's coming up soon. My name wasn't even mentioned in the news or anything. Yet without the internet, I can't prove any of this. But it's the honest truth.'

I didn't kill Janice. I'm telling you the honest truth, Detective. Please. It weren't me that hurt Janice. I'd never.

Penelope tried to shake the memory from her mind as Freddy continued speaking.

'. . . if the others find out that I was a suspect, even though I'm innocent . . . I'm the only Black man here. I think they're already suspicious of me. I mean, Frau Richter definitely is. And the others, I don't think it would take much to . . . you know?'

He stuffed his hands back into his pockets and waited for her answer.

I'm innocent, Detective Strand. I wasn't there when it happened. You have to believe me.

'I don't see any reason to tell them,' Penelope said, pushing the memory aside. 'Unless there's something about that crime that might relate to all of this.'

'There isn't,' he said. 'I mean there can't be. It was a random mugging that went wrong.'

'If anything does come to mind, just bring it to me, all right?'

Freddy nodded.

The two of them returned to the room. Everyone was shouting at one another, trying to prove they were the intended victim. Only Tonya seemed to notice they had gone, but she said nothing. Once the group finally settled down again, everyone seemed at a loss for what to say.

Finally, Alison asked, 'So what do we do now?'

'The emergency signal has been reactivated,' Penelope said. 'And I've used the master key to disable the door to the communications centre. No one will be able to get in and turn the signal off again. At most, a ship will be here in three days. Maybe sooner if someone's got suspicious as to why all the staff are on their way back to Earth. The best way to ensure that we're all safe is if we stick together from now on. No exceptions.'

'You mean at night?' Sasha asked.

'I mean at all times. Night. Day. Meals. Bedtime.'

'One big happy family,' Tonya sighed.

'I know it's not convenient and I know it won't be comfortable. But our priority right now is to each other. None of us wants to end up like Bobby or Jackson. Agreed?'

For better or worse, they did.

Chapter 30

22:00 UTC

The remainder of the day passed in tension-filled silence. The group camped out mainly in the Sunrise Lounge and only left in groups of three or four to use the toilets and get food, or other items with which to divert themselves. Penelope would start to worry when someone was gone for longer stretches, like when Freddy, Sasha and Dr Wyss had been gone for over fifteen minutes, and would only visibly relax when they returned. In that particular case, they had gone to their suites to change clothes and freshen up.

But no matter how much they scavenged from one area of the hotel, no one seemed interested in the books or card games they brought back with them. It was a miserable affair, as if everyone was waiting for something else to happen. The tension continued to build, so that even when something innocuous happened, like a chair getting bumped or someone coughing, the entire group jumped at the sound. Alison, Sasha and Tonya chewed copious amounts of nicotine gum, all longing for a real cigarette. Frau Richter self-consciously performed an exercise routine in the corner, her grunts grating on Penelope's ears. Sasha opened and closed her notebook, writing nothing, sometimes unfolding a letter she had tucked between the pages. Uchida and Dr Wyss silently played chess while Freddy read another book in between his constant glances at everyone in the room.

'I've had enough of this,' Alison said after they'd eaten dinner – last night's reheated leftovers. 'Can we all go up to bed already? I'd rather at least try to sleep than sit around doing absolutely fuck all.'

With no good argument against it, they all agreed and trudged up the stairs together, so that they could more easily stop at each person's bedroom on the way. Each person quickly changed into their pyjamas or grabbed anything else they needed for the night. Sasha was nervous about entering her room alone, so Penelope and Uchida went with her while the others waited in the hall.

When they entered the penthouse, Earthshine – triggered by the presence of the room's assigned guest – spoke to Uchida in Japanese. He responded and Penelope recognised that Japanese word for 'goodbye' as he turned off the system. Penelope had almost forgotten Earthshine since she had turned off her own system on the first day, and entering suites with the master key did not activate it. She linked the seemingly omniscient AI voice to the threatening message on the security system then quickly dismissed it. This wasn't an AI takeover like in a sci-fi film. But still, it reminded her that something or someone was – and always had been – watching them.

Uchida then used the control panel to switch the lighting system from automatic to manual. Those who had been to the penthouse before immediately chose a place to settle down while those seeing it for the first time gasped.

'You paid how much for this?' Frau Richter asked.

'That is not any of your business,' Uchida replied as he turned down the sheets on the king-size bed.

'Whatever it was,' Alison said, tossing herself onto the grey chaise longue, 'it was worth every penny.'

After Freddy, Dr Wyss and Penelope had carried in additional mattresses from some of the unoccupied rooms, between the mattresses and various sofas, everyone had a place to lie down. Penelope tried to inconspicuously choose a mattress by the door, but it was clear from Tonya's look that at least one person knew what she was doing.

It seemed to take hours for everyone to take turns in one of the two bathrooms and get settled in their beds. When the lights finally dimmed and went dark, the tension that had existed throughout the day remained. No one, it seemed, wanted to be the first to fall to sleep.

Alison's voice rang out in the darkness. 'I suppose this is a bad time to ask, but does anyone here snore? I forgot my ear plugs.'

No one answered.

'I'll take that as a no. Goodnight then, everyone.'

No one said goodnight back.

Penelope lay with her eyes open, letting them adjust to the dark so that she could make out the shapes in the other beds. She stayed awake for as long as she could before her body eventually gave way to sleep.

The halls of the Hotel Artemis were silent except for the endless cycle of 'Fly Me to the Moon' echoing from the lobby. The music drifted like a ghost through the hotel while the guests, isolated in the penthouse, slept. Amongst the music, a soft beep sounded, one that would not have been heard had there been any other noise in the hotel at the time. It sounded again. The noise came from within the communications centre, whose door remained locked. The computer beeped once again, indicating that another message had come through. The messages glowed on the screen, although there was no one there to read them.

What are you doing?
There isn't much time.
Do not forget our deal.

Day 4

Chapter 31

Penelope awoke from a misremembered dream with a strong urge to pee. She'd forgotten how many cups of tea she'd had yesterday as they'd wasted the day in the Sunrise Lounge. The bathroom was about halfway down the penthouse on her left. Before getting up, she propped herself up on her elbows and let her eyes adjust to the darkness. The penthouse was quiet. No snoring, only the sound of steady even breaths that came with sleep.

Quietly, she slipped off her mattress and padded over to the bathroom. She closed the door behind her and locked it but didn't switch on the light. She didn't want to assault her eyes. Besides, with the amount of starlight, she didn't need artificial light. A long rectangular window provided a view of space even here, so that a guest could admire the view while in the bath or, in her case, on the toilet, without worrying about anyone observing them from outside.

Despite everything that had happened, and everything that could happen, she still could not get used to that awesome sight of the size of Earth and how small it made her feel. Even after she'd finished, she sat there and stared. In spite of her phobias, she wondered what it would be like to go outside there, away from the safety of the hotel where it was easy to give in to the illusion that they were on Earth. What would it feel like to be truly out there? A single dot on the landscape of the moon?

Penelope sat up straight.

'Oh my God. I'm an idiot.'

She quickly wiped and flushed, wincing as the sound – similar to that of an aeroplane toilet – pierced the night. But when she opened the bathroom door, the noise had not seemed to wake anyone. She tiptoed back to the door, pausing at one of the mattresses. At first it looked like someone was sleeping there, huddled under the duvet, but she looked closer. It was just the crumpled duvet. The mattress was empty. Tonya. This was where Tonya had been sleeping.

Penelope kept moving. She didn't have time to worry about where Tonya was. Besides, it was possible that Tonya, also, had needed the bathroom and, knowing one was occupied, went to the other one on the upper level. Penelope put on her slippers and fingered the two master keys she'd been sleeping with in her pyjama pocket. She still had both of them. Just in case, she also took a small statue with a good solid base from a table in the penthouse entranceway, though she hoped she'd have no need to use it.

Dimmed lights illuminated the hallway outside the penthouse. According to hotel time, it was the middle of the night, and the silence of the place reflected this. Penelope took the stairs down to the ground floor where the scent of decomposition mingled with the cold, recycled air.

There was more light in the lobby, but these lights, too, had automatically dimmed to reflect the night-time hours. 'Fly Me to the Moon' continued to play, albeit at a lesser volume. She wondered what the hotel would normally be like at this time of night once it had fully opened. Guests laughing at the restaurant bar, the clinks of glasses, staff idling at Reception, tapping at their touchscreens, trying to pass the time until the end of their shift. But the bar and Reception, these were not the places that interested her. Not at the moment. She passed under the grand staircase and made her way to the rear of the ground floor, where the empty casino sat in darkness. But this, too, she passed.

Most of the hotel's amenities had sounded appealing to her, and she had made a plan to try everything at least once. All except one thing. This one she had dismissed immediately, and so had forgotten about it entirely. It had taken enough courage – and some hypnotherapy – on her part just to get on the ship. There was no way anyone was going to get her to go on a bloody moonwalk.

She stood at the airlock. A shiny brand-new metal sign proclaimed 'Moonwalks – Meet Here'. To her right hung three spacesuits emblazoned with the Hotel Artemis logo. There were hooks for four. She peered through the porthole into the airlock, checked that the outer door was closed, then tapped the master key. The inner door slid open. She did not step inside.

If someone got trapped in this airlock without the proper protection, they would suffocate to death in a matter of seconds. The only air would be what was held in their lungs, which would be ripped out of them by the vacuum of space if they did not immediately exhale. If they did exhale, they would gain a few more seconds of life as they stood there, suffocating in the opened airlock, banging on the inner door to be let back in while their skin and tissue began to swell as the water in their body vaporised in the absence of atmospheric pressure. Finally, they would gasp but there would be nothing to inhale. Penelope knew all of this because she had nearly given herself a panic attack reading about what happened to bodies in space.

She now looked at the floor of the airlock. Lying there was the fourth spacesuit, obviously damaged. A hose to the oxygen pack had been disconnected. The person wearing it would not have been able to reach back to fix it.

A tear came to Penelope's eye. 'Oh, Bobby.'

Penelope crept back up the stairs, images of Bobby's death still forming in her mind. Someone had sabotaged a spacesuit then lured Bobby into the airlock. This was why there were no marks on his body. He'd suffocated in space. Then his body had been transported to the restaurant for its horrific display. She now knew the how, but was still lost as to the who and why. If Bobby had not been the primary target, as the mysterious message indicated, why had the murderer needed to get him out of the way? The most logical answer was that he had indeed discovered something that put the murderer's plan at risk. However, the sabotaged suit indicated premeditation, and Bobby was killed on their first night. Yet if Bobby had been killed for something he'd discovered, it would have been so easy to make his death appear accidental. So why the show? It didn't make sense. The murderer had been absolutely foolish to put them all on guard like this.

In her discovery of Bobby's manner of death, she had not forgotten Jackson. Jackson most certainly had known something. Even though it seemed he had no intention of revealing what that was, clearly the murderer hadn't wanted to leave anything to chance. Plus, there was no big production in Jackson's death. Obviously his body was going to be discovered, but there was no staging of the body like with Bobby. And the door to his cell had been firmly shut, so that his body was hidden from view. Two murders. Two very different MOs. Which could mean that there was more than one murderer. Or that the murderer was playing it by ear, doing what they could when they could as they waited for the opportune moment to take out their intended target. And until she had a motive, they were all potential targets.

Penelope opened the exit at the top floor stairwell and heard movement down the hall. Someone at the door to the penthouse. She gripped the statue tightly. In the dim light, she couldn't make out who it was. Simply saw the robed figure hunched over the door. Penelope approached slowly, the statue raised in a defensive position.

Just as she was about to shout, the figure turned, jumping when she saw Penelope.

'Good God!' Tonya gasped. 'What are you doing?' She eyed the statue. Penelope lowered it.

'I was going to ask you the same thing.'

'I locked myself out,' Tonya said.

'What were you doing out of the room anyway?' Penelope asked.

'Me? What about you?' Tonya crossed her arms. 'First you don't tell me about these files you found and now you're—'

The scream inside the penthouse ended their conversation.

By the time Penelope had opened the door, all the lights were already on. Everyone was either out of bed or sitting up where they lay. Everyone was accounted for. Everyone was breathing. Everyone was looking at Frau Richter. She stood against the wall, one hand clutching her dressing gown, the other pressed to her throat. Alison and Sasha were the closest to her, but they dared not approach her.

'Stay away from me! Don't come any closer!' she shouted.

'What is it?' Penelope asked. 'What's happened?'

'Someone tried to kill me! To strangle me!'

Murmurs swept through the group.

'Are you sure?' Penelope asked.

'Am I sure?' Frau Richter repeated in a mocking tone. 'What kind of a question is that? Am I sure?'

'I mean, we've all been through a lot of stress. Are you sure it wasn't a vivid nightmare? A night terror?'

'What do you think I am? A child who cannot tell the difference between dreams and reality? I felt fingers around my neck! His fingers!' She pointed directly at Freddy, who stood on the opposite side of the room.

'Me? What are you talking about?' Freddy said. 'I was asleep. I wasn't anywhere near you!'

'It was you. I know it was you!'

'Did you see him?' Penelope asked.

Frau Richter hesitated. 'I fought him before I opened my eyes. I felt his fingers around my neck and then I opened my eyes.'

'If you didn't see who it was, then why are you assuming it was me?' Freddy asked. 'I've never touched you, so how do you know what my fingers felt like?'

'Because,' she said. 'Because they felt . . . dirty.'

This comment set off another round of shouting. Penelope

herself wanted to shout at Frau Richter for her racist remarks but she knew further shouting wouldn't solve the immediate problem. Restraining herself, she instead tried clapping to get everyone's attention. When that didn't work, she crawled up onto the table and whistled.

'Enough! We're not going to get anywhere if you all keep shouting at one another. Now, did anyone else see anything?'

No one answered.

'Did anyone hear anything?'

'Only when she started screaming,' Dr Wyss said.

'That's what woke me up, too,' Freddy said. 'I was all the way over here. I didn't—'

Penelope held up her hand to quiet him. 'All right. OK. I think we're all very tired and all very stressed.'

'So you're dismissing my assault. Is that it?' Frau Richter snapped.

'No one is dismissing anything,' Penelope said. 'I just think we all need to get some sleep and we can talk about it in the morning.'

'I'm not going back to sleep. Not with him in here.' She glared at Freddy.

'You can't kick me out.' He sounded afraid. 'There could be someone out there. I don't want to—'

'No one's kicking anyone out,' Penelope said.

Frau Richter's face darkened. 'Fine. Then I'll leave.' She started gathering her things.

'You don't have to go,' Penelope said.

'Yes, you could sleep on the upper level or lock yourself in the bathroom,' Tonya said. Penelope couldn't tell if she was being facetious or not.

262

'No. I refuse to sleep in a room where someone tried to strangle me and no one else believes me. No. I'll take my chances out there.' She juggled her belongings in her arms and clumsily bumped into everyone on her way out.

'Frau Richter, wait.' Alison scrambled off her mattress. 'I'll come with you.'

At the door, Alison turned back to the group. 'I'll keep an eye on her and make sure she turns up for breakfast.' She closed the door behind her.

Those that were left began to resettle in their beds. Freddy came up to Penelope as she climbed down from the table.

'Penelope, I didn't. I swear I was asleep. I didn't—'

'It's all right, Freddy. Just go back to sleep.'

Freddy nodded and turned away, hurt. As Penelope settled back onto her mattress, she realised why. She had not said she believed him.

Tonya waited by the penthouse control panel.

'I suppose we can talk tomorrow. Goodnight, Penny.'

'Goodnight, Ms Burton.'

Tonya turned off the lights.

Chapter 32

Penelope hadn't been to a sleepover since she was thirteen. She could still remember coming down the stairs wondering where her friends were, only to discover that everyone else had woken an hour before her and decided to go and ride their bikes, leaving the late-sleeping Penelope to have an awkward, silent breakfast with her friend's parents, the father asking her random questions about school and, for some reason, politics.

Now, an adult herself, waking up amongst a group of strangers was no less awkward. Uchida was already sitting up in his bed, leafing through a book. He and Penelope noticed each other, but he said nothing and neither did she. She looked at the others. Tonya, Sasha, Dr Wyss and Freddy were all present and all asleep, or pretending to be. More importantly, they were all still alive. She hoped the same was true of Frau Richter and Alison.

Penelope took the opportunity to use the empty bathroom and, by the time she came out, the others were stirring. Last night it had seemed safer for them to move together as a group. Now it was cumbersome and awkward. Who wanted to share their private morning rituals with strangers? The open-plan penthouse had few partitions and allowed little privacy. Sasha gathered her clothes and hurried into the walk-in closet. Dr Wyss brushed past Penelope and into the bathroom as soon as she put one foot out the door. Freddy sat on his bed, trying to change his clothes underneath his blanket, a task made harder because he kept looking over his shoulder. The others were throwing him glances but not saying anything to him. Penelope hurried over to her mattress, Tonya watching her the whole way. She clearly wanted to talk about last night and Penelope felt the same. Part of her wanted to apologise to Tonya for not telling her about the files, but the other part wanted to question her over what she had been doing out of the room last night, though she knew she'd face the same question in return. Either way, they needed to wait for a moment alone, difficult when their survival depended on staying together.

Eventually, after much awkward silence, the group of six made their way down to the Sunrise Lounge. No one spoke. Penelope hoped Frau Richter and Alison would already be there, but the lounge was empty when they arrived.

'We should look for them before we get settled,' Penelope said, but no one acknowledged her. 'Alison and Frau Richter,' she repeated. 'We should—'

'They will find us when they're ready,' Dr Wyss said. 'I'm not hunting anyone down. Not today.'

Penelope wavered in the doorway. The other five gathered their breakfast as if they had put up a wall between themselves and all that had happened in the last two days. As if by not acknowledging that Frau Richter and Alison could possibly be in any danger that the danger did not exist. Penelope looked from the terrace back to the inner hall. It was foolish of her to go searching on her own. It would only put her in unnecessary danger. But what if something had happened to the two women? What if their lives were hanging in the balance and there was no one to help them? But if Penelope went searching on her own, she could end up in harm's way, just like them, and what good did that do anyone? Also, there remained a good chance that whoever was responsible for Bobby and Jackson's deaths was in the Sunrise Lounge with her right now. It could be just as beneficial for Penelope to stay here and keep an eye on all of them. The logical choice – the choice with the least risk – was to remain with the others and hope that she could convince them to search for Alison and Frau Richter once everyone had finished their breakfast, or hope that the two women reappeared on their own before then.

Penelope toasted a bagel in the kitchen then looked for a place to sit. The tables they had pushed together the other night for their group dinner remained in that position. Tonya sat on one side of the square, and Freddy on the other. Tonya picked at a banana that had started to spot while Freddy had a bowl of cereal. Neither seemed too interested in speaking to one another, or to Penelope.

Penelope looked over her shoulder and saw Sasha, Uchida and Dr Wyss were seated on the enclosed veranda. Since they were out of earshot, Penelope decided she should apologise now to Tonya about not telling her about the files, but she also didn't want to look like she was calling out Tonya in front of Freddy for leaving the penthouse unaccompanied. She also wanted to apologise to Freddy for not clearly stating that she had believed him when he said he didn't attack Frau Richter. But how could she tell him in front of Tonya that her knowledge of the incident in New York hadn't coloured her perception of him without breaking her promise that she wouldn't tell the others? She stood there with her bagel, wondering further why she should have the urge to apologise to either of them anyway. These people were strangers. She'd known them barely a week. Why shouldn't she be suspicious of either of them despite the fact that instinct told her she could trust them? Was it because she couldn't trust her instincts?

Penelope finally sat at the table with Tonya and Freddy, choosing a seat closer to the latter.

'Freddy, I—'

'I didn't try to strangle anyone last night,' he said. 'Not last night. Not ever.'

'That's not why I—'

'I was on my mattress the whole time. I only jumped up after she screamed. Where were you two?' He looked across the table at Tonya. 'You two came running through the door last night. I thought we were all supposed to stay together.'

'I don't know where Tonya went last night—' Penelope started.

'Oh, of course. Make me out to be the suspicious one,' Tonya snorted.

Penelope looked around the lounge to see if any of the others were listening in, but Sasha and Uchida had chosen the table furthest from them on the glass-domed terrace and appeared to be in quiet conversation with one another. Dr Wyss had picked up his empty plate and now headed into the kitchen.

'I had a hunch about how Bobby died, and I wanted to investigate it,' she said. 'I was right.'

That got their attention. She motioned for them to move closer, so that she could speak more quietly. After they were re-seated, Penelope told them about the airlock and the spacesuit, gauging their reactions. Both seemed genuinely surprised.

'Why didn't we think of that before?' Tonya said. 'We're in space. Of course you don't need a weapon to suffocate someone. You just need to get them outside.'

'None of us thought of the airlocks,' Penelope said. 'Not even when we were searching the hotel. There's no place to go outside, so we didn't think of going there.'

'Where's the spacesuit now?' Tonya asked.

'I put it – I put all of them – in a secure location.'

'OK. Fine. Keep another secret.' Tonya stood up again.

'I'm not keeping a secret,' Penelope said, which she knew was untrue as soon as she said it. That was exactly what she was doing and Tonya knew it. 'I just . . . the fewer people who know, the better.'

'Why don't you come right out and say you don't trust us?' Tonya asked.

'Because I don't know that I don't.'

'What does that even mean?'

'It means, I guess, I don't know.'

'*You* asked us to help you, remember? You wanted our help. I was perfectly fine staying out of this whole mess, but you came to me. And Freddy. You trusted us enough then, or was that just a part of some plan? And what would you like me to do now, thank you for sharing this information?'

'It's more than you've shared with me,' Penelope said. 'I've told you what I was doing out of the room last night. What were you doing?'

'Maybe I had a hunch, too,' Tonya said.

'Which was?'

Tonya crossed her arms. 'Like you said, maybe I don't know that I don't trust you. Or maybe I don't know that I do. Either way, maybe the real reason is that I'm done with this so-called investigation. Maybe I'm far happier to sit back and let the Apollo Group handle everything once they do manage to get here.'

Freddy leaned forward. 'So you can accept their pay-off?' he asked. 'So you can pretend Bobby died of something like a heart attack and live off whatever the Apollo Group gives you to stay quiet?' He looked back and forth between Penelope and Tonya. 'You know, I don't know if I should trust you two, either. But I know that no one trusts me, not really. Not after what Frau Richter said.'

Tonya rolled her eyes. 'God, Freddy. Neither of us believes what that woman says about you.'

'You're saying that now. But neither of you was quick to come to my defence last night in front of everyone else. But I guess I shouldn't be surprised.'

Penelope sighed. 'Freddy, we were tired. Everyone was tired.'

'Too tired to say there was no way that I one hundred per cent could not – would not – have tried strangle someone?' he asked.

'I'm never one hundred per cent certain about anything,' Tonya said.

Dr Wyss exited the kitchen and the three of them fell silent. Penelope waited until he sat down at a table near Sasha and Uchida.

'Can we focus on Bobby's murder?' she asked. 'We know someone killed him in the airlock. But then they had to get his body from the airlock to the restaurant. How? It would've taken time and effort. He's a big man. Was a big man.'

Tonya sat back in her chair and looked away. 'I told you I don't want to be involved with this anymore.'

Penelope waited, trying to figure out what she could say to change Tonya's mind, and decided to keep talking out her thoughts.

'People always think it's easy to move a human body until they have to move a human body,' she said. 'We're very awkwardly shaped for carrying. Whoever moved him, no matter how strong they are, would've needed time and lots of luck so as not to get caught.'

Freddy suddenly sat up in his chair and looked at Penelope. 'What about pushing? Like in the hotel's laundry carts?'

'The laundry room is right near those airlocks,' Penelope said.

'I'm not listening,' Tonya said.

Penelope ignored her. 'They killed him, put his body in the cart – which they could have covered up with linens and things – then pushed him to the restaurant.'

'And we know they grabbed a white sheet to use as their flag,' Freddy said.

'You found that wheel,' Penelope said to Tonya. 'The wheel you found in the walk-in fridge. Could that have been from a laundry cart?'

'I'm not some sort of wheel expert,' Tonya snapped.

Penelope looked back at Freddy. 'They could have used the service corridor that runs from the laundry to the kitchens. But when they got there, they saw you passed out on the couch in the restaurant, so they had to wait. They put the cart in the fridge until you left and the wheel broke off either when they pushed it in or pulled it out.'

'I saw a three-wheeled cart,' Freddy said. 'Before Jackson died. I made a note but I didn't tell you. I . . . I forgot. Mr Uchida was trying to move it.'

'What was Uchida doing with a laundry cart?' Penelope asked.

'You want to know? Why don't we ask him?' Tonya waved her arm. 'Mr Uchida! Oh, Mr Uchida!'

'What are you doing?' Penelope asked.

'Your suspect is right there, Detective. Why don't you interrogate him now? Unless you want to keep another secret?'

'What do you mean "another secret"?'

But Uchida was already making his way over to them.

'You require my attention?' he asked, clearly annoyed.

Tonya responded. 'You were moving a laundry cart the other day and the good detective would like to know why.'

Penelope looked at the clock on the wall and then to the doorway, where Alison and Frau Richter had not yet appeared. 'I'd much rather know where Frau Richter and the professor are, at the moment.'

'But surely this incident with the laundry cart must be of importance to you, Detective.'

Penelope didn't like how Tonya kept using that word, as if she was putting extra weight behind it. As if she knew something.

'The cart was in my way.' Uchida glanced at Freddy then back at Penelope.

'In your way of what?' Penelope asked.

'Searching the hotel.'

'But this was before the search. Before Jackson was murdered,' Penelope said.

'I was not going to wait for your command, Detective Strand.

Early on, I suspected there may have been someone else in this hotel, so I acted on those suspicions.'

'And did you find anything in your preliminary search?' Penelope asked.

'No. I did not.' His face was unreadable.

'Where was this cart when you found it?' she asked.

'Why this obsession with the cart, Detective?'

'I asked you first.'

'In a service corridor on the ground floor.'

'But you can't get into those corridors without a master key,' Penelope said. 'Or did you manage to crowbar your way in after all?'

Uchida's eyes narrowed. 'I went to the offices and borrowed the additional key.'

'When did you return it?'

'Later that day. You have both in your possession now, do you not? Is your obsession with this laundry cart what spurred you to leave the penthouse last night? When we were supposed to be sleeping?'

'So you admit you went into the offices before Jackson's death?' Penelope asked.

'I spent no significant time there,' he said.

'Just long enough to break into the cabinet of tablets?'

'I did nothing of the sort.'

'Someone did. I noticed it yesterday. This wasn't a door that had been left open by accident. Someone had prised it open. Probably with something like a crowbar. Everything inside is gone,' Penelope said.

'And when were you going to share this information?' Tonya scoffed.

'Now you accuse me of stealing as well as murder,' Uchida said.

Voices rose behind them. As they all turned to look, Sasha stood up and slapped Dr Wyss across the face. Everyone began shouting.

'Lies!' Sasha was saying. 'He is saying lies about me. I never spoke to you that night. Never!'

Dr Wyss was holding up his hands in acquiescence, but his voice was warm. 'I wasn't trying to imply anything.'

'You are!' She looked at Uchida. 'He is trying to say that I had something to do with Bobby's murder.'

'Isn't the person who finds the body usually the suspect?' Dr Wyss looked at Penelope.

'See?' Sasha said. 'I told you. He is trying to put the blame on me.'

'And the detective,' Tonya said, 'is trying to put it on Mr Uchida. So maybe they're both right. You two have spent a lot of time together.'

Now Uchida and Sasha started yelling at Tonya.

'Why would you say that?' Freddy asked, which is what Penelope was also thinking, although she hadn't said it out loud.

'I thought you'd be happy I wasn't accusing you,' Tonya replied.

The five of them continued shouting insults and accusations at one another while Penelope closed her eyes and massaged her temples.

'We should find Frau Richter and Alison,' Penelope said, but she spoke too quietly. 'We've waited long enough, we should—'

Underneath the arguing, Penelope heard another sound. She looked over her shoulder then headed for the door, the sound becoming clearer. Music.

273

'Quiet,' she said. When no one responded, she shouted, 'I said quiet!'

All five of them stopped and stared.

'Do you hear that?' she asked. Finally, they listened.

Piano music. Not a recording – 'Fly Me to the Moon' continued its endless refrain in the lobby – but live piano music. There was only one room in the hotel that had a piano.

Penelope hurried out of the door, not caring if the others followed her, and ran down the hall to the Cold Moon Piano Bar. Seated inside were Frau Richter, at one of the small tables, and Alison at the piano, who was plunking out a tune. Frau Richter wore black, restrictive leggings and a zipped athletic jacket while Alison wore a flowing silk blouse in a dark colour that blended her body with the darkness of space behind her. She almost looked like a disembodied head and hands at the piano.

'Morning,' Alison called out, still tapping away on the keys.

'Where have you two been?' Penelope asked, knowing she sounded far too much like her mother.

'We came down for breakfast, but you all were yelling at one another and we didn't want to get involved,' Alison answered.

'I hope you were busy determining who tried to strangle me last night,' Frau Richter said.

Penelope took a deep, calming breath before answering. 'We've established everything we could about what happened to you last night, Frau Richter.'

'Oh, you have, have you? And who is this *we*? You and your friends? One of whom is the prime suspect?'

'They're not my friends,' Penelope said, then wished she

hadn't. She saw Freddy wince. 'I don't know what you expect me to do. I'm not locking anyone up without just cause, and I'm especially not putting anyone in the cells with Jackson's body.'

'So my word is not good enough?'

From across the room, Alison laughed.

'Be quiet!' Frau Richter snapped. 'I had enough of your nonsense last night. I don't need to hear any more of it today. All she did was moan, moan, moan. She's lonely. She wants a cigarette. She wants to go back to the others. Such a child.'

'Child?' Alison stood up. 'I'm nearly thirty. And how many children do you know with doctorates, *Fräulein*? Yes. Fräulein. Not sure why you insist on everyone calling you Frau when you're not even married to Herr Richter anymore. Or do you prefer Frau because you're old?'

'I will not respond to insults from little whores.'

'That's enough,' Dr Wyss jumped up. 'Charlotte, there's no need to speak to her that way.'

'Of course you would come to her defence. How many times have you fucked her since we've been here?'

'Whoa!' Freddy gasped. A chorus of embarrassed throat clearing and low whistles followed.

'And you.' Frau Richter turned on Freddy. 'Why do you insist on lying? A real man would come out and tell the truth. You tried to kill me last night. Why? Was it because I saw you?'

'Saw me what?' Freddy asked.

'Leave the security office. Before Mr Smith was found dead.' A smirk curled onto Frau Richter's lips as the group began to whisper. 'Ah yes. I saw you, but you did not see me. Is that when you killed him?'

Penelope jumped in. 'Enough! No one is accusing anyone of murder without evidence.'

'My eyes are not evidence?'

'Did you see any blood? Jackson's death was bloody. Freddy would've been covered in it.'

Frau Richter hesitated, not long but long enough. 'How would I be able to tell? His skin is so dark.'

Penelope grimaced. 'I've had just about enough of that.'

'Just about?' Freddy said. 'So you could listen to more?'

Frau Richter ignored them both. 'I am simply telling the truth,' she said.

'Then why don't you tell the truth about why you were in the manager's office,' Alison said. Dr Wyss looked at her. He seemed worried to Penelope but said nothing. 'Tell her you broke into the tech cabinet.'

Alison was the one who looked triumphant now. Frau Richter looked at Dr Wyss, betrayed. Dr Wyss looked away.

'Did you?' Penelope asked Frau Richter.

'Only because I was trying to find more information about this place. Names of employees. Information on who might've sent the staff away. On who may have vendetta against me.'

'Against you?' Penelope asked. 'The cabinet was broken into before Jackson was murdered. Before we read those messages, why did you suspect before then that someone was after you?'

Frau Richter crossed her arms. 'I have my reasons.'

'Yeah,' Alison scoffed. 'It's called delusional paranoia.'

'Says the person who was spying on us.'

'And did you find anything useful in that cabinet?' Penelope asked.

Frau Richter continued glaring at Alison while she answered. 'No. Just the tablets. The tablets I'm assuming were supposed to be in our suites. But you needed a password to access anything. I tried all zeros just to see. When that didn't work, I decided not to waste any more time.'

'What did you do with the tablets?' Penelope asked.

'I left them there. I had no use for them.'

'But they're gone now?' Uchida asked.

'The cabinet was empty yesterday when I looked,' Penelope said. 'Someone took them.'

Penelope walked to the back of the lounge to the grand piano to confirm what she suspected. There was a depressed key in the piano's upper registers. A high C.

'Just like someone took the C string from this piano and used it to garrotte Jackson.' She pointed into the open grand piano. This was why the key was depressed. The string for that note had been removed. 'This string has been missing since before Jackson died. I noticed this the same day we discovered Bobby's body.'

'So whoever took it,' Uchida said, 'is the murderer?'

'We all had access to this room,' Dr Wyss said. 'But I haven't been in here before.'

'Neither have I,' Frau Richter was quick to say.

'Sasha was,' Penelope said.

'And Tonya,' Freddy said quietly.

'Just as quick to accuse others as he was to defend himself,' said Frau Richter.

'Is that what you're doing, Freddy?' Tonya asked, clearly hurt.

'No! No, I . . . it's just a fact.'

'You think I could kill someone?' Sasha asked Penelope.

'That I could've taken that wire and put it round that poor man's neck? Do you?' She looked at Freddy.

'I don't know!' Freddy tossed up his hands. 'That's just it. I don't know. I don't know any of you. Like Detective Strand said, we're not friends. We're strangers. So I don't know.'

'Why keep asking all of these questions?' Dr Wyss asked Penelope. 'Why keep stoking suspicion of one another when there could be a third party?'

'I'm not trying to stoke suspicion,' Penelope said. 'I'm trying to stop anyone else from getting hurt.'

'I'm sure Jackson would appreciate the sentiment,' Frau Richter quipped.

Tonya put a hand on Penelope's arm before she could retort.

'There's nothing to do and we're letting our boredom and fear get the best of us. Let's drop the questions and try to do something fun. Or at least diverting. I happen to know the casino has an excellent selection of mind-numbing activities and beverages. What do you say?'

With reluctance from some and enthusiasm from others, they all agreed, though they kept their distance from one another as they filed out of the bar. When Penelope started to leave, Tonya's light touch on her arm became firm.

'You can only push people so far,' Tonya said.

'I'm not pushing anyone.'

'Just enjoy yourself for a little bit. And, while you are, think about why you're really trying so hard to solve this, *Detective*.'

Penelope didn't like the knowing emphasis Tonya put on the word.

Chapter 33

The casino chips were located in a vault inside the cashier's cage, a vault whose passcode was conveniently located in the cash-out drawer of the cashier's till. They divvied out an equal amount between themselves and took to their favourite tables.

Sasha and Alison sat at a roulette wheel with Uchida, who took on the role of dealer. Frau Richter and Dr Wyss took over one of the blackjack tables and dealt cards to one another. Tonya played an entire row of slot machines by herself. Freddy leaned on the bar like Penelope, but kept his distance from her. No one who came to the bar to help themselves to drinks spoke to either of them. And there were so many drinks. Everyone other than Penelope and Freddy was imbibing copious amounts of alcohol. Empty glasses soon littered each table as most would fill a new glass with a new drink rather than refilling the old. Alison had figured out how to get the speaker system to work and music blared throughout the casino, some sort of loud jazz that kept Penelope's nerves on edge, but which at least wasn't 'Fly Me to the Moon'.

It was a funhouse image of their party that first night. Where then the joy and laughter had been real, now it was plainly forced

– people who thought they could have a good time if they were pretending to have a good time. Revellers pretending they couldn't see the axe swinging above their heads. Penelope made her way down the bar to Freddy, who visibly tensed when she neared. She chose to ignore that.

'I don't understand why they won't take this more seriously,' she said.

'They do take it seriously,' he said. 'Or at least they did. It's just . . . they all think they're safe, don't they? Or they all want to think they're safe. People never want to think the worst could happen to them. Those things always happen to someone else.'

'There's a one in seven chance that the killer is after them. How can they not care?'

'I think those are odds they're willing to take,' he said.

'But anything could happen to anyone at any time.'

Uchida spun the roulette wheel once again, the sound of it barely audible over the music and Tonya's slots. It must have landed on Sasha's colour because Alison groaned and stacked more chips on a different number as Uchida took her others off the table. Across the room, Frau Richter laughed and nearly fell off her stool, saved only by Dr Wyss's arm around her waist. Alison saw them and slammed another stack of chips onto the table. Sasha kept her eyes on Frau Richter. One of the slots rang out and spat chips out faster than Tonya could collect them.

'People can't be on guard all the time. Most people,' he added, 'they just want to feel safe. They've been living through this storm, and now they just want to hunker down until it's over. I mean, so do I.'

'So why don't you?'

He didn't answer.

'Did you go and see Jackson?' Penelope asked.

'Like you said, Detective, we're not friends. So I'm not sure why I should trust you.'

With that, Freddy left the bar and headed over to the slot machines.

Penelope let him go. She had no right to ask him anything else.

She also knew he was right. Everyone knew they were in danger. That was why they wanted to feel safe. Why they wanted to create the illusion of safety. Of course they would get angry with Penelope. She kept breaking that illusion. She kept reminding them what the dangers were. They wanted to watch a film, and she kept turning on the lights.

Yet while she did that, the killer couldn't act. No one could move in the shadows if someone kept shining a light in all the dark corners.

Penelope looked out of the windows that overlooked the bar. The casino faced away from Earth, giving a view of the vastness of space towards the dark side of the moon. The sight of all that space made her shiver, as did the thought that she was increasingly alone. Tonya was displeased with her. Freddy was becoming distant. And the worst thing she could right now was isolate herself. In order to protect them, she needed them to trust her, even if they didn't trust each other. Penelope turned her back on space, topped up her sparkling water and walked over to the roulette table.

The wheel was spinning as she arrived, the ball clacking round and around. Alison's intense gaze gave no indication that this was all for fun, that she wouldn't actually win any money. Sasha leaned on the table, with her back to a wall and not the door, Penelope noticed. Uchida had turned round and was talking to Dr Wyss.

Penelope placed her glass on the edge of the table.

'Placing a bet?' Sasha asked.

'Oh, I never bet. Not even for fun.'

'Afraid of losing?' Frau Richter asked over her shoulder.

'Not a fan of unnecessary risk. Sasha—'

'I can't answer any more questions. Please.' Sasha waved a hand in front of her face.

'It's not that. I wanted to apologise. I didn't mean to put any suspicion on you, back there in the lounge. Everyone had access to that piano. We all know that.'

Sasha's expression softened, but before she could say anything, Frau Richter interjected.

'You shouldn't be sorry. Why not single her out? She spent the most time in that lounge the other day, making all of those foul-smelling coffees. She had plenty of opportunity to take the piano string. Damn. Red again.'

'You don't have to comment on everything, you know,' Alison said.

Uchida turned around, immediately displeased to see Penelope. 'Interrogating us again? Tigers and their stripes, I see.'

'No,' Sasha said. 'It wasn't that at all. It was Frau Richter who decided to bring up nasty things.'

'Yes, blame it all on me,' Frau Richter said, but there was no anger in her voice, simply resignation. 'Blame the German. Blame the lawyer. My ex-husband did. My clients. It is only natural.' She placed a stack of chips on black.

Alison shrugged. 'Fine with me.'

'Why would your clients blame you?' Penelope asked.

'Because divorces are messy. Nobody gets what they want. Not really. Because what they want is their old life back. The happiness they felt on the day of their marriage. Or even their life before they met the other person. But that is impossible. People change us. That can't be undone by who gets what car or how many days they have with their children. So they remain unhappy. And then they get mad at me. Even if they got everything they asked for.'

'I wasn't blaming you for anything,' Sasha said. 'You just want to make everything about you.'

Frau Richter leaned back on her stool. 'What's made you so bold all of a sudden?'

Sasha blushed. 'I'm just speaking the truth. And I am bold. Usually. Sometimes. It's just, this place has shaken me. I haven't been myself.'

'You don't need to justify yourself to anyone,' Uchida said.

'Even to your wife?' Frau Richter asked. 'I bet she would love all of the flirting between you and Ms Eris.'

'Do not pretend to know anything about my personal life, Frau Richter. You say people always blame you unnecessarily, but you seem to make a habit of purposely antagonising everyone you come into contact with.' He spun the wheel and tossed the roulette ball.

'Or perhaps I simply have little faith in people who do not believe me when I say I was assaulted. Everyone here is a coward.'

Alison laughed. 'Go on, Fräulein. Tell us how you really feel.'

And then Alison struck a match and lit a cigarette.

Penelope watched as if in slow motion. She knew the action

was wrong, but her brain couldn't register why it was wrong. The realisation that lagged behind suddenly hit her like a truck. She and the others started yelling at Alison. Even Tonya ran over from the slots.

'Whoops!' Alison shrugged but kept smoking. 'To be fair, I tried really hard with the gum.'

'Where on earth did you get a cigarette?' Tonya asked.

'The hotel we stayed at the night before the launch.'

'How did you get it here?' Penelope asked. 'That's contraband. No cigarettes or cigars. No sources of flame.'

'It wasn't that hard. I slipped a few in my pencil case and my makeup bag. Sprinkled some matches in, too. They weren't really being that careful about checking our bags, if you hadn't noticed. I guess you hadn't. But it's not like any of you mind, right?'

Dr Wyss grabbed the cigarette from Alison's fingers and stubbed it out on the lacquered edge of the roulette table.

'Do you know how dangerous that is?' he shouted. 'You've put everyone at risk! We're inside the equivalent of a hermetically sealed bubble and you light a flame?'

He was as angry as Penelope had ever seen him, his tanned face turning red, the muscles in his neck taut.

'Aren't we all in danger anyway?' she asked, but without her usual laissez-faire attitude.

'Do you have any more?' Penelope asked.

'Now look what you've done, Erik. You've got the police involved,' she tried to joke. It fell flat. 'A few, yes. Sorry.'

'How many times have you smoked in this building?' Sasha asked.

Alison averted her gaze.

'Jesus Christ,' Tonya sighed.

'We're confiscating them,' Dr Wyss said. 'Now.'

'Erik, I'm sorry. I didn't think—'

'Do you realise how much danger you've put us in? What would happen if there was a fire here? How it would burn up the oxygen? And who would be coming to put it out, hm? What fire brigade would reach us? How could you be so careless?' He waved his arm. It wasn't to strike her. He was gesticulating in frustration. But Alison flinched. Penelope saw how the group was ganging up against her. How quickly their frustration could turn to something more.

Penelope placed a hand on Dr Wyss's arm. 'We'll confiscate the rest of the cigarettes and matches. But what's done is done. Nothing burned. There was no fire. And Alison is sorry. Right, Alison?'

She nodded.

'We should put her in the cell. With Jackson,' Frau Richter said. 'What's left of him.'

No one immediately objected.

'Let's just get the cigarettes, all right?' Penelope said. 'Are they in your room, Alison?'

'Yes,' she said.

'We'll all go together. We can soak them in the sink or something and that will be that.'

After a pause, Dr Wyss nodded. Then so did the others.

'All right, let's go. Then maybe we can get some food,' Penelope said. 'I think maybe we've all had a bit too much to drink and not enough to eat.'

They started for the door.

'Hang on,' Tonya said. She stopped and looked around. 'Where's Freddy?'

Penelope looked. Counted. There were only seven of them.

Freddy was nowhere to be seen.

Chapter 34

'He was here a few minutes ago. We were talking at the bar, and then he went over to play the slots. Tonya, you didn't see him?'

Tonya looked over her shoulder at the slot machines, as if Freddy would magically appear. 'I don't know. Yes. Maybe. He went on the other side because I was playing this whole row. But I was so involved . . . I didn't . . .'

'Did anyone see him leave?' Penelope asked.

'If we had seen him leaving, why would we let him go?' Frau Richter snapped.

'He can't have been gone long,' Dr Wyss said.

'Yes,' Uchida agreed. 'You were only at the roulette wheel for a few minutes, Detective Strand. He must be near.'

As a group, they hurried out of the casino, calling Freddy's name. Alison – the drunkest of them all – stumbled at the rear. Dr Wyss ignored her, but Sasha saved her from falling with an arm around her waist. In the main lobby, the smell of Bobby's body was stronger than ever. Penelope covered her nose and took a cursory peek into the restaurant but did not see Freddy. Upstairs, they first checked the library and then the Sunrise Lounge, but there was no sign of him.

'What suite is he in?' Penelope asked.

'You honestly think he would go to his room?' Frau Richter asked.

'Why not? Maybe he wanted to grab something and didn't want to bother the rest of us.'

'The Khonsu Suite, I think,' Tonya said. 'Level 2A.'

They proceeded up the stairs. Penelope readied the master key, but when they arrived at his room, it was obvious they wouldn't need it. The door was open. Penelope took it as a good sign. She was right – Freddy had simply come up to grab something.

'Freddy?' she called into the room. 'You in there? We noticed you left the casino and got worried.'

There was no answer. Penelope looked back at the group. It was clear most were more suspicious than worried.

'Freddy?' she called again. She hoped to hear the toilet flushing. For any sign that Freddy just couldn't hear her. But there was only silence. Not even Earthshine spoke, but Penelope remembered that, at the party their first night Freddy had mentioned turning Earthshine off.

With a deep breath, she crossed the threshold. Before she could tell them not to, the others followed. She steeled herself for the sight of another body. When she saw that there wasn't one, her brain began to register other details.

The suite wasn't as neat as she'd expected. Freddy was always simply but well dressed. Put together. The backpack he carried around with him was an orderly collection of books and notepads, organised by type and size. But his hotel room was a mess. The bed was unmade. Clothes strewn across the furniture. Books and other belongings scattered and stacked on surfaces.

Maybe there had been a struggle, but no. The room held no sign of any trauma or attack. It was simply messy. Disorganised.

'Penelope,' Tonya called to her from across the room – the doorway to the bathroom. She hadn't thought about the bathroom. She pictured Freddy's body lying there, spread out on the tiles or in the tub. 'You should see this.'

Everyone turned to look at Penelope. She squared her shoulders and walked confidently across the room, prepared to face whatever she might see. Tonya stepped aside so Penelope could see.

There was no body.

But there was blood.

On the bath towels and staining the sink.

The kinds of blood trails left when someone has tried to clean themselves up.

When Penelope said nothing, the others crowded behind her to catch a glimpse. The comments started immediately, Frau Richter's voice the loudest.

'I told you. I told you!'

Penelope turned around and held out her arms, barring anyone from entering, not that it seemed they wanted to.

'Everyone calm down. We don't know what this means,' she said.

Frau Richter scoffed. 'Only a fool would say that. It means exactly what it looks like. He was covered in blood and cleaned himself up. And why would he be covered in blood? Because he cut off Jackson's head!'

'So it was Freddy all along?' Sasha asked, looking between Frau Richter and the bloody bathroom towels. 'It was always Freddy?'

'He could have just hurt himself,' Penelope said. 'Or someone could have hurt him. Or the killer could have cleaned up in here on purpose. The door was open. We don't know, and we shouldn't make assumptions.' Penelope waited for someone – Tonya – to come to Freddy's defence. Tonya leaned with her back to the wall, eyes closed and arms crossed, like she was trying to shut everything out.

'Have you seen these books?' Dr Wyss asked. 'They're all on criminology and crime. Books on evidence. Blood splatter analysis. Famous killers. Detective novels.'

'He's a criminology student. Of course he'd bring those books with him,' Penelope said.

'I didn't bring any psychology books with me,' Alison said.

'No, you were just content to take notes on all of us for an unknown source. And smoke until you got caught or blew us all up,' Penelope snapped. She hadn't got cross with anyone this whole time, not even when Frau Richter made her racist remarks. But she was at her wits' end now.

'It's obvious,' Frau Richter said. 'He's the killer. I do not understand why you are bending yourself backward trying to defend him.'

'Because she doesn't want to be proven wrong,' Tonya said, her voice just above a whisper. The group waited for more. Penelope hoped that was the end of it. It wasn't.

'She put her trust in Freddy. She'd eliminated him as a suspect, even though she shouldn't have, and doesn't want to accept that she was wrong.'

Tonya finally opened her eyes, straightened herself up. 'I read the files,' she said. 'Last night.'

'You broke into my room?' Penelope asked. 'How? I have both keys. I checked . . .'

She reached into her pocket and pulled out both. Tonya reached into her own pocket and pulled out a third.

'One of those is a blank,' Tonya said. 'The manager's office has a stack of uncoded key cards. I can't code them, but I took one as a dummy. Took a risk and swapped it out with one of the real ones when you were asleep. Can't keep a journalist out of a locked room, can you? But I guess you're not as light a sleeper as you think you are. I didn't know you'd be leaving the room, too. It's just good luck that the one you chose to use was one of the real ones and not the dummy. The only luck I've had on this trip, apparently.' She tossed the real key card back to Penelope. 'Why didn't you tell us that Freddy had previously been arrested for murder?'

Curse words in all languages rippled through the room.

'Because he wasn't. That's not what the file says. He was brought in for questioning in a murder investigation – once. And released. Freddy told me himself. The real murderer was caught and will be standing trial soon. Freddy had nothing to do with it,' Penelope said.

'The file doesn't say what happened in that case,' Tonya said.

'I know. I said Freddy told me.'

'And you believed him?'

'I didn't have a reason not to.'

'Why didn't he tell us?' Sasha asked. She seemed genuinely confused.

'For this very reason,' Penelope said. 'He was afraid he'd be accused of the murders. That people would throw suspicion on him.'

Frau Richter laughed bitterly. 'He has certainly achieved that.'

'Look, we don't know why he's gone missing,' Penelope said. 'Let's find him first and—'

Alison groaned. 'I am so fucking tired of running around this hotel trying to find people. Can we please not?'

No one made eye contact with her.

'OK, yes. Everyone hates me right now, but I'm right, aren't I? We know it's Freddy now, so all we have to do is stay away from him. Who cares what he's doing? If he wanted to, like, sabotage the whole place or something, he would have done it already. All we need to do is watch our backs until the ship arrives. So I'm grabbing a shit-tonne of food, some more bottles of wine and locking myself in my room for the next twenty-four to thirty-six hours or whatever it is. Anyone with me?'

'Listen,' Penelope said, 'we can't just hide our heads in the sand. Something is off here. Trust me.'

'Why?' Tonya asked.

It was not a question Penelope expected from her.

Tonya continued, 'I told you I read the files last night. I read all of them. *Detective.*'

Everyone heard the emphasis on the word. Their gazes shifted once more to Penelope.

'I am a detective,' she said.

'Suspended.'

'On leave.'

Penelope and Tonya stared each other down.

'What's the difference?' Tonya asked, her old sarcasm staining her voice.

'One is by choice. The other isn't. I chose to take a leave of absence.' She turned to the rest of the group. 'I have not been suspended. And when we return to Earth, I'm going to give my boss my final decision on whether or not I want to return.'

'So you're using us?' Uchida asked. 'Using this as some sort of test to see if you should remain a detective or not?'

'No. Absolutely not.'

'Why did you leave?' Frau Richter asked. 'What did you do?'

'I didn't do anything,' Penelope said, backing up as the group crowded around her.

'Was it one of those "either you choose to leave or we suspend you" things?' Alison prodded, clearly pleased not to be the most hated person in the room anymore.

'No! It was a personal choice. That's all. And it has absolutely no bearing on what's happening here. There is a killer in this hotel and—'

'And now we know who it is,' Uchida said. 'As much as I loathe Professor Crane for her reckless actions—'

'Why thank you.' Alison rolled her eyes.

'—she is right. Enough chasing ghosts and killers. All we need to do is protect ourselves. The ship will arrive, and the proper authorities will handle Mr Nwankwo. Farewell.' He bowed then offered his hand to Sasha. She took it and, after one last backward glance at Frau Richter, left the room with him.

'I don't want to be the last to the kitchen,' Alison said by way of goodbye and she, too, was gone.

'I told you,' Frau Richter sneered. 'I was right. And now you've let him walk free.' She turned on her heel and stomped out of the door.

Dr Wyss didn't seem to know what to say. He looked like

he wanted to make some comment but departed without a word.

Tonya and Penelope were left alone.

'Why would you say those things?' Penelope said. 'Freddy is sweet and kind. He's more likely to be the victim here. Not the perpetrator.'

Tonya looked tired and, Penelope wanted to believe, ashamed. 'You're a detective. You know the correct answer is usually the simplest.' She waved to the bloody towels. 'And the simplest is that you were wrong about Freddy. We were both wrong.'

Penelope could hear the pain in her voice.

'I didn't say those things to be cruel,' Tonya said.

'Of course you did. It's what you're good at.'

Tonya took a deep breath. 'I know about the Bevan case. I know how much it affected you. Affected all of the detectives involved. But just because you were wrong then doesn't mean you're right now.'

Tonya raised her hand as if she was going to squeeze Penelope's shoulder. But then she drew her hand back. Penelope kept her eyes on the floor until she was left alone in the mess of Freddy's room.

Chapter 35

17:45 UTC

The body of Timothy Alan Brian Bevan was pulled from the Thames near the Prospect of Whitby pub in Wapping exactly three months, twenty-seven days and six hours before DS Penelope Strand received the simultaneous email and phone call from a 'Becky' of Apollo Group public relations, informing her that she'd been selected as one of the ten guests in the Hotel Artemis contest. Penelope knew that was the exact amount of time because she had plugged the date and time the body was found into one of those timer apps on her phone. The police therapist said this was unhealthy and Penelope didn't necessarily disagree. She just wanted, for a time, to feel the weight of every second since the consequences of her mistake came to light.

It wasn't just her mistake. The police therapist had made sure she understood that also. It was a collective mistake. A collective failure of Scotland Yard (not that they would say that publicly). Penelope wasn't the only detective who'd suspected Bevan in the murder of his girlfriend, Janice Long. There had been a history of altercations between them, neighbours had witnessed an argument the night of the murder and Bevan had no alibi at the time. He never confessed. Kept proclaiming his innocence. Said he had driven off to Marlborough the night of the fight to stay with his parents and clear his head. The detectives couldn't corroborate any of it, got a warrant for his arrest and brought him in.

They should have double-checked the CCTV footage that was sent in. They hadn't.

Footage from the 24-hour Tesco where Bevan said he'd stopped for snacks showed him arriving in his car at exactly the time the murder had occurred in Tower Hamlets. But the local police had first sent the Yard the wrong footage – footage from the night prior to Janice's murder, not from the night itself. They didn't realise the mistake until after Bevan had been arrested and the news of the arrest released to the media. Janice had been killed in a botched phone-snatching outside her tower block. The suspect remained at large.

Bevan was released, but despite the press reports clearing his name, his community ostracised him. Since the real murderer hadn't been caught, they all believed him responsible. They made up rumours that he had hired someone to stab her. That it had been a lookalike on the name-clearing CCTV footage. It went on for months.

One drunken night, no longer able to cope, Bevan tried to hang himself with the noose that hung outside the Prospect of Whitby in Wapping – a novelty for the tourists who travelled to see the historic pub where the infamous 'Hanging Judge' Jeffreys had sat to order executions. Several patrons and staff stopped Bevan at the time, but he returned to the river later that night, hiding on a barge and jumping off before the crew even noticed he was there.

All the detectives would've needed to do was double-check the date on the CCTV footage before issuing the warrant. And now an innocent man had killed himself because of it.

Penelope remembered sitting with Bevan in the interview room, seeing the pleading look in his eyes as he proclaimed his innocence. He was young, barely twenty-one. He and Janice were getting help, he said. They'd made an appointment with a couples therapist. Most of their arguments were about money, but they'd both got new jobs recently. Penelope had heard many a suspect profess their innocence. She had heard so many lies – lies that broke down as the evidence revealed the truth or the suspect could no longer maintain them. She knew she could not be gullible and take every suspect's word at face value.

Instinct had told her there was more truth in Bevan's story than not, but she had ignored it. She had ignored her instincts and so had her colleagues because the case fitted every stereotype and profile for a murder of this kind. Penelope was angry for Janice, at the thought of her bleeding out on the pavement alone from a single stab wound to the abdomen, and Bevan was the easiest suspect. The right suspect.

Except that he was innocent.

Penelope lay on the bed in her suite, her door secured, the curtains closed – she didn't feel she deserved that remarkable view – as memories of that case ran through her head.

Had she wanted to believe Freddy because what he said *was* the truth? Or because she didn't want to make the same mistake? Like Bevan, Freddy had once been a murder suspect but had been innocent. Or at least that was what he had said. But the Apollo Group surely wouldn't have allowed a murder suspect to go on this trip. There's no way Freddy would've been allowed out of the States. But someone had manipulated the list and the entire outing anyway. Anyone with any past could've been put on that ship. So why couldn't they have manipulated safe passage for Freddy? It would've been easy for him to manipulate her with a story like his – just enough similarities to the Bevan case to make her doubt herself, to make her *want* to believe him, no matter the evidence. She couldn't separate her emotions from her instincts. It was why she had decided to accept this trip despite her phobias. She thought it would be a shock to her system. A way to reset her body and mind. A recalibration. And here she lay, more mixed up than ever. All she could do now was stay here, barricaded in her room, alone, like the others. Wait for help to arrive. Let someone else hash out the truth – or cover it up – before she screwed things up even more.

Then she thought of Jackson, likely also innocent. Jackson, whom she'd failed to protect.

'Stop feeling sorry for yourself,' she said.

She sat up.

She could solve this. She could put both her emotions and instincts aside and focus on the cold, hard facts. She gathered her hair into a braid and sat down at the writing desk, where she pulled out a sheet of the monogrammed Hotel Artemis paper and the personalised pen and wrote a single question at the top, the one question that still bothered her more than any other:

If Bobby died in the airlock, where did the blood on Jackson come from?

Chapter 36

If saying the wrong thing was an Olympic event, Tonya would have a gold medal. Several, more likely. She sat curled up in the window seat of her suite, looking out at the horizon of the moon and Earth in the distance. What had she done to earn this view granted only to the privileged few? Nothing, and she knew it. She warmed her hands around what was possibly the last hot cup of coffee she would have until she returned to Earth. Like the others, she had quickly gathered supplies and hurried back to her room.

But if she was a master of saying the wrong thing, she was also a master of self-preservation. She would stay in her suite until the ship docked and she could be certain Freddy wouldn't kill her.

It sounded wrong even as she thought it. She'd said it herself to Penelope – the evidence pointed to Freddy. But she couldn't square the image of the eager young man who earnestly peppered her on the ship with questions about writing and journalism with that of a cold-blooded killer who could wrap a length of piano wire around another man's neck.

But, as with her stories, she couldn't let her personal feelings interfere with the evidence she'd collected. After all, hadn't she done the same with young Dalia? Something had seemed off with the young starlet, but Tonya hadn't been able to suss it out. She thought she just felt sorry for the girl and so had shut off that part of herself – the part that cared for other people – and hadn't dug any deeper.

She sipped her coffee but didn't really taste it. Didn't the incident with Dalia prove that she was wrong now, too? After all, if she had pursued the issue further, she could've discovered the truth about Dalia's age. And instead of writing an eviscerating tell-all about an under-aged girl, she could have written an eviscerating tell-all about a horrible stage mother who was ruining her daughter's life.

'It's not the same.'

She said it out loud to affirm that it was true.

'Freddy left the casino on his own. He disappeared. And his room was filled with bloody towels. And he is, or was, a murder suspect. I'm right this time. I know I'm right.'

She put her questions out of her mind. She wanted to enjoy her coffee while it was still hot.

Alison, shivering in her silk blouse, gently rapped on the door.

'Erik, will you talk to me?'

She waited. No response.

'Erik, please. I'm sorry. It was stupid and selfish, I know.'

'You should go to your room, Alison. It may not be safe for you out there.'

'It's not safe anywhere. And I wanted to see you. We need to talk about . . . about what we're going to do. Please, Erik.' She waited, kept a hand pressed to the door.

'There is no "we", Alison. Now go to your room. Please.'

She said nothing more but lingered, hoping he might change his mind and open the door. But a full minute passed and she heard nothing. She withdrew her hand and balled it into a fist, punched herself in the thigh as she walked down the hall.

Cigarettes. How could she have been so stupid? Why had she smuggled cigarettes into the hotel? He had every right to be mad with her. They all did. No matter how much it felt like it at times, this wasn't an ordinary hotel. It was a space station, and she'd put them all at risk, herself included. Didn't her father always tell her she was selfish? That she was just like her mother and thought only of her own needs?

'What he thinks doesn't matter,' she whispered to herself. 'It doesn't matter.'

But it mattered what the doctor thought. She had to get back on his good side before this trip was over. It seemed impossible now. What else might he say to the others? What might he try to blame her for if he got caught? She would have to find a way to talk to him one way or another before that ship arrived. Whether he wanted to or not.

Sasha curled her feet up on the chaise longue in the penthouse, hugging the velveteen blanket around her.

'Thank you for letting me stay here,' she said as Uchida brought her a cup of tea.

'It is no trouble.' He handed her the tea and sat across from her. 'Besides, I do not think you are a murderer.' He smiled, but Sasha looked away. She couldn't bear to see the kindness in his eyes.

'Why did you want to come here so badly?' she asked.

Uchida sighed. Sasha followed his gaze through the window, to the only colour in the vast darkness of space – Earth.

'Do not laugh. But, when I was a child, I wanted to be an astronaut.'

Sasha smiled. 'I think that's true of most kids, to be fair. Although I wanted to be a fireman–princess–veterinarian.'

Uchida returned her smile. 'It turns out, I have no aptitude for science. Maths, yes. But not science. I lacked a ... curiosity. A desire for discovery and innovation. At least according to my teachers.'

'I was never good at anything,' Sasha said. 'Nothing I did ever felt right. And if it didn't feel right, I would give it up. A lack of ambition. A lack of focus. A lack of everything. My parents heard those comments for years. Until I found architecture. Knowing I could draw something and then see it come to life, there is no feeling like it. Knowing you can create instead of destroy.'

'My mother said similar things for years,' Uchida said.

'About creation?'

'About motivation. Or my lack thereof.' He stood up and went to the open roll-top desk where he picked up a photograph. 'My father doted on me, but he died young. I am not sure my mother ever desired children, but she felt it was her duty. After my father's death, she made me her sole focus. She wanted me to succeed at all costs.'

'I would say you have,' Sasha said.

'I used to tell her I would bring her the moon if it would make her happy. She would mock me. "Go get the moon then, Dai. What are you doing here?"' He set the photo down.

'I suppose you better get some moon rocks before we go then.'

Sasha sipped her tea. 'You have a reason to be here. I like that. It's something else I like about architecture. There is a reason for everything. Every bit of the design has a purpose. A justification. Nothing is done without reason. Nothing happens because of coincidence.' She looked away from the window. 'I was wrong. I thought I was meant to be on this trip. That it was a sign. But there's no reason for me to be here.'

Uchida returned to her side and took her hand. 'Do not think so lowly of yourself.'

'It's not that.' The tears welled in her eyes. She wiped them away before they fell. 'You said I wasn't a murderer. But there is a woman who is dead because of me.'

Frau Richter's dressing gown billowed behind her as she paced her suite, the latest origami stork crumpled in her fist. The others filled the bin. Hiding in her room was the best way to remain safe, yes, but how could she sit around another day or more waiting for someone to kill her? He had already tried once, and he would certainly try again. He would find a way into her room. He had before. And who would protect her? No one. The doctor had flirted with her only to be cruel. They were approximately the same age. He should have preferred her to the simpering Professor Crane who, doctorate or not, was still very much a child. No, he did not care to protect her.

Detective Strand – or was it former Detective Strand? – might, but only out of a sense of duty. Penelope did not like her either. Might even let her die because she did not agree with her accusations.

But they weren't just accusations. There had been hands around her throat. And they had been *his* hands, she knew it. She was certain. Why? She didn't know. Nor did she care. It had to do with her ex-husband, surely. He had paid one of these guests to kill her. He did not have money like Dai Uchida had money, but he had enough. She knew exactly how much because she had tried to take all of it.

She looked in the bin at the crumpled paper storks. Why storks, though? What was it supposed to mean? Storks had nothing to do with her former husband. She reached for the bottle of wine she'd brought with her to her room. Then stopped. That dinner. There was something about the dinner they held after Bobby's death that niggled at her mind. A moment of déjà vu. She looked again at the wine bottle.

This was about her. She knew it. But there was something she needed to check first, in order to prove it to the others. It would mean leaving the safety of her room, although if someone had entered at will to leave her those storks, was her room that safe to begin with? But even if someone could get in, couldn't she more easily defend herself here, as long as she remained alert to the door? Leave or go? Why was it so hard to decide?

People were always trying to take things from her. Her clients, her husband. And now someone wanted her life? No. No, she wouldn't let them. And she wouldn't stay holed up in her room, sheltering like prey. She would do as she did in court. Do what she should've done days ago. She would go on the offensive. She shrugged off her dressing gown, slipped on her zippered jacket and shoved the latest paper stork into her pocket.

Chapter 37

A knock woke her. It had been quick, sharp, and then gone. Penelope hadn't even realised she'd fallen asleep. When she realised she must have – her left arm tingling with pins and needles from serving as her pillow at the desk – she thought perhaps she had dreamed the sound.

She shook out her arm, the feeling slowly coming back as she approached the door. She saw no one on the video monitor, but this provided only a limited view no better than a peephole. She emptied the vase on the centre table of the now-wilting sunflowers. With her left hand, she disengaged the deadbolt and, with her right, kept the vase primed to strike.

She pressed the button that opened the door and brandished the vase. But the hall was empty. Something, though, had been left at her door – a tablet. She scooped it up and quickly returned to her room.

Penelope took the tablet to the desk and sat down. Without even turning it on, she knew what it was. The back of its black leather case was embossed with the Hotel Artemis logo. This was one of the tablets stolen from the manager's office. She pressed the home button and the main screen with all of its apps popped up. Either Frau Richter had been lying about needing a passcode or someone had unlocked this tablet before leaving it at Penelope's door.

She looked at the different apps. She didn't recognise any of them. There was no email app, and there did not appear to be any sort of internet connection. She did recognise a calendar. When she opened it, she saw the same schedule of activities that had been in her welcome pack, only more detailed – colour-coded to indicate different categories such as meals versus spa treatments, etc. It also indicated which staff members were responsible for which activities and the times they needed to report by. The calendar was also personalised to the whole group, with notes indicating which guests would most likely partake in which activities. This was no generic timetable, this was the intended two-week schedule for all their inaugural visitors. The staff had planned on being here. So who had told them to leave, and why would they have agreed, knowing the guests were on their way?

Penelope closed the calendar and opened another app with a grey and purple logo. The app name – Earthshine – appeared on the screen while it loaded, the same name as the AI concierge program. Within the app, their list of ten names appeared in alphabetical order. Penelope tapped on her own name first.

Her picture appeared – the official press photo they'd taken of her for the contest winners announcement – and a list of information such as likes, dislikes and preferences. She remembered filling out some of this information on an electronic form prior to the trip, but there was far more detail here than what she had given them. It included the last several hotels she'd stayed at on Earth and her reasons for those trips. There was information about her favourite music, films and television shows. Penelope stood up and checked the programmable sound system in her room, which she'd barely touched since the first night. It included all of the artists and albums on the list on the tablet – the complete electronic catalogue she streamed at home. There was also information on her preferred drinks – single malt Highland whisky with one ice cube in a highball glass. She'd never told them that. Then she remembered how she'd requested one on the first day of the flight, before she discovered there was no alcohol onboard the ship.

She went back to the main menu and selected the other guests' profiles. Uchida's was the most detailed, with information concerning his stays at all the world's top hotels – the Ritz-Carltons, Four Seasons, the Burj Al Arab, etc. Penelope had heard that luxury hotels had methods of keeping track of their guests' preferences. When she had investigated a series of thefts at the Savoy early in her career, the staff had been able to provide her with detailed information on the guests who had been robbed. Earthshine, apparently, was the Hotel Artemis's system.

She closed that app and opened another called Syzygy.

This app contained a detailed floor plan of the hotel that included all public and private areas – exactly what Penelope had needed for their earlier searches. The map had different modes – guests and staff – and could be viewed in 2D or 3D. It also could tell a person the quickest route between two points. Penelope tapped on the option that read 'Staff'. Nothing happened. She tapped on the option that read 'Guests'. Several pulsing red lights appeared on the map.

'What in the . . .'

She counted them. Eight. Eight red dots, each labelled with a code not a name. There was one red light in her own room. Carrying the tablet with her, Penelope walked to her door and – after checking carefully – opened the door and went out into the hall. The red dot from her room moved into the hall.

Penelope quickly returned to her room, locked the door and sat down at the desk. She noted the ID number of her dot and wrote her name next to it. Her next thought was that the two missing dots corresponded to Bobby and Jackson, but as she examined the map, she noticed the stationary dot in the restaurant and the one in the small cell. She noted those numbers along with Bobby and Jackson's names. She knew Tonya's suite and saw the dot there, and there was one dot in the penthouse, which she assumed was Uchida. That left five guests, but there were only three dots left. Someone was in the lobby near the shop. Someone else was in the main kitchen near the Harvest Restaurant. Someone was heading down the stairs towards the lobby.

Somehow, the hotel was tracking them. And somehow, two of the guests were not being tracked. Either they'd discovered the tracking devices and intentionally removed them or had inadvertently done so. But how was the hotel doing it? Penelope tapped her pen on the desk. Her first thought was that they'd implanted some sort of device inside her. They'd all had to comply with a physical and a series of vaccinations in order to come on the trip. But the vaccination was the only procedure they'd done to her, if it could even be considered a procedure. And despite what conspiracy theorists said, the technology for a tracking device small enough to fit through a standard needle and syringe didn't exist. Not to mention the significant human rights violations involved. Although, as Bobby had pointed out, no one had fully read the contracts they signed. But no, an implanted device was far too unlikely. Penelope swivelled around in her chair.

'What else then?' she asked.

The hotel clearly wanted to keep track of the location of all the guests and staff. So what would a person carry on them at all times? For the staff, it could be almost anything, especially if they were informed of the trackers and required to keep them on. But what about the guests? Clearly they hadn't been informed of a tracking device. There had been no mention of them in the safety videos or welcome packet. A hotel key was the obvious answer, but guests didn't use keys here. Just their palm print.

'What else do you need on you when you leave your room?'

Clothes were the next answer, but all of the clothes were her own except the hotel dressing gown, bathrobe and the flight suit they'd been required to wear at launch. But no one would walk around the hotel in any of those.

'Walking!'

Penelope looked down at the weighted trainers the hotel had provided. She slipped them off and, with nothing sharper to hand, started digging into the rubber soles with her pen. In the heel of the right shoe, she found it.

A small microchip.

She went to the closet and examined the other hotel-provided shoes – the flats, the slippers. In the right heel of each she found an identical chip. The hotel had said the weighted shoes were required to help counterbalance the moon's lighter gravity since the hotel could not yet fully replicate the weight of Earth's gravity. Everyone was required to wear the weighted shoes outside of their rooms.

Bobby had been in his hotel slippers.

Jackson had been wearing his hotel trainers.

Penelope went back to the tablet.

Her dot had disappeared from the screen. She went into her closet and found the last two pairs of shoes – a second set of trainers and pair of silver flats. She put on the trainers. As soon as her full weight was on them, her dot reappeared. But what if guests were sitting or lying down? The dot remained as she did these things and even remained on as she removed her feet from the shoes and set them in the hall. Her dot indicated she was in the hall. When she put on the silver flats, her location changed to within her room. She retrieved the trainers and sat back down at the desk. It seemed that the trackers were weight-activated, and they remained active in one pair of footwear until a guest put on different footwear. Then, the tracker in the previous footwear switched itself off as the person's weight activated the tracker in the new footwear. Removing the trackers from the other pairs of footwear must have damaged them and turned them off.

Leaving the tracker in the silver flats active, she tapped on her dot. Several options were given. She tried turning location services off but received an 'Authorisation Required' error. She tapped on 'Location History' but received the same error message. She went back to the map.

Some of the dots remained stationary. Others were moving. And two guests remained unaccounted for.

Penelope slipped on the first pair of trainers, now sans microchip, and put the tablet and notes in her bag. After once again checking the monitor, she carefully opened the door. The hall remained empty. She looked at the tablet. Her dot remained in her room. Quickly and quietly, she hurried up to the next floor.

Chapter 38

Tonya checked the video monitor, sighed and unlocked the door. Penelope hurried in and Tonya quickly closed it behind her.

'I'm not apologising and I'm not changing my mind,' Tonya said.

Penelope took something from her bag and thrust it into Tonya's hands. A tablet.

Tonya looked it over. 'Where did you find this?'

'Someone left it at my door. Look at this.' Penelope tapped on the tablet a few times and pulled up a map – a map with blinking dots.

Tonya stared at the screen. As she made her way to the bed and sat down, Penelope explained about tracking devices in the shoes and the missing guests.

'This dot was in your suite, so I was hoping it was you.'

Tonya looked down at her slippered feet. 'So someone's known our movements all this time?'

'At least since they stole the tablets. I don't know if these devices can be monitored down on Earth or not.'

'Why would someone give one to you?' Tonya asked.

'Obviously someone wanted me to know.' Penelope didn't meet Tonya's eye.

'You think it's Freddy,' Tonya said.

Penelope shrugged.

'If he was innocent, why wouldn't he just come to you and tell you what he knows? Why leave this at your door and run off?'

'I don't know. Because he's afraid? Because someone's after him?' Penelope said.

'Or it was someone else and they're afraid of being discovered. Maybe Frau Richter? She told us she didn't steal the tablets and doesn't want to be called out as a liar? Or someone else who doesn't want to admit they were in the manager's office around the time Jackson was killed?'

'If we could access the location histories, it could solve a lot of questions,' Penelope said. 'But I still think the key to this is figuring out why Bobby and Jackson were killed when they weren't the real target. They must have discovered something. Something bigger than just the fact there was no reality show. Either together or independently.'

'They were pretty upset with each other that night,' Tonya said. 'So I would suspect independently.'

'Or Jackson went to Bobby to apologise – or vice versa – and were together whenever . . .' She waved her arms.

'But they were killed a day apart. If they'd both witnessed something at the same time, the killer left Jackson alive long enough to tell us what happened,' Tonya said.

'Except he didn't. He wouldn't tell me anything and wasn't inclined to,' Penelope said.

'He could've been threatened. Or maybe thought he'd made

a deal with the killer?' Tonya guessed.

'Or he didn't realise what he saw, or what he knew. Not until it was too late.' Penelope chewed on her lower lip.

Tonya looked over the map again. 'You still want to find out where the blood came from. The blood on Jackson,' she qualified, thinking of the stained towels in Freddy's room.

Penelope nodded.

'There's at least one place we haven't checked yet.' Tonya showed her on the map.

The medical bay was located in a recessed corner of the hotel, a long way from the restaurant where Bobby's body still lay. No one wanted to be reminded of illness or injury in a luxury hotel, so the medical bay was inconspicuous, almost hidden. Penelope suspected it was mostly for staff and for storing supplies. Guests were probably meant to be treated in their own suites unless it was an absolute necessity to come here.

'Who was supposed to search this part of the hotel?' Tonya asked, keeping watch as Penelope retrieved the master key from her pocket.

'Uchida's group,' Penelope said, unlocking the door. It slid open with a *whoosh*. 'But they split up and our search got distracted when Freddy and Alison discovered the cameras. I'm not sure which of them came down here, or if any of them ever did.'

The lights turned on automatically when they entered. Tonya closed the door behind them and made sure that it was locked. The medical bay was a single room, and it was clear from a quick glance that they were alone. The privacy curtains were pulled back, the space under the two treatment beds visible and open, and there were no cabinets big enough for a person to hide in.

It was just as obvious that someone else had been here in the past. Bloody gauze was piled on one of the counters and a box of butterfly bandages had been torn open. Ripped purple jeans lay in a heap on the floor. Tonya bent down to pick them up.

'These are Jackson's.' She fingered the tear – a slice down the thigh of one leg.

'I thought he was wearing his pyjamas,' Penelope said. She found a torn open plastic wrapper. In an open closet were individually wrapped tracksuit bottoms and long-sleeve tops that matched what Jackson had been wearing when they found him.

'So the blood was his own?' Tonya asked.

'He injures himself that night. Comes here to clean himself up.'

'Then why were his hands still bloody when we found him staggering in the hall?' Tonya asked.

'Maybe the wound reopened? Depending on how deep it was, the butterfly bandages might not have been enough. He knew Erik was a doctor. Maybe he was going to him for help.'

Penelope walked over to the beds. One had clearly been slept in, the sheets and pillow rumpled, with some bloodstains, while the other was crisply made.

'So he hurts himself doing what?' Tonya asked. 'Helping to move Bobby's body? Unless he was involved, I don't see why he wouldn't have just told us the blood was his own.'

'He was scared,' Penelope said. 'He saw something and it frightened him enough to keep quiet. Maybe he preferred to be in that cell. That if we let everyone assume he was the murderer and he stayed locked in that cell, the real murderer wouldn't come for him. Or at least wouldn't be able to get to him.'

'Well, if it had been me, I would've just told you who the murderer was. You're the detective after all,' Tonya said.

'I thought I was an ex-detective?' Penelope quipped.

Tonya sighed. 'Either way, I would assume you could be the most impartial. If I didn't want to be accused of pointing the finger at someone else and didn't want to tell the whole group what I knew, I would've at least told you.'

'Unless . . .' Penelope tapped her fingers on the rail of the bed.

'Unless?'

'Unless he didn't know who the murderer was.' Penelope turned to Tonya. 'Let's assume Jackson had nothing to do with Bobby's death.'

'Well, you know what they say. When you assume, you make an—'

Penelope held up her hand. 'Please, don't. Anyway, that night – Jackson is drunk. We all saw that. Or at least still tipsy. By his own admission, he was wandering the hotel much of the night. What if he wandered near the spacewalk airlock. He sees what happened, or some of it, but not who because . . .'

Tonya snapped her fingers. 'Because they're inside the spacesuit.'

'Those suits are bulky. Not the cool sleek ones you see on TV. They're clumsy and bulky enough to hide any body type and even somewhat disguise our true height. Plus, they have reflective face shields. So he wouldn't be able to see a face. He runs off, hurts himself in the process, comes here. He doesn't know the full extent of what's happened until the next morning when we all find him. He realises – for certain – that he's witnessed a murder and realises the murderer could have been any one of us. So he decides to keep his mouth shut and stay locked in the cell until the rescue ship arrives.'

'But he let someone in. I mean, anyone could've found a way to open the door, but he let someone get close enough to him to wrap that wire around his neck,' Tonya said.

'Someone tricked him. Gained enough of his trust. Probably whoever knew that there were trackers in our shoes, so that they wouldn't be spotted – just in case – by the system's tracking data as being in the cell with him,' Penelope said.

'Which means they could have also worn someone else's shoes to try and frame someone, in case the tracking data was ever found. Freddy is one possibility. Who else?' Tonya asked.

'Before we start accusing anyone, I want to confirm some of our suspicions. One, that Jackson does have an injury to his leg and two, where in the building that injury occurred. It's still possible he was an accomplice and injured himself moving the body.'

Tonya looked at Jackson's ruined jeans. 'So this means, we're going to have to . . .' She paled. 'Can we see if there's any anti-nausea medication in these cabinets first?'

Penelope and Tonya made it to the managerial hub without incident. The hotel was eerily quiet, even more so than when they'd all first arrived. They closed the door to the office hallway and barricaded it with a chair. Penelope alone went in to examine Jackson's body. She offered for Tonya to join her, but Tonya went white at the thought.

'I'll, um, I'll stand here. In the doorway. But I don't think I can . . . No, I definitely can't.'

So Tonya stood back from the open doorway, avoiding the blood on the floor, her back to the cell, while Penelope snapped on the rubber gloves she'd taken from the medical bay. She did her best to avoid looking at Jackson's face and neck. It was the leg that concerned her after all. She knelt down carefully, trying to avoid the congealed blood that covered much of the floor. There was no smell yet but that didn't make approaching the body any more appealing. There was blood everywhere. She wasn't an expert in blood splatter analysis, but it looked like some of the blood had been smeared as if someone had either fallen in it or tried to wipe it up and gave up.

With a pair of medical scissors, she cut a straight line up Jackson's left trouser leg. She peeled back the fabric, then leaned back on her heels.

'We were right about the leg wound.'

'We were?' Tonya started to turn around. 'Oh God. Nope. Can't.' She braced herself on the door frame. 'Tell me what you see.'

'A cut – a gash, really – about four inches long on his left thigh. Seems fairly deep. There are two butterfly bandages still attached but two others that have come loose.' She lifted the cut fabric, saw the bloodstains inside. 'It did start to bleed again, which would make sense. It's definitely a wound that would require stitches. There's a bit of bruising around it, which makes me think he hit something with a good bit of force rather than just scraping his leg against something.'

'So, likely, he was running and ran into something?'

'Or something moving fast ran into him.' Penelope stood up and left the cell. Tonya immediately closed the door while Penelope pulled off the gloves.

'So there should be a trail of blood, shouldn't there?' Tonya asked. 'He didn't get that injury in the medical bay. He went there because he was injured.'

'His jeans might have soaked up some of the blood to start. How far he needed to walk to get to the medical bay would affect how much blood would've fallen.' Penelope tossed the gloves into the nearest bin.

'So, going on the accomplice theory, it would've had to happen after he moved Bobby's body. There's no blood in the restaurant, and I haven't seen any in the kitchen any of the times I've been there,' Tonya said.

'And going with the witness theory, he would've been somewhere near the spacewalk airlock.'

'Somewhere he wouldn't have been seen easily because if the killer had known he was there, they probably would have finished him off that night. The killer didn't know until the next day that Jackson had seen something.'

Penelope took the tablet from her bag. 'So let's find out the possible routes from that airlock to the medical bay.'

The tablet's map showed that there was no one in their vicinity – at least no one who was being tracked. Tonya kept watch while Penelope examined various locations in view of the spacewalk airlock. This airlock was near the end of a corridor at the south-western corner of the hotel. Two different corridors were close by – one that cut through the hotel at a diagonal, providing a more direct route to the centre of the hotel, and one that went north – a path up the western side of the hotel where the medical bay was tucked away.

Because of the confluence of corridors, there were several places Jackson could have viewed the airlock without being seen by anyone entering or leaving it, especially someone hindered by a bulky spacesuit. What was less obvious was how Jackson could have hurt himself. His wound was a gash, not a puncture – something he would have had to drag his leg across. But the corridors and doorways were all smooth, their edges rounded. The floors there carpeted – soft and spongy, giving the guests the feeling of walking on memory foam. The entire hotel was practically baby-proofed.

'Anything?' Tonya whispered.

'Nothing,' Penelope said, putting her hands on her hips. 'We know he ended up in the medical bay, so let's try working backwards from there. Tonya?'

Tonya squinted at the tablet.

'Something wrong?' Penelope asked.

'No, I thought someone moved, but . . . no. All the dots are in the same places. Sorry. Medical bay you said?'

Once they reached the door to the medical bay, Penelope crouched down and examined the floor around the entrance. The carpet was a gradated grey meant to mimic the surface of the moon. The pattern also helped to conceal stains. Penelope ran her fingers over the carpet, feeling the fibres. She stopped when she came across a different texture – more brittle. When she noticed the texture was different, she noticed the coloration was off. This small patch was somewhat darker where it should've been light.

'Here,' she said. 'There was a stain here but someone's cleaned it up.' She explained her findings to Tonya.

'Well, it certainly wasn't housekeeping.'

'Help me look for another,' Penelope said.

They found a few more spots as they drifted away from the medical bay. Penelope hadn't cleaned much blood off carpet, but helping at her parents' dog shelter, she'd dealt with her fair share of urine, faeces and vomit. No matter how high quality the carpet – how stain proof it was advertised as being – or the quality of the cleaning products, there was always some sign left behind in the altered fabric. Whoever had cleaned up those stains had done a good job, but once Penelope and Tonya knew what they were looking for, spotting the trail became easier.

When they reached the intersection where the corridor split, they lost the trail.

'Well, he didn't just start magically bleeding,' Tonya said.

Penelope examined the corridor to the left. There was an unmarked door only a few feet away.

'Where does this door lead to?'

Tonya tapped on the map. 'Nowhere. It's a utility closet according to this.'

Penelope pulled out the master key to unlock it but it wasn't necessary. The lock on the motion-activated door wasn't working properly and automatically opened when she went near. She found the light switch. The room lit up.

'Bingo,' she said.

In the middle of the room was a large metal cart – empty but possibly meant for holding cleaning or other maintenance supplies. A sign on it read BROKEN – DO NOT USE. One metal piece was clearly out of place, a sharp end protruding out and down as if it had broken off or not been assembled properly, at the perfect height for cutting a leg if the person wasn't paying attention.

'This door's faulty,' Penelope said. 'It's been left or stuck on automatic open.' She stepped out and the door closed behind her.

'So,' she said, beginning a re-enactment. 'I'm Jackson. I'm still somewhat inebriated and I'm making my way down the hall. I see something going on at the airlock, so I stop. Watch. Try to figure out what it is.' She stopped at the corner, the airlock visible.

Tonya continued, 'And you see what's happening to Bobby. Although you don't know it's Bobby at the time. You see someone pounding on the airlock from the inside while there's someone else in a spacesuit watching.'

'You lose it. You're already in a heightened state of emotion from the alcohol and the fight with Bobby and, well, being on the moon, probably. So you panic and turn to run,' Penelope said.

'But you stumble because you're drunk and the weighted shoes take some getting used to, even when you're sober,' Tonya said.

'And as you're trying to run, this door' – Penelope stepped in front of it and it automatically opened – 'suddenly opens and you fall inside, onto this damaged cart someone left just inside the entrance.'

'The murderer likely didn't hear Jackson because of the spacesuit. I'd imagine the helmet muffles most sounds. Isn't that why they put radios in them to communicate?' Tonya said.

'But Jackson doesn't know that. So he stays in here for a bit and then stumbles out, bleeding quite a bit.'

'He sees the signs for the medical bay,' Tonya continued. 'And goes there.'

'He still doesn't know if anyone saw him or not, so he decides to spend the night in this cupboard because it might be safer than his own suite,' Penelope said. 'From the medical bay, it would've been hard to hear Sasha scream. It's the complete opposite end of the hotel, and sound doesn't travel well in these back corridors. So when he wakes up, his leg is bleeding again, and he decides to risk going to see Erik – the only medical doctor here – for help.'

'But our whole group finds him first and screams bloody murder before he knows what's going on.'

'It's then that the murderer suspects Jackson might have witnessed something that night. Because why else isn't Jackson screaming that he's innocent? The murderer knows Jackson didn't do it. Jackson knows he didn't do it. But he says nothing because he's scared,' Penelope said.

'And while we all go about our business that day, the murderer comes back here, finds the trail of Jackson's blood and realises what must've happened,' Tonya said. 'They clean it up and at some point decide Jackson has to go.'

'It could have been any of us,' Penelope said. 'Each of us was exploring all over the hotel that day. We need a timeline. Try to establish who was where around what time. I remember when I spoke to everyone but outside of that . . . What?'

Tonya was giving the tablet an odd look again. 'One of the dots,' she said. 'It's moving. Moving fast.' She showed the tablet to Penelope. 'And if it's moving that fast, it must mean that . . .'

'Someone's running,' Penelope said.

Whoever it was, they were up on Level 2A. Penelope and Tonya were a floor below, in one of the service corridors, when the dot suddenly stopped.

'They've stopped moving,' Tonya said.

'Hurry.'

They raced up the flight of stairs, hearing nothing as they emerged onto the second floor. The red dot they were after remained stationary in the pool area. The door was open. They stopped and listened.

Nothing.

Penelope peeked inside the room.

There was the pool, the water undisturbed, the deckchairs in a neat row, and there in the doorway of the changing rooms, a body.

Penelope rushed over, Tonya close behind, and knelt by the body.

'It's Freddy,' Penelope said. She first felt for a pulse. 'He's alive.'

She turned him onto his side, in the recovery position, checked his airway. He was breathing. His only injury appeared to be a blow to his head. Two blows – one on his forehead from where he had fallen on the hard tiles, and one on the back of his head, where someone had initially struck him. Penelope looked at his feet. He was wearing his weighted trainers and they were intact – no evidence that he had removed, or tried to remove, the tracker.

Tonya looked at the tablet.

'He didn't . . . this dot is his. He was running. And he didn't remove or . . . There's still two dots unaccounted for. And Freddy's had his tracker on the whole time. Then who . . .'

'We'll worry about that later,' Penelope said. 'Right now we need to get him out of here. Someone's tried to kill him and if they realise they haven't succeeded . . .'

'One of the unoccupied suites,' Tonya said.

Tonya handed Penelope the tablet and she put it back in her bag. Whoever they were looking for couldn't be tracked anyway, so there was no point in staring at the map while they moved Freddy. Tonya took his feet while Penelope hooked her arms underneath his shoulders. Freddy gave no sign that he was coming to. Though he was alive, his body was a completely dead weight.

They were both panting by the time they got him to the pool entrance. After checking that the hall was clear, they slowly carried him towards the nearest unoccupied suite, pausing now and then to readjust their grip. They were both sweating by the time they reached it. Penelope tapped the master key and, as quickly as they could, they shuffled him inside.

'Bed or couch?' Tonya asked.

'Couch. It's firmer.'

They lifted him up onto the couch and propped his head up with a pillow. Tonya stared at his unconscious form, lines of worry creasing her face.

'I'll get some towels,' she said quietly.

Penelope examined his wounds. The one at the back was more severe, but his skull hadn't been cracked open as far as she could tell. She had once investigated a possible homicide where the victim had fallen down a series of concrete steps. She remembered seeing the grey of the victim's brain through the broken-open skin and bone. There was none of that with Freddy.

Still, head wounds were tricky, and she only had basic first aid training. Dr Wyss could probably do more for him, but it was possible the doctor was the one who had attacked him in the first place.

'Here,' Tonya said. She handed Penelope one towel and held on to several others.

Penelope pressed the towel to the back of Freddy's head, then gently lowered it to the pillow-padded armrest. His own weight could be used to apply pressure to the wound. The bump to his forehead was more superficial but Penelope dabbed at it with a wet cloth Tonya handed to her.

They watched him in silence for several minutes, keeping an eye on his breathing, noting his pulse. Both remained steady, which Penelope took as a good sign, but he still showed no signs of consciousness.

Tonya spoke first.

'So was it the murderer who went after him?' she asked.

'Or did someone go after him thinking he was the murderer?' Penelope asked.

'This is my fault,' Tonya said. 'I shouldn't have accused him. I shouldn't have . . .'

Penelope stood and placed her hand on Tonya's arm.

'We all saw what we saw,' Penelope said. 'And we still don't have an explanation for those bloody towels. But whoever did this, for whatever reason, no matter what Freddy did or didn't do, this wasn't right.'

Tonya nodded then lowered herself into the nearest chair.

'So what do we do now?' she asked.

Penelope went to her bag and pulled out the tablet and her notebook.

'We sit with Freddy for a bit. Make sure he remains stable.'

326

She handed Tonya the tablet. 'And then we figure out who isn't being tracked.'

Frau Richter ran into the Sunrise Lounge, panting for breath. She closed the door quietly behind her, but although she appeared to be the only person in the room, she still felt too exposed. Trying not to make a sound, she crept to the back of the room and slipped into the kitchen. The lights automatically turned on when she entered and she looked desperately for a way to switch them off but could not. She could only hope they had not heard her, although she had heard them.

The murder of a woman. They had been discussing the murder of a woman. But no women had been murdered here. Not yet.

She didn't speak for fear of being heard but, in her mind, she thought, *I knew it was me. I knew it.*

Frau Richter was running out of time. But why? Who had put them up to it? She had been wrong about Freddy Nwankwo. She knew that now. But who was left that she could trust? Who might believe her before it was too late?

Chapter 39

Dr Wyss flexed his elbow underneath the cold water. Ice would've been better, but he didn't want to venture down to the kitchens to find some. The swelling wasn't so bad at the moment, but he needed to wrap it. Unfortunately, he had access to a compression bandage and sling as easily as he had access to ice.

He turned off the water and gingerly dried the sore area with his last clean towel. As he stepped out of the bathroom, someone knocked on his door.

'Alison, I told you—'

'It's not Alison.'

Dr Wyss grabbed a sweatshirt and slipped it on, wincing as he pulled his arm through the sleeve. With his arm covered, he checked the monitor before opening the door.

'Charlotte, what do you—'

'Can I come in?' She entered without waiting for his answer.

He looked up and down the hall, saw that it was empty and closed the door.

As she paced back and forth, Dr Wyss instinctively went to cross his arms but it hurt when he tried. He lowered them to his side.

'What is it, Charlotte?' he asked.

'You're the only one I can trust,' she said.

Dr Wyss restrained himself from rolling his eyes. 'Of course I am,' he said.

'Can you please take me seriously?'

He stood there, silent, and waited for her to continue.

'Someone here *is* trying to kill me. But it's not Freddy Nwankwo.'

'And what do you expect me to do about it?' he asked. He caught a glimpse of the shirt she had on underneath her jacket. 'Is that blood?' He pointed to the stains.

Frau Richter looked down, seemingly surprised to see the speckled stains dotting her shirt. Then she waved her arm in front of her face as if she could wave them away.

'It's nothing. I had a nosebleed.' She zipped up her jacket. 'I heard something while I was out,' she said.

'Out?' Dr Wyss looked out the window at Earth and the surface of the moon.

'Not *out* out. Outside of my room. I was . . . it doesn't matter what I was doing. But I know now for certain that the killer is after me and—'

Dr Wyss raised an eyebrow. '"Peter and the Wolf". Isn't that a story of Germanic origin? Surely you must have heard it growing up. Cry out a false warning so many times, no one's going to believe you, even if it's real. Do you forget I slept near you last night? When Freddy supposedly strangled you?'

Frau Richter's hand went instinctively to her throat. 'He did. Someone did.'

'No one went running by me after you screamed. If someone

did attack you last night' – he stepped closer – 'they were much nearer to you than young Mr Nwankwo.'

Frau Richter took a step back.

'If, of course,' he continued, 'it even happened at all.'

'I am not a liar,' she said, holding his gaze.

Dr Wyss broke eye contact first. He turned away from her and opened the door.

'I cannot help you, Charlotte. If you truly suspect someone is after you, you should take what you've found to Detective Strand. Good evening.'

He stood there next to the open doorway until Frau Richter reluctantly passed through. In the hall, she turned back to face him.

'If I die,' she said, 'it will be on your hands.'

'Frau Richter, didn't you know? That's what I do for a living.'

He shut the door in her face. Then he held his breath until, on the monitor, he saw her walk away.

Dr Wyss let out a gasp of pain and grabbed his elbow. He'd barely been able to hold it together while Frau Richter was in the room. It hurt far more than a sprain now. Perhaps it was broken after all. He hurried back to the bathroom and began running his elbow under the cold water again, still his best option in lieu of ice.

He hadn't meant to be so cruel to her, but he needed her to stay away. Hopefully now she would.

'He won't want to talk to us,' Tonya said.

'We're not going to give him a choice,' Penelope replied.

'People have died. More are at risk. I'm done tiptoeing around him just because he's rich.'

'Mega rich,' Tonya corrected.

'We're all the same up here. We all have access to the same supplies and are facing the same dangers. His bank accounts are on Earth. Not here.'

They arrived at the penthouse where the tablet indicated there was one blinking dot inside. As Penelope stuffed the tablet in her bag, she noticed a crumpled piece of paper on the floor by the door. She picked it up and examined it as she knocked.

'Mr Uchida? It's Penelope.'

'And Tonya!'

'We need to talk.'

'What is that?' Tonya asked Penelope as they waited.

'I don't know. Looks sort of like a bird?'

The deadbolt disengaged, and the door slid open.

'Sasha!' Penelope said, surprised.

'Dai isn't here, sorry,' she said. 'Do you . . . do you want to come in?' Her fingers picked at a thread on her shirt.

'If you don't mind,' Penelope said.

Sasha stepped aside and ushered them in. She closed the door behind them and immediately re-engaged the deadbolt, which didn't require the assigned guest's handprint. The penthouse still bore the chaos of their sleepover the night before, with mattresses and blankets scattered across the lower level.

'Where is he?' Penelope asked, picking her way through the clutter.

'He went to get us some food,' Sasha said. She rubbed her arm and wouldn't meet Penelope's eye.

'Alone?' Penelope asked.

'He said he would be fine, and that it would be safer for me to wait here. He hasn't been gone long. What is it you wanted to talk to him about?'

Penelope made her way to Uchida's closet. 'A few things. And we also wanted to make sure he was safe.'

'Is he in danger? Did something happen?'

'No more than the rest of us.' Tonya smiled reassuringly. 'And no, not that we're aware of. Why? Have you heard anything?'

Sasha very quickly shook her head. 'No. I've been up here with Dai this whole time. It wouldn't surprise me, though,' she added. 'Not with everything else that's been going on. What are you doing in there?' Sasha had noticed Penelope entering the walk-in closet.

'I just want to see something.'

Sasha crossed the room. 'Those are Dai's personal things. I've told you before. He's very private. You shouldn't be in there without his permission.'

Tonya casually intercepted her. 'It's nothing,' Tonya said. 'Why don't you have a seat, darling?'

Sasha didn't sit, but she didn't advance. She stood, her arms hugged tightly across her chest.

'He's not what you all think he is. He's a very kind person. He cares about people. He has no choice but to come across as serious and quiet. He never knows if people are after him for his money or if they genuinely like him. He won't like you snooping around his things,' she said.

'Technically,' Penelope said, 'the shoes aren't his. They're property of the hotel.'

She re-emerged with a pair of Uchida's shoes. After setting the crumpled paper bird on the table, she pulled out her pen, and used it to dig into the heel of one of the shoes.

'What are you doing?' Sasha gasped.

Penelope felt around inside. 'Hm,' she said.

'What is it?' Tonya asked.

Penelope tried two more pairs before she answered. 'They're not there,' she said. 'No trackers.'

'You're joking,' Tonya said, even though it was obvious Penelope was not.

Penelope abandoned the closet and took the tablet out of her bag.

'Trackers?' Sasha asked. 'What are you talking about?' But she became distracted by the paper bird. She picked it up and examined it while Penelope opened the map and zoomed in on the penthouse, seeing more detail of its lower and upper floors. There was only one red dot in the whole of the penthouse. She looked at Sasha's feet. She wore the hotel-approved trainers. Penelope pulled out her notebook.

'ID number 0009 is Sasha,' she said.

Tonya explained about the tracking devices in their shoes, but Sasha's focus was on the bird.

'Where did this come from?' she asked.

'We found it just outside the door,' Tonya said.

Penelope tried to write down Sasha's name and ID, but a piece of rubber sole had become lodged in the tip of her pen. Rather than fight with it, she dropped the pen back into her bag and went to Uchida's desk.

'But you just said Dai's shoes didn't have a tracker. Why would we be tracked and not him?' Sasha asked.

Penelope opened the roll-top desk.

'That's one of the things we're going to ask him when he gets back,' Tonya answered.

Instead of reaching for a pen, Penelope picked up a grey, dusty rock about the size of her fist. She knew immediately what it was. She'd been up here for days now, seen the surface of the moon up close dozens of times, but this was the first time she'd touched a piece of it.

'Some souvenir,' she said. 'Why didn't I get one?'

'The billionaires get all the perks,' Tonya said.

Sasha bristled. 'Stop saying things like that. They didn't give that to him. Dai went and got it himself.'

Penelope froze. 'What did you say?'

'Dai collected that himself. It's a gift for his mother. It's a long story and, frankly, one he shared with me in confidence. But I am so sick of everyone assuming he is simply given everything because he's rich. He's a person with feelings and he's worked hard to—'

Penelope turned round, the moon rock still in hand.

'How did he get it?' she asked. 'Did he tell you how? Or when?' She looked at Tonya, whose stricken look informed Penelope that she was thinking the same thing.

Sasha had picked up on the tension and stopped her defensive rant.

'He went on a spacewalk. He said he knew he wasn't supposed to, not without the trained staff present, but he's a certified scuba diver and the concept was similar, except the lack of atmospheric pressure. So he decided he would be fine.'

'When? When did he go on a spacewalk?' Penelope asked.

'I'm . . . I'm not sure. He didn't say exactly, but I think it was shortly after we got here. Why? What is it? What's wrong?'

Penelope didn't say. Instead, she looked at Tonya.

'We need to find him. Now.'

'That goddamned . . .' Alison screamed in frustration and returned the bag of ice over her eye.

It was basically all that was left in the kitchen. Those vultures had picked practically everything else clean. As if they would need that much food. The ship was on its way. It would be here soon. Time was almost up. She needed to let go of her anger, stay calm. But the lack of cigarettes was making her nervy. And she couldn't find her nicotine gum. She might've simply misplaced it, or one of those vultures had stolen it from her on purpose. People were always stealing things from her.

'Stop it,' she whispered to herself. 'Stay calm. Stay rational.'

She practised the anger management techniques that a therapist had taught her years ago. As she did her breathing techniques, she wondered if her contact from the Apollo Group would've asked her to do this if they'd known about her past – the time spent in the group home for teenagers after her mother's death, what had happened there. They must've known. It wasn't a secret. She'd even told a few colleagues once after a few drinks at Kingston's faculty Christmas party.

All Alison had wanted to do was talk to Dr Wyss. Wanted to tell him that he wouldn't get away with it, not without her help. When he said no, she'd tried to push past him and Alison had ended up with an elbow to the eye.

Feeling calmer, Alison gathered up her bag of ice and left the kitchen using the service corridor. She had just opened the door to her floor when she heard the voices. She stepped back, hiding herself, but keeping the door open a crack.

Two people, whispering. Alison couldn't make out what they were saying and waited for them to pass down the hall – Tonya and Penelope. Penelope was carrying something. Alison tried to get a better look. It was a Hotel Artemis tablet.

'Where did she get that?' Alison whispered to herself. She waited until she was sure they were gone. Then she hurried back to her room, the bag of ice cold in her hand.

Slipped underneath her door was a note:

We need to talk about Eguisheim.

In the quiet of the unassigned suite, Freddy began to stir. His fingers twitched, his face winced in pain. With great effort, he tried to open his eyes, but when he did, the light was too bright and his eyelids too heavy. His dry tongue stuck to the roof of this mouth.

''Lo?' he called out weakly.

No one answered before his body dragged him back into unconsciousness.

Chapter 40

That the hotel had only allowed him to bring one measly little suitcase was ridiculous. Uchida had at least three bags that Dr Wyss had seen. But there was certainly no way he could ask to borrow one. With his elbow in a makeshift sling, Dr Wyss rolled Jackson's suitcase as well as the silver suitcases he'd taken from the Hotel Artemis shop out of the closet and clumsily lifted them onto the bed. Alison had retrieved Jackson's suitcase for him. She said it would be easy to slip it in with the rest of the luggage, easier than the Hotel Artemis branded suitcases that there was no record of anyone paying for. He hadn't asked her how she'd come to have it. As he tried to open Jackson's suitcase, the zipper kept catching. He needed two hands, but his left arm was getting stiffer by the minute.

He yanked and yanked on the zipper, each tug more vicious than the last, and let out a frustrated scream. A single lock of hair tickled his forehead. He brushed it back with his good hand, took a deep breath and then managed to free the zipper. He flipped the suitcase open and started pulling out Jackson's clothes. Jackson wouldn't be needing any of these things anymore. Dr Wyss wondered if anyone would notice he was loading

Jackson's suitcase onto the ship. No, it would be hectic when the ship arrived. The bigger problem would be retrieving it when they returned to Earth. As long as Jackson's family weren't there to claim it, he might have an easier time of it. And why would they be? No one outside of this hotel knew what had happened to him yet. But they would be on that ship for three days, and the ship would communicate with Earth, and likely there would be investigators waiting for them. Why not family, also?

Dr Wyss steadied himself and took another deep, calming breath. The Apollo Group wouldn't give him – any of them – trouble. They clearly had a serious internal issue going on. They would be embarrassed that someone in their organisation had ruined their big debut. They would let him have whatever he wanted.

He finished unpacking Jackson's suitcase. There was one item at the bottom – an 8 x 10 glossy headshot of Bobby. Jackson had talked to him about gathering up the nerve to ask Bobby to sign it. It seemed he never did. Dr Wyss picked up the photo, considered throwing it onto the pile of clothes, but then laid it back in Jackson's suitcase.

The suitcase otherwise empty, he began the slow one-handed process of refilling it.

Hotel Artemis monogrammed towels.

Hotel Artemis branded soaps and lotions.

Hotel Artemis drinks coasters.

And a set of Hotel Artemis electronic tablets.

Penelope doubted that Uchida would be up on the observation deck, so the only other place to go was down. She had tucked the moon rock into her bag, and it now thudded against her back as they hurried down the stairs.

'Do you think he's looking for Freddy? Does he want to check if he's dead?' Tonya asked.

'I don't know, but we'd better check on Freddy just in case.'

They first looked in the pool area. Whoever attacked Freddy – if it was Uchida – wouldn't know she and Tonya had moved him and might have doubled back to finish him off. But the pool was empty and quiet. There weren't any bodies this time, either. They slipped down to the suite where they'd hidden Freddy. Inside, Freddy remained alone, alive and unconscious.

'Up or down?' Tonya asked as they reached the staircase.

'Down,' Penelope said. 'With the ship definitely on its way, maybe he's starting to panic and has returned to the crime scene to make sure he didn't leave anything behind.'

The lobby appeared empty, but the smell was becoming overwhelming.

'God,' Tonya gasped, plugging her nose. 'Are they ever going to be able to get that out?'

'I have some menthol in my room. It helps me sleep. I should've brought it.'

Penelope crept over to the makeshift curtain she and Sasha had set up what felt like ages ago. She peeked behind it. No movement. No one there but Bobby and the pole in his back.

'Penelope.' Tonya's voice had dropped to a whisper. She pointed. The door to the managerial hub was open.

As they approached, they could hear someone inside, pounding on a door. Slowly, she and Tonya rounded the Reception desk. They couldn't see who it was yet, but the two of them hadn't been noticed either. As they reached the entrance to the managerial hub, a frustrated male voice spoke in Japanese. Penelope held up her hand, indicating for Tonya to wait. She didn't know any words in that language, but from Uchida's cadence and tone, he seemed to be speaking to himself. And he seemed more upset than angry.

The only way out of the managerial hub was through the doorway Penelope and Tonya now guarded. Uchida would have to go through them, but Penelope didn't know whether or not he was armed. Whatever he was trying to do, however, he did not appear to be succeeding. It was only a matter of time before he gave up and would want to leave. It was better if they could keep him cornered in the corridor.

When Penelope nodded, she and Tonya moved forwards. Tonya remained in the doorway while Penelope moved closer. Uchida didn't notice them. He was crouched in front of the communications centre door, pounding his fists on the keypad that Penelope had locked with the master key.

'Mr Uchida?' Penelope said.

He spun around, his expression one of fear. He tried to conceal it after he recognised Penelope, but traces remained. He couldn't fully gather the cool composure he'd demonstrated most of the trip.

'Apologies, Detective Strand. I wanted to reach someone at the Apollo Group or on the ship, to check the status of the ship's arrival. But it appears I cannot get through the door.'

'It appears not,' she said. 'I told everyone I disabled that door, remember?'

'Yes. You did. I simply . . . never mind. I will be happy to be done with this place as, I am sure, are you.' He finally noticed

Tonya. 'And Ms Burton. If you'll excuse me, I promised Sasha some food. I should—'

Penelope held out her hand and stopped him.

'Actually, there is something I wanted to ask you.' She reached into her bag and pulled out the moon rock. 'How did you get this? I mean, my dad would love a souvenir like this, but I haven't seen any around the hotel.'

'It was given to me,' he said without hesitation. 'It was in my penthouse when I arrived.'

'Really?' Penelope said. 'Because we were just with Sasha, at the penthouse, and she said you got it yourself on a spacewalk.'

He hesitated. 'I may have told her that. It may be what she believes.'

'So you lied to her? Or are you lying to us now?' Penelope continued holding out the moon rock. Uchida couldn't take his eyes off it.

'I don't see why it matters where I got it. I have it and I'll be bringing it back to Earth with me. My only souvenir of this whole ghastly affair.' His voice wavered as he spoke.

'I found the spacesuits, Mr Uchida. I know how Bobby died. What I don't know is why you did it.'

Penelope braced herself. Suspects behaved in all sorts of ways when confronted with such an accusation.

Uchida dropped to his knees. Tears fell down his face.

'Please,' he said, 'I cannot justify it but I can explain.' He looked down at his hands. They rested on his thighs, palms up in supplication.

Penelope crouched down to be eye level with him. Tonya remained standing, but closed the door to the managerial hub.

'Please understand, I never meant for Mr Rannells to come to any harm. Never. What happened was . . .' He took a deep breath, closed his eyes, and continued. 'I was angry when we arrived and the staff were not present. If there was supposed to be some sort of stunt such as Mr Rannells described, I should have been informed. I can look after myself. That is not the issue. But my sole reason for coming here – my dream – was to walk on the surface of the moon. It is the closest I will ever come to walking on another planet. I'm not an astronaut. I won't be going on a Mars mission.' He sighed.

'The hotel has very strict procedures for spacewalks. They are only meant to proceed with a trained astronaut and a minimum of two people. Never solo. I knew, when it was only the ten of us here, that the spacewalk would not happen as I intended. I could have booked another trip, I know. But the waiting list is extraordinary, even for someone with my wealth and my connection to the board. I called in too many favours to secure this maiden voyage. It will be at least two years before I can return. So many things can happen in that time. My father died at age forty-five. I am the same age now. We never know when death will come for us. This was my only certain chance.'

He wiped his eyes with his sleeve then continued.

'It was a foolish risk, but I convinced myself it would be less foolish if I had a partner. At our celebration that first night, Bobby told stories about his scuba-diving escapades. So I knew he had some training. He also seemed to be the only one who would be willing to flout the rules. I went to his room that night, knocked on the door. Explained what I wanted to do. He was excited. Thought it would make good footage for the show. A good storyline. He also agreed that we should do it right then, when everyone else was sleeping, so that no one would know what we were doing or talk us out of it. He didn't even bother to get dressed. He was just going to put the spacesuit on over his boxer shorts.

'So we went down to the airlock, put on the spacesuits. I operated the airlock controls. I've been studying them for weeks, and there was no security code needed to activate them. The airlock depressurised. The outer door opened. I stepped out onto the surface of the moon. And I was lost.'

A glimmer of a smile appeared on his face.

'Lost?' Penelope asked.

'I had been waiting my whole life for that moment. And the feeling . . . it was indescribable. Indescribable, Detective Strand. My whole life, I had never felt so fulfilled. And so I was lost. Lost in the moment.'

The smile vanished.

'I didn't . . . I did not realise . . .'

The tears flowed freely again.

'I did not realise Bobby was struggling. That there was a problem with his suit. Not right away. I had forgotten all about him. When I turned around, he was on his knees, grasping at his throat. I grabbed him immediately, helped him back to the airlock. I knew what was happening but my mind . . .'

He dropped his head into his hands.

'I panicked. I forgot how to operate the airlock. My mind had gone completely blank. I was hitting every key. Punching the control panel. And all the while, Bobby is lying at my feet, suffocating, his face swelling, and I couldn't . . . I failed to . . .'

He lifted his head. His eyes were red. His whole body shaking.

'By the time the door finally closed and the airlock pressurised, it was too late. It was far too late. I tried to learn what had happened. I could see there were error warnings on the backpack life support system but my mind was too confused, too in shock, to decipher them. I . . . I left him there and returned to the penthouse, still wearing my spacesuit. I didn't even remember I had collected a moon rock until hours later, when I finally had the strength to undress. I didn't return the spacesuit until the next day. After I failed to open the staff door – foolishly, with the crowbar – I searched the offices for another master key and found one. There are usually many, one for the head of each department. Freddy caught me bringing the suit down in the broken laundry cart. I returned it to its hook and hoped no one would notice it had been gone. Then returned the key to the office.'

He reached for the moon rock in Penelope's hand, but instead of taking it, closed her fingers around it.

'I am a coward, Detective. I should have woken you all immediately. Informed you of what happened. But I was afraid. I was not thinking clearly. So my plan was to forget it happened. Pretend I did not know. I thought someone would find him in the airlock, assume he had tried to do a solo spacewalk and ran into trouble. When I heard Sasha scream, I thought that was what she saw – his body in the airlock.'

He looked Penelope in the eye.

'I did not move his body. I had nothing to do with that. I was as shocked as the rest of you. And I truly thought Jackson had done it. That it was perhaps some sort of blackmail or extortion or simply a cry for attention. But when Jackson was murdered . . .' He looked in the direction of the security centre and shuddered.

'I truly believed there was someone else in the hotel. I did not think any one of us was capable of killing. The Apollo Group did extensive background checks and psychological profiles on everyone, myself included. It is a requirement, a condition of the trip. They want to confirm everyone visiting is of sound mind. Because if something were to happen . . . well, we've all seen the films.'

With that, he seemed to have run out of things to say, and Penelope decided she could ask her questions.

'Mr Uchida, when did you remove your tracker?'

He shook his head. 'I never had one, but I knew about them. It's meant to be a safety precaution, a simple way to make sure guests can be accounted for at all times. But I refused them, and that request was honoured. That was why I left you the tablet. I was hoping you—'

'*You* left me the tablet?'

He nodded.

'Do you have the rest?'

'No, I don't know what happened to them. When I came to return the master key, the cabinet was open and I took one tablet out but left the rest there. Today, I finally accepted there was no one else here. But admitting to you that I was wrong was too difficult. I hoped you could use it to uncover the responsible party.'

He fell quiet, awaited her verdict.

Penelope opened her hand, looked again at the moon rock, then slipped it into her bag.

'I think whoever moved Bobby's body was planning a murder

the whole time. Just not his. The messages seem to confirm that. And it was only bad luck that Bobby chose the damaged suit. It could have just as easily been you. Or both of you could have chosen uncompromised suits. When the ship arrives, whoever is in charge, whoever investigates this, you need to tell them everything you told us. And you can't let the Apollo Group cover this up. Bobby's and Jackson's families deserve to know the truth.'

He looked her in the eye. 'I swear to you, it will be done.'

'So what now?' Tonya asked. 'We still have a psychopath running around out there who is trying to kill someone and a psychopath somewhere on Earth' – she waved at the door to the communications centre – 'who is waiting for that murder to happen.'

'We should get everyone back together,' Penelope said. 'The killer can't kill if we're all watching them.'

'We could say Uchida confessed to everything,' Tonya said.

'No, the killer will know it's a lie,' Penelope said.

'But we could say the ship has made contact,' Uchida said. 'And that the captain has requested that we gather and await their arrival.'

'It's worth a shot,' Penelope agreed.

With their plan in place, Tonya opened the door. Before they could get to the hotel intercom system, however, Dr Wyss came racing down the main stairs, cradling his left arm.

'Erik?' Penelope asked.

'Oh, thank God,' he cried upon seeing them.

'Erik, what happened?'

'It's . . . it's Charlotte,' he said. 'I think she's done something.'

Day 5

Chapter 41

They got Dr Wyss to the medical bay where, under his instruction, they fitted him with a proper sling.

'All this blood . . .' he said, seeing the jeans and gauze Jackson had left behind.

'We'll explain later,' Penelope said. 'Tell us again what happened.'

He sighed and ran his good hand through his hair then looked up at the ceiling.

'She came to my room. I wasn't going to let her in, but she was insistent. Seemed to be in distress. The first thing I noticed was the blood on her clothes. She kept babbling, mixing German and English. I couldn't get any sense out of her. When I tried to confront her about the blood, she lashed out.'

He adjusted his arm and winced.

'The blood wasn't hers. Couldn't have been. She didn't have any visible injuries. When I tried to get her to leave, she managed to grab my arm and twist it and then she ran off. I have no idea where she is or what she's doing.'

Penelope and Tonya shared a look.

'What is it?' Uchida asked.

'Someone attacked Freddy. We found him at the pool,' Penelope said.

'Is he . . .' Dr Wyss started to ask.

'He's injured, fairly seriously, but he's alive.'

'I should look at him,' he said.

'He's safe and stable for now,' Tonya said. 'We don't want to lead Frau Richter to him.'

'But we need to find her,' Penelope said. 'Did she give any indication as to where she was going?'

'No, she just ran out.'

Penelope pulled the tablet from her bag. 'Was she fighting to go or fighting to stay?'

'Where did you get that?' Dr Wyss asked, seeing the tablet.

'Long story,' she said. 'So Frau Richter – was she trying to stay or trying to go? When you two got into that physical altercation and she hurt your arm?'

'She wanted to stay but I wanted her to go,' he answered.

'But then when she got the upper hand, she ran off anyway?' Penelope asked.

'Yes. I don't know. I suppose injuring me frightened her.'

'Hm. OK.' Penelope opened the Syzygy map. 'All right, so this dot is Sasha. Here in the medical bay is Dr Wyss. Which means this dot here is either Frau Richter or Alison.'

'And that is Alison's room, isn't it?' Tonya asked.

'Frau Richter could have also located and disabled her tracker,' Uchida said.

'Wait. Tracker? What tracker?' Dr Wyss asked. 'Someone is tracking us?'

'Something else we'll explain later,' Penelope said, stuffing the tablet back into her bag. 'What we need to do now is find her.'

Dr Wyss started to get up from the bed.

'I can help,' he said, but stumbled a bit and grabbed his head. 'I'm sorry. My head.'

'Stay here,' Penelope said. 'Rest. The three of us will go look for her.'

Dr Wyss nodded weakly and sat back down.

'As soon as we hear anything, we'll let you know,' Penelope said, and she led Tonya and Uchida from the room.

As soon as the door closed behind them, Penelope used the master key to disable the door as she had done with the communications centre, locking Dr Wyss inside.

'What are you doing?' Uchida asked.

'Who gets dizzy from a bump to the elbow? And that was a bump. It wasn't twisted. Plus, running down those stairs yelling at us didn't make him dizzy but standing up did?'

'Then he is the one?' Uchida asked.

'I don't know. But he certainly wanted to be left alone. Now he'll get what he wants, and we'll know where he is. We had four people unaccounted for. Now it's just three. I think we better find Frau Richter.'

Frau Richter slipped into the wine room and closed the door behind her. It had taken her a long time to locate this place – too long – but she was here now. She had not been before. It was Tonya who'd selected the bottles for their dinner party. Like the journalist had mentioned, it wasn't a cellar but a special climate-controlled room near the main kitchen. Frau Richter was afraid of turning on the light – afraid someone might see – but there was no other way for her to see what she was doing. The room was pitch-black. She took off her jacket and shoved it along the crack at the bottom of the door. That would have to do. She found the light switch and pressed it.

Her eyes had been in darkness long enough for the light to come as a shock. As soon as they adjusted, she began pulling out the various bottles and examining the labels. She had to be right. This all had to do with her. But *why*? It was right there at the tip of her brain, something from the past, long forgotten, that was now trying to scratch its way to the surface. Every time she thought it was in her reach, it vanished again.

She pulled out another bottle, read the label and put it back.

A sound came from the hall.

She froze. Waited to hear it again. Had it been footsteps? A thud? She wasn't sure, but she did not hear it again. Not yet. She continued down the racks.

She hadn't been imagining things. If she found the right bottle, she knew she would remember. She had seen it at dinner, hadn't she? The room had been dim, but she remembered the label. Or had that label only looked similar to what she remembered? There were only a few bottles left to check. Doubt crept up on her.

She wasn't crazy. She wasn't. It was here. She pulled out one more bottle, read the label and smiled.

'Of course!'

She gripped the bottle by the neck and carried it back to the door. She switched off the light first then scooped up her jacket. She opened the door and screamed.

The bottle fell from her hand, but one of the three figures standing before her caught it before it smashed onto the floor.

'Well,' Tonya sighed. 'He was right about the blood.'

Dr Wyss waited until he was sure they were gone, then he leaped up from the bed. The sling fitted well and, while his elbow remained sore, he felt fine otherwise. Now while the others were concerned with Frau Richter, he could sneak back up to his room. Hopefully his story had been enough to keep them away from his room. While they were looking for Charlotte, he could gather his bags and take them to the loading bay.

He pressed the button to open the door. A red light flashed on the keypad. The door remained shut. He took his arm from the sling and pressed his palm against the keypad. The red light flashed, and the door remained shut. He tried again and again and again but each time the red light would flash and the door would remain shut.

Dr Wyss kicked the door and let out a string of the most creative curses he knew in both German and French.

Chapter 42

'I'm telling you, the blood is mine! I suffer from nosebleeds.' Frau Richter sat in a chair in the Sunrise Lounge, Penelope, Tonya and Uchida all facing her.

'You didn't have nosebleeds on the flight here, did you?' Penelope asked. 'Or in the whole time we've been here?'

'How would you know?' Frau Richter crossed her arms.

'Because,' Tonya said, 'you're the type that would use something like that to try and gain sympathy from others.'

Frau Richter scowled at Uchida. 'What are you doing here? You don't even like them.'

'I am not terribly fond of you, either, at present,' he said. 'You had nothing good to say about Mr Nwankwo when we were searching the hotel together.'

'Him?' She looked between them. 'This has to do with him? What's he done now?'

'Nothing,' Penelope said. 'Not that we're aware of. But you've disliked him ever since you set foot on the ship.'

'I told you. I don't like his . . . type.'

'Yes, well,' Tonya said, 'you've made that quite obvious.'

'When was the last time you saw him?' Penelope asked.

Frau Richter crossed her arms. 'In the casino. The same as everyone else.'

'You're sure about that?' Penelope asked.

The woman glared at her. 'Yes.'

'What have you been doing since we found the towels in Freddy's room?'

She looked down at her shirt then back up at Penelope. 'Ah, so that is what this is about? You think I've done something to your little protégé?' She laughed. 'I certainly wanted to. But that was before.'

'Before what?' Penelope asked.

'Before I was certain someone is trying to kill me!'

Tonya rolled her eyes. 'Because you dreamed someone was strangling you the other night?'

'Because I heard you!' She pointed at Uchida. 'You and Sasha were talking. The door to the penthouse hadn't closed all the way. I could hear you. You were talking about murdering a woman.'

'That is ridiculous,' Uchida said.

'Then why has Sasha been in my suite?' Frau Richter dug into the pocket of her dressing gown. She held up what she'd retrieved – a paper origami stork.

'A bird?' Tonya asked.

'A stork,' Frau Richter clarified.

'And you took this to mean someone wants to kill you?' Penelope asked.

'I didn't know what it meant at first. I didn't even realise it wasn't something from the hotel. I thought that the staff had left it there, like that cruise line that folds towels into the shapes of animals. I threw it away. Then later I returned to my suite and it was back. Someone had taken it from the bin and placed it on the centre of the table in my room, pointed its face towards the door so that it was facing me when I came in. So that I knew it was intentional. And it certainly wasn't housekeeping. That meant someone had been able to access my room without permission and they intended this stork to mean something. I threw it away again. But every time I've returned to my suite, it's been there. I've received dozens.'

'Why do you think it was Sasha?' Penelope asked.

'Because we had an argument the first night. After the dinner party. She cornered me in the hall, tried to tell me how sorry she was about my husband, but the way she said it' – Frau Richter shook her head. – 'she was taunting me. I knew she was. She wanted to distract me. To make me suspect this had something to do with my husband. Somehow, she got into my suite, kept moving that stork around. Kept leaving more. Moved my wedding ring from where I had left it.'

'So what does the stork mean?' Penelope asked. 'Why would she leave them for you?'

'I didn't know.'

'Didn't? So you do now?'

Frau Richter looked down. 'I have a memory from a long time ago. I've been trying to place it.' She looked over at the bottle of wine she'd found. It now sat on a table near Uchida. 'That's why I went to the wine room. We had a bottle of that the other night at dinner, before Jackson's murder. The label was vaguely familiar, but I did not think on it much until the stork reappeared in my suite.'

Uchida picked up the bottle. 'Belle Cigogne Wine.'

'It's from the Alsace wine region, specifically a small French village near the German border. A village that is an *elsässiches storkadorf*.'

'A what now?' Tonya asked.

'It means storks live in the village, specifically white storks.' She nodded to the paper stork in Penelope's hand.

'What's your connection to the village?' Penelope asked.

'I handled a few cases there early in my career, before I moved to the Rhine Valley. But it was over twenty years ago. So much has happened to me since then. I can't recall anything specific.'

Penelope crossed her arms. 'If Sasha's leaving you threatening paper storks, then she knows exactly why she's doing it.'

'That's why I need to speak with her,' she said. 'I didn't think anything of it at the time, but she sat next to me at that dinner. She began to pour herself a glass of that wine, but when she saw the label, she stopped. I thought perhaps she simply didn't like that brand. But now, now I think she has some sort of connection that place.'

As Frau Richter spoke, blood suddenly fell from her nose and onto her shirt, overlaying the spots of dried blood that were there previously.

'Ah.' She leaned forward and pinched her nose. Penelope handed her a cloth napkin from a nearby table. 'See? Nosebleeds.'

Many people instinctively tilted their head back with a nosebleed, but this resulted in swallowing the blood. Leaning forward was what you were supposed to do, and what regular sufferers of nosebleeds knew.

'It happens mostly in times of stress,' Frau Richter said through her pinched nose. Penelope handed her another cloth napkin. 'I was not stressed on the flight. I've only been stressed since learning someone wants to kill me.'

'We don't know they want to kill you,' Penelope said. 'But they certainly want something from you.' She looked at Tonya and Uchida. 'Let's go and speak to Sasha.'

'What about her?' Tonya asked, nodding at Frau Richter.

'What do you mean what about me?' she sneered.

'She'll come along,' Penelope said. 'It'll be a group effort.'

The muzak version of 'Fly Me to the Moon' played in the lift as the group of four rode it up the penthouse.

'I swear to God,' Tonya said, 'if I have to hear that bloody song one more time—'

'Please don't say you'll kill someone,' Penelope cut in. 'That's sort of what we're trying to prevent.'

'Oh, she's funny now,' Frau Richter said, still dabbing the napkin to her nose. 'When did you get funny?'

The door dinged and slid open.

They gathered at the door to the penthouse. Uchida knocked.

'Sasha, it's me. I apologise for taking so long. Detective Strand and Ms Burton are with me.'

The view on the security system was limited, so Penelope and Tonya both said hello to prove they were there.

'What about me?' Frau Richter said.

'Frau Richter is here, too,' he said.

No answer.

'Sasha?' He knocked again, then used his palm to unlock the door.

The penthouse was empty. They called out Sasha's name, checked the bathroom and the upper floor, but there was no sign of her. Penelope was pulling out the tablet to check the map when Tonya pointed to something near the couch.

'Look,' she said, picking up a small microchip.

'Her tracker,' Penelope said.

'Tracker?' Frau Richter asked. 'What tracker?'

'We'll explain later,' Tonya said.

'What about Sasha?' Uchida asked. 'Where did she go?'

'Let's check her room,' Penelope said.

They took the lift back down.

Sasha's door was shut. No one answered it when they knocked, so Penelope opened it with the master key. She called Sasha's name after she opened the door, but the room was silent.

Sasha's suite looked the same as the last time Penelope saw it. As Frau Richter plopped herself into a chair and Tonya and Uchida searched other parts of the room, Penelope noticed something new. Sasha's desk drawer was slightly ajar. She opened it. When she saw what was inside, she took it out and called to the others.

'A paper stork,' Tonya said.

Penelope unfolded it. 'On her own monogrammed paper.'

Sasha's name was printed across the top, underneath the Hotel Artemis logo. Frau Richter removed her paper stork and unfolded it.

'I never thought to . . .' she said quietly. She read the name then showed it to the others – 'Sasha Eris'.

'But Sasha's an intelligent woman,' Tonya said. 'If she meant to threaten you, why use paper printed with her own name?'

Uchida lowered himself to a chair.

'There is something I should tell you,' he said. 'Sasha only told me this today. Frau Richter was somewhat correct in what she overheard. Sasha said that when she was younger, she was responsible for the death of a woman. A man with whom she'd had an affair – his wife discovered their tryst. The couple divorced, but the man got everything. The wife was left with nothing, not even the children. A few years after the divorce, the wife—'

'Killed herself,' Frau Richter said. 'I remember now. It was one of my earliest cases. The husband had an airtight prenuptial agreement. There wasn't much I needed to do. And the wife was unstable – setting fire to the vineyards, to the house, when the children were inside. She claimed she hadn't known the children were there, but that was more than enough to grant the husband full custody.'

'That's what you couldn't remember?' Penelope said. 'That seems like it would be hard to forget.'

'I told you it was over twenty years ago! And setting property on fire is hardly the craziest act a client of mine has done. Besides the suicide wasn't until years later. I saw it only briefly in the paper.'

'Right, so all of this remembering is wonderful,' Tonya snapped. 'But where is Sasha now?'

'And where is Alison?' Penelope asked.

Alison hurried down the service corridor that ran behind the hotel shop. The ship would be here soon enough. Then she'd be flying home, and three days later they'd be on Earth. She'd figure out what to do then.

The entrance to the shop's stockroom was just ahead of her. She'd helped Dr Wyss break in that first night after she'd discovered his plan to loot what he could and resell it back home. She needed nicotine to help her think clearly and, with her cigarettes gone, she needed more gum. She'd seen the cases of nicotine gum – which was sold in the shop – on her earlier trips. Alison looked around carefully to make sure there was no one around. Then she hurried into the room and closed the door behind her. With a sigh of relief, she flicked on the light and started prising open the crate.

A noise sounded behind her. Alison spun around. She was no longer alone.

Sasha stood in the doorway, a knife in her hands.

'I told you we need to talk about Eguisheim.'

Chapter 43

'The name of the village,' Frau Richter said. 'Eguisheim. And the winemaker is Johannes Vogel. He's even more successful now than when the divorce occurred.'

'This wine is a favourite of several members of the Apollo Group board,' said Uchida.

'So someone on the board possibly arranged this?' Penelope asked.

'To what end? Get revenge on Frau Richter for something that happened twenty years ago?' Tonya asked.

'Did this woman have a sibling or something?' Penelope asked.

'I don't know,' Frau Richter said. 'She wasn't my client. The husband was. I don't remember much about her. The only family I'm certain she had were the children.'

'We're missing something,' Penelope said. 'This is all far too elaborate just for someone to kill Frau Richter. No offence.'

The woman grunted.

'But, really, think of the money that must have gone into organising this. This is serious vindictive behaviour. How old were the children?' she asked.

'I don't know exactly. Young? The oldest was maybe eight or ten? The younger about five or six?' Frau Richter recalled.

'Could one of them now be a board member?' Penelope asked Uchida.

'No, everyone on the board is in their forties or older.'

Penelope nodded. 'I better go check on Freddy. You should all look for Sasha and Alison. If you find either of them, bring them to the manager's office. Use the intercom system at the front desk if you need to call me. And leave Dr Wyss locked in the medical bay for now.' She handed Tonya the second master key.

'Why is Dr Wyss locked in the medical bay?' Frau Richter asked.

'For being shifty,' Tonya answered.

'Shifty?'

'He says you assaulted him.'

'I never touched him!' Frau Richter scoffed.

'See? Shifty.'

Penelope grabbed her bag. 'If you see Sasha just be careful. We don't know what sort of state she's in right now. All right?'

They all nodded.

Penelope quietly let herself into the suite and closed the door behind her. When she rounded the corner into the main part of the suite, she froze. Freddy wasn't on the couch. Before she could further investigate, she heard the vacuum-suck of the toilet flushing.

'Freddy?'

A moment later, he appeared in the doorway of the bathroom, holding a towel to the back of his head. He gave no indication he'd heard Penelope call his name and, when he saw her, he froze in fear.

'Freddy, you're awake!'

'Am I not supposed to be?' he asked, somewhat suspicious.

'You've been unconscious for hours. Tonya and I were—'

'You and Tonya?' he asked.

'Yes. We're the ones who found you. You were unconscious at the pool. Someone attacked you.'

'I didn't think you and Tonya were getting along,' he said. 'I heard you arguing. Outside my room . . . I heard . . .' He closed his eyes and seemed a bit dizzy.

Penelope hurried to his side and helped him to the nearest chair. Before she could ask him how he was feeling, he continued talking.

'You were all in my room. You saw the towels. Tonya thought I was the killer.'

'She doesn't think that now.'

Freddy tried to nod, but it clearly pained him and he stopped.

'What happened?' he asked, prodding the back of his head.

'A lot, actually.' She gave him the short version of Uchida leaving her the tablet, the tracking devices, of using that information to trace Freddy to the pool. 'We didn't see who attacked you,' she said. 'You were already on the ground by then. We brought you here to hide you. The ship should be here late tomorrow. If nothing else, we were hoping to keep you safe until then.'

Freddy listened intently, never interrupting as she spoke. When she'd finished, he remained silent. Penelope couldn't tell if he was simply trying to take it all in or fighting being sick or a combination of both. She missed his usual loquaciousness.

'What's the last thing you remember?' She waited patiently for his response.

'Leaving the casino,' he said. 'I went to my room to get something, and I was on my way back when I heard all of you. I was about to ask what was going on when I heard what you'd found. How everyone thought I was the killer. I didn't want to be rounded up like Jackson, so I hid. Can I have some water?'

Penelope fetched him a cup. He took a few sips before continuing. He looked a little better, though, his colour returning.

'I don't know how I ended up by the pool. I wanted to keep out of sight until the ship arrived. I thought I'd have better luck explaining what was happening to the crew or whoever than pleading my case with you guys. But' – he rubbed his head – 'I remember running. Running away. And feeling scared. But I don't remember getting attacked.'

'So you didn't see who it was?'

'I don't remember seeing who it was, but I might've. And I have a pretty good guess.'

'Who?' Penelope asked, when he didn't say the name right away. Freddy looked at the towel he held, spotted with his own blood.

'Detective Strand, I owe you an apology. Frau Richter was right about one thing. Not the strangling thing! I didn't do that. But I did lie. I should've told you – at least you – right away. I did talk to Jackson.' He closed his eyes as if in pain, but Penelope didn't know if it was internal or external.

'Did he tell you anything?' she asked.

Freddy nodded. She waited for him to continue.

'He asked if I could help him and I said I would, but before I could, he was dead. I promised him but . . .' Freddy dropped his head into his hands. She could hear him crying. Penelope stood up and put her arms around him, hugged him while he let his emotions out.

When he had stopped crying, he thanked her, went to wipe his face on the towel, but stopped when he saw the blood. Penelope fetched him another towel from the bathroom.

'You can still help him,' she said, handing him the clean towel. 'Tell me what he told you.'

He nodded again, wincing less.

'When I went to him, he didn't want to say anything at first. He thought you'd sent me. But I told him you had no idea I was there. He must have believed me because once he started talking, he wouldn't stop. He kept saying he was innocent. That he hadn't done anything but he didn't know who he could trust. He made me promise that whatever he told me, I would keep it to myself.'

'If he said he didn't trust anyone, why did he trust you?' Penelope asked.

'I'll get to that. But the first thing I asked him was where the blood had come from. He pulled up his pants and showed me the cut on his leg. Gross looking. He said the blood was his and he got hurt running away from Bobby's murderer.'

'I've seen the cut,' Penelope confirmed. 'Tonya and I found where he'd hurt himself. So he saw the murderer?' She hadn't yet told Freddy about Uchida's involvement.

Freddy nodded. 'Yeah. He saw her.'

'Her? How did he know it was a *her*?'

'Because he saw her moving Bobby's body – hoisting it into the laundry cart.'

'So he didn't witness the actual murder but the aftermath?' she clarified.

'That's what he said. He said he'd been stumbling around the hotel, and came across her flipping a body into a laundry cart. He didn't see whose body it was. He didn't know it was Bobby until we told him, accused him, the next morning. But he saw the feet. He knew it was a dead body.'

'Who did he see moving the body?' she asked.

'Well, this is why he didn't trust you. The woman was wearing the Hotel Artemis sweatpants and sweatshirt they gave us, but she had the hood up. So he could tell it was one of the women from her height and body shape, and he could hear her grunting from the effort of moving the body. But he didn't know which of the women it was, so he didn't trust any of you. And he told me I shouldn't, either.'

'So he saw a woman moving a body, panicked and hurt himself, and decided not to tell me what he saw because he didn't know who exactly was responsible.'

Freddy nodded. 'He wanted to wait until the ship arrived. He didn't want the murderer to know he was a witness and thought that since we had decided to lock him up, he was as safe there as he was anywhere. I told him I could try to find out more. He said I should worry more about protecting myself. Made me promise that I wouldn't tell anyone what he'd told me. I said I would and that I'd bring him any updates. But before I learned anything useful he was . . .' Freddy couldn't finish his sentence.

'I got a little paranoid then,' he said. 'That Jackson had been right and I couldn't trust even you or Tonya, which is why I denied it when you asked me if I'd spoken to him. I thought I'd do my own investigation. I went back to his body on my own. But the blood . . . there was so much and I slipped . . .' He grimaced at the memory. 'I've never seen that much at once. I went back to my room to clean myself up. That's where the blood you found came from. I thought about telling you then what I'd learned, but I still wasn't sure. Not until the casino. That's when I knew—'

'Hang on,' Penelope interrupted. 'What did you find?'

'I found something with Jackson's body. I collected it as evidence and hid it in my room. When we were all in the casino together, that's when I realised who it belonged to. I ran back to my room to get it and, well, I already told you the rest.' He reached into the pocket of his trousers and handed her a little plastic bag.

The intercom system crackled. Tonya's voice sounded over the speakers.

'*Detective Strand, get to the airlock – now.*'

Penelope didn't have to ask which one.

Chapter 44

Chaos greeted Penelope at the airlock. Alison was bleeding from a split lip while Tonya was trying to offer her a towel, but Alison kept pushing it away. Uchida was asking her what had happened and where Sasha was, on the verge of yelling, while Frau Richter was also yelling, asking questions like, 'What do you know? How long have you known it?' Penelope was glad they had Dr Wyss locked in the medical bay. It was one less person she had to deal with.

She tried to whistle the way she did for her parents' dogs, but the recirculated air made her lips too dry. She settled for shouting 'Oi!' and clapping her hands.

'What is going on?' she demanded. 'What happened?'

'We went looking for Sasha and Alison,' Tonya said. 'We heard screaming and found Alison here bleeding.'

'She went crazy!' Alison shouted then winced and prodded her injured lip. Tonya offered her the towel again and, this time, Alison took it. 'She tried to shove me into the airlock.'

Penelope held up her hands. 'Start from the beginning. When did you first see her?'

Alison took a deep breath. 'I left my room to look for more

nicotine gum. I figured there had to be more somewhere. Sasha must have followed me or something while I was searching. Somehow, she knew where I was. Came up right behind me with a knife.'

Tonya nodded at Alison's feet. She was wearing the hotel-assigned footwear.

'The knife was one of those big ones from the kitchen. She made me go with her. She was jabbering the whole time.'

'What was she saying?' Penelope asked.

'I don't know. Most of it didn't make sense. Things about death and guilt. Some religious nonsense. And she mentioned a placed called Eguisheim?'

'Then what happened?' Penelope asked.

'She led me here. Said I had to "atone for my sins" and then she tried to shove me into the airlock. I fought her off but she punched me in the process.' She prodded the lip again.

'What about the knife?'

Alison nodded to the airlock. 'It ended up in there.'

Penelope looked through the viewing window. A large butcher's knife was lying on the floor.

'Where did she go?' Penelope asked.

'I don't know. I was bleeding by this point. She ran off, I guess. She's not very strong. Once she lost the knife, I had the upper hand.'

Penelope nodded.

'We need to find her,' Uchida said. 'She is clearly unwell. She may cause herself harm.'

'We can split up,' Tonya said. 'If we—'

Penelope held up her hand.

'Alison,' she said, 'do you know anything about this?'

From her pocket, she pulled out a paper stork. Alison's eyes went wide.

'I found one of those in my room! I thought the hotel had left it. And then I kept finding more. It seemed like every time I left and came back, there was another one.'

Penelope nodded. 'And you said Sasha mentioned Eguisheim?'

'Yeah, she kept saying she wanted to talk about it, but I have no idea what she was on about. I don't know what it is.'

'You don't remember the place you were born?' Penelope asked.

A hush fell over the group. Penelope looked at Alison. Alison glanced at the others.

'I'm sorry. I don't . . .'

'The file on you, that had been prepared for Bobby as part of the reality show ruse, it listed your birthplace as Germany. But you told me you were born in France. Eguisheim is a German word, but the village is located in France. Whoever prepared that false file on you got it wrong, either intentionally or on purpose, but you – accidentally or not – told me the truth. And then you complained about not having a good sense of smell or taste because you smoke too much, but you were *very* particular about the vintage of wine selected for dinner. Made a big show of sniffing and sampling it. Made sure Sasha saw the bottle.'

'I don't know what you're implying,' Alison said.

'Jackson wouldn't tell you what he saw, would he?'

Alison went pale. 'I never spoke to Jackson. I mean, not after we caught him and put him in the cell. I never saw him again until . . . until you showed us his body.'

'And you'd swear to that?'

'Yes.'

'On your father's life?'

'Of course.'

'On your mother's?'

Alison said nothing.

Penelope called over her shoulder. 'Freddy?'

Freddy appeared from around the corner. He was tired from standing, but Penelope saw how pleased he was to see Tonya smiling at him.

'Freddy, could you hand me the evidence you collected from Jackson's crime scene, please?'

'Certainly, Detective.'

He reached into his pocket and retrieved the small plastic bag, which he handed to Penelope.

'This is yours, isn't it?' Penelope held up the plastic bag.

It contained a bloodstained cigarette butt.

'Did it fall out of your pocket when you were garrotting him with the piano wire or were you stupid enough to smoke a cigarette in there before or after you killed him? I didn't notice any ash, but maybe it's just hidden by all the blood.'

Penelope kept the bag raised. Alison said nothing.

'That's why Freddy left the casino. When you were drunk enough to light up a cigarette, forgetting where you were. Or was that intentional? Did you want us to think that cigarettes were the only thing you were hiding so we wouldn't suspect you of more? Not realising you had left a cigarette butt with a dead body? Freddy knew it was you as soon as he saw you smoking and he went to get this. But by the time he found us, we had already decided he was to blame, so he stayed hidden. But you knew he must've known something. So you used a tablet that you stole from Dr Wyss to track him down and attacked him. You didn't have time to make sure he was dead, though, because Tonya and I were too close behind. So you left him and hoped for the best.'

Penelope finally lowered the bag.

'Where is Sasha?'

Alison glared at her. Then, with an overly dramatic sigh, she leaned against the wall and crossed her arms.

'It was supposed to be a lot simpler than this. We were all going to enjoy our two-week holiday, assume we were being recorded for a TV show, and then Frau Richter and Sasha were going to have some sort of altercation, resulting in Sasha's tragic death before our return to Earth. I've tried my best to stoke the paranoia between them. Even pretended to strangle Frau Richter last night. I thought with her anger management problem that would be enough. She did used to hit her husband. But she was so hung up on Freddy. Racists, God.' She rolled her eyes. 'But even if I couldn't get Frau Richter to kill Sasha, I was going to ensure it looked like she did. But there is no greater fallacy than man's hubris, is there?' She looked at Uchida, who could not keep her gaze.

'Oh no, the billionaire and the washed-up actor decided they didn't have to play by the rules. They chose to go on a little spacewalk of their own, while intoxicated, and one of them – surprise, surprise – ended up dead. I watched it happen on the monitors in the security centre. Which I locked down right after so no one else could see the footage. See, I realised I was going to have to work much faster than I originally intended.

As soon as you all found Bobby dead, the emergency signal would be activated. We'd all get sent home. A second accidental death would probably look too suspicious, but make Bobby's death look like murder? Put everyone on edge? Make us all suspect one another? Maybe I wouldn't have to kill anyone at all. Maybe I could get one of you to do it for me.'

'Where is Sasha?' Penelope asked again.

'Hang on. I'm getting to that. See, I tricked Sasha into deactivating the emergency signal the first time. Left her some old letters from my father and added a few instructions of my own. Amazing what a few anonymous threats can do to a person who's already being stalked. I can thank my father for that at least. That bought me a little extra time. Stole some stationery a few times from her room, too, to leave Frau Richter those lovely little storks Sasha once taught me how to make.'

'Tell us where Sasha is.'

'Don't you want to hear about Jackson? Now, I didn't want to kill him, but he'd obviously seen something, you're right about that. I found his trail of blood in the hall, figured he must've injured himself. I knew he must've seen me and not Mr Uchida because I'd been watching the cameras when Bobby died and, at that time, Jackson was passed out on the opposite side of the hotel. So if he saw anything that scared him, it must've been me moving the body. I didn't need a witness and I didn't want him screaming, so I . . .' She shrugged. 'It was actually very easy. My benefactor made sure my biometric data was given access to every room in the hotel. I have my own master key right here.'

She wiggled her fingers.

'I stripped Bobby out of the spacesuit and used the laundry

cart to move him, but a wheel broke when I tried to move him through the kitchen. I had to hide the cart in the pantry because Freddy was passed out in the restaurant. So I had to wait until he woke up and left. Did you like the flag? I thought it was a nice touch. I actually wasn't going to leave a flag at first but then I found some paint in a cupboard when I was returning the laundry cart and the sheets were right there. Thought it would add a little spice to everyone's paranoia. Quite hard to shove it in there though. I admit I maybe did go too far with that.'

'But why?' Frau Richter asked. 'Why do you want Sasha dead? Why did you try to implicate me?'

'No,' Penelope said. 'There's time for those questions later. She's stalling. Where is Sasha? What did you do to her?'

Alison put on an expression of mock innocence. 'Me? I haven't done anything.'

She examined her fingernails. 'Sasha is guilty enough. Ruining a family like that. Separating a mother from her children. Making a woman's life so miserable, she would rather be dead than carry on.'

'You're his daughter,' Penelope said. 'Johannes Vogel's daughter. Sasha had an affair with your father.'

'Vogel means bird,' Frau Richter said. 'You changed your name to Crane.'

'Father has never let us forget the affair. Even after our mother killed herself, he cared nothing for her. It was always dear Sasha, poor Sasha. His true love who had abandoned him.' She no longer tried to hide the hate in her voice. 'He's obsessed with her. Still! Follows her career. Tried to get in touch with her. And he'll never move on. He'll never properly grieve for his own, true wife until she's gone.'

'Your mother tried to burn you alive,' Penelope said.

'No! She didn't know we were there. She thought we were with our grandparents.'

'Where is Sasha?' Penelope repeated. 'Is she still alive?'

'Well, it depends on how much courage she has,' Alison said.

'Courage?'

'Courage like my mother. Courage to end her misery.' Alison looked out the airlock window. 'Sasha knows how much she's hurt my family. She told me so. That's why she came to me and wanted to talk. So we talked. I'm a very good psychologist, you know, even if I don't practice. Sasha knows she needs to make amends, so she's going to finally do what she's contemplated so many times before. It's the only way for her to atone.'

Penelope followed Alison's gaze.

'I wonder how far she's walked by now. Those spacesuits only hold so much air, you know?'

Chapter 45

With five against one, it wasn't difficult to detain Alison. They tied her wrists and ankles with cable ties from the nearest utility closet and Tonya kept a roll of duct tape around her wrist just in case. Alison didn't seem much interested in running, though, now that she'd achieved what she had set out to do. As she sat in the corridor outside the airlock with Frau Richter and Tonya guarding her, Penelope suited up.

Penelope had hidden all four spacesuits in a nearby supply cupboard, making sure to keep Bobby's faulty suit separate from the other three. However, Alison had known the location of the hotel's additional suits and had directed Sasha to them. Penelope suspected Alison's original plans for Sasha's intended murder involved the spacesuits and that the suit Bobby had chosen may not have just been faulty but purposely sabotaged. There was no time to ask her now, though. Not if she wanted to reach Sasha in time.

Her hands shook as she pulled on the gloves. If she had eaten full meals over the last twenty-four hours, she would be vomiting them back up now. Fortunately, she hadn't had much of an appetite. That didn't stop her stomach from doing somersaults or keep the sweat from breaking out on her face.

A shadow appeared over her as she secured the second glove and locked it into place.

Uchida stood beside her, fully dressed in a spacesuit, the helmet tucked under his arm.

'You don't need to do this,' Penelope said.

'Neither do you,' he said. 'And you shouldn't go alone.'

'But Tonya or Freddy could—'

'Ms Burton is doing an excellent job handling Professor Crane. And Mr Nwankwo remains injured.'

'We could get Dr Wyss out of the medical bay. Whatever he was up to, it didn't involve Alison or—'

Uchida held up his hand. 'Detective Strand, I appreciate what you are trying to do. That you would take my personal feelings into account even after I . . .' He shook his head. 'But this is something I must do, and not only because I care for Sasha. I will explain later, but I am as much to blame for all of this as Alison, and I must take responsibility.'

Penelope paused. 'You know who Alison's benefactor is, don't you?'

Uchida handed Penelope a helmet. 'As I said, I will explain. But after we find Sasha. Are you ready, Detective?'

Penelope's hand continued to shake as she took the helmet from him.

'I have to be,' she said.

Penelope had never been snorkelling or scuba diving. She had never jumped out of a plane or gone zip-lining. Whenever she crossed the Channel, she stayed inside the ferry with her eyes closed, and she never took the Eurostar because she shouldn't bear the thought of being underwater for any length of time, even though most of the journey was above ground. She took a train instead of a plane when she could. She had yet to visit her brother in the States because crossing the Atlantic by either air or sea had seemed too risky. No unnecessary risk. This had been her life's motto for as long as she could remember.

And now she was securing the helmet of a spacesuit to her head. Now she was standing in an airlock. Now all the air was about to be removed from her atmosphere. The atmosphere, itself, was about to be taken away. She hadn't seen Bobby die, but she had seen his lifeless face in the restaurant, had heard Uchida's description of what happened. She remembered what she'd read on the internet. She could picture everything. She closed her eyes. No one would blame her if she changed her mind. If she allowed Uchida to go after Sasha alone. They would understand why she didn't want to expose herself to an unnecessary risk.

But this wasn't an unnecessary risk. Sasha's life was at stake.

Penelope opened her eyes.

She and Uchida did the final checks on their equipment. Everything was ready to go.

It was not just her hands now. Her entire body was trembling. Her breaths came in short, rapid bursts. Her vision blurred.

'Ready?' he asked.

She took two deep breaths before answering. 'Do it.'

Uchida operated the controls and then Penelope could feel the air around her being removed. Even though she was breathing the oxygen provided by her suit, her brain told her to panic. Her brain told her the air was running out.

Uchida squeezed her shoulder.

'Breathe normally,' he said, his voice staticky over the suits' radio system.

She nodded and tried. It was easier once the airlock had depressurised and everything around her had stilled. A light turned from red to green. The doors in front of her slid open.

There at her feet was the moon. The barriers between them removed.

The spacesuit covered every inch of her. The shield of glass covered her face. But it was so different from being contained inside a structure made of steel and glass. She looked at the grey dusty ground in front of her. At first, she couldn't move. Her body, still shaking, was frozen to the spot. Fight or flight – it couldn't decide.

She forced herself to think of Sasha – Sasha out here somewhere, alone, intending to harm herself. She thought of Timothy Bevan, who had felt equally alone, ostracised, and had taken his life because of it. Because Penelope hadn't done her job well enough. She thought of his body on the gurney by the river.

Penelope made her body take the first step.

The ground was both harder and softer than she imagined. Her space boots sank into the moon dust about an inch before hitting firm ground. When she looked towards the sun, the moon's surface appeared light brown, but the surface in the shadows appeared grey. It reminded her a bit of the rocky cliffs she and her brother had walked along as children on their trips to the seaside. If she kept her eyes on the ground, she could almost pretend this was just another cliff. But she looked up into the infinite stars, infinite space. There was nothing between her and those stars except distance. Straight ahead, there was Earth, blue and shining.

Something dripped on her cheeks and she panicked, thinking her suit had sprung some sort of leak even though it was impossible for any liquid to get in. But they were only tears. She had started crying without realising it.

Uchida stepped up beside her. 'I know,' he said.

'Let's find her.' Penelope stepped forward.

Locating Sasha would not be a problem. With no wind to blow them away, her tracks remained imprinted on the moon's surface – a solo pair that went straight from the airlock towards the moon's horizon – yet it was difficult to tell how far she had gone. Penelope was having trouble gauging distances. But Sasha's single pair of footprints emerged from a tangled mess left from Uchida and Bobby's ill-fated excursion. Penelope didn't need to see Uchida's face to know he was reliving that moment. Though she knew he wouldn't feel the comfort of her touch, she squeezed his shoulder.

'Straight ahead,' she said.

He nodded.

Together they followed Sasha's prints. No, she would not be difficult to find. The only question was whether or not they would reach in her time. The silence stretched between them like the distance between the stars. As soon as they started moving, judging distances became easier. She tried to only focus on Sasha and on following the footprints she had left behind. But it was difficult, the strange differences she hadn't considered between walking on Earth or in the hotel and walking on the surface of the moon. She asked Uchida if he was experiencing the same issue with his perception.

'Parallax displacement,' he said. 'Because the moon lacks an atmospheric haze, it becomes difficult for our eyes to distinguish distances when we stand still. When we move, our brains can process how much we've moved from one distance to another – that is parallax displacement.'

'I didn't read about that,' she said. 'Just about how space will rip the air out of our lungs. How our bodies would freeze and not decay.'

'Yes, there is that, too.'

Talking helped Penelope not shake as much inside her suit. Her breathing felt more normal. So she kept talking.

'So my selection,' Penelope said, 'for this trip – I really was chosen? I really did win?'

'As far as I am aware. Although it appears I was not aware of as much as I thought I was.'

'I never win anything,' she said.

'Then allow me to say congratulations.'

'You know, I was thinking of asking for my money back.'

'I could possibly arrange another trip for you.'

'Let's not get ahead of ourselves. I still need to survive the flight home.'

Talking distracted her from where she actually was and what she was doing. The air in her suit was fine. She was fine. Sasha's trail curved to the right. They followed it.

'Did they actually read the essays?' Penelope asked.

'What essays?'

'I guess you didn't have to write one. It was the last part of the contest application. A five-hundred-word essay on why you should be given the opportunity to experience the Hotel Artemis.'

'I see. I don't know. Possibly. It could have been a useful way to weed out those with ill intentions.'

'Fat lot of good it did then,' she said.

They were going uphill now. She always thought of the moon as mostly flat with some bumps and ridges, but those bumps and ridges she could see from Earth were actually miles high and miles wide. Sasha's feet led them up what Penelope would consider a steep hill.

'What would you have written?' she asked.

'I was never a good writer. Probably I would say some words about dreams and exploration. Fulfilling a childish wonder. Most likely I would have passed on these ideas to someone who could express them well and paid them to write it for me.'

They were almost at the top of the hill now. Penelope glanced over her shoulder and could see the hotel glowing in the distance. It made her dizzy. She closed her eyes, took a breath and continued upwards.

'What did you write?' he asked.

'Just a sentence, actually. I mean, the application did say the maximum was five-hundred words, not the minimum.'

They were almost at the crest of the hill now. Uchida reached it first then offered his hand to help her up. She hadn't realised she'd been slowing down, that her body was trying to make her stop.

'And what was the sentence?' he asked.

Penelope took his hand.

'"Because it scares me",' she said.

'I believe, technically, that is a sentence fragment.'

Penelope smiled but stopped.

There, on the rocks a few metres ahead, a lone figure in a spacesuit sat at the edge of a wide crater.

Sasha was alive, looking up at the stars, gently turning her head to take in the view. If she noticed them, she gave no sign. They approached slowly. Penelope could tell from a light on Sasha's suit that she had her communications device switched off. No matter if they called out her name. Sasha wouldn't hear them.

As they approached, Sasha remained seated but looked down into the crater. Penelope saw the way her gloves gripped the rock she sat on, but she couldn't tell if Sasha was gripping the rock to keep herself seated or preparing to push herself up.

Sasha looked away from the crater and noticed them. She jumped to her feet, her movements slowed by the lack of gravity. Uchida stepped forward, his arms held up to indicate he intended no harm. Penelope stayed back.

'Hello, Sasha,' he said.

Sasha searched a moment for the correct button then turned on her radio.

'Please leave me alone.'

'Detective Strand and I did not venture all the way out here to allow you to do this.'

'It's not up to you, what I'm allowed to do,' Sasha said.

Penelope stepped forward. 'Sasha, we've spoken to Alison. We know what happened in the past. Between you and her father.'

Sasha looked away. Penelope could see that the crater was miles wide and miles deep. If Sasha stepped into it, she'd float into that empty space, out of reach.

'How did you know it was her?' Penelope asked.

'The stork. I taught her how to make those storks when she was a child. I used to babysit her and her brother. She loved making those storks with me. As soon as I saw it, I realised that one of the children was here. Alison was the only one who was the right age.'

Penelope took a step closer.

'We know she killed Jackson. We know it was her plan to kill you, too. But we're not going to let her do that.'

Sasha took another step towards the crater. 'When I realised who Alison was, it finally made sense. Why I was brought here. I thought I didn't deserve to be here, but I do. Because I can remain here. Up here, alone, where I'll never hurt anyone again.' She looked up at the stars. 'I dedicated my life to building churches because I thought bringing beauty and tranquillity and sanctity into the world helped bring others peace. But this was just another example of my own pride. To really help others, I need to stay away from them.'

Uchida stepped forward. 'Sasha, that is not true! You are a good person. A kind person. Alison has only wanted to convince you of these things because of her anger.'

'Her anger is justified,' Sasha said.

'You did not kill her mother any more than her father did. Her mother made her own choices, and if Alison cannot accept that, she must deal with it. Not you.'

'But my choices destroyed her family,' Sasha said. 'I could blame it on being young and stupid, but that doesn't make up for the fact that I was wrong and that the choices I made hurt people.'

'But it also doesn't mean that you have to die,' Penelope said. 'You want to atone for what happened, I understand. And maybe building churches wasn't the way. But there might be something else. Something that allows you to contribute to the world instead of subtracting yourself from it.'

Sasha looked into the crater.

'We all make foolish mistakes,' Uchida said. 'Foolish, terrible mistakes that can result in terrible consequences. But it is hubris that makes us believe ending our lives is the appropriate solution.'

'It is not hubris,' Sasha said, 'if it is what is owed.'

'It's my fault Bobby is dead,' Uchida said.

For the first time, Sasha seemed to snap out of her own world. Alison had clearly not revealed this information.

'We were drunk and careless and because of that he died out here. My mother was right. Like my father, my hubris is my downfall. But if I end my life, I will have no opportunity to make amends to Bobby's family. I must have the courage to accept the consequences of my actions.'

'I've tried for twenty years,' Sasha said. 'Twenty years I've tried to make up for what I did and what good has it done?'

She took a step back. Her foot slipped on the edge of the crater. She started to fall. Without thinking, Penelope leaped forward, floating in space, and grabbed her wrist as Sasha fell backwards. But Penelope's feet were not anchored to the ground. The weight of Sasha's movement pulled Penelope towards the crater, too. They would both float into the emptiness until the oxygen ran out.

Then something grabbed her foot and held. Uchida yanked Penelope's body down to the moon's surface. She still held Sasha's wrist and Sasha kept drifting towards the crater, but Penelope was now stationary. Penelope reached with her other arm and got a firmer grip on her.

'Pull!' she shouted.

Uchida dragged her back, her stomach scraping against the rocky ground.

When Sasha was half out of the crater, Uchida let go of Penelope's ankle and hurried forward to grab Sasha's other arm. Together, they pulled her the rest of the way out. Uchida hugged her close.

'There are other ways. Don't let her spite be the end of you. Look.' He pointed to the stars. 'Look at them all, Sasha. Your light belongs in this world, too.'

Chapter 46

The ship was less than a day out. Expecting the worst, the crew included medical doctors and security from a private firm. Apparently, dismissing the entire staff and having them evacuate in the emergency shuttle upon the guests' arrival had set off red flags at home, at least once the powers-that-be found out about it. That, coupled with an inability to communicate with anyone at the hotel and a rescue ship had already been sent prior to Penelope activating the emergency signal for the second time. The staff who were supposed to be at the hotel had been told, like Bobby, that it was all part of some reality show stunt, but no one in charge of the Hotel Artemis knew who had approved or arranged such a stunt. The PR women who had accompanied the group on the trip had been fired immediately, and the highest-ranking officials of the Apollo Group were fighting amongst themselves.

Alison, now resigned and unwilling to die on the moon as Bobby and Jackson had, had given up the password that fully unlocked the full capabilities communications console, giving Penelope full access to the satellite radio that allowed them to communicate with the ship and the main base at Cornwall Spaceport. So Penelope and Uchida had learned what happened from the captain of the ship en route who informed them they should wait in the hotel lobby until they arrived. Penelope informed him that, due to certain factors, they'd be waiting upstairs in the Sunrise Lounge. Communicating with the ship had been Penelope's first action once the computers were fully unlocked. The second was turning off 'Fly Me to the Moon'.

At the top of the stairs, she and Uchida paused and looked down into the lobby. It glistened as bright as it had on their arrival, but there was no escaping the smell of decay emanating from the restaurant.

'I hope they can get the smell out,' Penelope said.

'I'm sure they will find a way. Although you are more likely familiar with crime scene clean-up than I. There should be a memorial to them,' Uchida said. 'A plaque we can install there.' He pointed to a wall of the lobby.

'The first men to die on the moon,' Penelope said. 'They'll be famous.' She leaned her arms on the railing. 'That name you gave the captain. The name you said he should radio to Earth.'

She didn't have to ask the rest of the question. Uchida leaned on the railing beside her.

'"There is no greater fallacy than man's hubris",' he quoted Alison. 'My father died racing Formula One cars as a hobby. For fun. On his own personal track. He was an amateur with no professional training. He would take his car out, race it around the track, destroy it, buy another. But walking away from every crash made him think he was invincible. Until one day he wasn't. I was young. I didn't fully understand what happened to him. He had brought me to the track to watch and I got too close, wanted to see more. When he crashed, a piece of debris flew up and cut me.' He ran his finger over the old scar. 'I almost did not survive. When I woke in hospital, I asked my mother how my father died, she would say, "Hubris. It was hubris that killed him. And it will kill you, too."'

Uchida pushed himself up to standing but kept a grip on the railing.

'My mother has been vehemently opposed to this hotel from the start. She's even funded some of the protests against it. When I told her I was going, that I paid for a place, she called me Icarus. Said this hubris would be the death of me. She said she would do anything to see this hotel burned to the ground. She has not spoken to me since.'

'You think she's Alison's benefactor,' Penelope said.

'When my mother is afraid, she attacks. Besides having access to a great deal of money, she has a very violent temper.' He looked up at the security camera in the corner. 'She would do anything to see this hotel fail.'

'Including arranging for an obsessive woman to have access to the person she hates the most. I suppose she thought a murder in the hotel would derail its opening.'

'And it may delay it,' Uchida said. 'But it won't be destroyed. Too much money has been spent to make it happen.'

He turned and faced the observation window.

'People will pay for this view. To feel this close to God. Murder will not stop them.' He stepped back from the railing. 'Detective Strand, may I get you a drink? We may all need more alcohol before the ship arrives.'

He ushered her into the Sunrise Lounge.

The breakfast from their first morning was still laid out on the side table. None of them had ever cleaned it up. But the others had brought in a fresh selection of alcohol and snacks while the two of them had been in the communications centre.

Alison had been tied to a chair in the corner, a strip of duct tape over her mouth. Frau Richter sat close by, never taking her eyes off her.

After Uchida had fetched a glass of whisky for Penelope, he went and sat with Sasha on the opposite side of the room. Sasha had remained quiet and somewhat vacant since their return to the hotel, but Penelope saw her take Uchida's hand when he offered it.

Dr Wyss sat alone at a table in the centre of the room. No one seemed to want to talk to him since they released him from the medical bay.

Penelope took her drink to the table near the kitchen door, where Tonya and Freddy sat.

'You get him to talk?' Penelope nodded to the doctor as she sat down.

'Oh, you'll love this,' Tonya said. 'Freddy, you found it out. You tell her.'

'Well, apparently, as soon as Dr Wyss found out he was selected, he decided he could earn some extra cash by selling hotel amenities – towels, pens, slippers, glasses, you name it. If it wasn't nailed down, he took an order for it. But he didn't realise we were all given a luggage limit. He stole some of the suitcases from the shop and a bunch of other things. He had taken more orders than he could handle and didn't know how he was going to get it all back to Earth. He'd already taken a deposit from people, too. Alison spotted him that first night, stealing stuff, and he thought she was going to nark. He said that *she said* she wanted in and so they started working together to steal stuff. But my guess is that Alison panicked when Dr Wyss spotted her roaming the halls that night and she just used that as a cover. It gave her an excuse to be lurking around if she was helping him, so at least he wouldn't suspect her. When you guys all went in my room and she saw the blood on my clothes, she must have realised I had been to see Jackson's body and that I must have found something, and she decided to, well, take me out. I guess. But you guys finding me so quickly, she must have heard you and didn't have time to, you know, finish the job. Which was really cool of you. I don't think I said thanks.'

'Well, it's very cool that you're still with us.' Penelope took a sip of her drink. 'I'd hate to lose a friend I just made. I don't make them very often.'

Tonya cleared her throat and turned to Penelope. 'I want to apologise. It wasn't my place to bring up your leave of absence in front of the others. And I probably shouldn't have sneaked into your room and read all of the files without your permission.'

'And I'm sorry, too,' Freddy jumped in. 'I should've told you both what I knew. I shouldn't have lied. It wasn't cool. I shouldn't have—'

Penelope held up her hands. 'I don't think I can handle any more apologies. We're all strangers, really. We were strangers. We didn't know who we could trust.'

'You know, I'm not sure if I'll be able to read any more detective novels after this.' Freddy shook his head. 'I'm going to go home, finish my degree and get a job in a lab. Lab work is cool. I like lab work.'

'And you, Tonya? Back to the paper?' Penelope asked.

'Just long enough to tell them to fuck off,' Tonya said. 'Being on the moon really gives you perspective, you know? I may have ruined Dalia Joy's life, but I don't have to do it to anyone else.'

'How noble. So you mean you're going to write about what happened here,' Penelope said.

'Abso-fucking-lutely. Christmas number one bestseller, here I come. International sensation. Film deal. Can you imagine? I suppose I can count on you two for interviews?'

'As long as you don't call me Penny.'

'Deal.'

They shook on it.

'What about you, Detective Strand?' Freddy asked. 'Are you going to go back to the Met?'

Penelope looked at the people scattered around the room then at the vast, star-specked blackness of space. The awe remained, but the fears that had underlain so much of that awe were gone. Or at least neatly catalogued and tucked away for the time being.

'I don't know,' she said. 'I could get used to it up here.'

Ten Months Later

r/hotelartemis

u/moonshot_mike 16 h

Burton Book – Banger OR Bogus?

So I just finished it and I still don't know what to think. Like, I want to believe her and if Apollo allowed her to publish it, it must be true. But I don't know? You know?

What do you guys think?

⇧ 29.6k ⇩   💬 11.9k   ⤝ Share   🎁 Award

> **apollorox** 16h
>
> Definitely true. Apollo would have sued the pants off her otherwise.
>
> ⋮   ↩ Reply   ⇧ 19.7k ⇩

> **luvspace** 15h
>
> Uh, total FICTION. Why? BECAUSE Apollo hasn't sued her. They CLEARLY told her what to write. I GUARANTEE the truth is WAY worse.
>
> ⋮   ↩ Reply   ⇧ 17.1k ⇩

> **yomammasanasteroid** 14h
>
> Yeah, more than two people died, I bet. In fact, there's pretty convincing evidence that the whole group

was murdered and the ones they brought back are replacements. It was a total massacre up there.

⋮ ↩ ⇧ 2.6k ⇩

noplanetb 14h

Replacements? Don't you dare bring up lizard people.

⋮ ↩ ⇧ 2.6k ⇩

yomammasanasteroid 14h

I'm not saying lizard people. But haven't you noticed the social media presence of most of the guests is practically non-existent? Except for the person calling herself Tonya Burton?

Sasha Eris? All privacy locked.
Dai Uchida? No photos? For a billionaire? When it's so easy to see Gates and Musk and Bezos?
Penelope Strand? Nothing! And she barely showed up for the pressers anyway. She's probably not even real.

Everyone died – from life support malfunctions, space psychosis, aliens. I don't know. But they did. I'm not alone in thinking this. There are whole websites dedicated to it.

⋮ ↩ ⇧ 9.3k ⇩

Apollorox 12h

Websites set up by those eco-nuts. Maybe not believe everything you read online.

⋮ ↩ ⬆ -2.0k ⬇

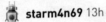 **yomammasanasteroid** 12h

Maybe not believe everything Apollo tells you.

⋮ ↩ ⬆ 718 ⬇

 starm4n69 13h

It's total fiction but for the opposite reason. No one was murdered. No one even died. Bobby Rannells wanted to retire and decided to pull a hoax. He's on a beach in Thailand now or something.

'Jackson Smith' was an actor. Everyone knows Canadians aren't that blond. He was just some punk from LA Rannells hired. The rest of the group was totally in on it.

⋮ ↩ **Reply** ⬆ 1.7k ⬇

culf 13h

Seconded. My cousin lives in LA and he knows a guy who met 'Jackson Smith' at a bar in Hollywood right after the news broke. His name's Steve.

⋮ ↩ ⬆ 1.0k ⬇

starm4n69 13h

I knew it! And doesn't Penelope Strand work for the
hotel now or something? Total hoax.

⋮ ↰ ⇧ 417 ⇩

 2ruth 12h

not a hoax
bobby rannells died at the hotel artemis but
they're lying
he wasn't the first

⋮ ↰ ⇧ 212 ⇩

 culf 12h

source?

⋮ ↰ ⇧ 26 ⇩

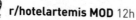 **r/hotelartemis MOD** 12h

This post has been removed the moderators of
r/hotelartemis. Moderators remove posts from feeds for
a variety of reasons, including keeping communities safe,
civil and true to purpose.

Acknowledgements

I like to travel to the specific places I write about, but that wasn't really an option this time. So apart from staring up at the sky at night, two books I found incredibly helpful were *A Field Guide to the Moon* from Wildsam Field Guides and *Moon: A Brief History* by Bernd Brunner. Thanks to the pandemic (and my bank account), I also was unable to stay at the luxury hotels I researched to bring The Hotel Artemis to life. For insight into the running of these hotels, I turned to Micah Solomon's *The Heart of Hospitality*. Apologies for manipulating many actual hotel processes and procedures meant to help guests and staff for my own nefarious purposes.

Unlike the guests of the Hotel Artemis, when it came to writing this book, I wasn't left to my own devices. Thank you, Kelly Smith, for trusting me with this idea in the first place, and thank you to the entire team at Zaffre for bringing the book to fruition. Thank you as always to Sandra Sawicka for her guidance during the writing process.

Thank you, Jannicke Bevan de Lange, for giving me permission to kill her husband, and thank you to the real Tim, for allowing himself to be killed. I promise it won't happen again. (Maybe.) Thanks to my older sisters, Cherie and Lindsey, to whom this book is dedicated. (See – I do more than stay at home all day.)

Thank you, Harry, Gizmo, and Watson – my faithful, fuzzy trio who let me talk to them about my ideas without judgement. And thank you Mom, for everything.